LITTLE DISTRACTIONS

LITTLE DISTRACTIONS

K.G. Brightwell

For Nami, who gave me a push in the right direction.

Freshman Year

1 Mission

People aren't really my thing. That might be an understatement. I don't much like the phone either, but since Tea is one of the few people I can stand, I agreed to these weekly calls. She calls them "proof of life." As if I'm being held hostage on my college campus.

"So, Richard, are you making any friends? Or are you being your usual self?"

"Forget it. I don't actually want to talk to you," I say. "Hanging up now."

Tea laughs. "Is your roommate still irritating the crap out of you?"

"Who, Matt the stoner? No. He's not here much anymore. Haven't seen him in more than a week when he stopped by to get his soccer cleats. He has his own stoner girlfriend now with off-campus housing. I pretty much have a super single."

"Sounds super."

I sit down and put my feet up on my desk. There is no way to be comfortable in this room. The bed is too narrow. The desk is too low. The chair doesn't even lean back. I hate the shade of the curtains. They're in between royal blue and steel gray. I think they only became this color after years of constant exposure to sunlight. They look tired. I never thought I cared about these things. Apparently, I do.

"I guess this Matt person is not going to be your new bestie at college." she says.

"Bestie? Really?" I pick up a pen from the desk and twirl it between my fingers.

"Yeah. You know, close pal, buddy, partner in crime, compadre?"

"I know what the word means. And no. He's not a bad guy, but Matt will not be my 'bestie.' I don't need one anyway. I came to college to get a degree, not make friends. The course load for biochem is killer—twice as many lab classes as the other majors. I can't afford distractions."

I know Tea is frowning. I can hear it in her voice. "If by 'distractions' you mean human contact, you are wrong. You are so very, very wrong. Okay, maybe bestie isn't the right word. But Richard, you can't stay in your room every day and only come out for meals and classes."

"Have you been spying on me?"

Tea laughs. "I've known you for a while now. And I'm telling you that you need to take off your lab coat once in a while and socialize with other humans. You, my friend, need to find your people."

"Yes. Well, as you say, you've known me for a while. And I don't like people. This is the chief benefit of having a super single."

"Fine. I'll cut you some slack." Tea sighs. "We can start slow first semester. Forget 'people.' But at least find a *person*. I'm not saying you need to become some sort of social butterfly and attend epic campus parties. But I'm afraid you will need to talk to more than one individual in order to find an appropriate candidate."

I stop fiddling with the pen and set it on my desk. "Candidate for what?"

"For your bestie. Weren't you listening?"

"I thought we decided against the use of that term. And against the waste of time trying to find this mythical person." The light is shining in my eyes through a gap in the tired curtains. I turn in my chair to face the other direction.

"So. Not bestie. I get it. What term would you prefer? Best buddy? BFF?"

"No. I'd prefer if you left it alone. I'm fine. Look, it's not like I'm hidden away from the world in some cave. It's a big campus. I spend enough time outside my room. And I talk to plenty of people."

"Really?" Tea pauses. "Prove it. What's your lab partner's name?"

"Uh…" I actually can't remember her name. "Chem?"

"Sure, chem. Or biology. Either one. Who's your lab partner?"

"No. That's her name—my lab partner for chemistry. I call her Chem. She calls me Bio. Gives me crap about majoring in biochem since she's straight up applied."

Tea pauses to let this information sink in before saying, "So… you're telling me that you don't even know the name of this person you spend hours and hours with every week?"

"Possibly. Unless her name is actually Chem. It could be. You never know."

Tea scoffs. "Okay, we'll start even smaller. Your assignment is to find out her actual name. I'll give you the whole week to muster up the courage to ask her."

"It's not courage. It's that I don't care what her name is. I don't like her. And she smells like dryer lint."

"You don't need to like her. This is practice for speaking to someone more likely to suit our purposes. Think of it as training to be an actual functioning human. Ask her name. Tell her yours. Make small talk."

"Can we appreciate the irony of you trying to teach me to make small talk."

"Hush. I'm a pro now."

I laugh harder than I expect at that, partially falling off the chair before clearing my throat so I can speak again. "Yeah. I'm sure that's true."

I am completely unprepared for Tea to shout into my ear when she gets a sudden flash of inspiration. "Oh! I've got it! Forget finding out Chem's name. That is no longer your mission for the week. You, my friend, are going to attend a freshman orientation activity," Tea says triumphantly.

"Pretty sure I've already been orientated." I've been at school for a month.

"Nope. If you had been *successfully* orientated you would be out with actual people instead of forcing me to speak on the phone."

"Who's forcing who? I can always hang up."

Tea ignores me. "Okay. I found it. I love when they put such detailed schedules out in the universe for all to see. There is a freshman mingle in your dorm this afternoon. Go. Think of it as an early birthday present."

"This is the crappiest birthday present I've ever received. And my sister once gave me a pair of used socks."

"I meant an early present for *me*. Seriously Richard, I worry about you."

"Why? I'm not getting in any trouble with administration, I haven't stormed out of any classes, my grades are better than expected, and the cafeteria serves brownies with fudge icing on Fridays. Life couldn't be better."

"Person," Tea says firmly. "Mingle. Go."

"This will make you happy?" I ask.

"Ecstatic."

"Okay."

"Really? That easy?" She sounds shocked.

"Don't get all excited. It wasn't because of your amazing powers of persuasion. I'm going as a favor to you. So you know that you don't need to worry." When Tea gets worried, she sometimes worries herself right into the hospital. Only once, and it was for reasons, but I don't want to bring her any more stress than she brings on herself.

"Okay bye!" Tea sounds overly excited.

"Wait, just like that? Done talking? What about filling me in on how things are going with you? Aren't these regular phone calls supposed to be two-way conversations? I know I suck at small talk, but I am familiar with the concept of dialogue."

"Yeah. Whatever. We can catch up later. I don't want you to miss out. What if your person is waiting?"

I don't tell her this, but I'm pretty sure that she's my person.

*

There are posters up in the hall advertising this afternoon's event. I've managed to avoid participating in any scheduled activities in the dorm since opening week. I wonder if all the dorms have so much programming or if it's just the ones that cater to first-year students.

Grey waves at me from across the lobby. It looks like they will be running the mixer or whatever. Good. I actually like Grey.

"Richard! I'm so glad you could make it," they say with a smile.

I nod. "Yeah. I promised a friend." Their hair looks different, but I'm not sure how.

"You like it? The hair?"

Oh. I remember. Their hair used to be dark brown. Now there are silver highlights. "It's like your name. It suits you."

"Thanks!" Grey smiles.

Grey is one of the first people I met here and one of the few people I know by name. They're the resident assistant for my hall, and have a room directly across from me.

I don't know anyone else at the mixer or mingle or whatever, and I'm not sure I want to. I am even less interested in meeting new people after a tall guy across the room calls out, "Grey told us to stand over here, didn't she?"

Idiot.

How hard is it to remember someone's pronouns? We have all lived here for a month. Grey being nonbinary is not new. I mean, sure I don't know anyone else here by name—but there are only four RAs in the building, and even *I* know them all on sight.

Grey has us do a bunch of stupid ice breakers. If some teacher was requiring this in a class I would probably walk out, but Grey's a nice enough person, so I go along with their plans. I follow directions. I behave. Mostly.

Of course I only manage to behave by avoiding the people who have already managed to get on my nerves. The tall dude who can't remember pronouns steers clear of me on his own. I think he caught me glaring after he misgendered Grey.

After doing some aimless wandering and answering pointless questions, we do this activity where we put one of our shoes in a pile and then have to locate the person whose shoe we have. We're supposed to get to know them somehow. This doesn't seem like the basis for any kind of friendship.

My shoe is picked up by some kid from India named Ravi. We talk for a while. He asks me some questions. All I remember about him is that he is a music composition major, and we both wear size ten.

The person whose shoe I picked up is a girl from right here in Indiana who uses a wheelchair. She's white, has very long hair and a crooked nose. She tells me she had to threaten a lawsuit against the college so they would correct the slope on the ramp to our building. She's a design major and did some genius modifications to her chair. She seems badass. I don't remember her name; it was something unusual.

None of the kids I talk to are majoring in science. They are mostly fine arts and humanities. The chem and bio labs are clear on the other side of campus, so it makes sense there aren't a lot of science majors here. It never occurred to me how much the dorms would be segregated by major. The walk across campus is not a hardship.

I didn't choose this place for its location. Hanover was the old student center. It has a small movie theater and bowling alley in the basement. That's why I picked this dorm, as far away from the science labs as it is.

I don't care about bowling, but I do care about movies. Genre doesn't matter much to me. Lately I've been partial to older films for whatever reason. Mostly they show second-run movies, but they have a regular schedule for the classics.

I only stay until the official activities are finished. I can check this off of Tea's growing list of things I must do in order to be a "fully functioning human."

Mission accomplished.

2 Collision

I'm not particularly a morning person, but I don't mind getting up early. I know some people plan their whole class schedule around not getting out of bed before noon. But I get up whether or not I have a morning class. Force of habit.

I wake up at my usual time and head out for breakfast. I like to get there before the rush and leave in plenty of time to get clear across campus before my first class.

My feet collide with something solid right outside my door. "Holy fucking hell!" I catch myself at the last moment, managing not to land on my face. But I lose hold of the stack of textbooks I'm carrying.

There's a person seated directly outside my door, which wouldn't be a problem if I exited my room while staring at the floor. But I don't. So before I notice he's there I *almost* step on him, and I *do* drop my books on his head—which is hardly my fault given that he's the one who chose such a poor spot to sit.

He winces and rubs his head. They are chemistry textbooks. Not light.

I feel bad for yelling at him, but honestly he scared the crap out of me.

Why is he sitting in the hall wearing his bathrobe? It's obvious he recently got back from the shower. Besides the blue terry cloth bathrobe and the matching flip flops, which are dead giveaways, his hair is wet and he's got a shower caddy full of supplies on the floor next to him.

But why is he sitting in my doorway?

I think I recognize him from around the dorm. He's the short kid from the end of the hall. His hair is very black, his eyes are very dark, and his skin is a pale tan color. He's Asian, I think. Or Hispanic. Something less white than I am, anyway.

I take his hand to help him up. But he winces and I drop it quickly. "Crap. I didn't mean to hurt you. Sorry."

He shakes his head. "That wasn't you. I mean, the books were totally you," he says, putting a hand to the back of his head. "But not the wrist. I injured it at rehearsal. One of the perils of being a dancer."

"Oh. I never thought of that. Wrists, I mean. How's your head? And why are you here? This is a bad place to sit."

He smiles at me as he pushes himself off the wall and stands up. "The head is okay. I'll live, anyway. And I didn't mean to be part of your morning obstacle course. Sorry. I left my key in the room and got locked out." He gestures vaguely down the hall.

"What about your roommate?"

"Not home."

"Grey?" I point at the door across from mine.

He nods at the sign on the door: "Out for a run."

I should have noticed that. "Oh. Well, you'll have a long wait. They're hardcore. I think they're training for a marathon."

I stand there wondering what else to say. Is there a right way to handle things when you trip over an unknown, mostly naked person outside your room and nearly give them a concussion with your organic chemistry textbooks?

"Do you want some clothes?" I ask.

The kid laughs. "I'm sorry, what?" He looks me over slowly from head to toe and raises one eyebrow. I am easily a head taller.

"I know. My clothes will be too big for you. But you can borrow some for a while anyway. Until Grey gets back. That way you can eat. If you want."

"You are too sweet. Thanks."

I let him into my room and he sits in the chair at my roommate's desk while I look for something he can wear. Stoner Matt wouldn't like this. He could be kind of a dick about his stuff. But he's not here so he can't object. Besides, it's university furniture, not his.

I find some clothes that are least likely to fall off of this kid. He's even smaller than I thought. I hand him some drawstring sweats and a Pink Floyd T-shirt that my sister got for me.

He looks ridiculous wearing my oversized clothes with his flip-flops. Nothing fits, of course. He has to roll up the pants so he doesn't trip over them when he walks.

"Well, you look like a homeless person. Let's go."

He looks amused, which means I probably said something offensive, but he doesn't seem overly offended. That's good. People who are easily offended are not good company. Or rather, I am not good company for them.

"I suppose I should ask your name," I say as the door swings shut behind us. "I'm Richard."

He gives me a crooked smile. He has very white teeth. "I know. We met at orientation."

"Oh." Sometimes I'm not very good with faces. Or names.

He's still smiling. "I'm Jesse."

"Okay." I nod.

When we get to the cafeteria, Jesse follows me to a table and takes a seat beside me. This surprises me. I thought he would probably have friends to sit with. Maybe they aren't up yet.

I'd never seen Jesse at the dining hall before. At least I hadn't noticed him. I tend to eat pretty early when the dining hall is still quiet. Also, I usually eat alone, and it takes about five minutes, and then I leave. I don't pay much attention to who else is in the cafeteria.

Jesse eats slowly and keeps asking me questions in between bites.

"I haven't seen you around much since orientation. What are you studying?"

"Biochemistry."

He nods. "That explains it. There's probably no overlap in our schedules. I'm majoring in theater with a concentration on contemporary dance. I thought of doing ballet, but I'm really not built for it. I need a few more feet."

"That was a terrible joke. Also, you're not that short."

"Thank you, darlin'." He bats his eyelashes. "But you haven't seen me standing beside a prima ballerina. We look like we are entirely different species."

He can't be much shorter than my friend Tea. But I think she's short for a girl. And that would make Jesse really short for a guy.

"So Richie…" He puts his elbows on the table and rests his head on his hands. "When you click your heels together three times, where do you end up?"

"Richard." I correct him. But I don't know how to answer his question. I'm not sure what he's talking about. Maybe it's a theater joke.

Jesse shakes his head with a small smile. "Home, sweetie! You know...there's no place like it? Where are you from?"

"Oh, like the Wizard of Oz. Minnesota. West of Minneapolis. And no, I do not ride a moose to school." For some reason a lot of people ask this. Indiana isn't even that much further south.

Jesse grins. "I was born in Harvard. The town, not the college. Located in the heart of Idaho, the gem state."

I thought it was the potato state.

"You're thinking it's the potato state, right? I'm also a mind-reader."

"Huh." I'm more interested in how he ended up stranded in the hallway than where he went to high school. "Who's your roommate anyway? And how can you forget your keys?"

"Easily. Besides reading minds, my other superpower is losing things. I hate that the doors shut automatically. Stupid fire codes. And my roommate is Nick. I'm sure you've seen him around."

I think I met Nick. If I'm right, he's in my calculus class, and I don't like him. He's wrong a lot of the time and doesn't like being told that he's wrong. "Is Nick about my height? Brown curly hair?"

"Yeah. That's him."

"I don't like him."

Jesse looks up from his bowl of cereal with his eyes wide. I wonder if I've offended him.

"My friend Tea says I can be a real ass. If I say something stupid, don't take it personally."

"Noted. And...Tea?" Jesse tilts his head to the side.

"A friend from home. She has a stupid long name, but no one calls her that except her mom and there's no reason for you to know it since I doubt you'll ever meet her anyway."

"Okay." He nods slowly. "Friend? Girlfriend?"

"I asked. She said no. Probably for the best, since she's a lesbian."

Jesse laughs at that, but not a mean laugh. "So, she's a member of the rainbow brigade too."

"Yes, if you mean she's gay. But she doesn't like rainbows."

Jesse laughs again and shakes his head.

"Oh, and I'm not. Gay."

"I never said you were." Now he does look upset, or at least uncomfortable. I'm not sure why.

I look right at him even though Tea says sometimes this puts people off. I want to make sure he knows what I mean, though, so I need to see his eyes. "You said *too*. That she's a member of the rainbow brigade too. And I'm not."

Jesse shakes his head. "Yeah. I wasn't saying that. I meant me. Clearly." He gestures to the clothes he's wearing—my clothes. "That's right, ladies and gentlemen, and people of all genders: you are in the presence of the one, the only gay Filipino boy from the great state of Idaho. I assumed you could tell by my amazing fashion sense," he says with an exaggerated feminine voice and a flip of the wrist. "Plus, you know, theater major," he says as if that is supposed to mean something.

"You don't need to be gay to dance."

Jesse smiles. "True. But it helps."

I don't know why, but I stay at breakfast until he's done eating. I finished my food long before. But he keeps talking to me. And I keep listening.

There's something about him that makes me want to stay. Maybe it's that he reminds me of Tea. He doesn't make me miss Tea, or anything. But I think of how I wouldn't want her to be alone.

Or maybe it's the clothes. They make him look even smaller than he is, like he's way too young to be in college. I'd feel bad leaving him by himself.

Could be it's like he's a stray cat. They show up on your doorstep and you feel bad for them. Give them some food. See if you can help them find their way back to where they belong. You need to make sure that they're okay.

The cafeteria starts to fill up and pretty soon all the friends I had expected him to sit with show up. They are loudly exuberant and overly touchy. When he introduces me, this girl with a round face and curly pink hair greets me with a hug, which I don't much like, but it's better than the face full of kisses that she gives Jesse before sitting down.

One of the newcomers—a chubby black kid—briefly sits on Jesse's lap and throws his arms around his neck. He's followed by a slight, pale, blond dude with horn-rimmed glasses who gives a two-fingered salute as a greeting.

Jesse introduces me, but their names slide right past. I think the big guy is Danny. Jesse seems happy to see them; I'm glad they showed up. I'm still not sure why I worried about him before they arrived or why I didn't feel comfortable leaving him alone.

In any case, Jesse seems like he's okay now, surrounded by a bunch of friends, so I get up and leave.

"What's with your new friend?" I hear the girl say as I put my tray on the conveyor belt to the kitchen.

Jesse says, "Richie? He's great."

I realize then that I forgot to say goodbye. At least Jesse wasn't offended.

3 Classics

On Saturday night they're showing *Singin' in the Rain* in the dorm. While I don't mind watching the classics on a small screen, it can't beat the authentic cinematic experience.

I show up early so I can get a good spot, not that these things tend to be crowded. I like to sit slightly off center about a third of the way back. After I find the perfect seat, someone walks through the whole empty row to sit right next to me. There are plenty of other places to sit. I don't know why people do that. I'm about to tell whoever it is to find a different spot, but when I see who it is, I keep quiet.

"Fancy meeting you here," he says with a smile. I hadn't seen Jesse around much after that first morning. A glimpse in the cafeteria. Or a brief sighting of him leaving the dorm.

"I didn't picture you as a fan of musical comedies, Richie," he says.

"Richard. I like classic films. Also, Kelly and O'Connor are comic geniuses."

Jesse nods. "That may be true, but I'm here solely for Cyd Charisse. That woman has legs. Hell, that woman *is* legs."

As the movie plays, he leans over to tell me things I didn't know. It feels strange because I'm usually the film expert—but musical theater is not my main focus, and it's part of Jesse's major.

I find out that Gene Kelly did his own choreography to make sure no one could tell he was shorter than Cyd Charisse—who incidentally had polio as a child.

Jesse doesn't whisper, which I appreciate. Whispers carry in a quiet theater. He knows how to speak softly, his head near my shoulder, so only I can hear.

I do know some things about the movie; at one point we turn to each other to share the same information: "They mixed milk with the water so the rain would show up better on film," I say.

"Which made Kelly's wool suit shrink. And he was running a fever for the whole shoot," Jesse adds.

After the movie we head to the bar down the street that serves deep fried pickles, which are unexpectedly decent when dipped in ranch. I don't know why I agreed to go with him. I had planned to head back to my room, but I enjoy his company more than expected. And it's not like I have anything better to do.

Jesse orders for both of us. Whoever is carding people is not even trying. Jesse looks like he's fourteen. Well, maybe not—he's not that scrawny. But he doesn't look anywhere near twenty-one. He orders a fruity drink for himself and a Coke for me.

"You're not drinking?" he asks.

"The beer tastes like piss here. And I don't drink much anyway." We take a seat at one of the narrow booths and wait for our appetizers to arrive.

"Maybe you haven't found your drink yet. Wanna try this, Richie?" He hands me his glass.

"Richard." I take a sip. It's so sweet it makes my tongue curl.

Jesse grins at my expression. "So—neither beer nor mai tais are for you? Hmm… Don't worry. I'll find your drink. My brother was a bartender. I helped him study for the test so I know just about every drink there is." He rattles off a list of ones he thinks I might like.

I'm not much concerned with finding "my drink." But I enjoy watching Jesse when he's talking about his long-term plan to educate my palate. He talks with his hands when he gets excited. And he keeps smiling—showing all his teeth—which on some people looks fake, but on him seems quite natural.

"Okay, movie guy…" Jesse fixes me with a serious look, tapping his fingers. "Best classic movie?"

"How classic? Color or black and white?"

"Gimme one of each," he says.

"Alfred Hitchcock's *Rope* is the finest movie ever made. And for black and white? *Roman Holiday*."

Jesse nods thoughtfully. "I've actually never seen *Roman Holiday*."

I frown and shake my head. "Are you even allowed to be gay if you haven't seen it? I'm pretty sure they kick you out of the club."

Jesse waves a finger at me. "Ah, well... That's a common misconception. It is suggested, but not required, that you are familiar with Audrey's entire filmography. I've seen *Breakfast at Tiffany's*."

"Not her finest. I mean, she's phenomenal in it, of course. And the imagery of New York is iconic. But it's not a favorite. What's *your* classic film?"

"I don't actually know a lot of old movies. Oh, how about *White Christmas*?"

I grimace.

"What? It's a classic," he says.

"It's a ripoff of *Holiday Inn*, but in color and without Fred Astaire. Although it does have a few fine points, I guess, like the lack of overtly racist blackface performances. But the plot is non-existent and all the songs are simply rehashing old material."

"Okay, okay! New topic," Jesse says, waving a white cocktail napkin in surrender. "Tell me about your family."

"One older sister. She's the rebel."

"Ooh... how does she rebel?" Jesse rests his head on his hands.

"By not graduating from college in a timely fashion—she keeps switching majors. And by dating girls. Although I'm not sure they know about that." I keep meaning to ask her if she's out to them.

"I've got two older brothers: Caesar and Berto. Bastions of industry. Manly men. Nice guys, though. Then there are the twins—Max and Angel—who are little terrors. And Maya, the baby of the family. She's the only one who doesn't tower over me. But that will likely change in the next year."

I don't remember what else we talk about. I know I say some things that come off as rude or insensitive, because Jesse laughs at me quite frequently and shakes his head.

A lot of people take things I say the wrong way. It's a pain in the ass to navigate constant misunderstandings with people I don't know, so it's nice that Jesse can figure out what I am actually trying to say. And he thinks it's "cute" when I'm too direct and say things that might be rude.

16

"You look terrible," I tell him after his second mai tai. His cheeks are flushed and he looks ready to pass out.

"Wow. You really know how to make a gal feel special."

"ALDH2," I say.

"What?" Jesse turns his bleary eyes toward me.

"That's why you're flushed. And also why you probably feel like crap. The enzyme to break down alcohol doesn't work. Common in people of Asian descent."

Jesse stares at me with his eyes wide open, unblinking. Like I'm speaking a foreign language. I guess I am. "Biochemistry major," I say.

"Huh. Biochem for the win. Also—even alcohol is racist? That totally sucks."

I put down some money for the tip. "We should go back to the dorm."

Jesse stumbles when he stands up and I grab his elbow to steady him.

"Looks like your boyfriend has had enough," the bartender says as we walk past. Then he mutters as an aside: "You're welcome," and gives me a wink.

I stop and slap my hand on the bar. "Did you do something to his drinks? Maybe make them a little too strong?"

Jesse puts his hand on my arm. "Whoa there, tiger. Leave the poor man alone. You already explained the chemistry to me, science boy. And honestly I should know better than to drink above my weight class."

I walk close to him so if he stumbles I can help keep him on his feet, but he doesn't seem that unsteady. When we get back to the dorm there is a note on Jesse's door that says: "Stay Out. Busy." There are muffled moans coming from behind the door.

Jesse shrugs. "Guess I'll be couch surfing again." He fumbles for his phone.

"Does he do this a lot? Kick you out? Without warning?" This sort of behavior is not making me think any better of Nick.

"Often enough. I've got friends in other dorms. There's a reason you haven't seen much of me."

"I've seen plenty of you. Your bathrobe leaves little to the imagination."

"Richie! A gentleman does not divulge such indelicate information." He gasps in pretend shock, clutching his hands to his chest.

I take out my keys to unlock the door to my room. "My cover is blown. Not a gentleman. You should stay here."

"You mean in the hallway? Because that isn't a very appealing choice. I mean, it's a fine place to linger for a while, but it doesn't really have what I'm looking for in terms of amenities for overnight accommodations."

"Not the hallway. My room. I have an extra bed. You can go get the stuff you need from your room in the morning. Unless you want me to pound on the door for you now. I'm pretty sure Nick is afraid of me."

Jesse laughs. "Yes to the room, no to the intimidation. Although it's a kind offer. I can tell that it comes from a place of love."

Matt's bed doesn't have bedding on it, but I have a spare set of sheets. I toss them at Jesse. "Here." I also get him a water bottle and a couple of ibuprofen.

"Friends don't let friends go to bed drunk and dehydrated," Jesse says before knocking back a few pills. Then he blows me a kiss and strips down to his boxers.

When he changed out of his robe before I hadn't actually seen anything, since my back was turned. But my back isn't turned now. Before he gets under the covers I get a clear view of his dancer's physique.

And... damn.

4 Recital

I see a lot more of Jesse after that. Sometimes I eat lunch with him at the cafeteria if he's on his own. He'll stop me to talk in the dorm lounge if he sees me. So it's not too surprising that he invites me to his studio performance, I guess.

I've never been to a contemporary dance recital before. Or any kind of dance recital. I went to a lot of Tea's piano performances though, and this feels quietly formal in the same way.

I sit in the back, as far away from Jesse's friends as possible. I wouldn't mind them if they weren't all so friendly. Despite the fact that I am terrible with people, I have managed to learn their names at least.

Kit and Danny are dating. Danny is the heavyset biracial kid. He likes to slap people on the back as a greeting. But he doesn't do that to me. This makes me like him.

Kit is a platinum blond trans dude who has horn-rimmed librarian glasses and wears exclusively black and white clothing. He also has fake tattoos on his left arm. They are all black and show up really well on his pale skin. First I thought they were real, but they kept changing every few days. He's an art major, so I guess that makes sense.

Bailey, the ringleader of the group, describes herself as penta-racial. She has pale brown skin, light brownish green eyes and curly pink hair—but it's not natural. The curls are. Not the color. That's what she tells everyone: "I'm not a natural pink-head."

Bailey is the worst. She keeps trying to find me a girlfriend even though I have told her that I'm not interested. When she asked if maybe she should be looking for a boyfriend instead, Jesse declined on my behalf.

He thinks I'm pining for Tea. I don't think that's true.

I can't imagine enjoying the process of going out with someone Bailey finds for me, especially if they were anything like her. She's fine, I guess. But not what I'm looking for in a partner.

I find most people dull or exhausting. Sometimes both. Jesse's fine. He's easy to be around. Unfortunately, spending time with him means spending time with these energetic friends of his. They are not dull. And they are certainly nice enough. But they are endlessly exhausting.

"Richard!" Bailey has spotted me. "We saved you a spot. And look, it's by the aisle so you can escape quickly. There's even a spare seat on the other side. See? Personal space. I'm learning." She shows off the empty seat with a flourish.

Kit tells her to leave me alone, but Bailey presses on. "You know we rarely bite. You'll see much better up here. And Jesse will be so happy to see you... Come on, Richie."

"Richard," I say automatically.

I don't think Jesse will see me in the audience regardless of where I sit. I think stage lights make it impossible for performers to see who's in the audience. I decide to placate Bailey in case she is right, though. I know my presence is important to Jesse for some reason. He kept asking if I was coming even though I told him I would. More than twice.

Why would I lie?

There are several dances before Jesse. The first one is embarrassingly sensual. I don't feel like we should be watching it. There is no music, just a guy and a girl on stage wearing costumes that match their skin tone precisely, going through a series of very intimate poses.

The second is a group of male dancers. The dance evokes waves crashing across the stage. Their costumes sometimes look like they're solid and sometimes fluid. I have no idea how they accomplish this. The lighting coordinates flawlessly with the music, which is almost recognizable. I didn't pick up a program. I don't care about the other dances. I'm only here because Jesse asked me to come.

His piece is third.

Jesse is dressed all in white. His shirt has long ties attached to the sleeves that exaggerate the movement of his arms. As he walks on the stage, the audience goes quiet. His bare feet don't make any sound. When he reaches the center of the stage, the lights go out. When they come on again, there is only a spotlight.

Jesse doesn't look small on the stage. Standing there motionless he looks powerful. Commanding.

When the music starts, he comes to life. His arms and legs cover impossible arcs. I don't have the words to describe what I'm seeing. His hands communicate things so clearly that it's almost like sign language, but more fluid. And I'm not quite sure what he's saying.

Jesse lowers himself to the floor slowly, with impossible strength. And then somehow he's upright again. At one point in the piece he is flying. Only for a moment, but I swear he stops in mid-air.

I have never seen anything like it.

When the lights come up again, Jesse looks straight at me and smiles so wide that I know he can see me. I'm glad I sat so close. I give him a nod and a thumbs up.

I watch the rest of the recital, and come to the conclusion that I am not a fan of contemporary dance. But I am a fan of the way Jesse moves.

I could watch an entire recital if it was nothing but him dancing.

After the show Jesse meets us outside. He has changed into his regular clothing—pale ripped jeans, a pink T-shirt and a denim jacket embroidered with pink and white lotus flowers. He loops his arm in mine and rests his head against my shoulder briefly. "Thanks for being there for the performance, Richie darling."

"I told you I would. And you asked three times today. And twice yesterday. The answer was always yes."

Bailey pinches Jesse's cheeks and gives him a kiss on his forehead. "You were amazing!" He shrugs off her attention and I step in between them. I don't know if he wants her to pinch his cheeks, but I don't like it. She shrugs and gives me a crooked smile.

"Did you like the show?" Jesse asks.

"I liked your piece. The other ones made me uncomfortable. Except the one with the waves. That was interesting. The costumes anyway."

Jesse grins, "I think you'd look great in a sarong. I can see if they have one to spare."

"Too drafty."

Jesse smiles wide at this and Danny laughs out loud. They start talking about some of the other dances and I stop paying attention. I watch Jesse's face as he talks. I thought he talked with his hands, but he talks with his face too.

Kit waves a hand in front of my eyes to get my attention. "Hey, we're going to hang out at Bailey's. You wanna come?"

Jesse tugs at my sleeve. "Please?"

"Fine."

Bailey's dorm isn't too far from ours, but it's an entirely different setup. It is more like a traditional apartment building and it is a lot newer. The walls are painted a soft blue color and are hung with art done by former students—some of them famous alumni. A lot of the grad students live there. Bailey won the housing lottery and hit the jackpot.

She has a quad with a common room so there is a lot more space than I was expecting. There is a long couch, two armchairs and a handful of floor cushions arranged around a low table. The room is on the corner of the building and has windows on two sides. One wall is hung with a giant canvas. There is a bookshelf with small cans of paint and a clay jar of paintbrushes arranged like a bouquet.

"Work in progress," Jesse says, noticing my gaze.

"What?"

"That's the title of the piece." Bailey walks over to the canvas and grabs a paintbrush. She holds it out toward me. "Care to contribute?"

"No."

Jesse pokes me in the ribs. "Not even a teeny bit? Not even one brush stroke?"

I don't bother to answer.

Bailey's roommates are out for the evening, which she says is pretty common. It's a quiet dorm and they go for more raucous entertainment.

For this post-recital gathering, there is nothing on the agenda but hanging out. At least I don't have to worry about making small talk. They all know me enough by now.

Bailey puts on some music—but I quickly improve her selections. Her tastes run strictly to meaningless, pre-packaged, bubble-gum pop. My playlist includes pretty much everything but that. Time to broaden her horizons.

Kit takes a turn at the canvas, adding some angular branches to the outer edges, framing the lower left side. Danny sits cross legged on the floor, offering color commentary.

Bailey folds her legs up under herself on one side of the couch and takes out some knitting. I think it's a fuzzy pink scarf. Or a horribly misshapen sweater. Possibly an arm.

I finish making adjustments to the musical selections. Jesse is sitting on the couch opposite Bailey. He pats the seat beside him. "Here babe, I saved you a spot." He winces as he moves his arm, reaching back to rub his shoulder. I'm not surprised he is sore now that I've seen him dance.

"I saved you a spot too." I point to the floor in front of the seat. Jesse looks at me and raises an eyebrow. "Trust me," I say, pushing him off the couch and taking his spot.

He sits between my legs with his back against the couch. I begin by resting my hands on the top of his shoulders, palms against his shoulder blades. I let my hands warm his muscles for a while. Jesse sighs and relaxes into me before I even start. When I do, his back feels like it's made of wrought iron. It's easy to find the knots. Harder to work on them. Jesse sucks in air through his teeth when I press on a tight spot near his shoulder blade.

I back off on the pressure, but Jesse puts his hand on mine, holding it in place. "No, it's good. Keep going."

It takes a long time to release even a small amount of the tension in his shoulders. I have to use my elbow on the left side. It will take more than one half-assed massage sitting on the floor of Bailey's dorm room to deal with that. I wonder if it's merely tight from the performance or if there is an old injury. I wonder how he can move so gracefully with so much tension. He must be in pain. A lot of pain.

When I'm done, Jesse lays his head on my leg and gives a long sigh. "Fuck, Richie. That was better than sex."

"Do me next!" Bailey says, raising her hand.

"Back off. This one's mine," Jesse growls, which makes everyone laugh.

5 Take Care

"I found a person."

"Why hello Tea, how are you? Fine thanks. And you?" Tea says.

"Right. Hello. All of that."

"See? Not so hard. We'll make a fully functional human of you yet. So, tell me all about your person. What's their name? Where did you meet?"

"Jesse. We met in the dorm."

"Ooh! I told you to go to the mingle. Tea for the win!"

"Not there. In the hallway the next morning. I dropped books on his head."

Tea laughs. "Not a great start, maybe. But whatever. What's he like?"

"He's short. He's Filipino. And he is a dance major. He doesn't think I'm an ass."

Tea coughs. "Well, that's a good start. Although it doesn't say much for his intelligence."

"Hanging up now," I say.

Tea laughs again. "Kidding. What else?"

"I don't know. He has friends who are good to him. He smiles a lot. He's not interested in science or math. But that's okay. I'm surrounded by people who like science and math, and I don't really like any of them. Including Chem. Especially Chem.

"Her name is Finesse, by the way. She's black. That's not why I don't like her. And it isn't because she smells like dryer lint either. I don't like her because she likes it when people feel bad." Finesse isn't quite a bully, but she comes close.

"Jesse never makes people feel bad. He knows how to talk to everyone in a way that makes them feel welcome. Although he is weirdly affectionate, and I think he has to touch people when he talks to them."

"How's that going for you," Tea asks, barely holding back yet more laughter. "All that touchy feely stuff driving you crazy?"

Before I can answer, there's a knock on the door. Jesse. It must be lunch time. "Sorry, gotta go," I tell Tea before pocketing my phone.

I must've stood up too fast because the room spins and I have to put out a hand to catch my balance.

"You coming to lunch?" Jesse asks when I open the door.

Up until that moment, I was fully planning on following him to the cafeteria, but now the world is still tilting and the words that come out of my mouth instead are: "Not hungry."

Jesse pouts. "So I have to eat by myself?"

I scoff. "I doubt you'll be by yourself. You are never in danger of being alone." Even if his tight circle isn't there, Jesse always finds people.

"Wait, did you say you're not hungry?" Jesse does a belated double-take. "What's wrong with you!" He feels my forehead. His hand is wonderfully cool against my skin.

"You're burning up."

"I do feel a bit..." I sway on my feet. I swear five minutes earlier I felt fine. Now I feel like I've been hit by a truck. Headache, fever, weak as hell...

Jesse looks worried. "Wait here. No, lie down." He walks me over to my bed.

"I'm not tired," I say. But I am. I'm exhausted. It came on so suddenly I didn't realize.

"Of course you're not tired," Jesse says. "Don't be an infant. Now lie down." He's kind of scary in this nurturing mode of his. "Good. Under the covers." Fierce.

"Are you kidding? Under the covers?" I feel like it's a hundred degrees in the room already.

"You have a fever. You need to sweat it out," he says.

"I don't think that's true." I shake my head. "That can't be right."

"Tell that to my Filipino grandmother. Better yet, don't. You might not survive the lecture. Stay here. I'm going to find a thermometer and some Tylenol. Unless you have either of those things lying around?"

I shake my head. I don't usually get sick.

"Keys so I can get back in?" Jesse looks around the room.

I point at the dresser. Before he leaves, he tucks the blankets around me so I am in my own sweltering cocoon. I try to shake the covers off once he leaves, but I can't figure out how to escape, and only become more tightly entangled.

I must drift off for a bit because It seems like Jesse is back in no time at all. He looks very serious as he opens the white bag from the pharmacy and takes out the thermometer. "Open." He sticks it under my tongue.

At the sound of the beep I read my temperature at 102°.

"Here. Sit up." Jesse puts some pillows behind me—stealing from Matt's unused bed. He hands me a steaming mug of something. The smell burns in my nostrils.

"What is this?"

"Hot honey and ginger."

I take a sip, and it feels like my throat is dissolving. Maybe not that bad. But it is strong.

"Really what my grandma would prescribe is tying some herbs to your head. But somehow I didn't think you'd put up with that. Plus I don't have the right ingredients."

"Yeah. I'd rather avoid the leafy crown. It doesn't sound comfortable. Good call." I swallow the handful of pills he hands me. "I hope I didn't down a bunch of street drugs."

Jesse pats my hand gently. "Of course not. Now try and get some sleep."

I drift in and out all afternoon. Whenever I wake, Jesse is there to get me a fresh glass of water or encourage me to eat a few crackers. He has thankfully relented on the whole sweat-it-out plan. I'm free of my blanket prison. He lays a cool washcloth on my forehead.

"Ahhh. This is what *my* grandma would prescribe," I tell him as he lifts my arm and sponges it off with a damp cloth. I shiver as the air hits my damp skin. But when Jesse stops, I put my hand over his. "No, please. It helps."

Jesse keeps the cloth cool by dipping it in a bowl of water periodically. I've no idea where the bowl came from.

He takes my temperature again. I'm not sure what it is, but he doesn't look happy. "I'm staying the night," he says.

I'm in no condition to argue. Plus, Jesse is still in nurturing mode. I'm afraid to contradict him.

In the morning he's prepared to stay with me during the day as well, but I think that's ridiculous.

"I'm sick. You're not. Go to class. I'll be fine."

Jesse bites his lip. "I don't think you should be alone. Someone should stay with you. What if you need something?"

"I'm a grown ass human. I can take care of myself."

He narrows his eyes.

"I feel much better. My temperature has gone down since last night. It's not like I'm in danger of dying from a low-grade fever." I still feel like shit, but I'm not about to tell him that.

Jesse frowns at me and I shut my mouth. He only agrees to go to class when I promise to call him if I pass out, which is ridiculous. How can I call anyone if I've passed out?

Anyway, it's not really Jesse's job to take care of me, which I try to communicate, but apparently he doesn't agree. He takes my keys with him so he can come back in between classes to check up on me.

When he's not in the room all I do is listen to music and sleep. I can't even keep my eyes open to watch anything or play any games.

That evening, Jesse still insists on staying in Matt's bed overnight. But I'm not sure how much he actually sleeps there. Whenever I wake in the night he is by my side, sitting in the chair that he pulled up next to my bed.

The next morning the fever is better, but I feel like all my muscles are made of jello. Jesse wants me to go to campus health services but I already know what they will say. There's a flu that's been going around.

The day plays out much like the day before. I sleep. Jesse goes to class with great reluctance and comes to check on me frequently. He makes me ramen noodles with chili peppers and has me drink more hot honey and ginger.

On the third day of being sick as a dog, my appetite returns and I have enough strength to sit up and eat real food. Jesse pilfers some choice selections from the dining hall. It's not stealing. I paid for the meal plan.

"Are you feeling at all better?" He asks as he cleans up after my meal. Even though I told him he didn't have to.

"Almost completely well. I told you. You don't have to stay."

Jesse glares at me and I stop trying to persuade him to leave. In fact, although I don't need him, I've grown used to his presence.

My most recent symptom—a hacking cough—keeps me up most of the night. I know it wakes Jesse too, but he pretends to be well rested in the morning.

After returning from his afternoon class, Jesse has me remove my shirt. I expect him to hand me a washcloth so I can smell less bad—neither of us trusts me to take a shower just yet. I'm not all that steady on my feet. And even the necessary trips to the bathroom wear me out.

But instead of handing me a cloth, he rubs some oil on my chest.

"What are you doing? What is that? It smells weird."

"White flower oil." His hands feel cool on my skin even though I haven't had a fever in some time. "It's a Filipino cure-all. I finally managed to find a store that carries it."

It smells weird, but seems to help with the cough. I manage to sleep through the night.

I've never been this sick in my life. I'm not sure I've ever been sick for this long. I'm finally steady enough to walk around on my own, at least for short periods of time.

"I think you might be okay for a short trip to the cafeteria," Jesse says after I manage to make it from my bed to my desk without falling on my ass. It feels good to move around, although I am hardly at full strength.

Jesse insists on supporting me in case I topple over. "You're still a patient under my care, sweetie. Either you lean on me or I will carry you. It would hardly be more difficult than some of the lifts I have to do."

He is almost absurdly strong. He could probably follow through on his threat.

I opt for walking on my own two feet. But walking down the stairs I realize the importance of having the extra support. A short dizzy spell calls for a brief rest on the landing.

"Take it easy, big guy. It's not a race." Jesse puts his arm around my waist and drapes my arm over his shoulder.

On the way out of the dorm, we pass Jesse's roommate Nick and some friends in the lobby. Nick has very curly brown hair. His skin is three shades darker than a bowl of instant mashed potatoes. I've never seen his friends before. Or maybe I have, and never paid them any particular attention.

"Oh, there you are. I thought maybe you dropped out and left all your shit behind," Nick says, eyeing Jesse. "But I guess I can see what you've been up to." His lip curls back as he says this.

"Yeah. Nursing me back from the dead," I say before Nick can say something even more obviously homophobic. I already want to punch him in the mouth. And I don't do that.

One of Nick's friends mumbles something and grabs him by the arm, pulling him away from us. Pulling him away from me.

I've been told that my pissed-off face scares the crap out of people. It's a useful attribute in these types of situations.

"Take a breath, sweetie," Jesse says.

"How can you stand him?"

Jesse shrugs. "I've learned to ignore him."

6 Substitute

Jesse is lying down on his bed pretending to study for his art history class. I am at my desk actually studying for a biology quiz. It's all vocabulary. I think we should get foreign language credit for the class.

"Remember how you were a drummer in high school?" Jesse asks.

"Yeah. It would be hard for me to forget that I was a drummer. What with the kit in my basement and all." I put down my pencil and swivel around in my chair.

"Well, good." Jesse grins and clasps his hands. "Because I have a teensy-weensy favor to ask. My darling friend Marie plays with a band—she's the drummer—and is ever so briefly out of commission. She sprained a finger playing flag football, of all things. And I was wondering, well the band was wondering, if you would be willing to fill in."

"When? How long?"

"Only for their next gig. And—don't shoot the messenger—it's this Friday. So it would be intense practice sessions for a while, but then you'd be free."

"Do I have to sing?" I don't sing. Technically I *can* sing, but not well enough that I feel comfortable doing so in front of people.

"Good lord, no. At least I don't think so. Marie can't sing for shit."

I miss playing drums. And it's not an academically challenging week; no major tests or graded labs. I even feel confident about this bio stuff. "Sure."

Jesse jumps up and gives me a brief hug, which takes me by surprise.

The first rehearsal is that afternoon. I have no trouble finding the place. The guy who plays bass is a townie. He lets people store their equipment in his garage, including the drums. Jesse told me the drums came with the practice space; they belonged to some kid who graduated a while ago and just left them behind. I'm less disturbed about playing them once I find out they don't belong to Marie. I can be very possessive of my equipment. Most drummers are.

"Richie!"

I look up to see Jesse running toward me. Luckily this gives me time to brace myself for his exuberant greeting, so I'm ready for it. He gives me a tight squeeze and kisses me on each cheek. Which is unusual, but whatever.

"Darling! What are you doing here?" he says in an artificial sounding voice.

Oh. He's being funny.

"You two know each other?" the bassist asks. He's taller than I am and has blond dreadlocks. I think dreadlocks look ridiculous on white people. But I manage not to tell him this. Tea would be so proud.

Jesse puts a hand on my arm. He fakes a southern drawl. "Yes Dave, Richie and I are *quite* well acquainted."

The white chick with the guitar raises her pierced eyebrow. She has pale skin with freckles and long brown hair in two braids with bright green ends. "Oh, really?" she says.

"Yes. Jesse's room is down the hall from mine." I sit down at the drum set.

She gives me a knowing smile. "How convenient!"

"Why is that convenient?" I look from her to Jesse. "Oh. You mean for sex."

She makes a choking sound. Apparently my fantastic conversational skills are on full display.

Jesse pouts. "Sweet Chelsea, to my utter devastation, this one is straight."

"Ah. And here I thought you were developing better taste in men." Chelsea shrugs and looks away.

"I have *excellent* taste in men," Jesse says.

No one has any response to that. I wouldn't know. But apparently they have some inside information on his previous connections.

It's almost a relief to have sticks in my hands again, and my foot on the bass pedal. I didn't realize how much I missed playing.

When Nate, the lead singer shows up, Chelsea points at Jesse and then gestures with her thumb. "No groupies. They're a distraction."

"But I won't say a thing," Jesse whines.

"Out. Significant others are the worst." Nate shakes his head.

"He's not..." I start.

"Fine. I'll see you later, sweetie." Jesse blows me a kiss.

Chelsea looks at me with both eyebrows raised.

"We're really not," I say. "Not having sex, I mean."

Dave shrugs. "Whatever, man."

They are an okay band. They play an eclectic mix of covers so it's easy for me to fill in; I have an eclectic taste in music. And Jesse was right—practice is intense, but I have no problem with that. I like that they don't mess around during rehearsals. When we practice, it's all business.

It's a bit disconcerting playing someone else's kit; everything is slightly off from what I'm used to. But what actually bugs me the most is that the snare drum sounds fucking perfect. Mine always bugs the crap out of me. I can never get it quite right.

After practice Chelsea walks back to campus with me.

"So, you and Jesse are really not a thing? I mean I could see things going either way. You don't necessarily put off a gay vibe, but there's something about the two of you..." She squints up at me.

"Really not a thing. He's cool, though." I shrug.

Chelsea nods slowly. She doesn't say a lot for the rest of our walk. Which is fine with me.

*

The gig is part of a local band showcase at a club off campus.

Jesse volunteered to style me for the show. I figured what the hell. It makes him happy.

"Wait, all you have in your closet is some altar-boy white button down shirt? What is this even doing here?" He holds the shirt at arm's length as if it smells bad (which it doesn't) and stares at the offensive article of clothing.

"My mom made me bring it in case I have some formal event to go to. If you look in the back of the closet she made me bring a suit, too. But I don't think it fits anymore. I only brought it to humor her. I got it to go to my grandpa's funeral a few years ago."

"Well… where are the rest of your clothes?" He pokes his head into the closet as if more outfits will miraculously appear.

I point at the dresser.

Jesse rifles through the drawers, muttering under his breath. He despairs at the lack of any appropriate base outfits, the disappointing scarcity of accessories, and the fact that nothing he owns can possibly fit me.

"It's not a complete disaster. We'll start here. And fear not, I didn't come completely unprepared. Now, strip down to your skivvies and let's see how these look on you." He holds up a pair of ripped jeans. They're not my favorite, but they're comfortable enough.

"Not a single one of your shirts will do. Luckily I came prepared for this eventuality. I thought we could start with your own items if you had anything remotely appropriate. Which clearly, you do not. I don't know what I was thinking." He looks at me and shakes his head in mock-disappointment.

Once I have the jeans on, Jesse tosses me a black T-shirt he borrowed from Kit. Which is ridiculous. Kit can't be that much bigger than Jesse and is therefore much smaller than me. "I have T-shirts," I grumble.

Jesse shakes his head. "You don't have T-shirts, sweetie. You have tents. You gotta give people a hint of what you've been hiding underneath all those baggy clothes," Jesse says, patting my stomach. "I can't be the only one who knows you're sporting a six pack."

I do not have a six pack. "I feel naked in this shirt."

"Honestly, that was also an option I considered. But somehow I didn't think you'd be comfortable with an open jacket and a bare chest."

I shake my head. It's not that I'm all that self-conscious, but I sweat a lot on stage and appreciate wicking layers.

"Yeah. I thought not. Now try this." He hands me an oversized leopard-print jacket from Danny.

"No."

"Okay. Don't worry. I have other options."

I also decline the red pleather jacket, the pink and black plaid, a military-style thing with gold trim, and a denim jacket that would be okay if I could move my arms; it's too tight across the shoulders.

"Do I really need a jacket at all? It's hot as hell on the stage unless they are the one club in all of the Midwest that actually has adequate ventilation."

Eventually Jesse decides I'm fine wearing a deep blue satin shirt from Bailey in lieu of a jacket. She stole it from her brother, so it's big enough to fit me. I tuck in the T-shirt, put on a belt, and leave the shirt open, rolling back the sleeves. All of this under Jesse's critical eye.

He's not fond of my scuffed athletic shoes. I tell him no one will see them anyway. He spouts some nonsense about walking on and off the stage, but it's not like I have any better alternatives. Which Jesse finds appalling. What can he do, though? It's not like he wears my size.

For the finishing touch I let Jesse put in some dangling silver earrings. I have never worn dangling earrings. And then I make Jesse's entire year—according to him anyway—by allowing him to apply some eyeliner. It scares the crap out of me when he comes at me with the angled brush, but he doesn't poke me in the eye or anything. I survive.

"See? Not so bad, was it? I am a semi-professional with stage make-up, you know. You should have known you could trust me." He takes a step back and sighs as he examines his work. "Now you look like a proper rockstar."

"I feel like a proper fraud."

"Perfect," he says.

Jesse comes with me and the band so he can help set up. Marie is there too, but no one lets her lift anything. Her finger is in a metal splint. "I'm so sorry I let everyone down."

"It's okay," says Dave. "Your friend Jesse saved the day. The kid he brought us ain't half bad."

"You aren't after my job, are you white boy?" Marie asks, turning her dark eyes on me. She looks pretty white too, but Jesse told me she's Puerto Rican. And apparently she swears very creatively in Spanish. In ways that are untranslatable.

"He's too busy making explosives and torturing small animals in the science labs," Jesse says. "Don't worry about him putting you out of a job, querida."

Jesse and Marie stake a claim to the best table near the front. Just before the show starts, Bailey, Kit and Danny join them. The gig itself goes pretty well. A few missed entrances on the part of the vocalists, but we covered for them. I dropped a stick, but I recovered fast enough that I'm pretty sure only Chelsea noticed—and she did a fine job of hiding her smirk. I didn't break anything. No one fell off the stage. It was a good set.

At the end of our performance I join Jesse and the rest of the crew at the table. Marie is already backstage, once again being refused the opportunity to carry anything. I need to head back soon myself.

"You were amazing!" Jesse clasps his hands together and tilts his head to the side with a wide grin. "I'm so proud of you, sweetheart."

"Ooh, Richard, check you out!" Danny says, admiring my too-tight shirt.

Kit punches him. "Keep your eyes to myself."

"Hey, you know I only have eyes for you." The two of them congratulate me on a successful performance and then head out for the rest of their date. I think they're going dancing or something.

Bailey takes off as well, but Jesse stays to help with loading up the equipment and hauling it to Dave's house.

When we get back to the dorm Jesse's asshole roommate has left a note on the door again. "Busy. Stay out."

"Fucker," I say.

"Literally," Jesse adds, waggling his eyebrows at the moaning sounds coming from the room.

I snort. "You can stay in my room again. No problem."

Jesse swoons. "My hero!"

I keep Matt's bed made up with fresh sheets now. "Were you expecting company?" Jesse asks when he sees this.

"Yes. I'm running a bed and breakfast on the side, but I had a cancellation for tonight and don't have any paying customers, so the bed is yours."

"What a happy coincidence," Jesse says.

I'm about to fall asleep face first on my bed without even taking off my clothes, but Jesse insists that I at least remove my eyeliner, or what's left of it. The makeup remover leaves an oily film around my eyes even after I use soap. I am never wearing that stuff again.

7 Roomies

Something smells terrible. And it's me. I should have showered last night. I might have to burn these sheets. I slink off to the bathroom while Jesse is still asleep. When I get back from my quick shower, he is just waking up.

"Do you mind if I borrow a towel? And some of your product?"

"If by product you mean my generic cheap-ass unscented hair and body wash?" I hold up the bottle. "Go for it."

"Thanks. Towel?" I throw a spare one his way.

When Jesse gets back from the shower, I realize he has the same problem now as the first time we met. I mean, technically he has clothes this time. But they are only slightly cleaner than mine, I imagine. I should have thought to have Jesse keep a spare set of clothes here since apparently his roommate is a chronically self-centered bastard in addition to being a homophobic prick.

"You need clothes again," I say.

"That's okay. I can wear what I had on last night," Jesse says. "It wouldn't be a disaster. There are plenty of guys in college who don't bother changing their clothes for days at a time…"

"Not you. And it's clear they never took microbiology. We could see if your room is open for business by now."

Jesse shakes his head. "It's far too early for that to be true. Don't worry about it. I can drown in some of your clothing again for a while. It's comfortable. And trendy. The 'boyfriend shirt' is all the rage." He bats his eyelashes at me. "Or hell, give me a belt and I can make a fashion forward dress out of any of your voluminous T-shirts." He strikes a pose that makes me snort.

"Wear these. They might not fall off." I hand him a stack of clothes. At least they're clean.

Before, I thought Jesse looked like a vagrant when he had my clothes on. Now I think he looks ridiculous, but adorable. At least he has his own shoes this time. That helps.

Jesse and I arrive at the cafeteria after Bailey, Kit and Danny are already seated.

"Did you come together?" Bailey asks. She's doing something with her face.

"Yes. I think that's obvious since we arrived at the same time," I say.

"Oh sweetie." Jesse pats my arm. "She means did we come *together,* and the answer is yes. Sorry we were late. Richie is an absolute monster in the sack."

"Jesse wouldn't know. He slept in Matt's bed because his crappy roommate kicked him out for the night without warning. Again." Matt was kind of an ass sometimes, and smelled like weed all the time, but at least he let me sleep in my own damn room.

Jesse swats me lightly on the arm. "Spoilsport. We could have strung them along for a little longer. Where's your sense of whimsy?"

Kit teases Jesse about landing such a hunk, claiming that I'm a much better choice than other guys Jesse has gone out with. I wonder who he's gone out with? People keep mentioning his poor taste in men.

When we head back after breakfast, we bump into Nick on his way out. He's alone. I can't imagine who would want to spend the night with him. Maybe he's a "monster in the sack." They were loud enough anyway.

"Huh. I guess you're not 'busy' anymore," I say.

He sneers and looks from Jesse to me. "Together again, I see. So I take it you're a 'friend' of Jesse's. Funny, you don't look the part."

"I don't look like a friend?" I know what he's going to say, but I ask anyway.

"You don't look like a fag."

I do not punch him in the face.

I have successfully not punched anyone since elementary school when I knocked Josh Tyler off the monkey bars for calling one of the girls in our class a fat sow. I didn't even like her. And she was fat. But he made her cry, which really pissed me off.

He got a broken arm and a cool-looking cast, and I got a suspension from school and a therapist to help me work on my anger management issues.

Probably a good thing. My anger needs some management right about now.

"I don't look like a *fag*?" I narrow my eyes and walk toward him. "Well I was going to say you don't look like a homophobic, inbred douchenozzle, but that would be a lie."

"Whatever. Just keep your extracurricular activities out of the room. I don't want to walk in on... anything." His lips draw back in disgust.

Jesse comes to stand by me and pulls me away from Nick. "Richie, drop it," he says in a low voice.

"No. This is bullshit." I take another step towards Nick. "It's not *your* room, asshole. He can do whatever the hell he wants— since that seems to be the house rules. And you think Jesse and I want to walk in on anything? I doubt there's anything all that exciting to see, anyway." I glance toward his crotch.

Nick freezes. Personally I don't give a shit how big his dick is. But I get a certain sadistic thrill that I have made him uncomfortable at the idea that I am thinking about the size of his package. Before I can say anything else, Jesse grabs me by the wrist and drags me down the hall.

Once we're out of earshot, he drops my arm. "What part of 'leave it' did you not understand, Richie? I have to live with him."

"He's a dick."

"Agreed."

"You should report him. Get him transferred to another room."

"For what?" Jesse asks.

"Calling you a fag."

Jesse shrugs. "Technically, he didn't."

"He's a homophobic asshole."

"Given."

"You should move in with me."

"Sweetheart, we've only been on one date. Don't you think you're moving a bit fast?" Jesse says in a fake voice, putting a hand on my arm and doing that eyelash thing.

"I'll get Matt's key and tell him he has to take the rest of his shit to his girlfriend's room. It's mostly cleared out anyway."

Jesse shakes his head and loops his arm through mine. "Oh Richie, you are a sweetheart, but it's not necessary.'"

At lunch I call on the combined persuasive powers of Bailey, Kit, and Danny. That afternoon they help move his crap into our room.

*

Jesse is holding a handful of incense sticks in one hand and a ceramic elephant in the other.

"No."

Jesse frowns. "But it will make the room smell like something other than gym socks and cheese doodles."

"The room does not smell." It doesn't. "And what the hell are cheese doodles?"

Jesse pouts and deploys his giant puppy dog eyes.

They are not effective.

"No incense. It gives me headaches. Also no cigarettes and no pot. Same reason."

"No problem there. My dance instructor and my vocal coach would both murder me until dead if they caught me smoking anything. How about overnight *visitors*?"

I shrug. "Whatever. We don't need a rule for that, do we? I mean we can talk to each other and figure it out, right? Don't pull the kind of crap that Nick did. I want to be able to sleep in my own room more than half of the time, I guess. What about personal property? Matt was weird about his stuff. I'm not. You want to borrow something—fine. Sit at my desk—whatever. Use my bed—change the sheets."

Jesse snorts. "Good to know. And anytime you want to borrow any of my *fabulous* clothing, you are of course welcome to do so. But, I do get a wee bit possessive about my beauty products. So…"

I laugh. "Yeah, I'm good. I don't think we wear the same shade of foundation."

"Touché. Well, seems like a good set of house rules. Shall we shake on it or whatever you straight boys do?"

"We grunt and do that weird chin nod."

Jesse and I look at each other and at the exact same moment execute the straight-boy grunt-and-nod. Then we laugh our asses off.

"What the hell is wrong with you two?" Bailey asks when she walks in through the open door.

"Nothing all that important. Establishing rules of the room," Jesse says. "You're coming to our housewarming tonight aren't you? Nothing elaborate. Gifts unnecessary but not unwelcome. Very exclusive: invitation only. Oh, and there's a theme. But I'll tell you later once this one isn't in hearing range." He points a thumb at me and speaks to Bailey in a stage whisper. "It's a surprise."

Jesse kicks me out for the afternoon. I use the spare time to find an appropriate housewarming present. There's a shop in town that sells all kinds of cute crap. It takes me forever to pick something. The woman working the register is very helpful. "Would you like this gift wrapped?"

"Yeah. That would be nice. I suck at making things look good."

She nods. "Anything you'd like me to write on the card or should I leave it blank?"

"Um, write: 'In case the room smells of cheese doodles.'"

When I get back Jesse allows me into the room with a flourish.

I stand in the doorway with my mouth hanging open for some time before I enter. He has hung umbrellas from the ceiling, with glittering translucent streamers for rain.

He's borrowed one of the stage lights on a stand as a prop for the party. There are a number of raincoats hung on hat-trees that are also presumably from the theater department.

But what really stops me in my tracks is Jesse. He's wearing a jet-black chin length wig, emerald green heels, and a green satin flapper dress. He also has a narrow velvet choker, earrings that look like chandeliers, and a number of silver bracelets snaking up one arm. He waves at me with the cigarette holder in his hand. "Whaddaya think, sweetie? Do I clean up okay?"

"Holy shit." If Cyd Charisse were short and Asian, she would look exactly like this. "You have legs."

Jesse laughs. "Yes, darling. That's how I'm able to walk around."

"No. I mean. You are. Shit. Dancers." That is as intelligible as I'm going to get. I have seen his legs before, obviously. But this outfit really makes me realize how... shapely they are. "I guess I'm a legs man," I say.

"Thank heavens you're not a boobs man because I'm severely lacking in that department." Jesse squirms around and adjusts the bodice. "You think I need to add some stuffing?"

"No. It looks good. You look good. Do you have fake eyelashes on?"

He blinks his eyes slowly so I can admire his handiwork. "Why yes, I do. And of *course* I look good. I was born fabulous." Jesse takes me by the hand. "Now, for the big reveal..." He gestures toward my bed where he has laid out my costume: khakis, a white button down shirt, a bright yellow vest, and a red tie.

"Gene Kelly," we both say at the same time.

"I hope you don't think we're going to re-enact the dance sequence." I pick up the yellow vest. "You have no idea the level of my incompetence on the dance floor. It is legendary."

"Of course not, Richie darling. I thought this would be an appropriate theme considering our first date."

When Bailey and the guys arrive, they are all issued raincoats and handed drinks with tiny umbrellas and a slice of lime.

"Bright and Rainies," Jesse says. "Gin, peach schnapps, lime juice, and ginger ale. And for you, sweetheart, a Gin Buck, height of fashion in the roaring twenties. Trust me darling, the Bright and Rainies will be far too sweet for you."

I sip at the Gin Buck. It's not bad.

Jesse grins at me. "I know, right? It's a Bright and Rainy minus the peach schnapps."

Of course everyone brought gifts. Danny brought a doormat that says: "This *is* our circus and these *are* our monkeys." Kit brought a matching circus-themed cork board/whiteboard to hang on our door. And Bailey supplied us with "His" and "His" throw pillows with a subtle tan and blue pattern.

I am allowed to be in charge of the music. In keeping with the theme I play mostly show tunes. Kit and Jesse dance together, whirling gracefully around our room. Kit's okay. I mean, he holds his own. But the way Jesse moves in one fluid line—I'm not wrong. He is a diminutive, hot as hell, Asian reincarnation of Cyd Charisse.

It's only after everyone leaves that I remember Jesse's housewarming gift.

"Here. I got you this." I hand him the neatly-wrapped present.

"And I got you this," he says, holding out a gift bag with rainbow-colored tissue paper peeking out of the top.

Jesse opens his present first.

"Candles?" he says.

"Yes. Scented candles. The person at the store said they would make the room smell nice even if you don't burn them. And really, don't burn them because they will set off the fire suppression system."

Then he looks at the card and hoots with laughter.

I open my gift. It's a set of shampoo, soap, and after-shave in its own caddy. "In case you are tempted to use my products, now you'll have some of your own." I smell the soap. Not bad. It's lightly scented. Not the same as whatever Jesse uses. I like it, though.

"So, how do you gay boys thank people for a housewarming present?" I ask.

"Darling, you shouldn't have," he says, kissing the air on either side of my face.

"Uh… Darling. You are too sweet." I blow him a kiss and he nearly collapses with laughter.

8 Twenty Questions

"You don't need so much stuff. Oh. Except if you are going clubbing I suppose you might." Thanksgiving break is only a few days. Jesse has three suitcases. I have no idea what could be in them. I only have one bag.

Jesse ruffles my hair—which he can only do because he is standing on the steps of our dorm. "You are so adorable. How much of a thunderous flaming asshole would I have to be to go home with you and then dump you to have myself a gay old time."

"I thought we would go together."

Jesse almost falls off the stairs. I have to catch his elbow to steady him. My lips curve into that stupid smile I get whenever I surprise him. I like surprising him.

"Except I don't think I make a good wingman. I scare people off."

Jesse waggles his eyebrows. "You could always scare them in my direction."

"Sure. If you want."

Jesse shakes his head. "You let me get away with entirely too much, Richie. You shouldn't let me take advantage of your good nature. Nope. I'm going home with you and we are going to do whatever *you* like to do. We can visit Gaylandia another time," he says as he takes his place in the front seat.

"Okay. But I think you'll be bored."

"Not with you around, I won't," Jesse says. "You always keep me guessing. Now, tell me about the hometown friends."

I sigh.

"Please..." Jesse bats his eyelashes at me.

I shrug. It's not like I have anything better to do on the long car ride.

"Harris and Ben are the two guys who used to play with me in this band back in high school. Harris plays bass. Ben is on guitar."

"First things first: band name?"

"We didn't have a name. We just played stuff."

Jesse sighs extravagantly. "Boring… Describe them for me. What do they look like?"

"Like guys. I don't know. White. Like ninety percent of the other kids at my high school. Harris is kinda skinny. He keeps trying to grow a beard but it only grows on the sides so he looks like a Civil War reenactor."

"North or South?"

"What?"

"Confederate or Union soldier?"

I have no idea how to answer this. I never thought about it and I don't have much knowledge of Civil War era fashion trends. Jesse laughs at my confusion and rests his hand on my arm. "Okay, sweetie, we'll go with Union. How about Ben?"

"Ben has no sense of rhythm. He always comes in early. He thinks he can sing too, which is technically true. He has a solid voice, but once he starts playing, it all goes to hell. Nice guy though, I guess. He doesn't kick puppies or steal from old ladies anyway."

"And what did you guys do for fun?"

"Nothing."

Jesse gestures dramatically with his hands. "Nothing?"

"Yeah. They aren't those kinds of friends. We'd get together sometimes to play or hang out. Not fun."

"Okay… so why did you tell me about them when I asked about friends?"

"I was trying to think of people who aren't Tea."

"Ah… the infamous Tea. The one you don't ever talk about. Can you finally tell me something about her now?"

"Finally? I talk about her a lot."

Jesse shakes his head. "You really don't. You tell me all kinds of things that she's said to you, or about you, but I know almost nothing about her."

"I don't know what to say."

"What is she like?"

"She's like… herself."

Jesse groans.

"What?" I say.

"I sometimes don't even know how we can be friends! Okay. Start with a physical description and we'll go from there."

"She is short and has brown hair. Or maybe it's black. I think she has brown eyes too. Like yours."

"Good start. You know her from high school, I assume."

"Yes. We were in bio together freshman year. She passed out when they were showing videos of open heart surgery and I carried her to the nurse."

"Pity things didn't work out for the two of you. That would have been such an epic meet-cute. She's at college, you said. What's she studying?"

"Music. She plays piano."

"Is she seeing anyone?"

"Why, are you interested?"

Jesse raises an eyebrow. "Hardly, darling. I think we've established my particular romantic leanings by now. And even if she were the sparkliest diamond in the crown? Not my cup of tea, so to speak."

"Yeah. She wouldn't like you either."

"Thanks for that," Jesse says.

"I mean, obviously she'd like you. Everyone likes you. Tea was dating someone, but it was a big mess and didn't last."

"Who was the lucky gal?"

"Sophie. And Sean. They were all kind of dating. Until Sophie broke up with them."

Jesse rubs his hands together. "Ooh, drama. I'm assuming vee, not triad. So, tell me more about Sean."

"Why?"

"Because when you said his name you got a little tick in your jaw. Don't we like him? Should I spit in his beer? Tie his shoelaces together?"

I shake my head. "He's fine. He and Tea are still friends. That survived the breakup."

"Ah, I see." Jesse nods. "You're jealous."

I want to disagree, but he's right. "Yes."

"Well that's fine, because you have me now!" Jesse says, poking me in the ribs.

Wait, I have *him* now? How does that affect my friendship with Tea at all?

It takes me a moment to notice that Jesse is silently laughing at me. "I didn't mean to break your brain, sweetie. You can be friends with both of us. *I'm* not the jealous type."

Jesse put himself in charge of the music even though I'm driving. This breaks the rules that I have for my car, but he has good taste in music and he's very excited about being the drive time DJ, so I let it pass. Jesse listens to pretty much any genre, like me. But he has particular ideas about what makes for an epic road trip soundtrack. We end up listening to a lot of musicals, trucker-themed country music, and peppy retro tunes, but that's fine. Jesse sings along. I like the sound of his voice.

We aren't even across the state line when Jesse falls asleep. I wake him when we get to a rest stop.

Jesse punches me in the arm. Hard. "I told you not to let me sleep. I'm supposed to be keeping you company."

"You are. I like quiet company."

"Gee, thanks," he says. I think he's being sarcastic.

"Not an insult. I like your company even when you are not quiet. You don't choose irritating topics. And you have a nice voice. Talking or singing, I mean."

Jesse grins at that, showing off his very white teeth. He links his arm through mine as we walk into the rest station.

A middle aged white dude in a red Make America Great Again hat stares at us, his head swiveling to watch as we approach. Jesse starts to pull away from me, but I clamp my hand over his and glare at the asshole who is making him uncomfortable.

"Stop staring at my boyfriend. I'm the jealous type," I say in a low voice as we pass Mr. MAGA.

Jesse comes to an abrupt stop once we are out of that asshat's line of sight. "Richard, You can't do that. It's not safe."

"What's not safe?" I feel bad because something I did made Jesse scared. I know he's serious because he called me Richard.

"You can't say things like that. You could get hurt. We could both get hurt."

"It's 2017."

"True," Jesse says.

"He's a backwater, anachronistic, bigoted asshole."

"Yes."

I take a long, slow breath. Jesse doesn't need me to lose my temper and do something epically stupid. He already looks scared enough. "He shouldn't look at you that way," I say.

"He was only looking." Jesse bites his lip. "It's okay."

"It's not okay." I put my hands on his shoulders and I can feel that he is shaking. "Fuck him. Does this kind of crap happen a lot?"

"Yes. Of course it does, when you look like me." Jesse removes my hands from his shoulders.

"Like what? Filipino?"

Jesse sighs. "You are such an innocent little flower, darling. No. Gay."

"Because of your clothes? That's stupid. Anyone can wear clothes."

"Ha! First of all, I take offense at that. There's no way you could pull off an outfit like this." He gestures to his fitted pink button down shirt tucked into black skinny jeans with black and silver embroidery on the pockets. For earrings he has dangling silver daggers on one side and silver hoops on the other. He's wearing shiny black shoes with a two inch heel. I was wondering why he seemed so much taller.

He's right. I couldn't pull it off.

"And it's not simply the clothes, Richie. It's the way I talk, the way I walk. Everything. You can't possibly tell me that even you didn't notice?"

Of course I noticed. He likes to wear feminine clothes and jewelry. He spends a lot of time styling his hair. He often wears makeup—especially eyeliner—but it looks good on him. Not overdone. And he doesn't have any now, I don't think.

He's small and has a gentle voice. And he always moves in this graceful way like a dancer. Because he *is* a dancer. He uses expensive shampoo and soap that smells like plants in a garden. But not in a bad way. Not too fruity or flowery.

All these things are supposed to mean that he's gay.

Which he is, but people shouldn't automatically think they know that about him. Unless they want to screw him, why do they even care if he's gay anyway?

I shake my head. "None of that means anything. You talk like you. The clothes you wear are yours. Narrow minded hillbilly homophobes can go to hell. And so can sophisticated urban homophobes."

"No arguments from me on that one. Still. Can you do me a favor and maybe dial back the jealous boyfriend routine while we're on the road? I should know better—I should always remember to keep my hands to myself at truck stops in the Midwest. Maybe wear a baseball cap and a sports jersey."

"That would look good on you too. But if you wear the wrong team's jersey you're in danger again."

The bigoted asshole is gone when we go back to the car. Jesse walks several steps ahead of me. He doesn't loop his arm through mine or put his hand on my shoulder.

This makes me sad. If we were on campus, it would be completely normal for him to be glued to my side. No one would bat an eye. And this distance between us doesn't feel normal to me. Not at all. I'm surprised that I miss the connection. I miss him being close.

9 Welcome

"My mom will ask you to call her Imogene. You don't have to."

I carry all of my things and most of Jesse's. He tries to take one of his bags back from me but I hold it out of his reach. Height has its advantages. He jumps in an attempt to capture his luggage with no success. Apparently he can fly on stage but can't manage to attain any height at all in real life.

He flips me off. "Dick."

I return the gesture. "Diva."

Jesse gives up and glares at me. He only manages to retain one of his pieces of luggage: a brown leather over-the-shoulder bag with his initials embossed in gold.

My mom is waiting in the kitchen when we walk in. She's wearing navy pants and a matching navy and white striped shirt. Her ash-brown hair is pulled into a messy bun on top of her head. I know it wasn't messy when she started cooking. I can smell ham in the oven. The table is already set for five.

"Is Gabby coming for dinner tonight?" My sister isn't always the most reliable when it comes to family get-togethers. Especially if she has a girlfriend, although I think she's between girlfriends at the moment.

My mom nods. "She might be late. And this must be Jesse."

"Yes. Obviously. Since that's who I told you was coming home with me."

"Pleased to meet you, Mrs. Hargrove." Jesse smiles brightly.

"You can call me Imogene," my mom says.

Jesse winks at me and I try not to snort.

"My room's upstairs."

When we get there I drop all the bags on the floor. Jesse looks around my room in fascination. Like he is on an archaeological expedition. There isn't anything all that remarkable. Bed. Desk. Bookshelves. There are some old model rockets I never bothered to get rid of hanging from the ceiling. Band posters on the wall. Well, drummer posters on the wall. John Bonham. Neil Peart. Longeneu "LP" Parsons.

"So, this is you as a high schooler?" Jesse says, running his hand along the desk.

"No. This is where my bed is. You wanna see me? You'll have to look elsewhere. Come on."

He follows me downstairs. We pass through the kitchen where my mom is folding cloth napkins and putting them under the silverware—a sign that Jesse counts as "real company."

Finally we end up in the basement. "This is me."

"Ah. The man-cave."

Jesse picks up one of the mallets for the marimba and picks out a tune I don't recognize. "Nice." He taps on the snare and runs a fingernail along the cymbal. It makes my skin itch.

"Sorry." He noticed. He always notices when I'm uncomfortable. Although this is probably not surprising; I have no poker face.

"Yeah. I don't really share my drums."

There's an old couch in the corner opposite the flatscreen TV. He collapses on the couch and pulls me down beside him.

"Gimme a shoulder. I'm tired."

He doesn't use my shoulder, though. He shifts to drape his legs over the arm of the couch and puts his head on my lap. "That is not my shoulder."

"This makes a better pillow. You're bony as hell."

"I am not bony."

"Well, your shoulders are. Your muscular thighs make a much more comfortable pillow," he says. "What's on the agenda? I doubt you brought me down here to seduce me," he says with a smile.

"No. I am now going to demonstrate the superiority of *Holiday Inn* over *White Christmas*. Then tell me I'm not right." I pull up a playlists and adjust the volume. Only the musical numbers—we don't have time for a full viewing of both movies. Not before dinner, anyway.

Once we've seen most of what the two shows have to offer, Jesse sits up. "I don't know... *White Christmas* has that 'Choreography' number that's pretty great. And Bing Crosby and Danny Kaye in drag? How can you not love that? I thought you were a fan of the comic genius."

I'm afraid that my plan has backfired. Because ignoring my strong dislike of the performance of the song "White Christmas" in the newer movie, I have to admit I enjoy a lot of the dance numbers.

"You're right."

"I am?" he says. "I win?" He claps his hands together and beams.

"Don't rub it in. You're right about the *musical* parts. It's the story that's less appealing."

"Boys, time for dinner," my mom calls.

Gabby is not there so it's just us and my parents.

My dad doesn't say much. He never does. He looks like an old, balding version of me. If male-pattern baldness is true, I should be in the clear, though. My uncles both have full heads of hair.

My mom asks Jesse all the usual questions. I don't pay any attention. The ham is good. She made golden raisin sauce and scalloped potatoes too. Jesse kicks me under the table.

"I wasn't listening," I say.

Jesse rolls his eyes. "Obviously. Your mom wants to know what we have planned for tomorrow."

"We're going to Jane's. Tea says there's a thing. We'll eat there."

"Oh. Your friend from high school?" My mom asks, as if there could possibly be more than one Tea.

When it's time for bed, Jesse asks if I want him to sleep on the floor.

"Why would I want you to sleep on the floor?"

Jesse looks at me with one eyebrow raised so I know it's a stupid question.

"Oh. Because you're gay? Don't be an idiot. Don't have sex with me and we'll be fine. That won't be a problem for you, will it?"

Jesse laughs. "No problem. I have successfully not had sex with you ever since we met. Before then, even. I have been not having sex with you for my entire life, actually."

It gets hot as hell at night with an extra body in the bed even though it's fall and plenty cold outside. In my sleep, I throw all the covers onto the floor. Violently. But in doing so, I also elbow Jesse in the face. Violently.

"Jesus Christ!" Jessie shouts quietly so his voice doesn't carry outside the room. He puts a hand to his face and it comes away bloody.

"Shit. I'm sorry." I feel sick to my stomach. It's not because of the blood. It's because I hurt Jesse. I don't even hurt people I don't like. I mean, I'd wanted to punch his ex-roommate. I would have been more than happy to deck the dude in the hat for looking at Jesse the wrong way. I hadn't laid a finger on them, but I'd given Jesse a bloody nose.

I wanted to protect him from them and I was the one he needed protecting from.

I grab a box of tissues for him so he can soak up the blood. I rub his back while he pinches his nose. I don't know what else to do. Am I supposed to get ice? Is he supposed to lean forwards or backwards? "I'm sorry. I'm so sorry. I'll sleep on the floor." I stand up and pull my pillow from the bed.

Jesse grabs me by the elbow. "Richie, you're sweet, but don't be an ass." He pulls me back down to sit beside him. "You'll sleep in this bed and that's my final word on the subject." Once his nose has stopped bleeding he lies down and falls asleep almost right away.

I lie down beside him but it takes me forever to get back to sleep. I scoot way over to the side of the bed until I'm nearly falling off. What if I turn over again and commit another assault in my sleep? I watch him for a long time. I don't hurt people. I don't. But I keep hurting Jesse. Grabbing his injured wrist, dropping books on his head, and now this.

I feel nauseous.

When I wake up in the morning, Jesse is already up and dressed and sitting at the foot of the bed scrolling through his phone. I hope I didn't push him off the bed in the middle of the night. He doesn't look much worse for the wear.

"Morning, sunshine!" he says cheerily.

I rub my hand over my face. How long did I lie awake last night? I feel like I could sleep another ten hours. Jesse looks perky as hell, despite my vicious night time attack. I'm relieved to see I did not give him a black eye. Of course, he slept quite a bit in the car while I was driving. He has an excuse to be well rested.

When we go downstairs, my sister Gabby is sitting on the couch. She stops us on our way to the kitchen. The left side of her head is shaved. Mom will definitely not be a fan.

"Welcome back, big sis. Your hair looks like crap."

"Hey there little bro. Your breath stinks. And it's Jesse, right?"

I scowl at her. "My breath smells fine. And why do people keep asking if he's Jesse? You know he's Jesse. You've even seen pictures of him."

"Really?" Jesse turns to me and raises an eyebrow.

I nod. "Yes. Official ones. From your recital."

"I'm flattered."

"You should be," Gabby says. "Besides the fact that you can apparently levitate—which is quite impressive—you are one of only two people that Richard talks about by name. And that we have photographic proof of their existence."

"Shut up."

Gabby and Jesse laugh together.

"Oh. Do Mom and Dad know?" I want to ask her before I forget.

"About..." Gabby starts to ask but then she realizes what I mean. "Ah. About my sapphic nature? Dad does. Mom doesn't. Unless he's told her, which I highly doubt."

"Fair." My dad doesn't care about people being gay. When he found out that Tea was gay he didn't say anything.

But my mom did. She kept asking if Tea was really sure that she was gay. She said maybe Tea would grow out of it or change her mind. Clearly my mom doesn't understand how being gay works, and I figure it's not my job to explain it.

"Do they know about..." Gabby gestures at Jesse.

"About 'the gay' who's cohabitating with their beloved son? Possibly corrupting his wholesome suburban morals?" Jesse whispers.

"Yeah," Gabby whispers back. They both look at me expectantly.

I'm confused by the question. "Why would I tell them? Not their business. Not anyone's business but yours."

"That is why I love this man," Jesse says, throwing his arm around my shoulders.

"Oh really?" My sister raises both eyebrows.

"In a purely platonic way," Jesse assures her.

"Of course." And then she winks at him.

10 Asian Adonis

I park out front of Jane's house and walk up the long driveway with Jesse's arm looped in mine. Her house is large and imposing, set back on a heavily wooded lot.

"Do I look okay?" Jesse asks.

"Of course."

He tugs on my sleeve. "You didn't even look."

I stop to look him over from head to toe. He's wearing one of his satiny pastel shirts and skinny jeans. A thin silver chain matches his favorite silver hoop earrings. He's wearing subtle eye makeup that makes his eyes look bright. I wonder if he's wearing lipstick. His lips look naturally pink anyway.

"You always look good," I say.

Jesse laughs.

We're greeted at the door by Jane herself. Her hair is in box braids reaching almost to her waist. "Richard! What a welcome surprise. And this is..."

"I'm Jesse. Richard's roommate from school."

"Well, make yourself at home. There are refreshments in the kitchen."

It's a pretty small crowd. Just people who have graduated high school and are going to school close enough to come home for such a short break. Jesse introduces himself to everyone, which is good since I have forgotten a lot of names. But it's not like he'll see most of these people again, so it probably doesn't matter either way.

Tea is there with Sean, of course. The two of them are still together. Kind of. Sean nods at me, but fades into the background without saying anything.

"Jesse. I've heard so much about you," Tea says. "The roommate, right?"

Jesse nods. "The friend, right?"

"The one and only." Tea grins.

"Not anymore, you're not. Now shoo." Jesse gives me a push. "I'm digging up all the dirt on high school Richie."

"Fine. I'll get drinks."

I'm driving, but Jesse likes white wine. I get him a small glass from the kitchen.

"Thank you, sweetheart," he says when I return. He leaves one hand resting on my arm as he takes a sip.

"You find out anything?" I ask.

He shrugs. "I'll never tell. But I thought it was only fair to give her a few tasty morsels on your life at college."

"Like what?"

Tea grins. "He told me you set fire to some rice in the communal kitchen in the dorm."

"That's only because I accidentally set the microwave for twenty hours instead of twenty minutes and didn't come back in time."

Tea's eyes widen. "Dear god, did you become *me* at college? That takes talent."

Jesse chuckles. "I know. Honestly, who can't cook rice? To the point where it actually bursts into flame?"

"It wasn't really flaming. It only smoldered. I'd never made rice in a microwave before. I wouldn't recommend it."

"Well, the whole dorm smelled for days. You're lucky I covered for you, Richie." Jesse pokes me in the ribs, in the only spot where I am ticklish. I grab his hand reflexively and give him a warning look.

He retrieves his hand, pretending to be hurt. I know I didn't hurt him. I was careful. He glares at me. "Dick."

I roll my eyes. "Diva."

Tea gives me a pointed look.

"What?"

She shakes her head and mouths, "Later."

Jesse is always popular in a crowd, but he gets even chattier and more charismatic when he has a glass of wine. He soon has a crowd of admirers soaking up his stories. I'm not surprised. He's the most interesting person here.

I leave him standing at the counter with his audience and go to the tv room. There's always a movie playing. This time it's *Bohemian Rhapsody*. I've seen it before. I like the music.

I'm surprised when Jesse walks into the room not too much later.

"You abandoned me." He flops down next to me, sticking out his lower lip.

I think he's joking. "You were having fun. I didn't think you wanted to watch a movie."

"Richie, I am your date for the evening. And it's poor form to leave me alone." He snuggles in closer.

"Right. Sorry." I'm still not sure if he's serious or not.

When he starts squeezing in beside me, people shift to make room on the couch.

"Oh, that's okay. I don't need much space," Jesse says. He sits half in my lap with his legs across mine.

"What about my space?"

"You don't need much either," he says, draping an arm around my neck.

"Fine." I sigh.

Part way through the movie he sends me to get more wine. "Are you sure?" I ask him.

"Yes, Mom. I'm fine. I won't get falling-down drunk from two little glasses."

Tea grabs me on my way to the kitchen and pulls me aside. "What?"

"So, Jesse seems nice," she says.

"Yes. He is. Did you drag me away to tell me that?"

Tea lowers her head and narrows her eyes at me. "Are you and Jesse maybe more than friends?"

"No. What do you mean? He's gay. I'm not."

Tea doesn't say anything for a while. "Are you sure?"

"Yes. He told me he's gay. And he has sex with men. Which is fairly definitive."

"No. I mean... Do you think *you* might be gay?"

I was not expecting that. "No. Why?"

"Well, you two seem very hands-on with each other. And also: Sweetheart? Baby? Darling... *Richie?*"

I shake my head and smile. "That's how Jesse is. He's that way with everyone.'"

Tea chews on her bottom lip. "But *you're* not that way. Except with Jesse. Have you thought about why that is?"

"Why what is?"

"Why are there different rules for Jesse? You'd bite my head off if I called you Richie. And we've been friends forever. Why are you okay with Jesse's nicknames for you? And what about being so close? Why are you comfortable with him sitting in your lap? You two look natural together—so clearly this is not new behavior. And there's something about the way you look at him."

"How do I look at him?" I ask.

Tea shrugs. "Like he's yours."

"Well, that was your idea. You said get a person. A friend. That's what he is. My friend."

Tea tilts her head to the side. "Maybe."

I frown. "We're friends. Like you and Sean are friends. I've seen the two of you together. You hold hands. You sleep on his shoulder. And you wouldn't do that with other people. Not even me. Different people, different rules. Isn't this the same?"

"Maybe. Maybe not. Be careful, Richard. I don't want you to get hurt. And I know you don't want to hurt Jesse."

This makes me think of the way I gave him a bloody nose and that sick feeling in the pit of my stomach—even though I know that's not what she's talking about.

I deliver Jesse's refill and he snuggles in beside me again. Tea is right. I don't simply *tolerate* him sitting in my lap—I like it. This feels natural. Because this is Jesse and it's how things are with us. How they have always been as far as I can remember.

Tea has me wondering, though. Why are there different rules for Jesse?

After half of his second glass, Jesse's cheeks are already tinged with pink.

He's not as bad off as he was the night of *Singin' in the Rain*. I still take the glass away from him before he finishes it off. "I don't know why you drink at all. Why would you ever touch alcohol when it only makes you sick?"

"It's not that bad. I feel okay now."

I get him a large glass of water and order him to drink the whole thing.

He grumbles about me being such a worrywart. "It's cute the way you look out for me, sweetie. But I'm fine."

He does seem okay. Just a bit sleepy. He dozes off during the last part of the movie. I have to put my arms around him to prevent him from sliding off the couch.

When it's time to go he tugs on my sleeve. "I'm tired. Carry me."

"No."

"Please?"

"No."

"Piggy back?"

I shake my head. "You can walk on your own damn feet. Lean on me if you need to."

I stand next to him and put my arm around his waist so I'm practically carrying him anyway. Tea gives me a knowing look on the way out.

"Shut up," I say too quietly for even Jesse to hear.

He might not be drunk, exactly, but the alcohol has clearly taken its toll. Jesse falls face-first into bed when we get back to my room. For such a small person he manages to take up a lot of space. All of the space, actually.

"Hey." I give him a shove, but he doesn't move at all. "If you don't want to sleep in your clothes you've gotta wake up at least partially. Work with me here."

He opens his eyes and glares at me. "Fine." He peels off his pants and fumbles to unbutton his shirt before collapsing again. I push his hands away and undo the buttons one by one. I pull his arms out of the sleeves while he mumbles wordless complaints. Once he's out of his constricting clothing, he settles more deeply into the bed, his breathing becoming deep and even. I envy Jesse for his ability to fall asleep without fanfare.

I take a few minutes to get ready for bed myself before shoving him gently to the side to make room. I can't complain about him being a bed hog because at least he doesn't commit violence on me in his sleep.

I look at Jesse's peaceful face and it strikes me that he is very handsome. This seems like something I should have noticed before. No, he is not handsome. He is beautiful. Not only his face, either.

I noticed from very early on in our friendship, dance has made him very fit. There is no part of him that is not well-defined from hours of practice. And I have seen every part of him. He is not shy, and we share a room. Not that I spend a lot of time ogling him. That would be rude.

He isn't built like a weightlifter. He isn't musclebound with bulging biceps. And he isn't gaunt like a distance runner. His physique is perfectly balanced. His muscles are subtly defined along every limb. And his skin is smooth and flawless. He looks like a classical statue. If the Greeks or Romans did statues of very fit Asian dudes and not cut Mediterranean dudes.

I lie there next to Jesse and close my eyes. The sheets are cool against my skin. There is only faint light coming in through the curtain from the streetlamp. A few cars drive by. I don't feel at all tired. I am very aware of Jesse's mostly naked body and how close it is to mine. I am aware of the scent of his body, which against all odds doesn't stink.

Damn Tea and her questions.

Why am I okay with him calling me Richie?

Why can he be so close to me?

Why do I care what his body looks like?

Why do I keep looking at his body?

My eyes are open again. Feigning sleep is no good. The light coming in through the window gives his skin a faint sheen. I wonder if it feels as smooth as it looks.

These are not the thoughts of someone who is straight, are they? People don't have these thoughts about their friends, do they?

I realize after what feels like hours of fruitless struggle that there is no way I can possibly get to sleep. Not with this Asian Adonis lying next to me. I slide out of bed, shuddering when my bare feet touch the cold floor. Jesse stirs a little, but doesn't wake as I steal out of the room.

If it weren't the middle of the night—early morning really—I'd play drums loud enough to shake the walls. But this would not be a popular choice with the other people in the house and I don't want my parents to sell my drum set when I'm away at college. So I'll have to leave the sticks alone.

I go downstairs and break out some old console video games. I need to find batteries for the controller, which means an extensive search of the junk drawer in the kitchen. I can't remember the last time I played this thing. I go through a few different games. I can see why I haven't played in a long while. The graphics suck. The music is repetitive and tinny. Eventually I realize that I'm not really playing games anymore; I'm staring at the screen and holding a remote in my hand.

It's just before dawn when I go back to my room. Too soon to get up and too late to go to sleep. Jesse has spread out to take up more than his fair share of the bed. I pick up his legs and move them. When I slide in beside him, he rolls over, facing away from me. I study Jesse's bare back in the half-light of morning. I imagine running my fingers lightly down his spine. It is more of a temptation than I thought it would be.

I think I figured out the reason the rules are different with him. Jesse is ridiculously outgoing, naturally flirty, and cheerful as hell. In spite of this, I enjoy his company. That's what he does to people—he puts them at ease. Of course I'm different with him. And of course he can call me whatever the hell he wants. That's friendship.

But in terms of physical attraction? I don't think so. I'm pretty sure it's only aesthetic appreciation on my part. Of course I love watching him on stage because who wouldn't? He is powerful, and ethereal, and almost heartbreakingly beautiful when he dances. And of course I like the way he looks when he is lying in my bed in the half-light of morning, his legs tangled in my sheets. Because he is a fucking work of art. I don't think that necessarily means that I'm gay. Not conclusively, anyway.

Somehow I manage to sleep a few hours. When I wake up, Jesse has his head on my chest and his leg thrown over mine. It feels nice. Other than the fact that he is like a small furnace and I have a partial boner.

But I'm pretty sure it's only morning wood.

11 Thanks

Jesse wakes well rested with no ill effects from the party last night. Thankfully I didn't clobber him in the few hours I managed to spend in bed. I feel like I could sleep for the rest of the day, but that is definitely not an option.

When we enter the kitchen on Thanksgiving morning, my mom is already in full-on meal prep. My dad is sharpening the carving knives while standing at the island in the center of the kitchen. Gabby is grating orange rind for my grandma's traditional cranberry sauce that we make every year that no one likes. My mom is murdering the corpse of the turkey with the power of her eyes.

"Back away. Back away slowly," Gabby whispers to Jesse. "Don't let her see you. And whatever you do, don't make eye contact." She nods at my mom, who is now trying to tie the legs of the turkey together with twine while pretending not to swear under her breath.

My mom doesn't seem like the kind of person who would even know half of the words she's using. She saves them up for special occasions.

I turn silently, pushing Jesse towards the door. A floorboard creaks, and I freeze.

"Too late," Gabby says.

My mom is looking straight at us. Then she points at me quite aggressively. "Whipping cream for the pie." She makes it sound like a death sentence.

Thank God that's all it is. At least this will get us out of the house and away from the danger zone.

"Food first," I say. It's a mark of my mom's single minded focus on preparing the perfect Thanksgiving meal that she hasn't instantly offered to fix Jesse a made-to-order hot breakfast. I think my mom can do guests, or Thanksgiving, but not both. That's fine. I can take care of the company. And the rest of the family can deal with her particular brand of holiday madness.

My dad gestures toward the table where there is a bag of bagels and cream cheese. Gabby tosses some bottles of juice to Jesse.

"We're not eating here?" he asks.

"Not a chance."

My mom's curse-word filter fails yet again as one of the turkey legs escapes.

"Ah," Jesse says. "I see."

I have the inside scoop on where to get whipped cream on Thanksgiving, since forgetting some crucial ingredient for the big meal is par for the course around here. Most of the grocery stores are closed already, but there is a gas station convenience store not too far away that carries some last-minute Thanksgiving staples: fried onions, cream of mushroom soup, canned green beans, creamed corn, jellied cranberries, whipping cream. I am sure we forget one or more of these items every year. Maybe that's how the store decides what to stock—whatever my family neglects to purchase on time becomes part of their order for the following year.

We have some time before the pie topping is necessary, so there is no need to rush our errand. I stop at a nearby lakeside park with a handy table for our chilly morning picnic.

"You have a great group of friends," Jesse says between mouthfuls of bagel. "Jane is charming. And Sean and Tea are positively adorable." I didn't even know he'd met Sean. "Although I can see why you don't like him if Tea was the object of your affection."

I shrug. "We get along fine."

"Right. I could tell that by the way you two greeted one another so warmly."

I'm not sure I greeted anyone. Social niceties are not my specialty. First Tea and now Jesse has taken the role of prompting me for appropriate responses.

Jesse perks up. "Hey, what was all that secretive whispering between you and Tea? Any juicy gossip you'd like to share?"

"She had some questions. She's curious about you. I'm not saying this for sympathy; I don't have many friends. I think she was surprised I brought anyone home."

"Ah. Checking out the competition," Jesse says, making ridiculous poses and kissing his biceps.

Once we're done eating, Jesse wants to go for a short walk along the lake. There is a paved path along the shore that leads back into a lightly wooded area of the park.

"This place must be beautiful with fall color," Jesse says.

"Yes. But now it's ugly."

"Poor November." Jesse shakes his head. "After fall color and before the icy sparkle of snow cover. The only claim to fame is a holiday that involves the butchering of birds and people gorging themselves on five kinds of stuffing."

"I think we only have one kind."

The trip to the store is brief and uneventful. We're in good company; the aisles are clogged with teenagers sent on last minute errands.

As soon as we walk into the house Gabby takes the whipping cream off my hands. "About damn time. She was about to call out the National Guard on you."

My mom might be a terror in the kitchen on big occasions like this, but she does put together a fine Thanksgiving spread. Roast turkey, plenty of outside-the-bird stuffing, homemade cornbread, green bean casserole, creamed corn, that horrible cranberry sauce, fresh-baked rolls, mashed potatoes and gravy... plus two kinds of pie for dessert.

"Mrs. Hargrove—Imogene—the turkey is absolute perfection." Jesse helps himself to a second serving.

I don't pay much attention to whatever he's saying. He's not talking to me anyway. I listen to the sound of his voice and notice the expressions on my parents' faces, though. My mom smiles at him a lot. And it isn't the fake, Midwestern smile she uses strictly for politeness.

My dad tells one of the three jokes that he has in his repertoire, which he doesn't do all that often. This joke is the one that's about a parrot. The punchline is, "And then when she takes him out of the freezer the parrot says, 'I'm terribly sorry for my uncouth language. But I have to ask, what did the turkey ever do to you?'"

Jesse laughs, and it's a real laugh that makes my dad smile.

Gabby can talk to anyone, so it's no surprise that she and Jesse hit it off. He gets her to tell us something about her classes, which is more than any of us have heard about school from her in the past two years.

"You're welcome back anytime Jesse," my mom says sweetly as Jesse and I are clearing the table. Everyone else was on meal prep, so we're on clean up duty.

"I think my mom likes you better than she likes me or Gabby," I say, with my arms up to my elbows in dishwater.

"Of course," Jesse says with a wink as he finishes drying a plate and stacks it neatly in the cupboard. "I'm exactly the kinda guy you take home to meet the parents."

12 Gaylandia

"Come on boys. Get off your asses. You have five minutes to get in the car," Gabby says. She's standing by the front door twirling her car keys.

Jesse looks up from his spot on the couch beside me. "Where are we going?"

"Out. Grab your coat. It's chilly outside."

After a day lounging around eating leftovers it will be good to get out of the house. Jesse looks at me with one eyebrow raised.

"She's got a plan," I say.

"And that plan is…"

"Put your coat on."

We all pile into Gabby's little car. For the entire twenty minute drive, my sister plays show tunes and she and Jesse sing along. My sister doesn't have a great voice, but Jesse more than makes up for that. Harmonizing beautifully. Always on beat.

It takes a while to find a decent parking place in the city, but eventually we find a good spot.

"Where are you taking me? I'm simply bursting with curiosity!" Jesse squeezes my arm as we walk from the parking ramp to our destination. His excitement is infectious.

"It's a surprise," I say.

Jesse rolls his eyes. "Well, I gathered that. Any hints? What about you, Gabby? Not even a scrap of information? Somebody, please… don't leave me dying of suspense!"

Gabby shakes her head and walks faster, leaving us a few steps behind. She's wearing a black velvet jumpsuit and ridiculous heels. I'm not sure how she can walk in them at all.

"Bitch," Jesse says without malice.

"Homo," she calls back without looking.

Jesse and my sister have bonded. Which no doubt means I'm in big trouble.

"We're here," Gabby says as we arrive at a nondescript brick building.

"And here is…" Jesse prompts.

I hold the door open and gesture for him to enter with a flourish. "Gaylandia."

"In these clothes?" Jesse says, his eyes wide. "And me without my face!" He fans himself as if he is going to faint.

He's wearing tight black pants and his favorite boots. His silky button-down shirt has red, cream and gray rectangles that look like stained glass or a Mondrian painting. And despite his comment about not having his face on, it looks like he might have some subtle eyeliner.

I smile and shake my head. "You look good," I tell him.

Gabby gives him a once-over with a critical eye. "My brother is clearly whipped. You look... passable. Don't worry. This place, not 'Gaylandia' by the way, is very low key. I didn't think my brother could handle the more flamingly queer clubs."

I shrug.

I've been here before. This place is one of my sister's favorites. When Tea and Sophie broke up or whatever, Gabby took her here a few times. I told her not to. Tea can't take loud noises. And she's not very good with crowds. I came with them the first time. I'm amazed there was a second time. Gabby insisted that Tea needed practice flirting. Probably true.

It's not too crowded the Friday after Thanksgiving. They have a live band playing. I haven't heard them before. They're not bad. I wonder if they're local.

Despite my sister's warnings to disavow all knowledge of me due to my inability to dance, Jesse drags me to the dance floor. I do have a sense of rhythm, obviously. But I never know what to do with my hands. Or my feet. Or really any part of my body.

"Oh relax, Richie. Nobody is looking at you. Oh wait, I think the positively adorable bartender is throwing some amorous glances your way."

I follow his gaze. "Not amorous. Probably murderous. She's Gabby's ex. She never liked me. I didn't like her much either. She didn't adjust the mirrors properly on her car."

Jesse snorts. "You find the oddest things to dislike about people. Like your lab partner in chem? Because of how she smells?"

"No. That's not why. I mean, she does smell like lint. But I don't like her because she's mean. Not as bad as your ex-roommate. Not homophobic. That's maybe one of her finer points: she's nasty to everyone without bias."

"Well, that's a solid reason not to like someone. So, what are my bad points, if I may ask? Don't worry about hurting my feelings. Thespians must develop thick skin to deal with the critics."

"Nothing," I say.

"Oh, come on. There must be something. Do I snore? Take up too much space in the room? You don't like the earrings I wear or how loudly I turn the pages of my books when I'm reading? I wear too much makeup? I'm embarrassingly effeminate? Too publicly affectionate?"

"No. None of those things. They don't bother me." I stop and think for a while before saying, "It bothers me when you get hurt."

Jesse shakes his head. "That's not quite in the spirit of things, Richie. Come on. There must be some idiosyncratic thing I do that drives you batty from time to time."

"I can't think of anything." And it's true.

I know he's not perfect, and maybe it was hard to figure him out at first. But now it's different. When I try to think of things that bother me about him, all I can think of is the things I like about him.

He's easy to spend time with. He's kind and funny and takes care of people without making them feel bad about it. He has a nice voice and can sing harmony even if he has only heard a song once. He's good at telling stories but he doesn't talk all the time and is fine with being quiet. He's tidy without being obsessive about it. He can handle my habitual rudeness without getting offended. And as for being overly affectionate? It doesn't bother me that he's always close to me. I like that he's always close to me. I miss him when he's not nearby.

"You're you. You're… just right." I shrug.

"Why Richie, you're making me blush."

"I don't know why. I'm only telling the truth."

Gabby comes to find us and shoos me away so she can claim some time on the dance floor with Jesse. My sister can dance. They look good together.

I sit at the bar and watch them. It's not like they're dancing all that differently from anyone else. Nothing elaborate. But there is a clear difference between the way they interact with the music and the way most other people here do. Gabby and Jesse don't just sway back and forth or jump up and down. They include small gestures that hint at details in the music. Pausing at exactly the right time, both of them in unison, as if they've rehearsed.

A blond guy wearing a sleeveless shirt sits next to me. He smells like citrus and mint. I glance at him briefly. His skin is flushed. He has a tattoo of a leaf on the inside of his left wrist.

"Can I buy you a drink?" he asks.

"No." I look back to the dance floor.

"Ah," he says, following my line of sight. "Your boyfriend's got some moves."

"Not my boyfriend."

The guy nods thoughtfully. "Good to know."

I get off the stool partly to get away from him and the prospect of having to deal with any possibility of conversation, and partly to find the men's room.

When I get back, Gabby is seated alone at the bar and Jesse is nowhere to be seen.

I sit down next to her. I'm about to ask if she's seen Jesse, but before I say anything she points at the far side of the dance floor. "Your hot little roommate is attracting a lot of attention. Not surprising. He's cute as a button."

I look over to see the blond guy with his body pressed up against Jesse. Jesse is laughing and a small crowd has gathered around them, cheering them on. They're dancing. That's all. But I don't like it.

"Um... little bro? Is there something you'd like to tell me?"

"About what?"

"Green is not a good color on you, Richie."

I spin on my stool to face her. "Don't call me that. And what do you mean?"

Gabby shakes her head with a sad expression on her face. "Jealous, much?" She nods toward Jesse.

"I…" I start to say something, but realize there is probably no other explanation for why I am gritting my teeth at the sight of blondie grinding against Jesse.

When Jesse comes back to find me, he drags me by the wrist to dance some more.

"You looked like you were having fun," I say.

"Yeah, I guess so. But it's not the same as when I'm with you, sweetie. All my other dance partners pale by comparison."

I can't be sure, but I think I might be fucking blushing.

13 Results Inconclusive

The rest of the visit went by without anything of interest happening. Other than my mom reiterating that Jesse was welcome to visit any time. I'm just glad to be back in our room and settled into our regular routine again.

"Jesus, Richie!" Jesse hisses as I press my thumbs into the space just beneath his shoulder blade. "I thought your regular massages were painful, but this is next level."

"Stay still and quit whining. You'll alert the whole dorm and Grey will come barging in to make sure I'm not murdering you. You're fine." He's face down on his bed so I have easier access. The room smells of white flower oil, which is apparently a Filipino cure for everything. It doesn't make a bad massage oil even though it smells a little bit medicinal. "If you don't want me to do this then…" I take my hands off his back.

"No no no. You're right. I'm fine. Maybe give a gal a little warning next time, okay sweetie?"

"Sure." I rub some more flower oil between my hands to warm it. "This is gonna hurt, but it's your own fault for reinjuring yourself."

It happened right after we returned to campus. He fell wrong during practice and wrenched his shoulder. He wanted to pretend like everything was fine afterwards, but he could barely undress himself and stayed up half the night in pain. I made him go to urgent care the next day where they gave him a prescription for heavy-duty anti-inflammatories.

The following week, when the doctor had given the go-ahead, I dragged Jesse to the trainer and had her show me what to do to help him as things healed—now that the best medicine wasn't simply to leave everything alone. She showed me a few things to avoid. A few tips for pressure points I hadn't known about. I had taken notes, which Jesse made fun of me for doing. But I wasn't going to be the one to ruin his shoulder by being an idiot. He was doing a fine job of that by himself.

Enough time has passed that I am able to use some of the techniques she showed me. Even though it doesn't hurt quite as much as it did at the time of the injury, it's still not a pleasant experience. Jesse moans into the pillow—well really it's more of a yell—as I rotate his shoulder gently and activate another acupressure point. I am extra careful not to push too far or use too much force. I hate the part of the massage when I feel him tense beneath my fingers as he goes utterly silent. I know then that he is truly in pain. And I'm the one causing it.

Finally I'm done with the excruciating parts of the massage. Now it's only for relaxation. I run my thumbs down Jesse's back on either side of his spine with only moderate pressure. His skin is smooth under my hands. I can feel the tension leaving his muscles. I like this part of the massage the best.

"I think you are a minor deity of some sort. Or the patron saint of massage. Ahhhhhhh." Jesse sighs extravagantly.

In the two weeks since Thanksgiving I have spent so much time worrying about Jesse's shoulder that I haven't thought a lot about Tea's proposal that I might be in love with him. Now that I have him half naked and moaning on his bed... It is a terrible time to be revisiting these thoughts.

The oil on his back has given his skin a faint sheen. I rest my hands on his back between his shoulder blades. As I let them slip down the sides of his back, he lets out another soft moan.

"Okay. Done here," I say, stepping away quickly.

Jesse turns so he is facing me. "Where did you learn how to do that?"

"Your trainer, asshole. You were there."

"I mean before that. You have always had an amazing touch." He says in an over-the-top husky voice. Is he flirting more than usual or is it just getting to me more because I'm overthinking the nature of our friendship?

"YouTube," I say, wiping my hands on a towel.

"What?"

"I learned massage by watching a lot of YouTube."

Jesse raises an eyebrow. "Okay... But why?"

"I thought it would be a good life skill. Plus my sister was a gymnast. She put me to work at her meets in between events. I was kind of the mascot of the team. In addition to being a good life skill, I believe basic knowledge of sports massage kept me alive during my pre-adolescence. She was scary."

"Not Gabby! Sweet, angelic Gabby?" Jesse gasps. "Well, that is the most adorable story. Did they have a cute mascot nickname for you?"

"Yes. They called me Richard."

Jesse laughs and I feel giddy at the sound, or maybe giddy at the thought that I made him laugh? It's a ridiculous feeling. I don't like it.

"Well, you're right. Richard is a cute nickname. Maybe I should call you Richard from now on."

"No," I say without thinking. Jesse raises an eyebrow.

"Richie is fine. For you, I mean." I shut my mouth and walk away to keep from saying anything more asinine.

It's late. I hand Jesse a glass of water and his prescription pain meds. I wait for him to swallow the pills and take the glass from his hand.

He grins up at me. "Thanks, Richie darling."

I feel my heart skip a beat when our eyes meet.

Fuck.

*

The next morning I'm tired as hell. I can barely pry my eyes open. The light coming in through the ugly curtains is particularly offensive. I slept poorly thanks to Jesse and his stupid dark eyes and flirty smile. Thanks to his impressive physique and the feeling of his skin beneath my hands. While he is washing up before breakfast I pull out my phone and find an online quiz: "How gay are you?"

It's twenty stupid questions long. And the answer is of no help whatsoever. Of course. The quiz was probably written by some pimply fourteen year old during a dull moment in ninth grade health class.

Can you imagine kissing someone of the same sex.

Who can't imagine that?

Do you think this person is attractive?

And of course they only put pictures of attractive people.

The results of the quiz inform me that "Traditional labels are meaningless to you," and goes on to explain how I am free to celebrate my sexuality, or lack thereof, in any way I choose. Which is stupid, because of course that is true for everyone.

The idea of whether I find certain people attractive or not is on my mind when Jesse comes back to our room with a towel slung around his waist and nothing else. It is definitely not the time to blurt out, "Tea thinks I might be gay." So of course I do.

Jesse stops in his tracks, looks at me from head to toe and then laughs so hard he gets tears in his eyes.

"What?" I didn't think it was that funny.

"I'm sorry." Jesse stops laughing finally. "And what makes Tea think you're gay?"

"I let you call me Richie."

"Right." Jesse nods slowly, wiping tears away from his eyes. "We all know the secret litmus test for gayness—tolerance of nicknames."

"She also thinks I might be in love with you—my sister too—and I'm wondering if they might be right. I took a quiz to see if I was gay, but it was inconclusive. And I think being in love with you is a separate thing anyway."

Jesse doesn't say anything for what is probably only a few moments, but feels like a long time. He faces me on the bed with a blank expression. He doesn't look like himself. I realize how rarely I've seen him without a smile.

"What..." he starts to say something but then trails off.

"I know that we're friends. But after I talked to Tea... She made me think about how things are between us. How close we are. How I am protective of you."

"That's who I am. And it's who you are. I'm a flamingly gay theater major who has no need for personal space. You are a gruff-seeming softy who can't stand to see anyone hurt. And... We. Are. Friends."

"Yes. I said that. That's what I told Tea. That's what I said to you. But she pointed out that you are the only person who can call me anything but Richard without it annoying the shit out of me. And I like it when you are close to me. Like this." I step toward him until we are close enough that our shoulders touch. The contact raises goosebumps on my arm. I rest my hand on his wrist. "And I know that I don't feel about anyone else the way I feel about you."

Jesse backs away so we are no longer in contact. His voice is almost cold. "Richard. Close friends. That's what we are."

I don't like that he called me Richard. I don't like the serious look on his face.

I'm not sure what to say that will make him stop looking at me like that. "Would it be a problem if I were gay? If I were in love with you?"

"Jesus, Richard. How am I supposed to answer that?"

"I don't know. Truthfully?"

"Do you want to fuck me?"

"What, now? I don't..." I don't have any lube, is what I almost say. But I don't have to because Jessie pushes me—not even that hard—and I trip and fall on my ass.

"What the hell!" I pick myself up off the floor.

At least Jesse doesn't have that serious expression on his face anymore. He is back to laughing. This time more of a chuckle. "No, not now, sweetie. Ever. Because if the answer is no, you aren't gay. And I'm right. I love you to pieces, darling, but we're only good friends."

There is a long and horrible silence before he speaks. And this time his voice is deadly serious. "You are one of the few straight male friends I've had. Now I'm wondering if it was a mistake—if I screwed everything up somehow. Maybe I don't know how to be friends with straight guys. Maybe I was too flirtatious with you since I knew it was safe. I didn't mean to confuse you. I should have given you more distance."

"But that's... I don't want distance. I'm not confused." Except, to be fair, I guess I am the very definition of confused.

Jesse shakes his head and closes his eyes. "I need to get dressed." He points at the door. I don't get the hint that he doesn't want to change in front of me until he says, "I'll meet you at breakfast."

Fuck. I think I just wrecked things.

14 Hookups

Things changed after that. Jesse gave me more space. And decided to pursue a more active social life. One that involved meeting new people.

Jesse makes a very brief appearance in our room to apply a fresh spritz of cologne before going out. It's my favorite smell, whatever it is. Not musky or floral. I told him it smells like freshly crushed leaves, which he thought was hilarious. He told me I could use it anytime I wanted. But I don't think I'm a cologne kind of guy. And it would be weird if I smelled like Jesse.

"Don't wait up, sweetie. I've got a hot date tonight. Wanna see?"

I don't.

Jesse holds up his phone. There's a picture of some very built sunburned white dude with a septum piercing and a partially shaved eyebrow.

I didn't exactly wreck things between us, but after my sort-of-confession a few weeks ago, Jesse started going out on dates. Lots of dates.

He doesn't bring the guys back to our room. I'm glad. But I feel like a dick for being glad. This is his room. I told him it was fine. I can find somewhere else to stay. The couch in Bailey's quad is available. She told us both we were welcome any time we needed a place to stay so the other person could have "conjugal visits."

I didn't exactly wreck things, but Jesse doesn't hang out with us as often anymore. Ever since that morning. He'll eat breakfast with me, but then I won't see him for the rest of the day. I've been spending more time alone with Bailey. She's nice enough. But she's not Jesse.

I don't feel like staying in my room while Jesse is with his hunky stranger.

I remember it's one of the days the bowling alley is open and I text Bailey to see if she wants to hang out there. It's an old bowling alley. We have to keep score manually, and I'm always in charge. As I'm tallying up my score, Bailey sits beside me and puts her arm around me for a moment before I slide away from her on the bench.

"Sorry." She folds her arms across her chest. "So, how are you doing since the breakup?"

"What breakup?"

Bailey does a double-take. "Uh, you and Jesse? Are we not talking about this?"

I frown at Bailey. "We didn't break up. We're friends."

She nods. "It's good you can stay friends."

"No, I mean we were never together. So we didn't break up."

Bailey's face freezes in mid-expression. "Not together? Sure honey, you can tell yourself that." She shakes her head slowly.

"You too?" I ask.

"What do you mean? Me and who else?"

"When we went home for Thanksgiving, one of my friends from high school thought I was in love with Jesse. That I was gay. So did my sister."

Bailey looks profoundly unsurprised. "And... Are you?"

"I don't know. We came back and..."

"Jesse started hooking up."

"He doesn't like that term," I say.

She shrugs. "He has sex with a series of guys that he doesn't care about. What would you call that?"

"Having a social life? That includes a healthy dose of sex? I don't know. I never thought about it."

"Richard, you are a surprisingly un-thoughtful dude sometimes." She taps her finger on the table.

"You are not the first person to mention this."

"Did you tell Jesse about this—your friend's assumptions?"

I put the short pencil back in the holder and tear off our scores. "Yes. He told me I was wrong."

Bailey nods. "That explains a lot. He's sending you a message."

"What message? And what made you think we broke up?"

Bailey twists a bright curl of hair around her finger. "The message is: we are not a couple. And about the breakup? Other than the fact that he is suddenly trolling for sex instead of hanging out with us? He gives you space."

I nod slowly.

"How do you feel about that?" she asks.

"I hate it." It's true. I want things back to the way they were. I want Jesse to steal my food and mess with my hair. I want him to share a chair with me even though there are plenty of other seats available. I want him to fall asleep on my bed some nights complaining that he is too lazy to get up. I want him to stop changing in the bathroom or waiting until I leave the room because he is afraid that I will see his dick. As if he is suddenly self-conscious of his body. I know he isn't.

"Hmmm... Interesting." Bailey strokes her chin.

"Do you think that means I'm gay?"

"I'm not sure. Only you can tell that. But I think you are probably in love with Jesse."

"He told me he doesn't know how to be friends with straight guys."

"Yeah, I'm not convinced that's what's going on here. Have you seen him naked?"

Now I roll my eyes.

Bailey grins. "Did you like what you saw?"

"You've seen him dance. What do you think?"

She holds her hands up in a gesture of surrender. "Hey, I'm only trying to help you determine whether or not you're gay. You know, where you fall on the Kinsey scale."

"I took a quiz."

She coughs and gets some pop up her nose. "And what did you learn?"

"Nothing. According to the very scientific online quiz, I don't care about gender or sexuality—mine or anyone else's. Apparently I'll screw anyone."

"And?" she prompts.

"And what?"

"Does that ring true for you?"

I scowl at her. "Don't know. And I don't really care."

"So that's a yes. Well at the very least you're not... un-gay? Do you want me to do anything about this?" she asks.

"About what?"

Bailey rolls her eyes at me. "The romantic tragedy of you and Jesse? Can I help you get your man?"

"He's not mine." But that doesn't feel true somehow. I told Tea I found my person. I think I was right. I think maybe she was right, too. Still, I shake my head. "He seems happy. I don't want to make things even worse between us. We're still friends now, at least. And I don't know for sure that I'm in love with him. I only know that… I miss him."

"Oh baby boy," Bailey says. "I really want to give you a hug. Can I give you a hug?"

"No."

*

I'm not sure why I agreed to the plan. But suddenly I'm getting ready to go out to the bar with Jesse. So he can introduce everyone to some guy he's been seeing. I don't want to meet the guy. But I can't say no to Jesse.

I comb my fingers through my wet hair and put in some black steel hoop earrings—my wanna-be-punk earrings as Jesse calls them. That's about as much preparation as I ever do before going out.

Jesse has been messing with his hair for at least half an hour. Luckily he's already finished with his evening-look liquid liner or we'd never make it out of our room before the bar closed.

"You sure you don't want even a smidge on your upper lids? Really make your eyes pop?" Jesse asks.

"Funny." He knows there is no way I'm letting anything come near my eyes again. It still freaks me out. Even if I were interested in making my eyes pop.

Jesse pulls on his current favorite item of clothing: a vintage French leather racing jacket. One of the sleeves says: "Follow me I'm famous." He's wearing black jeans and half-boots with a low heel. I notice his earrings match mine. Anyway, he looks good.

"You'll be cold in that," I say.

"Fabulous comes at a price." Jesse gives an imaginary hair-flip.

I have on my old blue jeans and the Pink Floyd T-shirt I lent him when we first met. I throw on my very unfashionable yellow winter jacket.

"Come on, darling." He loops his arm through mine.

"Bailey talked to you."

"What makes you say that? About what?"

"You aren't acting weird anymore." I look pointedly at his arm. Earlier that day he'd sat beside me at the dining hall, not an inch away from me. He even changed in our room without going through extraordinary means to hide his body. Not that I looked.

"She told me to stop being a dick to you. I'm sorry. I didn't notice." He squeezes my arm lightly. All of this feels bizarre in its normalcy after such a long time of him treating me like—everyone else.

By the time we arrive at the campus bar, Bailey, Kit and Danny are already seated. They take up one side of the table leaving the other side for me, Jesse, and Ewan. They already have their drinks and a basket of deep fried pickles.

We must be late because Danny is already finishing up a chocolate malt. I don't know why. The malts here are not good. They are too thin and don't have enough malt powder. Who goes to a bar for ice cream anyway? But Danny doesn't really drink—not much anyway.

"Where's your boo?" Kit asks. Today his tattoos are day-of-the-dead candy skulls and flowers. Not seasonal, but very well executed.

"Ewan's on his way," Jesse says after checking his phone for the third time.

Ten minutes later Ewan swaggers in wearing a worn brown bomber jacket and stained blue jeans. He looks exactly like his profile picture. Built, tanned from being in the sun, with what looks like a two-day old beard. His hair is wavy and shoulder length. He has part of it pulled back from his face. It's hard to see the color of his eyes because of the dim lighting. He sits on the other side of Jesse. "Hey babe, sorry I'm late."

He gives Jesse a peck on the cheek and throws an arm over his shoulder. "Let me guess," Ewan says in his "charming" Irish accent: "Kit, Danny, Bailey and... Robert?"

"Richard." My voice feels rusty.

"Right, right. Richard," Ewan says. He orders himself a beer and a fruity cocktail for Jesse.

I dislike Ewan.

Well, that didn't take long.

I don't like the way he makes sure Jesse is only looking in his direction, using his grip on Jesse's shoulder. I don't like the ridiculous stories he tells to make himself sound like a badass. I don't like the way he smells like a department store perfume counter mixed with sweat and axle grease, the odor strong enough that I could smell him when he sat down.

I don't like his beard, or his ambiguous eyes, or the way he toys with the bottle cap of his beer, spinning it on the table. I don't like how he whispers things in Jesse's ear. I don't like the way he orders for Jesse without asking what he wants.

When Ewan flags the server down and orders Jesse another drink, I put my hand on Jesse's arm without saying anything.

Jesse looks to Ewan and then quickly moves his arm. He turns away from me. "Sure I'll have another. Thanks, sweetie."

I don't like the way Jesse calls him sweetie. I hate it. I feel physically ill, actually.

Bailey announces that she needs to go to the ladies. She grabs my arm. "Come with me."

"I don't have to go to the ladies."

"Be a gentleman," she says, tightening her grip.

"Fine." The sound of my chair dragging across the floor is jarring on my nerves.

Once we are away from the group and out of sight, Bailey says, "You need to stop glaring at Ewan."

"He's not here."

Bailey growls at me. "You know what I mean."

"I don't like him."

"I know," Bailey says. "And so does half the bar. You need to tone it down for Jesse's sake."

"Okay. For Jesse, I'll try. But I don't like him."

Bailey nods. "Fair enough. No one is asking you to like him. Now let's head back, and be on your best—or at least your better behavior."

When we get back to the table, Jesse is on his third drink. I don't say anything. I very specifically don't glare at Ewan. Although I probably glare in his general direction. Bailey gives me a tight smile. I'm trying.

It doesn't take long before Jesse's face is flushed bright pink and he looks like he is about to pass out.

I put my hand lightly on his back. "Hey. Looks like you're about done for the evening. Let's get you home."

Jesse nods his head and tries to stand, but instead he staggers and falls into Ewan's lap.

Ewan laughs, pushing me away. "I think that's my job. Don't worry, Rich. I'll take good care of him."

I sit down and watch as Ewan guides Jesse out of the bar.

"I don't like him."

I don't even flinch when Bailey tousles my hair. "I know, sweetie," she says.

"Richard." Only Jesse can call me sweetie.

15 Person

We're at an end-of-semester event in the student union, sponsored by the Asian American Student Alliance. It's "Picnic in December" and there are red and white checked tablecloths spread all over the floor. The menu includes grilled Hmong sausage, chicken satay, Japanese rice balls with umeboshi, lychees in syrup, and boba tea—all the major food groups.

"Sit up straight. I need back support to properly appreciate this meal." Jesse scoots so we are sitting back to back on one of the picnic blankets. He tilts his head and rests it on my shoulder. "Thanks, sweetie."

I freeze, shocked by the physical contact and also the fact that he called me sweetie. Ever since that night at the bar, Jesse has been much more hands off. With everyone. Before he just acted weird around me. But now he ducks Bailey's kisses. He no longer throws his arms around Kit when congratulating him on an art project. He certainly doesn't loop his arm through mine when we walk to breakfast in the morning. Sometimes he sits all the way across the table from me. Like I'm contagious.

This is a brief return to normal, but it makes me uneasy. I know it can't last. I feel the warmth of his back against mine. I wish things could stay like this.

Some skinny Asian kid with a red beanie snaps a picture of the two of us and asks if he can include it on the official AASA webpage. "You two are adorable. Boyfriend goals, am I right?"

Jesse moves away, scooting so we are no longer within arm's reach, and shakes his head with a short laugh. "No. Just roommates."

I nod. "Yeah. Roommates."

"Well, even better!" He's so damn cheerful. I bet he gives campus tours to prospective families. He seems like the type. Entirely too perky and upbeat. "Can I get your names for the photograph?"

Jesse bites his lip.

"We'd rather you didn't," I say quickly.

Jesse visibly relaxes as the photographer leaves. He turns to face me, moving even further away. "You know it's not that I mind…"

I interrupt him. "Yeah. I know. It's fine." I know he is about to tell me that *Ewan* would mind if he saw us together.

Ewan would lose his mind if people thought we were dating. Because Ewan is an arrogant, self-centered, overbearing, hyper-controlling asshole.

"Thanks," Jesse says. I don't even think he realizes it when he sighs in relief.

He goes back to eating the rest of his picnic lunch far away from me. On the other side of the picnic blanket. I am struck with the impression that he is not himself. He is quiet and small and somehow less. Less everything. Again. His expression is dark. His smile when he turns to look at me is flat.

I hate it.

Ewan isn't even here and I can feel his fingerprints all over Jesse.

*

"You were right."

Tea sighs. "Hey Tea? How was your weekend? Gee, I'm sorry for calling so late. Is now a good time to talk? I'm so glad you asked, Richard…"

I didn't realize how late it was. Maybe it could have waited until the next morning. But I had to tell someone. The picnic incident had been bothering me all day.

"Yes. All of those things. But also, you were right."

"I see. What exactly am I right about—wait, are you gay?"

"Maybe. Yes. I really don't give a fuck. Which is apparently my sexual orientation. More importantly, I think you were right about me being in love with Jesse."

"Oh. Is that good or bad? Because from your tone of voice, it doesn't sound good."

"No, it's fine. It's fan-fucking-tastic. I'm over the moon. Other than the fact that Jesse is dating a pretentious muscle-bound douche who is 'good with his hands' and has a 'delightful Irish accent.' Ewan." I spit out his name like a curse.

I'm pacing back and forth, alone in our small room.

"Calm down, take a breath, and tell me what's going on."

"I don't know. Probably nothing. I haven't seen anything in particular to make me think anything is wrong, exactly. But I don't trust the guy."

"Ewan? Why?"

I try sitting down at my desk. "No reason. He's too charming. He's older. He smells like cheap body spray."

"Solid reasons."

"No. Listen. Jesse's different since they started going out." I get up and start pacing again.

"Well, people act different sometimes when they're in a new relationship."

"Not like this." I almost don't know where to start. "When we met, Jesse was... himself. Right away. You met him."

"Flirty as hell and all over you?"

"Yeah. All over me and everyone else. But not in a creepy way. I don't know how he does that."

"It's a gift," Tea says. "One that neither of us have."

"Given." No one would ever accuse me of putting people at ease. Even if I tried. "Well, if you met him now... his smile is weak, he gives everyone miles of space. It's that bastard he's seeing. I know it."

"You sure it's not your jealousy talking?"

"Yes. He's gone on dates with other guys. And that was mildly annoying. I missed him on nights he stayed out. Standard jealousy. Perfectly manageable. This is different. Jealousy is that I want him around more often. Jealousy is me wanting Ewan to keep his clever mechanic's hands to his damn self. Whatever has me so worried is in addition to the jealousy. Something is wrong."

*

The next day Jesse doesn't show up at dinner, which isn't all that unusual. I try not to make it obvious that I am watching for him, but apparently it is obvious. Because Bailey is looking at me with a very sad expression on her face. Pity, probably. She keeps trying to distract me by talking about things I couldn't care less about.

Kit and Danny are flirty and oblivious. They keep feeding each other French fries and making lewd noises. I think they're supposed to be mocking something or someone because they're clearly not serious. Maybe they're trying to distract me. It works from time to time.

"Do you like this design?" Kit straightens his arm. Today his tattoos are lines and angles and abstract shapes.

Danny tousles Kit's platinum hair. "Eventually you'll find something you want to make permanent."

"It's such a commitment," Kit says.

I don't care about tattoos. I don't care about the fact they are serving the famous brownies with fudge icing on a non-Friday. I don't care about Bailey's newly dyed fuchsia hair. I have no opinion on whether it suits her.

I stand up without saying anything. At least I remember to get rid of my tray before walking out of the cafeteria.

Jesse doesn't come back to our room after dinner, either. Which is unusual on Wednesdays. He has his early dance class the next day and typically tries to get extra sleep. And then gets me up ridiculously early so he has time to fuel up for the day and be fully awake for class.

Until Ewan, Jesse and I ate all our meals together.

Fuck. I am jealous. Jealous as hell. Even if I am not gay. Even if I am not in love with Jesse. Tea told me to find a person. I did. Jesse is my person, and this sucks.

And apparently, I am an overbearing, possessive asshole.

I guess this is not much of a surprise. I didn't take Tea's friendship with Sean very well and they weren't even dating. I don't like sharing my friends.

Why isn't he home? In our room, I mean.

No, he doesn't need to be here. He doesn't need to check in with me. We are not dating. Even if we were, he wouldn't need to answer to me. And while I'm pretty sure he's my person, that doesn't mean that I am his.

We are only roommates.

I try to study for the upcoming chem test, but either I already understand the material or I can't pay attention for long enough to grasp the concepts. The fact that the books I'm paging through are the same ones I dropped on Jesse when we first met does not help with my concentration.

I try gaming for a while, but my focus is off there too. I keep getting my ass shot up and no one wants to play with me. Can't blame them.

Eventually all I can do is lie flat on my back in bed staring at the ceiling. The streetlights from outside filter in enough light through the curtains that I can see the faint crack in the plaster that runs across the length of the room. I check the clock every fifteen minutes or so hoping either that I will finally be asleep, or he will finally be back.

Before Jesse moved in I liked having the room to myself. Hell, I was fucking ecstatic when Matt shoved off. The room was peaceful, predictable, empty, and mine. Now having the room to myself sucks. It's not only the room that feels empty. I can't make myself sleep.

I don't trust that Ewan will take care of Jesse. I don't trust him at all. I close my eyes and pretend that I can sleep through my worry. I think about texting him, but what would I say? You're out after curfew? I can't sleep without you here? Ditch your date and come home because I miss you?

Jesse stumbles in some time after three a.m. It scares the shit out of me because after one I was sure he was spending the night with Ewan and I finally managed to doze off. But it's not like I'm sorry to see him.

"Oh hell, did I wake you?" Jesse says, stumbling in the dark.

"Don't worry about it." I turn on the table lamp so he can see where he's going.

His clothes are in disarray and he smells of smoke. His face looks gaunt in the shadows thrown by the dim light.

"You look like shit."

"Charming as always." He struggles out of his clothes and I look away.

I want to lecture Jesse about being out so late. I want to tell him not to drink so much because of what it does to him. And I know what dancing on a hangover costs him. He'll pay for this tomorrow.

I want to tell him that Ewan is not good for him.

I want to tell him to take better care of himself.

I want to slide into bed beside him, wrap my arms around him, and hold him until the sun comes up.

Well, that's sappy. And kind of gay.

I don't do any of these things.

Instead I get him a glass of water and some pain killers and set them on the table beside Jesse's bed.

"Friends don't let friends go to bed drunk," I say.

"Thanks, sweetie. You're the best."

With Jesse in his bed, I can finally fall asleep.

16 Changes

Winter break was long and dull. Day after day of nothing to do and no one to do it with. Tea was only there part of the time since she and her mom planned a ski trip to Colorado. Gabby wasn't around either. My patience for dealing with anyone else was non-existent. I slept far too late every day, spoke to my parents as little as possible, and ate too much junk food while gaming all night.

"Can you give this to Jesse when you see him?" my mom asks. She hands me a care package full of sweet and salty snacks. "Tell him we miss him and hope he can visit soon."

The ten-hour drive back to campus is draining without any company. When I stop to get gas and stretch my legs, no one gives me a second glance. As far as anyone is concerned I am a straight, white, Midwestern guy who has every right to be there.

Alone in my car I can play whatever music I like as loud as I want. I find myself listening to a lot of the same tunes Jesse chose on our drive. But even with the music blasting it's hard to keep my eyes open driving across the vast, flat expanse of the American Midwest for hour after hour.

The drive seems twice as long as it did with Jesse. I haul my luggage up to our room, completely exhausted. When I open the door I'm surprised to find Jesse waiting for me. He greets me with an unexpectedly exuberant hug. I can't remember the last time he's done this. I'm so surprised, and he is so enthusiastic, that he almost knocks me off my feet.

"Nice to see you too," I say, finally able to set my bags on the floor.

I have missed him. God, I didn't realize how much. It seems like I've been missing him for so long. And not just during break. Since before break. Since before Ewan. Since I made my stupid half-assed confession.

"Hey, I need to talk to you about something." Jesse's voice is disturbingly serious.

I know I won't like what he has to say. "What?"

"How do you feel about having a super-single again?" Now his voice is artificially cheery.

"It wouldn't be my first choice." Honesty creeps out before I can think of a more neutral response.

Jesse looks at the floor.

"I suppose this means you are moving out." My voice feels mechanical.

Jesse nods, still not looking up. "Ewan asked me to move in with him."

"I see. Do you think that's a good idea? This soon?" I know I'm asking for selfish reasons. I am thinking of how little I see of Jesse when he is nominally living here. If he moves out completely I'm afraid I'll never see him again.

Ewan. I hate everything about him: his rugged good looks and his hipster piercing, his terrible self-congratulatory stories. And most of all his obnoxious implied ownership of Jesse communicated through every glance, every gesture, every syllable he uttered.

I want to tell Jesse that moving in with Ewan is a terrible idea. Because Ewan is a terrible human being. But I don't actually know Ewan well enough to say that. I haven't set eyes on him since we met at the bar. But based on everything Jesse has said about him, and the way Jesse's behavior changed so dramatically, Ewan is at the very least an overbearing and abrasive human being.

The same could be said of me, I suppose.

I look around the room. Jesse's desk is empty. The Indonesian tapestry he had above his bed is gone. The dresser is clear of his toiletries. There are no scented candles on the window ledge.

"You've already moved, haven't you."

Jesse winces. "I'm sorry. I was going to tell you before it happened. But Ewan had the day off yesterday and had the time, so we packed my things up and brought them to his house. I thought I should tell you in person. And it's not like Ewan and I are getting married. I can always move out again if things aren't working out. I mean that is if—"

I cut him off. "I won't be advertising for a new roommate. Technically this is still Matt's room anyway. Go ahead and keep your key. If you need to crash here, or anything."

"Yeah. Thanks. And we can still hang out."

I nod. "That would be nice. I don't like it when you're not here." Again, the inconvenient honesty.

Jesse nods. "I'll make sure to visit often, then. Maybe I can spend Wednesdays here. You know that Thursday morning class is a bitch."

"I know. Any time. I told you already: no one else will move in here."

Jesse gestures to the bed with a forced smile. "You never know. You could meet someone." He raises an eyebrow. He's trying to sound flirty and positive. But instead it feels sad and wrong.

"I know." I will not meet someone.

He leaves behind the "His" pillow from Bailey. I thought it belonged to Jesse. He assumed it was part of a set.

I put them both in the closet when he leaves.

Only later do I notice he's left the key on top of his empty desk.

*

Days go by without a word.

He shows up at lunch just as the rest of us are finishing our meals. Danny and Kit are trying to organize bowling for later in the evening. I have an early exam so I won't be attending.

Bailey is creating tabletop art using the unused silverware, napkin containers, salt and pepper shakers, and the laminated cards advertising the benefits of the campus meal plan. She is trying to convince us all that her creation looks like a brachiosaurus. It does not.

"Hey! How is everyone? Did you miss me?" Jesse sits across the table from me, next to Danny. He bats his eyelashes and frames his face with his hands.

I bristle at his question. Of course we've missed him. Jackass.

He looks good. I wish he didn't look quite so good. I wish the sight of him didn't make me excruciatingly aware of the effect he has on me. Seeing him reminds me of how much I miss him.

Seeing how good he looks reminds me of my inconvenient feelings.

He is dressed in jeans and a white V-neck T-shirt with one of his oversized button down shirts. This one is pale blue with wide cuffs and mother-of-pearl buttons. His fingernails are painted with opalescent nail polish, which really pisses me off for some reason. I'm pissed at Jesse, but I fixate on his damn fingernails.

We haven't seen him for days. I haven't seen or heard from him in days. And now he shows up when there is no time. I have to get to class soon. And he knows this. He knows my schedule, just like I know his. I have Philosophy 101 in twenty minutes. He has Fundamentals of Movement in an hour.

"About time you showed your face again. Too good for us now that you've got off-campus housing with that hunk of yours," Danny says with a flirty smile, matching the tone of Jesse's greeting.

Jesse laughs too loud. It sounds fake. "Yeah. I'm getting used to the commute. It's not the same as walking across the quad."

"Do you like the new digs?" Bailey asks.

Jesse smiles hesitantly. "I mean, I liked my old place too."

Everyone looks at me. I'm not sure what they expect me to say.

"Well, you'll have to have us over sometime," Danny says since no one else breaks the silence.

"Yeah. Sometime…" Jesse trails off.

Great. So we can't see him here or at Ewan's place. Which leaves me with nothing. Not that I have any desire to see Jesse in Ewan's environment. I don't think of it as a place that Jesse belongs. He should be here with us.

I want to tell him: "Date Ewan. Fuck whoever you want. Just stay here." But I keep my mouth shut. Jesse makes his own decisions, even if they are terrible decisions.

I am not responsible for him. He doesn't belong to me. But I can't stop thinking that he is my person. And it hurts like hell to see him sitting there with his fake smile. Knowing that when I leave he will go to class. And then instead of coming to find me after or waiting for me in our room to hang out, he will disappear. For who knows how long.

"Well, it's great to see you," Kit says. There is another long pause.

Bailey steps on my foot. I know this means I am supposed to say something. In the rules of conversation it must be my turn to talk. But I still don't know what to say. I don't have anything to say.

I stand up and walk away. Without clearing my tray.

17 Weeks

He doesn't eat on campus anymore. Or if he does, it isn't when the rest of us are at the cafeteria. Kit and Danny have taken to sitting on either side of me. It's weird, but I don't tell them to stop. Ordinarily I don't mind their lovey-dovey behavior, but their theatrical mealtime flirting was starting to get to me. And I am 99% sure it was meant to be a distraction.

Jesse and I have classes at different ends of campus, so there's no reason for us to meet by chance now that he doesn't live or eat here anymore. Kit and Danny see him in the fine arts building, but outside of class he's not around.

I leave the cafeteria fifteen minutes before I need to in order to walk across the quad to the science buildings. When I get to class I discover that I failed my fucking chemistry formative exam. Technically I got a D+. I have never gotten anything below a B in any of my science classes in high school or college.

Finesse, who I still call "Chem," laughs her ass off when she sees the expression on my face. "Trouble in paradise? What, your girlfriend refuse to give you a blowjob? Is that what put you off your game?"

I don't respond. Unless it's related to a lab, I do not interact with her. This pisses her off. A lot. It is a perverse pleasure of mine. I thought about making irritating the crap out of her into my new hobby, but decided against it. She's not worth the effort.

I try to pay attention in class. We're starting a new unit on nuclear chemistry, which is something we didn't cover much in high school. I usually take detailed notes. I usually take notes that other people borrow to check against their own.

When I look down at my notebook, the page is empty except for the heading: Nuclear Chemistry. Fantastic. Now I will have to copy someone else's notes. Chem takes the most detailed notes of anyone in the class, but there is a zero percent chance that she would let me borrow them. Or that I would ask in the first place.

I need to do something different. I can't focus. It's not even that I'm thinking of Jesse all the time. But I don't feel like myself for whatever reason. I had gotten used to having him around, and missing him has screwed with my head. I hate change.

I should take up running. Or boxing. At least hitting a punching bag. I could really get behind the idea of punching things. Things with more give than lockers. Lockers and tables were my go-to back in high school when I was beyond pissed. I had asked for a punching bag, but my parents had refused to get one because they thought it would encourage aggressive behavior. I know there are heavy bags in the gym. That would probably be a lot more satisfying than lifting.

I should not have failed that test. I have no explanation. All I do is eat, sleep, and study. It's been two weeks.

Jesse hasn't even fucking texted me.

*

I was sad for weeks. And then I wasn't.

I don't know what flipped the switch, but I'm done being sad. It's just as well; I don't know how to do sad. I have moved into the far more familiar territory of being angry all the time. Not explosive anger, but a more poisonous feeling that lurks right beneath the skin and accompanies me throughout my day.

I had found my person and he dumped me. He didn't need to date me. Hell, I don't even know if I wanted him to date me. But he needed to... not do this. He needed not to disappear without a trace and treat me as if I were nothing. Not even a friend. Not worth keeping in his life in even the smallest way.

So now I am living with anger. It's familiar territory. I spent most of high school in this state.

I've started running with Danny most mornings. He wants to lose weight. I want to get my mind off of things and get rid of some of the built up adrenaline from my constant simmering anger. I also go to the gym a few times a week to punch things.

It doesn't really help.

Maybe it helps a little. I'm still pissed off, but I've kept my temper in check. This is good. I have not stormed out of a single lecture in college. I'd like to keep it that way.

Hell, I haven't even spouted any choice profanities at Chem, and she knows how to push my buttons. Lately more than ever. All her talk of my imaginary girlfriend and whatever sexual favors she might be withholding... But I refuse to engage even to tell her there is no girlfriend. And no plans for a girlfriend.

I set an alarm and make myself go to the cafeteria for lunch every day even when it means I will have to see Bailey's sympathetic eyes or listen to Kit and Danny arguing about whether Andrew Lloyd Weber is utter trash or a complete genius. Back in the days of sad, I would lose track of time and miss lunch. Or class.

Now I go early to all my classes. Hell, I even attend some study sessions for whatever I had missed out on over the past few weeks where I was pining after Jesse.

I never see him. Not even a glimpse. It's like he's dropped off the face of the Earth. When I think about that, about how Jesse only exists in the alternate universe of Ewan, I am drawn out of anger and back into sadness, so I try not to dwell on it.

I'm not even mad at Ewan. Well, I am, but he isn't the main source of my anger. I'm kinda pissed at Jesse, but that's not what causes the simmering rage. In an uncharacteristic flash of insight I realize that I am mad at myself for taking this so hard.

I hate being fucking sad all the damn time.

*

One day nearly a month after he left, Jesse surprises me after class. He is waiting for me right outside the biology lecture hall when class lets out. It's the first I've seen or heard from him since that first week after he moved out. I don't know how to react.

He smiles that small, sad, un-Jesse-like smile. "I know I've been... There's no excuse. I'm a shit friend. Utter trash as a human. But I hope you will come to my studio recital. It would mean a lot to me. It's this Friday. Sorry for the late notice." His voice sounds stilted and unnatural, speaking in short, choppy sentences.

I nod. "Kit told me. I was planning on going anyway."

"Oh, that's right. He's helping with the set." Jesse touches my arm lightly and then flinches away like the contact burns him. Or like touching me is a habit he's been trying to break.

I feel like someone has stabbed me in the gut. I'm glad to see him again, even like this. Even though I know I will only get this moment with him before he disappears again.

He looks thinner than I remember him. Paler. His clothes hang on him like they are several sizes too big. Not just the oversized shirt, but everything. I feel like I'm channeling Bailey—I want to give him a hug. But given how he couldn't bring himself to touch my arm for more than a blink of an eye, I doubt that would be welcome. Instead I stand there stupidly. Blinking.

Eventually I notice that he is holding out an official invitation to his recital.

Jesse presses the thick, cream-colored card into my hand. "I'm an ass. I know. But it would mean a lot to me if you were there."

I shrug. "You aren't an ass. You just have different priorities."

"Hell, Richard. That makes me an even bigger ass. I never wanted to be the guy who bails on his friends when he starts seeing someone. Bros before hoes, right?"

"Yeah. Hooking up was easier."

Jesse's mouth drops open at the same time that his eyes go wide.

Oh. Misunderstanding. "I mean it was easier to spend time with you. Before Ewan. When you were with random guys."

"Aha. I thought you were trying to tell me something. Wondered who you were hooking up with." Jesse rocks back and forth on his heels.

"No one. At least not lately. I don't really like it. The sex is okay, but everything else is complicated and irritating."

"Richie! How did I not know this about you?"

"Know what?"

"That you were such a little tramp?"

I shrug. "I fucked around with some people before we met. But not since then." My use of the word "people" hits me hard. It is intentional. I don't want him to think of me as straight, even though I know he does.

"You go girl!" Jesse says with some of his old flirty self. "And here I always thought of you as more of a hopeless romantic waiting for just the right person."

"I think I am," I say. "Probably why hooking up lost its appeal."

Jesse nods and then is silent for what seems like a long time before saying, "So, you will be there?"

I look at the invitation in my hand. "Yeah. Just like I told you."

For a moment my Jesse makes a brief appearance. He claps his hands, jumps up and down, and then throws his arms around me. I stiffen. He still smells like his soap-scented cologne. But I also catch a faint whiff of cigarettes.

Fucking Ewan.

"He shouldn't smoke around you."

"What?"

"Ewan. He shouldn't smoke when he's with you. It's not good for you."

I stop short of saying "He's not good for you." I'm not sure that would be a good plan since this is the first we've spoken in weeks. And what do I really know about his relationship with Ewan anyway?

Only enough to be jealous as fuck.

18 Honesty

"Hey, come with me to pick up Kit for lunch," Danny says after we finish our run.

"Sure. Whatever." Once I'm done dealing with my sweaty clothes and my smelly body, I join him in the quad so we can walk together.

He forgot to mention that Kit is on the small stage in the fine arts building where Jesse's studio is having a dress rehearsal for their upcoming recital. I'm not ready to see him again. It took me a while to recover from our earlier encounter.

So of course we walk in right as Jesse's group is on stage while the rest of the studio is in the audience taking notes.

I had forgotten how beautiful he is when he dances. He is always stunning, but it's different watching him move like he does on stage. He has an amazing presence. He does not at all seem like the shortest person on the stage, although I know for a fact he is.

There are a bunch of other guys up there who are probably perfectly fine dancers. And I'm sure they have nice bodies as well. My eyes slide over them. I can only see Jesse.

I don't realize I'm staring until Danny bumps me with his shoulder. "You okay there?"

"Yeah. Great. I'm great."

"Hmm." He nods thoughtfully.

Kit is backstage. Danny drags me back there before Jesse has the chance to notice our presence. I hope. I'm not sure why I don't want him to see me. I don't want to know how he will react to seeing me. Will he be happy I'm here? Irritated that I'm in his space? Or worse, what if he doesn't show any reaction at all?

Danny and Kit become a disgustingly cute couple within moments of being five feet from one another. They can't help it. Danny oohs and ahhs over all of Kit's pieces for the set: a bunch of crates with mirrors on them in a mosaic pattern. A short flight of winding steps. A cool looking tree with withered black and gray leaves.

We haven't been back there long when there is a commotion from the stage and I hear someone shout, "Jesse!" There is a loud thud and the stage shudders.

I don't remember moving from one place to the other. I am somehow instantly by Jesse's side. He is lying still on the floor, his eyes closed.

"What happened?" I growl at one of the dancers who is standing there stupidly instead of being useful. "Who—"

"I'm fine," Jesse says faintly, his eyes fluttering open. "And don't go looking to beat anyone up on my behalf, cowboy. I pushed myself too hard is all."

"You're not fine." I don't precisely hold him down, but I do make it difficult for him to get up by looming over him.

Jesse's dance instructor shows up with a bottle of orange juice and a cold cloth to put behind his neck. I sit with him between my legs so he can rest supported by my chest while he drinks the juice. He is sweaty from practice and his back feels like a small furnace. I don't care. I have one arm around him, supporting him.

A bit of color comes back to his cheeks. I press the towel against his neck, then lean him back and hold the cloth to his forehead. He feels so frail against my body—his frame much smaller than I remember.

Kit and Danny are there now too. "What happened?" Danny asks.

Jesse waves a hand weakly. "Nothing. I'm just tired."

"You. Take him to the trainers' office." Jesse's dance instructor is talking to me. I think it's pretty clear I won't hand him off to anyone else. I help him to his feet.

"I'm fine, really." Jesse's voice is faint. He walks to the trainers' office on shaky legs, leaning heavily on me, with Danny on the other side.

The trainer looks him over and doesn't find anything terribly alarming. "You need to make sure to stay hydrated. Have you had anything to eat this morning?"

"Yeah."

She looks at him from under lowered eyebrows and he amends his answer.

"I was in a hurry," he says.

"Don't dance on an empty stomach. That's idiotic and irresponsible." She tells him to go home and rest for a while before trying to do anything. She tells him to eat something. To give his body a chance to recover before he can return to practice tomorrow or the day after, even.

Jesse starts to object, but I thank the trainer and steer him out toward the exit where Kit and Danny are waiting for us.

"Should we call Ewan?" Danny asks.

"Fuck that. Our room... my room is closer."

I send Kit and Danny to sneak food out of the cafeteria. Jesse needs something more substantial than ramen. "Pick up some electrolytes too. Or more juice if you can't find anything else." I think all I have in the room is gin left over from our housewarming party.

"I'm taking you back to the dorm."

Jesse nods wearily. "Piggy back?" he asks.

"Fine." I kneel down so he can put his arms around my neck. His legs are wrapped around my waist. Feeling his weight against my back brings me an odd sense of comfort. I carry him to my room, only setting him down to navigate the stairs.

"You are so good to me," Jesse says.

This doesn't do good things to my heart.

Once we are back in the room, I put Jesse down gently on my bed. It's the only one with sheets. Having Jesse's bed made up as if he were coming back didn't do me any good in my sad phase. And in my angry phase I knew it would only piss me off. So I use his bed as a flat surface to store my running gear. Clean, of course.

Jesse tries to sit up, but sinks back down into the pillows. "I'm fine. Really. Maybe a little run down."

"I'm sorry."

Jesse looks confused. "None of this is your fault. You have nothing to do with me collapsing. Why are you sorry?"

I have to think about my answer. The apology came automatically. I'm not used to apologizing, and it's really not something I do without reason. "I know I didn't have anything to do with what happened on stage. But I should have. I mean, I've been a crap friend too. I should be taking better care of you. You're not the only one who disappeared."

"How have you been?" he asks softly.

I stare out the window where his candles should be on the ledge. I look at the top of the dresser that should be covered with beauty products. At the empty wall that should be covered in fabric.

"Kinda shitty, actually. My roommate, this guy I was really close to, moved out. And we never saw each other after that. I miss him like hell. And I'm worried about him."

"Why? I mean, why are you worried?" Jesse sits up until I turn to give him a warning glance. Then he leans back against the pillows.

"Well, other than the fact that he was away for so long, when I ran into him again, he had changed." I sit down near him on the bed. Not too near.

"How so?" Jesse asks.

"He seemed sad. Quiet. Not himself." Why am I talking in third person? Why is this so hard?

"Have you told your friend about this?" Jesse touches my hand lightly.

"Yeah. But not until just now. It was damn hard to say anything when you were so persistently absent. And unreachable. What's going on? What the hell is wrong? Is it something with Ewan?"

Jesse takes a slow breath. "He's good to me."

"Really? How so."

"He drives me to campus every day. He brings me flowers all the time. He always pays when we go out. If I ever need anything—anything at all—he gets it for me."

"You sound like a kept man," I say without thinking. Jesse looks like I slapped him in the face. "I didn't mean that. I'm sorry. I say things without thinking them through. You know that. But I don't like that I don't see you anymore. That we don't see you anymore. Why did you stop coming to the cafeteria? Hanging out on campus? Why didn't you text me at least? Let me know how you were doing?"

His shoulders fall and he looks at the floor beyond me. "I didn't know what to say. And... I don't know how to be around you."

I shake my head. "Well, not like this. There has to be something in between. I don't mean you need to spend every spare moment with me. But can't we at least see each other sometimes? Why can't it be like it was before? Before Ewan."

Jesse is quiet. I sit there on my bed, careful not to get too close. So damn careful.

I don't think I should say more, but now that I've started, I can't seem to stop. "Things used to be so easy between us. I didn't worry about how I behaved around you. Now I'm afraid if I get too close to you that you will run off. The other day you couldn't bring yourself to touch my arm. Like I might hurt you. Are you scared of me? Did *I* do something?" I feel ice in my veins, and it's hard to breathe.

Jesse's eyes widen. He grabs my hands in his and squeezes them. "I would never be afraid of you. Don't ever think that."

I pull my hands away from his. I can't bear his touch right now. "I hate that I still feel like you're gone even when you're right here." My voice is shaky. I hate that, too. "Please don't leave again. Not like that. Don't disappear entirely. I promise I won't interfere with whatever you have with Ewan. But I don't want to lose you. You're important to me. Please."

I squeeze my eyes shut and clench my fists. I can feel my fingernails biting into the skin of my palms until Jesse puts his hands on mine again. This time I don't move away.

"I'm sorry. I didn't know how much I hurt you. I'm so sorry. I'm not going anywhere." He pulls me toward him. Then he leans over so his head is on my chest. "Is this okay? With me here? Can I rest here for a while? I'm so tired."

My arms drape around him naturally. This is where he is supposed to be. I am terrified of how much this feels like home. Feels right. His breaths grow slower and deeper as he falls asleep in my arms.

I text Kit to leave the food outside the door. I close my eyes. I'm afraid to move. I'm almost afraid to breathe. If I do, he might wake up. And I don't want him to wake up.

Because when he does, he will only leave again.

19 Stage Lights

It feels like a repeat of the recital from first semester. The hall is packed. Bailey saves me a seat. I think it is the same seat she saved before. This time she doesn't mention how happy Jesse will be if he sees me. I'm not sure he will be happy. We didn't talk after the day he collapsed. But she does mention *she's* glad I made it.

I look around the audience, reasonably sure that I am scowling.

"You looking for Ewan?" Danny asks. "He said he couldn't make it. Work, I guess."

I turn to look squarely at Danny. "You *talk* to Ewan?"

"Not really," Kit says, quickly jumping in. "We've been out with him and Jesse once or—" Bailey waves her hands to get his attention and he stops.

I turn to Bailey. "I see. You too?" I can feel my pulse beating in my temple.

"No," Bailey says firmly.

Danny nods. "It's more of a double-date kind of thing. And it's not like we've seen them all that often."

I clench my teeth. So it wasn't that Jesse dropped off the map. He'd only ducked out on me. I must look as shitty as I feel because Bailey can't help herself from giving my arm a squeeze.

I take a breath before speaking. "So... no Ewan."

"No Ewan," Danny says.

I am jealous beyond reason. Of Ewan, of Kit, of Danny. Of every ridiculously fit dancer in Jesse's entire goddamn studio who gets to see him every goddamn day.

I get up from my seat and pretend I need to use the restroom so I can walk some of my anger off. I have to walk for a long time. And it doesn't work.

I don't return until the lights go down to signal that the recital is starting.

This time Jesse is performing in three different pieces: a duet, a group routine, and a solo. Once again I have trouble paying much attention to any of the other dancers. I even nod off during one of the performances, so Bailey pinches me. Harder than she needs to. I'm pretty sure there'll be a bruise.

But when Jesse is on stage I am wide awake, fully aware of every move he makes, however subtle. I can't take my eyes off him.

His partner for the duet is a softly rounded white girl with very short reddish hair that curls around her face. She has the same infectious smile that he does. Their dance tells a story—friends to lovers.

And I am unreasonably, irrationally, heart-poundingly jealous of this girl. Even though there is nothing true about their dance, it *feels* real. By the end of it, Jesse has convinced me that the two of them are deeply in love. Soulmates even.

I want her hands off him.

Hell, I am more viscerally jealous of this imaginary girlfriend than I am of his real boyfriend. Probably because I have never been all that convinced of any sort of emotional connection between Ewan and Jesse—not that I'm basing this on anything but my gut.

I feel an ever-increasing surge of resentment towards the adorable chick who falls into Jesse's arms at the end of the dance. The feeling stays with me right up until the moment Jesse's eyes seek me out in the audience, somehow finding me as always, even with the stage lights. He smiles brightly for what feels like the first time in ages. And he winks. And suddenly everything is better.

This is not good.

I have no right to feel this way—so ridiculously giddy from a mere smile—but I do. Maybe it was a good thing Jesse stayed away. I don't know how to be with him either.

The group number is the one they were rehearsing when he collapsed. Now that I'm watching the entire dance from beginning to end, I am not surprised. It's a very athletic piece involving all the male dancers in the studio. They spend a lot of time throwing one another around on stage. Jesse is the lightest. They throw him highest and farthest. He could always fly, even without their assistance. Now he flies impossibly higher. They are all bare-chested and cut. And I don't care. Jesse is the only one who makes my heart beat faster. Not good.

Even though he is only a freshman, Jesse's solo is the final dance of the recital—the grand finale. He is dressed all in white again. His sleeves are translucent and flow gracefully with his movements as he dances. When the lights hit a certain way, you can see the definition of his arms through the thin fabric. There is no story. There are no athletic leaps. But the piece is so damn sad, the way he crosses the stage as if his limbs are moving through something heavier than air.

Maybe I was wrong about there being no story. As he dances, he slowly loses pieces of his costume—and not in a sexy way. I didn't realize before; his shirt is made of cleverly attached scarves. And each time a piece of fabric flutters to the ground, Jesse's dancing stutters. Like a piece of him has been torn away. I blink back tears at the expression on his face, at the way he holds his hollow frame as if he is in pain. It is excruciating to watch.

By the end, all that is left of his costume is his tattered pants and a shred of fabric draped across his torso. He finishes unmoving on the stage.

I'm not the only one who can't take their eyes off him. The entire theater is silent for several frozen moments after his dance finishes. Finally I can breathe and the entire audience seems to exhale at the same time.

Jesse gets a standing ovation. Maybe it's supposed to be for the whole studio, because everyone comes out to take a bow. But I know most of the applause is for him. He smiles at me in between bows. I give him a thumbs up. Why aren't things always like this? Like they were before. Easy.

The dancers head off to get changed, and we all wait for Jesse.

We wait for longer than it should take for him to put on his street clothes and remove his stage makeup.

"Maybe we should go check on him," Kit says.

"Good idea." Bailey pushes me toward the backstage area.

I expect him to be chatting with people in or near the dressing room. Losing track of time. Life of the party. But there is no party. Most of the other dancers have already left. There are only a few stragglers here and there. The sounds are muffled in the wings, swallowed by the heavy velvet curtains.

I run into Jesse's dance partner. She's changed into a checked green shirt and fitted black pants. Her face is scrubbed clean of makeup. She looks a lot younger than she did on stage.

"Hey."

She looks spooked when I speak, but I'm not sure why. I didn't surprise her in the dark. She saw me clearly before I said anything. I hope she isn't scared of me. I probably seemed like a jackass for chasing everyone away from Jesse when he collapsed the other day. I feel bad for possibly freaking her out. "Sorry. Have you seen—"

"You're looking for Jesse," she says softly.

When I nod, she points further into the recesses of the theater. She still looks nervous. I make sure I give her plenty of space when I pass. Then I thank her and continue my search.

Thick dusty curtains and walls lined with acoustic tiles absorb most of the sound. I don't hear anything until I pass the trainers' office. The lights are off. Of course no one is there.

Then I hear him. That fucking Irish accent grates on my nerves even before I can make out what he is saying. As I get closer, his voice becomes more distinct.

"...without me? You think I don't know what's going on between you two?"

"Nothing. There is *nothing* going on between us. There has *never* been anything going on between us. How many times do I have to tell you before you believe me? Richard was only ever my roommate. We're friends. He's straight, for God's sake."

"I saw you looking at him. I saw the way you smiled. And the other day when you didn't come home after rehearsal, where were you? You were with him, weren't you. What can he give you that I can't? Nothing. There's nothing he has to offer. He's just a boy." Ewan has Jesse by the arm. His fingers are biting into bare skin.

I have never wanted to punch someone so badly in my entire life. Of course if I come barreling in yelling, "Get your hands off him!" with fists flying, I am playing right into Ewan's paranoia. And I'm not sure how Jesse would take that kind of intervention. Or what Ewan might do to retaliate.

I don't mind if the "charming" bastard comes after me, even though I'm sure he could beat me senseless. But if he takes things out on Jesse...

I haven't had time to figure out what to do or say when Ewan sees me. His eyes widen in surprise before he whirls on Jesse. "So you arranged to meet him here? Thinking I wouldn't be around? That I wouldn't find out? Just friends my ass." Ewan snarls, twisting Jesse's arm until he winces.

I step forward, fighting to keep my hands by my sides. My heart is beating so fast that I can hear the blood singing in my ears. Jesse looks at me and pleads for something with his eyes. I'm not sure what. But I'm pretty sure he does not want me to fly off the handle and fail to beat the crap out of his overposessive, emotionally unstable, and very muscular boyfriend. Still, it takes absolutely everything in me to stay still. To do nothing. The bastard is still holding Jesse's arm at an awkward angle.

"Don't." Jesse mouths silently.

I try to look slightly offended instead of giving off any obvious signs of murderous rage. "Oh fuck off, Ewan. Jesse already told us he couldn't go out with us after the show since he wanted to get back home. To you. I only came back here to find the hot chick he was dancing with. Have you seen her? I'm pretty sure she told me to meet her here."

My rambling works well enough as a distraction that Ewan loosens his grip on Jesse, at least. I wait for a clear signal to leave, although every fiber of my being tells me to grab him and run.

"You shouldn't keep her waiting," Jesse says. His voice is so small. Ewan has his arm around Jesse's shoulders now. I want to vomit. Instead, I nod my head.

And then I turn my back on him and walk away.

I am shaking with the effort of keeping my rage in check. I need to get out of the theater. Away from Ewan. Away from the smirk on his face and the sound of his voice and the accusation in his eyes. I can't believe I left Jesse there alone with him. Maybe I made the wrong decision. Maybe I should go back. But Jesse had been very clear. Not the right time. Not yet.

I shouldn't have left him alone. He needed me and I turned my back on him. I walked away.

Fuck.

I walk right past Bailey, Kit and Danny without saying a word. I walk outside to the decorative stone wall surrounding the reflecting pool on the east side of the building. The rocks in the wall are different sizes—river rocks with smooth edges. Without pausing to consider the consequences, I put my fist into the wall. Harder than I mean to. The stone bites into my knuckles. A jolt of excruciating pain shoots straight through my hand and up my arm.

Jesse's friends—my friends—have caught up with me by then. I'm not sure how much they saw.

I grit my teeth and speak in a low and quiet voice. "Kit, I need you to take me to the ER to have someone take a look at my damn hand. I think something might be broken." I take a slow, shaky breath. "And then we need to get Jesse away from his sack-of-shit abusive boyfriend."

20 Babysitter

Having a fractured metacarpal is not as much fun as it sounds, and it doesn't sound all that great. It's not like I'm always aware of the pain. It's more or less a dull ache that is in the back of my mind somewhere unless I try to move the damn thing.

When Tea calls, I open with "I broke my hand."

"Richard!"

"Actually it's only a finger. Still, hurts like hell." I set my hand gently on my lap. At least I managed to injure my left hand. Almost as if I'd thought things through. Which I clearly had not done.

"How? Or do I not want to know…"

"It was a necessary sacrifice. It prevented me from being arrested for assault and battery. And given how Ewan's built, it may also have saved me from more significant injuries. Like a coma. As it is I only need to keep my fingers taped together for a while."

"What the hell happened?"

"I punched a wall. Harder than I meant to." Tea waits for me to elaborate, but I don't know how much to tell her. "I was right. About Ewan. He's hurting Jesse. I saw him after the show." I feel my anger rising to the point that it is difficult to breathe or speak. And of course it isn't simply anger. I'm worried sick. "And then I left. He told me to leave. And I have no idea what's going on."

"So you haven't been in touch with him?"

"How? I can't call him. I can't text him. What if Ewan is monitoring his phone? What if my contacting him provokes more violence? What if he hurts Jesse because of me?"

What if all of this is my fault.

"Breathe, Richard," Tea says softly.

I take a breath and start pacing the room like it's a cage. "I need to do something. No clue what. All the plans I come up with are violent and ill-advised. I need to enlist someone with a more level head than mine. Which at this point is literally anyone else. Kit is pretty solid. I already talked to him about this last night at the ER. He agrees that we should find a way to help Jesse. But we didn't really get as far as making a plan."

Tea listens to me for a while, but all I do is say the same things over and over again. Variations on a theme. "Please stay in touch. And let me know if there's anything I can do," she says before we hang up. But what can she do?

My lunchtime alarm goes off. I head to the cafeteria. Automatically. Mechanically. Because this is what I do every day. Hopefully Kit will be there. I need Kit to be there. If I don't have eyes on Jesse by the end of the day I might risk arrest and storm Ewan's house single-handedly. I need someone to talk me out of this. I need Kit and his plans.

The cafeteria seems louder than usual. The lights are too bright. I have trouble carrying the tray without full use of my hand, but I manage to make it to our table without major incident. I sit there by myself and try to shut out the noise. No Kit. No Danny. No Bailey. And of course no Jesse.

I can't think.

Bailey shows up toward the end of lunch as I am pushing cold mashed potatoes around on my plate.

"Hey Richard, how's the hand?" she asks as she settles in next to me.

I don't want her to sit next to me. I don't want to be comforted. It is an inappropriate response to the situation. "Have you heard anything from Jesse?"

Bailey doesn't say anything, which is not the answer I'm looking for.

I take a deep breath. Two. Three. "I want to beat the crap out of Ewan. Please tell me this is a good plan."

"Tempting," she says. "But probably not the best idea. Especially in light of your recent injury."

I glance at my bandaged hand. "I don't care. You didn't see what I did last night. You didn't see him. No one can talk to Jesse like that. And for damn sure no one can put their hands on him like that."

Bailey searches my face with an expression of concern. "Don't worry. He'll be okay, Richard."

What an asinine thing to say. "You can't know that. Ewan is dangerous. Unhinged. Jesse needs to get away. Needs to leave him. Today."

"Oh, honey." Bailey gives me a hug. I don't even have the patience to shrug her off. I don't need a hug. I need to find out what is happening, and Bailey is of no help whatsoever. Still I sit there and tolerate her sympathy or whatever this is.

"Great. Are you done? Now help me track down Kit and Danny. Maybe they know something. Anything."

"Well that sounds like a much better plan than marching over to Ewan's house to get the shit beat out of you." She's trying to smile but it isn't working.

"None of this is funny. Stop trying to make it sound better than it is."

"I know, sweetie. I'm sorry."

"Richard."

Bailey follows me back to my room.

Danny and Kit aren't responding to texts. I am slowly going insane. Bailey watches me pace back and forth in my room. It is a cage.

Why is Bailey still here? I don't need her here. "Don't you have to go to class?"

"Don't you?" she counters.

"Fuck if you think I could focus on anything besides Jesse right now."

"Yeah," she says.

Oh.

I look at Bailey. Something seems off. "Are you... babysitting me? You are. Kit and Danny assigned you to be their watchdog. You know something."

She looks away, which is very damning evidence.

"Bailey, I'm about to lose it here. Tell me what you know. Tell me anything."

"I promised I wouldn't say anything. But everything will be fine." She won't make eye contact.

"Get out." I point to the door. Bailey starts to object, but I push her out of my room.

Once she's gone I press my head against the door. It's cool against my skin. I'm burning up. It feels like I have a fever but I know that's not it. I'm frantic with worry and no one will tell me a damn thing.

My hand is throbbing. It has gone beyond being a dull ache. Sharp pains are shooting up my arm, no doubt aided by the monster headache I have acquired. I take some more of the heavy-duty pain meds that make me a little loopy. I can see why people get hooked on these. It takes the edge off my anger. I float in a semi-coherent haze, dozing on my bed.

I don't know how long I lay there, not really doing anything. I can't sleep, and I don't have the patience or mental capacity for anything else.

Fuck Bailey. Fuck Kit. Fuck Danny.

What the hell is going on?

And why the hell will no one tell me?

I fell asleep once the pain meds kicked in. I only know this because I wake to the sound of someone knocking quietly at my door. It doesn't sound like someone's trying to break down the door so I know it isn't Bailey.

"Knock knock." It is Jesse's voice. "Yoo hoo! Anybody home?" I wonder if I'm hallucinating. If I'm hearing Jesse's voice because it's what I want to hear.

I lurch out of bed, standing up so quickly that I feel dizzy and have to regain my balance before I can make it to the door.

"I... wait." I trip over my feet in my hurry to open it.

He's standing there. In the hallway. Right in front of me. He looks better than he's looked in forever. His eyes are bright and he's smiling an honest smile. His face doesn't look pale and thin. But again, I must be imagining these changes. I saw him last night.

It seems like I have been holding my breath forever until this moment. I feel all the air rushing out of my lungs.

"Can I come in?"

I manage to step aside so he can get past me. I catch the familiar scent of his shampoo. The dizziness hasn't gone away; I have to hold on to the door frame to prevent myself from falling.

"I come bearing gifts." How had I not noticed him carrying something. Not just something, a professionally-arranged fruit basket. With colored cellophane and a gold mesh bow.

"I wasn't sure what the traditional, 'I'm sorry my shitty boyfriend inspired such rage that you had to take it out on an immovable object and broke your damn hand' gift was."

"It was only a finger." I hold up my taped hand. "And I'm pretty sure the traditional gift for that is a fruit basket. So, good call." I'm pleased with myself for being able to make light of things. I can do that now. He's standing here. With me. Although I'm still not sure that he isn't a narcotics-induced hallucination. I can't be certain that I didn't wish to see him so badly that my brain conjured him up.

He sets the basket on his empty desk. It looks ridiculous in the room—oversized for a space this small. Jesse steps back and stands in the middle of the room, far away from me, shifting from one foot to the other.

"Richie... Richard, I have to say something."

"Richie," I correct him. "Say it. No. I have to say something first. You have to get away from him. I said I wasn't going to interfere with you and Ewan, but this is not okay. He's dangerous. You need to leave him." The last sentence comes out in a growl and I clench my fists before I remember that my finger is broken. Fuck.

Jesse steps toward me, but then stops as I hold up my good hand. I can't bear for him to be any closer. If he touches me I will fall apart.

"I'm sorry. I know," he says gently.

Why does everyone keep trying to comfort me? That's not what I want. I look into his eyes so he knows I am serious. But he always knows when I'm serious. "You aren't safe with him. You said he takes care of you, but that isn't true. I know it seems like I'm saying this for selfish reasons, but I saw the way he spoke to you. The way he had his hands on you." I'm trembling with anger. I start to pace back and forth.

"I know," Jesse says again, coming closer and placing a hand on my back. The contact stops me in my tracks. Stops my breath in my throat. Stops my heart in my chest. The place where his hand is touching tingles like pins and needles.

"You know?"

He nods. "I know. It's done."

I stare at him, my eyes wide. "You left him?"

Jesse nods. I take a breath and my heart starts beating again.

"Kit and Danny came this morning to help me move my stuff out. They borrowed Dave's van and brought him along for reinforcement. He is one scary-looking dude when he wants to be. I waited to break things off with Ewan until they were there in case he became violent. He never did that before, you know. Never hurt me."

At the mention of Ewan hurting Jesse I feel my heart rate double.

"Easy, darlin'. I'm here now. I'm okay," Jesse says, rubbing calming circles on my back.

I start to feel more human, more capable of rational thought. "Kit, Danny, Bailey, Dave… Why did you tell everyone but me? You made Bailey promise not to tell me. Why?" It hurts that I wasn't the one he turned to for help.

Jesse puts one hand on each of my shoulders and looks me in the eyes. "Partly to keep you safe. When I heard about your hand… But also because I wanted the story to be about me leaving Ewan. Not you swooping in as my rescuer. I know that's what you wanted to do. That's who you are, my gruff-seeming cinnamon roll. But I didn't want there to be any question that this was *my* choice. I knew I needed to leave him before the recital. I knew after we talked that day. I didn't think about how Ewan treated me until you mentioned I was a kept man. I didn't see it because I didn't want to. But you were right. He took care of me, but I don't think he ever really cared about me."

"I care," I say quietly, and my voice catches.

"I know," he says in his softest voice. "I know, sweetie."

My stupid heart stops. I may need cardiac care after this discussion. Perhaps a pacemaker.

"So where's your stuff?" I ask, looking around. "Are they bringing it up for you later?"

Jesse shakes his head. "I'm not moving back in. I'm staying with Bailey until I can find a new place. But even if I can't, she says I can stay in the quad for the rest of the year. Her roommates are cool with it."

Her roommates are cool with it.

"But I thought things could go back to normal now. That you were coming back. That we could be friends like we were before."

"They can. We can," Jesse says. His lips are smiling, but his eyes are sad. "Only not if I'm here. We just need some space. A little breathing room."

I feel like the rug has just been pulled from under my feet. I sit down heavily on my bed. "I told you already, I don't want space. This is your room. I don't need space."

"But I do." His voice is a whisper.

21 Normal

It's been a few weeks since Jesse moved out of Ewan's house, and things are back to the way they were.

Mostly.

Jesse has gone back to invading my personal space. He sits on my lap and plays with my hair or messes with my clothes when we're watching a movie. He steals my food. He leaps onto my back and demands that I give him piggy back rides. He calls me sweetie, honey, darlin'... Richie.

When he's tired and we're hanging out at Bailey's or wherever, he snuggles up against me and nestles his head against my chest. It makes my heart beat like crazy, but also somehow makes me feel calm.

He teases me all the time in that maddeningly flirty way of his. But he doesn't spend the night in my room. That's the only difference from when we were roommates.

It's an unseasonably warm day, which means that every college student on campus is outside with shorts and sunglasses throwing frisbees or "studying" on the quad. I fall into the latter category.

I am leaning against a tree reading Camus's *The Myth of Sisyphus*. Jesse is lying in the grass beside me describing the clouds as they float by. "Look at that and tell me it isn't baby Dumbo in a tiara."

"It isn't."

"Well aren't you two lovebirds completely adorable," Kit says, stopping in front of us with Danny close behind.

"Of course." Jesse sits up and rests his head on my shoulder. "We are always adorable. It's on brand for us."

"Big plans for the weekend?" Danny asks. He and Kit have both taken a seat. I guess I won't be getting any reading done. Not that I was able to read much before.

"Please tell me you have big plans for the weekend," Bailey says as she arrives. She is giving me a very significant look but I can't imagine why. Neither of us ever have big plans.

Most weeknights Jesse hangs out in my room while I study. On the weekends we go out with the rest of the group or spend time with the two of us—watching movies or at the Tap or whatever. What are these big plans Bailey is hoping for?

Jesse raises his hand. "Ooh, ooh, I've got a big plan! I thought we could hang out and watch movies. I was thinking Hitchcock. *North by Northwest* anyone?"

I'm pretty sure I'm the only one who actually enjoys old movies, but Jesse can convince the group to go along with anything.

"Sure, why not." Danny shrugs.

Bailey scowls. I guess this wasn't her idea of big plans.

"We can see if the theater is open if you don't want us crashing at yours," Jesse says.

"If you didn't want viewing parties, y'all should never have put up that flatscreen." Danny shakes his finger at Bailey.

"No. It's fine." She says this in a way that makes it very clear it's not fine. And it doesn't seem like she is about to explain herself. I'm getting used to not having the answers.

For instance, I still don't know what it means that Jesse doesn't want to move back to our room. And I am not going to ask him again. What we have is fine, as long as he doesn't treat me like I'm a casual friend—which he doesn't. I wonder, looking back, if he ever treated me like his other friends.

"Fantastic! Richie and I will take care of refreshments. I'll put you in charge of dessert because you're so sweet," he says with a wink. My heart rate picks up only a bit, but enough that I notice.

If my reaction to the whole Ewan situation wasn't enough to clarify my feelings, my reaction to flirty Jesse makes things very clear; I do not have platonic feelings for Jesse. Or I do, but then I also have a lot of non-platonic feelings layered over those.

I don't have any indication that Jesse feels anything for me but friendship, though. Because all this? The way he's acting now? This is how he was with me when we first met. Maybe all of this affectionate behavior means nothing to him, and this is how he does friendship. But this is not just regular friendship for me.

I know I am overanalyzing everything, but I'm not sure what else to do.

Spending time with Jesse is confusing as hell. He has his hands all over me, but I'm afraid to touch him. I don't want to scare him away by doing something stupid. But every time he so much as brushes against me, I feel tangible relief at the touch. I feel like a strung-out drug addict craving whatever contact-high I can get.

I feel this most acutely on Thursdays. Every Thursday when Jesse is done with his killer studio class, he stops by my room for a regular massage so I can undo some of the damage he does to his body every week. I have cleared off his bed for the purpose and purchased some of his preferred white flower oil. I like how the smell lingers in my room when he's gone.

I should not use these massages as an excuse to stare at his half-naked body while he's lying there with his eyes closed. I should not revel in the way his skin feels under my hands or the sounds he makes when I release the tension from a particularly tight muscle. I should not use a relaxing scalp massage as an excuse to run my fingers through his hair. I should not be staring at his beautiful face with his eyes closed, fantasizing about what his lips would taste like.

I fucking hate Thursdays.

Happily, today is Friday.

Kit, Danny, and Bailey take off, leaving Jesse and me on our own.

I go back to reading Camus. Jesse lies down with his head in my lap, which nearly short-circuits my brain. I don't know why we need humanities credits as science majors. I hate the readings. And it's very difficult to focus on anything when Jesse is so close. Not that I'm complaining, really.

"I missed this," Jesse says dreamily. "I'm glad we're back to the way things were."

"Yeah. Me too." It's a lie. But what we have now is better than nothing. Much better.

Even if it is slowly driving me mad.

*

By Monday I've managed to make a fair amount of headway on the philosophy assignment, even though literary criticism is definitely not my forte. Jesse is off at practice, so it's a lot easier to get things done. At least until someone starts pounding on the door of my room as if the building is on fire.

Before I let her in—and there is no question that I will—Bailey is already in mid-rant. "So, you utterly useless heap, you wanna tell me why the hell Jesse is still living with me instead of back in your room where he belongs?" Her fuchsia hair is free of its usual confines—bright coils sticking out on all sides. Somehow this makes her seem even more terrifying than usual. Plus, the expression on her face makes it seem like she wants to kill me.

I close my laptop and drum my fingers on the desk. "He said he needed space. And that you were fine with him being there. That's why."

Bailey's hair bounces against her shoulder aggressively when she shakes her head. "Bullshit. About the space thing. That boy never needs space. Not from you, certainly. Of course I am fine with him staying with us. Unless it's a damn excuse to avoid the inevitable." She shakes her head and bites her lower lip. "I don't understand what the hell is wrong with you two. So tell me, exactly why aren't you together?"

"I asked him to move in when he left Ewan. Jesse doesn't want that. He was pretty clear."

Bailey's eyes go impossibly wide and she raises both eyebrows. "Really? Even with everything between the two of you... Did you tell him how you feel?"

I nod. "Yeah."

"When? A hundred years ago when you took that stupid internet quiz?"

"Yeah."

Bailey scoffs. "I don't think that counts. I don't think he believed that to be any kind of evidence that you had feelings for him. You know, feelings of the gayer kind."

"He asked me if I wanted to fuck him."

Bailey chokes. "What? When?"

"The same time I told him I might be in love with him."

"Oh, baby." Bailey gets that irritating look of sympathy on her face.

I shake my head. "I should have figured out sooner. Maybe we wouldn't be together, but maybe he wouldn't have ended up with Ewan."

Bailey snaps her fingers in front of my face. "Not. Your. Fault. And it's no good overthinking the past. Time to focus on the present. And the future." Bailey grabs one of the remaining pieces of fruit, a granny smith apple, from Jesse's fruit basket. "You wouldn't let me help you before because you thought Jesse was happy. But I'm telling you he's not happy. So will you accept my help now?"

"Help with what? And what do you mean he isn't happy?"

Bailey rolls her eyes and gives an extravagant sigh before speaking slowly and clearly. "Can I help you get your man? And as for his state of happiness? He's moody as hell when you aren't around. It's only when he sees you that he breaks out that fantastic smile of his. When he's in the room all he can do is talk about you every damn minute: 'Doesn't Richie look good in navy? Come here and listen to this, it's Richie's favorite band. Richie said the funniest thing today. Can you invite Richie to come bowling with us?' I swear if I hear him say 'Richie' one more time I'm going to lose my shit."

"I don't understand." My head feels fuzzy. I'm fairly certain that what Bailey is saying is very straightforward, but I feel like she's talking in code. "You don't like it when he calls me Richie?" Well, that can't be it. At least if the expression on her face is any indication.

"Ahhhhhh!" Bailey tears at her hair, causing it to become even more chaotic. It looks like excellent nesting material for some sort of psychedelic bird. "I think Jesse has feelings for you. Of the romantic and lustful kind. And I think it's pretty obvious to everyone. Like, the entire western hemisphere."

I shake my head. "No. If he did, he would have said something. He would have stayed."

"He's scared to lose you." Bailey smiles. I don't know why that makes her smile. It doesn't even make sense.

"No. I told him I wanted him to move back in. That I didn't want him to leave in the first place. I confessed. Kind of. How could he lose me?"

Bailey sighs again. "It doesn't need to make sense. You're both besotted and afraid to say anything. Wake up and smell the romance. You two need to get your shit together and stop making everyone else's lives miserable."

I raise an eyebrow. "You're miserable?"

Bailey rolls her eyes. "Fine. No. But Jesse is irritating the crap out of me. And he hasn't even been living with me for that long. Can you *please* take him off my hands?"

I shake my head. I'm not sure what she thinks I have the power to do. "It's not up to me. I already told Jesse he can move back any time."

Bailey growls in frustration. "I don't care where he *lives*, you jackass." Bailey cracks her knuckles editorially, looking at me through slitted eyes. "You don't intend to do anything about the Jesse situation, do you."

"What would I do that I haven't already done?" I am no less confused now than I was at the beginning of our conversation.

Bailey raises her voice by a number of decibels. "You two are out to personally drive me insane, aren't you? You are already secretly together and just pulling this crap to mess with me. If you're not? If you and Jesse are both pining away for one another and neither one of you willing to do a damn thing about it? Honestly, you and Jesse need to put signs up: 'If dumb was dirt, we could cover half an acre.'"

"Thanks."

"Or how about this one right above the dresser: 'Caution: objects in mirror are stupider than they appear.' And y'all look plenty stupid."

22 Plans

We're in Bailey's quad doing not much of anything. As usual. Kit and Danny are playing cards. Bailey is painting her nails even though I told her it smells like jet fuel. It's her room, so it's not like I really have any say.

Jesse is sitting on the floor watching K-pop videos over and over to study the choreography. Sometimes he presses pause and goes through the motions without standing up or anything. How can someone look like they're dancing when they aren't even really moving?

Predictably, I can't take my eyes off him or focus on anything else. I think I'm supposed to be studying for something, but I haven't glanced at the book in my lap for some time.

"How about you, Richard, Are you in?" Bailey asks. Kit and Danny look at me expectantly. Jesse leans back and rests his head on my legs.

I have no idea what she's talking about.

Bailey throws her hands in the air. "Honestly, Richard! Spring break. You weren't listening at all, were you?" She lowers her head and looks at me over the top of her glasses. She has taken to wearing pink-tinted glasses that match her hair.

Jesse climbs onto the couch and as per usual drapes himself over me. "Aw Richie, you're so adorable when you're oblivious."

Bailey glares at me, making sure she has one-hundred percent of my attention. Which she nearly does. Jesse is toying with the cuff of my sweatshirt and his fingers keep brushing against my wrist, so that does hijack a few brain cells. I make a mental note: wrists are another weak spot of mine. Who am I kidding—anywhere Jesse touches me is a weak spot.

"Right," she says. "I'll start from the beginning: a getaway with the five of us. Within driving distance. Not any heteronormative, beach body, beer bong, spring break kinda place. I found a family run Airbnb resort. They have the sweetest little cabin on a lake in the mountains. Not for the whole week, but a few nights anyway."

"What about the other days?"

"Who cares?" Kit sighs. "I've missed mountains. And bodies of water larger than the municipal cistern. Ones you can actually swim in—although I guess it's still a bit early for that. And breathable air." He is from Vermont.

Jesse nods his head. "Yes to all three. Indiana is so unrelentingly flat."

"There are mountains in Idaho?" I ask.

Bailey widens her eyes at me before saying, "Yes. It is on top of the largest mountain chain in the US. What do they teach you here in flyover country?"

"Whatever. I guess geography's not my forte."

"Leave the poor boy alone," Jesse says, ruffling my hair. "Honestly, Idaho is the back of beyond and I hardly expect people to know anything about it."

"It's the gem state," I say. Which makes Jesse laugh.

"So where is this mystical vacation location?" he asks.

"Kentucky. It's close, inexpensive…"

"And right on top of the second largest mountain chain in the US," Danny adds with a mocking tone in his voice. Fine, everyone knows their US geography better than I do. What do I need geography for? I have GPS.

"Please tell me you don't already have plans, sweetie." Jesse looks up at me with his puppy dog eyes, which lately have been much more effective on me than they were in the past. I think he knows it too. Manipulative bastard.

"No plans. Which means I can drive home and spend a week with my parents, stay in my room by myself, or join you in Kentucky. That seems better."

Jesse claps his hands and gives me a quick hug. "Oh good! The trip would be absolutely abysmal without you."

"Hey!" Bailey objects loudly while Kit and Danny glare at him in unison.

"I mean, of course I'm pleased as punch that y'all will be there too," he says with an apologetic grin.

Bailey looks around the group with a serious expression on her face. "Time to divvy up the responsibilities. First off… Richard, can you drive? Your car is a lot less… problematic than Kit's"

Kit looks like he is about to object, but even he has to admit that his old junker probably would not survive the trip over the state line, much less on mountain roads.

"Yeah, sure." It will be a tight squeeze, but if it's only a few hours we should be okay.

"I call shotgun!" Jesse says, raising his hand.

Danny grumbles at that. "How is it fair that the person with the shortest legs gets the most legroom?"

"Because I am the most fabulous," Jesse says, framing his face with his hands and batting his eyelashes.

I should have known things wouldn't go smoothly.

*

Even though the whole trip was her idea, Bailey is the first to cancel. She breaks the news to us at lunch two weeks before break.

"I'm so sorry guys. But my sister just got engaged and she wants me to help shop for wedding dresses." She seems to be apologizing, but she doesn't look sorry.

I reach for a napkin from the center of the table. "Why don't you look online and send her some pictures."

Jesse gives me a gentle shove. "Honestly Richie, you clearly know nothing about how bridal shopping works."

"True. I have never once shopped for a wedding dress."

Jesse grins. "Don't worry sweetie, when it's your turn to pick out a gown you can count on me."

Bailey nods. "I can see him in something of a rose champagne silk. Perhaps off the shoulder."

"Fine. But I don't want one with a giant bow in the back."

Danny giggles. "Of course not. Wouldn't want anything to hide that fine ass of yours."

Kit punches him in the arm. "What is it with you and Richard's ass?"

I still think finding a dress for a wedding that is months away could wait until Bailey is home for the summer. But her sister has already purchased the plane ticket to Santa Barbara. So she's out. Which leaves the four of us.

The next to cancel is Kit. A week before the trip. I'm studying his tattoos when he brings up the topic. His arm is inked with Snoopy and the Red Baron biplane battles. If I ever get a tattoo I'm having Kit design it. I'm convinced he can draw anything. In any style.

Kit clears his throat to get everyone's attention. "I can't believe I have to do this, but I'm out, too. The show I'm dressing the set for has a huge build scheduled. I can't get away. I'm really sorry."

Danny looks at the floor. "Uh... I'm staying with Kit."

"Well of course you are, honey," Bailey says.

Figures. I mean, it would be weird for him to be on a trip with me and Jesse. Of course he'd rather spend time with Kit.

I look at Jesse. "What about you? It's only me and you now. You still want to go?" I'm not sure whether I hope he'll say yes or no. I know I don't want to be away from him, but a trip with only the two of us sounds like a particular kind of hell. Still I find myself hoping he'll say yes.

"Of course. What could be better than a trip to the mountains with you, darlin'?"

I feel a wave of relief wash over me. Why am I relieved? Is it because Jesse wants to spend time with me? Clearly he enjoys spending time with me—we are together every day. But a trip is different.

"Great!" Bailey says. "I'll change the reservation to the smaller cabin."

"I can't wait!" Jesse says. He gives me a kiss on the cheek and then takes off for class.

Leaving me sitting there. In the cafeteria. With Bailey, Kit and Danny.

Jesse has never kissed me before.

It doesn't necessarily mean anything. It's who he is, always flirting with everyone. Still, the stupid kiss has scrambled my brains. I'm having trouble putting two thoughts together.

Once I can put two thoughts together, they are not good ones.

A trip alone with Jesse? How will that be, exactly? Sure we're alone sometimes now. But it's in small doses when I have a chance to recover, or to steel myself for the experience ahead of time. Long stretches of time alone with Jesse? The two of us, uninterrupted? I am sure to screw everything up. Again. And we will come back no longer on speaking terms.

We'll leave after the first day since he won't want to spend any more time with me. In the car on the way back he'll start scrolling through his phone for hot, muscle-bound men to hook up with. He'll show me their pictures at the rest stops.

"Snap out of it," Bailey says, actually snapping her fingers in front of my face. This is becoming a new habit of hers. I don't like it. "Whatever you're thinking, it's wrong," she says.

"But what if—"

"Wrong," she repeats firmly.

23 Scenic Route

I don't keep my car on campus. It's too expensive. This is the college's way of discouraging students from going anywhere. It works. There is inexpensive long term parking available for students about two miles off campus with shuttles that run three times a day. I picked up my car the night before the trip.

It doesn't take me as long to find a parking spot near Bailey's dorm in the morning as I thought it would, so I arrive early. Not many people are out yet. I walk three blocks and pick up a bag of fresh muffins and some coffee. I can't stand hot coffee on the road. It steams up the windows. I get a regular iced coffee for myself and one of the dreadful concoctions that Jesse likes—complete with sugar-free caramel and an indecent amount of whipped cream.

After I walk back to the car, I check the time and discover with some irritation that I am no longer early; Jesse is late. He's never late. I wonder if he's changed his mind. Everyone else has canceled, after all. I check to see if I've missed any texts, but there is nothing.

Well, I for sure will not be driving to Kentucky to spend a few nights in a charming cabin on a lake at the foothills of Appalachia by myself. Although given how anxious I am about this trip with only the two of us, maybe a solo trip would be better.

I text Jesse again, but he has a habit of silencing his phone during dance practice and then forgetting to turn it back on, so I'm not really surprised there is no reply.

Bailey isn't answering either. But she sleeps like the dead and is rarely up before noon when she doesn't have a class. I think her flight to California is today, but doesn't leave until the afternoon.

I should have arranged to meet him in their room anyway. If he packed for this trip the way he did for our Thanksgiving trip he'll need plenty of help with his luggage. I leave the car and march up to the second floor. I pound on Bailey's door. "You're late and I'm not sure how legal my parking spot is."

Jesse opens the door. Shirtless. Pajama pants slung low over his hips. My mouth goes dry. "You. Are. Not dressed." I am too stunned not to stare until he starts speaking.

"I'm so sorry. I meant to be downstairs before you got here. And then I slept through my alarm and I had to get ice from the freezer and stock the cooler." He moves his arms around as he speaks indicating various locations. "But I haven't even showered yet and then I didn't get your texts until just now…" He holds up his phone.

Jesse is cute when he's flustered. I try to ignore this thought; it's not helpful. "Glad you decided to join me. Take your time. I'll bring your crap to the car and meet you back here. We can leave when you're ready."

Jesse points me toward his luggage and then disappears to wash up. He only has one small suitcase and a messenger bag. I can't believe he is bringing fewer things on this trip than he brought home with me for Thanksgiving. I haul his things down to the car and shove his bags in the trunk. There's no room there for the cooler, so that goes in the back seat. It takes up more room than anything else.

When I knock to be let back in, it's Bailey who stumbles to the door in a fuzzy purple bathrobe, rubbing her eyes. She has matching fuzzy rabbit slippers with ears that trail along the floor. "That boy of yours was up all night packing and repacking. Kept us all up. I swear if you don't sort things out with him on this little trip I will strangle you with my bare hands upon your return. With zero remorse. So get your fucking act together and claim your man." She pokes me in the chest for extra emphasis.

"I told you. How many times have I said this? He turned me away. He moved out. He said no."

Bailey reaches out, puts her hands on my shoulders and says very slowly and clearly: "He wants to say yes. Give him a reason."

When Jesse reappears, he looks like he is ready for a photo shoot. He's wearing a button down white linen shirt with the cuffs rolled up. I have to make a conscious effort not to stare at him again. Especially not at the triangle of skin exposed by the number of buttons undone at the top. He looks very good in white. It contrasts with his warm skin and dark hair. It makes his smile look brighter than usual.

Bailey grabs me by the hand on my way out the door. Jesse is already halfway to the car. "Give him a chance. I'm serious. He's waiting for you."

"What if you're wrong?" For some reason I say this in a whisper.

"Oh honey," Bailey says. She can't help herself and gives me a hug.

*

It doesn't take us long to get out of the city and into farm country. Jesse stares out the window. "Does the entire Midwest look like this? It is so unrelentingly flat!"

"I don't think this is the Midwest. We're too far south now. And east."

Jesse starts to unbuckle his seatbelt to get something from the back seat, but I put my hand over his.

"I need to get something from the cooler. Won't even take a second."

"Wait." There is no traffic. It is a straight, flat road. I don't move my hand. I pull over and come to a complete stop. Even then I don't really want to move my hand from his. He is always the one to reach for me first. This feels different, his hand warm under my palm. Eventually I let go so he can get whatever he wants.

"Such a mother hen," he teases. "I would have been fine."

Jesse opens the cooler and retrieves a ziplock bag of something before taking his seat again. I pull back out on the road as soon as he's buckled without even looking at what he was after.

"And now I present to you: the ultimate road snack." Without warning he leans over and puts a frozen grape in my mouth. His fingers brush against my lips and I have to tighten my hands on the wheel. The lingering sensation of his touch is very distracting and the icy feeling of the grape on my tongue is absurdly sensuous.

Driving while distracted is easily as ill-advised as driving while drunk. It's a damn good thing we are on a flat stretch of empty road.

"Get off the highway at the next exit," Jesse says, studying the route on his phone.

"That's not the right way." I know. I looked.

"Oh Richie. You must know there isn't one right way." He shakes his head in mock sadness. "I found a more scenic route that will take us through the national forest. We can stop and take perfectly posed selfies on the way to make our flaky friends jealous." He grasps my arm in his hands. "Please?"

"Fine." I am becoming such a sap that I will say yes to whatever he asks. I manage not to shiver as his fingers trail against my skin when he lets go of my arm.

The forest roads are narrower, but the view is much better. We take a break for photos at a "scenic outlook." He has me take a selfie of us because my arms are longer. I hate taking pictures. I always look angry. Maybe Bailey is right and I do have "resting homicidal face."

Jesse links his arm through mine as we go back to the car. Nothing new. Nothing special. But even this friendly gesture is increasingly difficult for me to handle. It puts his body in closer proximity than I can tolerate. And the car will be even worse. In such an enclosed space I am surrounded by the subtle smell of his cologne. I'm at the mercy of his constant, innocent touches. There is no escaping.

Has he always had his hands on me this much? Yes. But it hasn't always affected me like this. Not to such an extent anyway. Maybe because the contact always comes as a surprise while I'm driving. I have no clue when or where he will suddenly have his hands on me.

I can hardly keep an eye on him, because I am supposed to have eyes on the road, and when I look at him that's impossible to do. So I don't have any advanced warning before he rests his hand on my thigh, or toys with my earring, or brushes my hair out of my eyes, or feeds me a fucking grape.

The road is getting narrower and narrower and the trees are blocking more of the sunlight. It's a much more pleasant drive than having the afternoon sun beating through the windows, even if I am starting to be concerned that I'm driving into the middle of nowhere.

"Are you sure we're still going the right way?" I ask.

Jesse squints at his phone. "Yeah. Eventually this exits on the other side of the park and re-joins the highway."

That might be true, but the road we're on now isn't paved. And parts of it seem to have washed away either quite recently or long ago. My car might be more reliable than Kit's, but it still isn't made for off-roading. I slow down to a crawl. At this rate we won't make it to the resort until long after dark.

As we round a corner, three does come bounding across the path. I swerve abruptly to avoid hitting them. Unfortunately, this involves swerving off the questionable road entirely. And when I turn to get back on the road, nothing happens. Well, something happens. The car doesn't move, but I hear the sound of tires spinning.

I try rocking the car back and forth, but that gets us nowhere.

"Take the wheel." I get out and Jesse climbs over into the driver's seat.

I try pushing from the rear as he steps on the gas. All I accomplish is getting splattered with mud.

Jesse gets out of the car and joins me to survey the situation. We try both of us pushing, but that doesn't help at all.

There is no question that we are stuck.

24 Camping

I get back in the car, but I'm not sure why. I guess because standing there staring at a car that is going nowhere seems pointless.

Jesse wipes some mud off my face with a bandana he produces from his bag. "Richie, I am so sorry."

I shrug. "I don't see why. You had nothing to do with the deer. And you weren't driving."

"No, but this route was my idea."

I look the road up and down. For a road in the middle of nowhere, it's not that bad. As long as you stay away from wildlife and avoid the patches where the road is missing. "It's a nice drive. Better than the highway. Don't be sorry. You were right."

Jesse takes out his phone. "Good thing I have triple A."

While he's on hold with roadside assistance, I change out of my mud-splattered T-shirt. The person he speaks to is very sympathetic, but they tell him we can expect a wait of two to three hours. We are, after all, in the middle of nowhere.

"What do you want to do while we wait?" I instantly regret asking when I see the glint in Jesse's eyes.

"I have several ideas of how we might stay busy for a few hours. Or did you mean things we can do outside the car?" He trails a finger along my arm as a joke.

I nearly swallow my tongue.

"Outside. Definitely outside." I open the car door and leap out.

Jesse follows my lead. "Well then, how about a walk through the national forest?" He changes into some stylish hiking boots. He also has a windbreaker and some mosquito repellent. I didn't think to bring any of these things. And I can't believe how many useful things Jesse managed to pack in his tiny suitcase.

"City boy, did you bring anything with you at all that's appropriate for a trip to the great outdoors?

I slip on my hoodie, thankful that it escaped the mud. "I brought warm socks."

"Oh sweetie. You are too adorable. 'Warm socks.'" He laughs softly and pats me on the arm.

I'm not sure what is so adorable about warm socks. "I don't like cold feet."

Jesse loops his arm through mine as always before we head off down the road on foot.

The woods smell like new leaves and recent rain. We walk along the packed gravel road for about a mile before we find the marked trails that lead further into the forest. It's starting to get cold. I'm glad for Jesse's warmth against my side.

"I take it you don't spend a lot of time in the woods back home?" he asks.

I shake my head. "Nothing like this. I mean, I've been up north with my cousins a few times, but my parents aren't really into the whole 'nature' thing, so most of our family vacations involved well equipped hotel rooms and nearby outlet malls."

Jesse shudders. "I grew up with woods like this in my backyard, more or less. My dad and my older brother work for the forestry service."

"And there are mountains."

"Yes, sweetie. There are mountains. You should come see them sometime." He gives my arm a little squeeze.

We come to a bridge over a shallow stream. Water makes whispering noises as it passes over tumbled rocks. "Here," he says, handing me his phone. "Take a few pictures of me here." His white shirt and pale blue raincoat stand out against the browns and greens of the surrounding woods.

Jesse smiles and strikes various poses. Most of them are ridiculous. He sticks out his tongue. He winks. He makes various kinds of finger-hearts. Then he wants a selfie of the two of us despite the fact that he has seen what my selfies look like. After I hand his phone back, he surprises me and takes a photo when I'm not looking at the camera. That one turns out okay because I'm looking at Jesse.

"I know this wasn't the plan, but is it terrible that I'm enjoying the hell out of this?" He leans against the railing of the faded wooden bridge, looking down into the rushing water.

"I like it too. Here, I mean. With you." I'm more relaxed here than I have been for a long time. We stand there for what feels like hours listening to the wind and the sound of the water. I keep stealing glances at him. His skin is pale in the filtered light, which makes his hair look even darker. He catches me looking at him when he turns his head and we make eye contact.

"Richie, I never noticed it before, but you have a hint of green in those beautiful brown eyes of yours."

I stare into his eyes for several seconds before I manage to look away.

"Oh." I clear my throat. "We should probably head back." I don't know how much time has passed. I just needed to find something normal to say.

It's still early enough in the spring and we're still far enough north that the sun sets early in the evening. The light is already getting dimmer. I should have paid attention to what time we left. I'm sure it has been at least an hour since Jesse called for a tow.

"Have they called back yet to let you know how soon they'll be here?"

Jesse pulls out his phone. He looks at the screen and grimaces. "Uh... my battery is dead." He holds the black screen towards me.

"We can charge it when we get to the car," I say.

Only we don't get back to the car. We walk a mile down the road and get to the spot where the car should be. There is the rut on the side of the road where our wheel spun helplessly in the mud. There are deep tire tracks, presumably left by the tow truck. Then there is only empty road as far as the eye can see.

I pace back and forth, staring at the ruts in the road left by the tow truck. "Call them back."

Jesse holds his phone out as if that's some sort of an explanation. Oh, right. It's dead.

"But you can look up the garage. It's Peterson's Service Station," Jesse says.

I find the number and dial. Unfortunately they aren't picking up their phone. Their recorded message says they close at five. And their voicemail box is full.

"Now what?"

"I don't suppose Lyft comes out this way." Jesse smiles weakly.

I check, but I already know the answer: no. No one comes out this way. We are in the middle of nowhere.

My battery is running low as well. I call Danny to let him know the situation

"Dude. That's rough."

"Yeah. I thought someone should know where we are." I send him a pin for our location as well just in case. Just in case what? It's not like he can do anything from back on campus.

Jesse raises his voice to add: "And to let you know we're fine. It's a grand adventure. Don't worry, Danny. I'll take good care of our clueless urban youth."

"Not clueless," I say before hanging up.

I search the map of the trails on my phone until I locate the rangers' station, which according to the park's website is about two miles down the road. They're not answering either. But at some point tomorrow presumably someone will show up for work and at the very least help us charge our phones.

"Shall we go, sweetie? It's a nice night for a romantic walk." He slips in beside me and once again I am thankful for the warmth. We walk side by side down the passable sections of the road. I match my stride to his pace. I'm used to it.

We can't be halfway to the station when it starts to rain. And not a little rain, either. At least the trees block some of the downpour.

It's a good thing Jesse is wearing a raincoat, but I'm not. My hoodie offers little protection from the rain, although it hasn't soaked through yet.

Jesse drops my arm, grabs me by the hand and starts running down the center of the road where we have the best chance of even ground. "Let's see if we can beat the worst of this," he says.

I have trouble keeping up with him even with my long legs and despite the fact that I've kept up my running regimen with Danny. Compared to Jesse I am still woefully out of shape. Dancers.

The rangers' station is a single story building with a wraparound covered porch. It looks a lot like the weathered gray bridge. Rain is running in fast rivulets down the gutters into the parking lot. There is a stack of firewood as well, but no place we could start a fire. No picnic shelter with a fire pit. That would be too convenient.

At least there is part of the porch facing away from the wind so it is relatively dry. Jesse pulls me to sit down next to him on the steps near the door.

"Oh sweetie, you're turning blue!"

I do feel cold, but it's not that bad. "I'm from Minnesota. This is nothing. Summer weather." Although I'm sure my comment doesn't sound very convincing through my chattering teeth.

"It's only going to get colder when night falls. We should get you warmer right now before you get cold enough that it's a problem. Much easier to prevent hypothermia in the first place than to treat it later."

"I do not have hypothermia."

"I know. Didn't you hear what I said? *Preventative* measures, Richie. It's a good thing you have me here, city boy, or I'm afraid you wouldn't last the night." He sounds like he's joking, but he has a very serious look on his face.

"I'm sure I'd be fine," I say. But he doesn't look any less worried and I know he's unlikely to let this drop. Scary nurturing Jesse is about to make an appearance. "So, what's your plan, boy scout?" I ask.

Jesse takes off his jacket and then unbuttons his shirt. I see where this is going. Just because I don't have a lot of experience practicing survival skills doesn't mean I don't know anything about them. Like I told Jesse, I'm from Minnesota. We know about cold weather.

"I don't think that's necessary at this point," I tell him as he tugs at my wet sweatshirt, pulling my arms out of the sleeves. My T-shirt is fairly dry, but he has me remove that as well. "I think I'll be fine."

"Shut up. We need that for insulation. At the very least we can prevent you from getting chilled to the bone."

Even exposed to the elements, I am in no danger of becoming chilled at the moment. In fact the sight of him without his shirt on is making me plenty warm before we even get to the next stage. When he sits between my legs with his back pressed against my bare chest I can feel my whole body going up in flames. My teeth are no longer chattering, but I feel a shiver going through my entire body that has nothing to do with the cold.

He grabs my hands and wraps my arms around his waist before draping his shirt and raincoat over us the best he can. He throws my damp hoodie on top for good measure. I feel warmth radiating from his body. I hope I won't siphon off all his body heat and cause him to catch a chill. I wrap myself around him more tightly.

"I'm sorry," he says, squeezing my arms against him and pressing his head into my chest. "This isn't how I hoped we'd be spending spring break together."

"It's okay. At least the company is good." I rest my chin on top of his head. Is it crazy that part of me is glad this happened? That I'm glad to be here with him in my arms?

Yes. It is.

25 Check-in

I wake with my arms still wrapped around Jesse. The morning air is chill. It didn't get cold enough for frost to form on the grass, but there is a light fog that has yet to burn away in the early sunlight.

"Morning, sunshine," Jesse mumbles from his position. His voice startles me. I thought he was asleep.

He carefully separates himself from me. The air on my bare skin takes my breath away. I hurry to put on some clothes, as does Jesse. My sweatshirt is still damp so I leave that alone, but I pull my T-shirt on. Jesse buttons up his shirt.

"How did you sleep?" he asks.

"Well, I wouldn't recommend the mattresses here. Although they are plenty firm, I guess." My joints are stiff, but that should improve once I've moved around. I stretch out my arms and shake my hands.

Jesse laughs. "I mean, did you stay warm enough?"

I nod. "You?"

"Absolutely. You have one hot body, Richie."

I can't think of a single way to respond to that. Which makes Jesse laugh some more. "Don't die of embarrassment on me, sweetie. I don't want to deal with the paperwork after being found with a dead body on federal land."

"Ah. Right."

The park rangers arrive at nine o'clock, an hour before the garage opens. One of them is a black woman with a close-shaved head. The other one resembles a bearded lumberjack with what looks like permanent sunburn.

"Hello... Joseph, were we expecting company?" The woman looks us up and down and then turns to her partner.

He snorts. "That's Brenda's way of asking if you boys are okay."

"We are cold, wet, and hungry," I say at the same time that Jesse says, "We're fine."

"And he's right. We're fine," I add.

Brenda brings us some warming blankets and Joseph scrounges up some food from the kitchen in back. Instant oatmeal and some sour apples. I'm most grateful for the terrible coffee he provides us. I warm my hands around the mug.

I'm still hungry and damp, but I feel a lot better than I did before.

The garage is very apologetic about the mix-up with the towing company. They offer to send someone to pick us up.

"Yeah, we can use a ride," Jesse says.

Joseph overhears and interrupts. "No need. I can run you into town."

"You sure?" Jesse asks.

"Yeah. I can use a break from this one." He points his thumb at Brenda, who rolls her eyes.

Jesse climbs in front while I take the back. The car smells like damp firewood and dirt, although it is perfectly clean.

"You boys don't look like you planned on roughing it in the forest." He nods at Jesse's once-pristine white shirt. "Where are you headed?"

"Oh we're bound for a charming little Airbnb in Kentucky," Jesse says.

Joseph nods. "I wonder if it's one of the places on my sister's list. She's looking for honeymoon locations off the beaten path and really liked a few spots in the mountains there." He pauses before continuing. "I don't know if it's okay for me to say this, but the two of you make a really cute couple."

I start to contradict him. Why? It never bothered me before when people thought we were together. Hell, I went out of my way to give bigoted assholes the impression he was my boyfriend. I think about that MAGA dude on the way home for Thanksgiving.

But now it feels too close to an impossible reality. I would love to be a cute couple. But we're not. I don't get the chance to say anything, though, because Jesse answers for both of us. "Why thank you, sir. I think so too." It's the kind of joke he would make with our friends. But it surprises me here.

The car is waiting for us with a full tank of gas, compliments of Peterson's Service Station. Jesse offers to pay, but they won't hear of it.

"You boys have been through enough, staying out in the rain all night. Should never have happened."

Once we're back in the car, I head for well paved roads and marked highways. I get no argument from Jesse.

Our national forest detour added quite a bit of mileage to the trip. We get to the resort in the late afternoon.

The outside of the main building looks like logs, but it's really siding made to look like a log cabin. Inside, the walls are painted a blank white. There are a few bland paintings hanging on the walls. It's a stark contrast to the rustic exterior.

The woman at the reception desk gives us the keys to our cabin and brochures with information about the amenities and nearby attractions. We won't be here long enough to enjoy any of the nearby attractions. I wonder what kind of amenities this place has to offer. Whatever. It has what I'm looking for. Running water. Heat. A roof.

The cabin where we're staying is at the base of a smallish looking mountain, right on the lake. When we get out of the car, the air smells like pine trees. Which makes sense, because we are surrounded by pine trees. It also smells like a lake. Not fishy, precisely, but very wet.

The cabin is made of real logs, unlike the offices. It's a lot smaller than I thought it would be. A lot smaller than it looks in the brochures. When Bailey said she downsized for us, she wasn't kidding.

There is only one room.

And one bed.

"I think this was a mistake," I say. And instantly regret it when I see the hurt expression on Jesse's face. "I mean, I think Bailey reserved the wrong place. Isn't it meant to be a two-bedroom cabin?"

Jesse studies the pamphlet that the person at the front desk handed him. "Well, it's obviously not two bedrooms. According to this, our cabin is a two *bed* cabin, not two bed*rooms*."

I look around the room. "Where is the other bed?"

Jesse calls the office. "I see. Are there any others available? No, it's fine." He hangs up and looks at me nervously. "She says they recently renovated their cabins and forgot to update the promotional materials."

This is the Kentucky mountain version of the honeymoon suite. I was right. What I accidentally blurted out to Jesse is exactly how I feel. This was a mistake. A terrible idea. And I am pretty sure she set up this single-bed cabin on purpose. So it had been Bailey's terrible idea. I doubt any of them ever planned to join us.

Also, what kind of a place doesn't have the option for two beds? I always thought you could just separate the bigger one into two singles. Maybe not at a family-run b&b. I wouldn't know. Like I told Jesse, my mom was really not into roughing it by any stretch. I'd only been to fancy hotels with indoor pools and complimentary breakfast buffets.

I look from Jesse to the bed. It is full of country charm with its handmade quilt of multicolored squares on a navy background. The bed frame is made out of varnished logs.

I can't stop staring at the bed, so I notice every detail. A knot in the wood on the left side of the headboard. A flaw in the pattern on the quilt where they used the wrong color in the alternating pattern—blue where it should be green. There are four pillows, but two of them seem decorative. They look too thin to be of any use. They are covered in material that matches the quilt.

It doesn't matter what the bedding looks like or how comfortable the pillows might be, I can't possibly sleep in the same bed with Jesse. Not now. Last night was one thing, when there was some sort of excuse for him to be in my arms. And Thanksgiving was an entirely different lifetime.

Jesse's voice interrupts my spiraling thoughts. He pats my arm and I nearly jump out of my skin. I didn't know he was so close. "Don't worry even a little bit, sweetie. I can take the couch. I'm used to sleeping on one anyway."

"It's not that..." But I don't know what to say. It's obvious that I'm not comfortable sharing the bed with him. I look at the pale blue couch shoved up against the wall. It looks new enough, and probably doesn't have springs sticking through the cushions, but it's narrow and stiff-looking and covered in coarsely woven fabric. There is a thin navy blue blanket draped over the back.

"No. Two nights here, right? We'll each take the couch one of the nights."

"Rock paper scissors?" he asks.

"No. The bed is yours tonight. Since you were my rescuer last night, let me pretend this makes up for it." I plan to see if we can get better bedding from the resort before he has to sleep there. Maybe a rollaway, although that was nearly guaranteed to be full of uncomfortable steel springs. "Also, you need a break from couches."

"Richie, I'd argue with you, but I know somehow that would be pointless. I might have rescued you from the cold, but I'm also the reason you were in trouble in the first place. You are too sweet to me." He stands on tiptoe and kisses me on the cheek. Again. The ghost of his lips remains on my skin. I shiver involuntarily, hoping that he doesn't notice.

I stand there like a permanent fixture of the cabin while Jesse goes about exploring our accommodations and unloading food into the refrigerator.

I think I'll stand here for the duration of the trip. At this point it's all I have the mental capacity for. Twice now. Twice. Not a real kiss either time. Only a peck. And still it scrambles my brain.

Jesse finishes putting things away, and eventually I manage to move from my position.

"Cards? Booze? Some other vice?" He waggles his eyebrows suggestively.

"Is sleep a vice?" My voice comes out in a monotone.

I must sound as monumentally tired as I feel, because instead of continuing with his teasing manner, Jesse says, "Oh honey. Of course. You must be wrung out."

It's not that late, but between the regular fatigue that comes from driving unfamiliar roads for hours, the discomfort of spending the night on a wooden porch, and the extra exhaustion of dealing with Jesse and his constant distractions (because he did *not* keep his hands to himself in the car), I am done.

"Let's get you all cozy and tucked in for the night." Jesse locates the towels and some fluffy white bath robes in the built-in closet that I had failed to notice. After a scaldingly hot shower, I grab one of the functional pillows from the bed and head for the couch.

It is smaller than I thought. The fabric is every bit as uncomfortable as it looks. I can feel it even through my T-shirt. At least my sweats offer some protection. It doesn't matter. I could sleep in the car. I could sleep on the floor. Hell, I could sleep outside on the open ground as long as it's not raining. I'm not sure I've ever been more tired in my life.

I pull the insubstantial blanket over myself and close my eyes before Jesse gets back from washing up. He decided to turn in early as well. When I hear him come back into the room, I don't open my eyes. The last thing I need is to see Jesse in nothing but his boxers, with his toned body on full display.

"I'll hit the lights," he says.

But before he turns off the lights he starts laughing softly. I open one eye and am relieved to see he is wearing flannel plaid pajamas instead of his more common nighttime attire.

"What are you laughing about?"

"That couch is not made for someone of your stature."

My legs are nearly falling off the edge of the couch, my toes poking out from underneath the blanket.

"It's fine. I don't sleep this way."

"No, you sleep curled up like an adorable little pill bug."

"Pill bugs are not adorable."

"Maybe not, but you are. Goodnight, sweetie." He blows me a kiss before turning out the lights.

26 Amenities

The next morning Jesse drags me out of the cabin far too early, luring me with the promise of fresh coffee.

The air is crisp. It's cold enough that there's a mist rising off the lake and I can see Jesse's breath when he exhales. There's a bench just wide enough for two overlooking the lake. I hesitate before sitting down. How do I tell Jesse not to sit so close, not to lean against me, not to hold my hand, without making things uncomfortable between us?

It hurt like hell when Jesse backed away from me. I don't want to hurt him that way—to make him think I am backing away because I don't want him close to me. Especially since it's really the opposite. I'm a mess. I want him close, but not too close. I want him to give me space, but not too much space.

When we sit down, of course Jesse snuggles in close and leans against me.

I close my eyes for a moment and breathe in the cold morning air. I look out over the lake. The mountains are hidden in the mist.

As we're watching, a great blue heron flies in and lands not a hundred yards from us. There are mourning doves cooing in the background. If we were together, this would be perfect. Everything about this place would be perfect. The two of us. Breathtaking scenery. Hot coffee.

This place is romantic as hell. And I'm sitting here next to the person I love. When I breathe in I don't smell the scent of pine trees anymore. I don't even smell the mug of coffee in my hand. I am too close to Jesse.

If we were together this would be perfect.

But we aren't. So instead, it's painful.

After breakfast we go for a walk on a path beside the lake. Jesse takes my hand and pulls me along whenever he sees something he needs to show me: a particularly stunning view of the mountains, a pair of swans drifting past, a collection of butterflies in a sea of wildflowers. He has me take pictures of him in all these places.

And then he has us pose together—always standing much too close.

At lunch we have a picnic. Jesse has thought of everything.

"I didn't bring anything." I help spread out the blanket while he unpacks the refreshments.

"Well, that isn't a problem, is it? You were only responsible for bringing yourself, sweetie. What more could we need?" He gestures at the spread of tiny sandwiches, fruit kabobs, and bottles of lemonade iced tea.

I sit down on the blanket and Jesse takes his place beside me. He holds out a skewer of fruit and I put out my hand to take it from him before he decides to feed me. I remember the disaster with the grapes. This doesn't prevent our hands from touching, though.

Am I the only one who can feel the sparks? Not static electricity—something far more dangerous. Jesse gives no indication that there is anything out of the ordinary.

It is official: I will not come out of this trip alive. Constant encounters like this will definitely kill me. Sooner rather than later.

After he's done eating, Jesse lies down and rests his head on my lap. I've almost become accustomed to this particular brand of torture.

"If you could have anything you wanted, what would you wish for," he asks as he stares up at the clouds.

I very nearly say: you. Instead I remain silent for a long time. "I don't do that," I say eventually.

"You don't want things?"

"Of course I do. But I don't make wishes. I've never seen the point. Things will happen, or they won't. Wishing has nothing to do with it."

Jesse stops looking at the clouds and looks directly at me instead. I'm not prepared to meet his gaze; I have to remind myself to breathe.

"That is a very dark way of looking at the world, Richie. I will have to wish for you then." He closes his eyes and clasps his hands together.

"What are you wishing?"

"I told you. I'm wishing for you," he says, as if his words are not devastatingly open to interpretation.

After lying there in silence for a few moments, Jesse stands up. I start to get up as well, but he puts his hands on my shoulders. "Nope. I'm sensing a lot of tension from you. My turn." He presses his fingers against my shoulders.

I let out a soft moan completely against my will. It sounds pornographic.

"I know I don't have your level of expertise, but I have learned a thing or two from my weekly sessions." He runs his fingers lightly across my back using exactly the right amount of pressure until he finds a knot I didn't know I had. When he presses in the right spot, tears spring to my eyes.

"Fuck, Jesse. Is this what it feels like when I work on you?"

He chuckles. "I'm not sure. Tell me when I'm done. If it hurts badly enough right now that you're barely able to contain your screams of agony, then I'm on the right track. If you feel like gravity doesn't quite have the same hold on you and you've landed on your own private piece of heaven when I'm done? Then yes. That's what it feels like."

It's almost a relief to have his hands on me like this—pressure to the point of pain—instead of his maddening barely-there fingertips feathering my skin. I close my eyes and concentrate on breathing deeply, on releasing all the tension I've been holding. Even though I feel like maybe tension is the only thing holding me together.

When Jesse finishes, he kneels down behind me and rests his head on my shoulder. "Better?" he asks, his hands snaking around my waist.

Well, it *was* better until he held me like this and I could feel his warm breath on my neck.

"Yeah. Better. Thanks," I quickly move away, gathering up the remains of the picnic and shoving everything in the cooler.

"Can we rest here a while longer?" Jesse asks. He leans back and pats the blanket beside him. I can't read the expression in his eyes. But there is a pleading tone in his voice that makes it impossible for me to refuse.

The sun is hidden by stupid puffy clouds. The weather is the right amount of cold to be comfortable without a jacket. I lie down on the blanket beside Jesse at a reasonable distance. He scoots over so there is only a whisper of space between us.

He sighs as he stares up at the sky. "I'm glad we came here, just the two of us. I can't think of a more perfect place to be."

Our hands are touching—that not-quite contact that is almost impossible to bear. Then he winds one of his fingers around mine. I'm not sure I hear him right, but it sounds like he says, "You're my favorite."

And then he is asleep.

*

I go for a run in the afternoon partly in the hopes that it will deal with the pent up adrenaline from the stress of being in this "relaxing" environment with Jesse. This is the first break I've had from him other than last night when I was sound asleep. And that hardly counts.

I run along the same paths Jesse and I took in the morning. The bench where we sat. The site of our picnic. The place we saw the birds' nest... If I was hoping this would be a respite from thinking about him every minute, I was wrong. I see him everywhere.

I run faster than I usually do. I push myself harder. I am out of breath, my legs shaking by the time I return to the cabin. And I still have the same problem I did when I set out: I'm confused as hell and I don't know what to do. About Jesse. I don't know how to be around him, but I don't want to be without him.

I walk down by the lake shore after my cool-down. I want to stop sweating before I take a shower. Otherwise there's no point. I find a few flat stones and skip them across the water. I'm picking up another stone when something hits me like a compact, but very solid freight train.

Before I'm really aware of what is happening, Jesse has picked me up and thrown me into the lake. And damn if it isn't colder than ice. Mountain lake. Early spring. Go figure.

Jesse is laughing his ass off.

I pick myself up and walk toward him. Slowly. He could easily escape, but he seems rooted to the spot. Water is dripping from my hair, from my hands. "Come here." My voice is raspy from the dunk in the lake.

Jesse's eyes go wide and he finally starts to back away, but he doesn't move fast enough. I lunge toward him and put my arms around his waist, hoisting him over my shoulder. He might be strong as hell, but he is still smaller than me.

"Richie, I'm sorry!" He's laughing, beating my back with his fists and kicking his legs, making it difficult to keep my balance. "Put me down!"

"I only want you to experience the lake the same way I did. It's quite refreshing." I fling him into the water and he comes up sputtering, but he also has an arm around my leg, and he takes my balance so we are both on our asses in the shallows.

Neither of us is interested in staying in the lake for very long. It's so cold it steals my breath and makes my skin itch. I make my way to the shore with Jesse close behind me. His teeth are chattering and his lips are dark with cold. He huddles close to me for warmth. I can feel his whole body shaking.

I flick him in the forehead lightly. "Jackass. Now you're going to die of pneumonia and ruin the trip for the rest of us."

"But I have you to keep me warm."

I shake my head. "How's that working for you?"

He pulls me closer. "Ask me later," he says with a wink. His voice is huskier than usual.

And now it isn't the cold that is taking my breath away. Does he know what he's doing to me? Does his flirting mean something more? Or is this all just... Jesse?

As we walk toward the cabin, he skirts around the side instead of going through the front door. I follow behind him.

"I don't think now is a great time to go for a walk. I'm kind of not kidding about the pneumonia thing."

Jesse gives me a shove. "You are such a worrywart. And an utter sweetheart. Don't tell me that you didn't notice the list of amenities for our little cabin in the woods?"

All I had noticed was the single bed. And the narrow couch. "What amenities?"

As we round the corner to the tiny back porch, Jesse throws out his arms and proudly announces: "Hot tub with a mountain view. Last one in's a rotten egg!" He starts stripping out of his clothes. All of his clothes. I don't move at all. I look away—at the sky and the distant mountains and the wind chimes hanging from a nearby tree.

"Richie! Snap out of it, love. You'd better get in here quick—or you'll die of pneumonia and spoil the trip for the rest of us."

He splashes me with water from the tub. It's scalding against my chilled skin, which at least reboots my brain. I stand there without moving, still, but at least now I can look at him. He's immersed up to his neck.

Jesse laughs softly. "Why Richie, are you turning shy on me?" he asks.

"Yeah, right." But my voice gets caught in my throat.

I take off my clothes, very aware of how long it is taking me to remove each article of clothing. I don't want to seem like I'm rushing. Or stalling. I slide into the hot tub inch by inch and it feels like my skin is being parboiled. I think I preferred the lake.

Once I am fully immersed in the hot water, I'm fine. I don't usually like hot tubs—especially the smell of the chemicals. But whatever they use here isn't the same. It's not like a chlorinated hot tub with water jets. It's made of wood and the water smells like cedar.

Jesse lowers his head into the water and blows bubbles.

"I don't think this water is sanitary."

"Noted," Jesse says quite seriously before hitting me in the face with a great wave of water.

I splash back in his direction, but not with any force. I'm not in the mood for a water fight. Now that I don't feel like I'm being slowly cooked to death, all I want to do is be still and relax, taking in the scenery, and the sounds. There are unseen birds singing. And frogs too, I think. But it's the underlying silence that I hear the most. We are far enough away from civilization that there are no car noises. It's been a long time since I've been outside of a city.

Jesse sighs. "This feels like home."

"Lucky you," I say.

He smiles softly. "I know." He looks directly at me with his impossibly deep brown eyes and I have to look away before I say something stupid.

After we're both ready to get out, Jesse announces that he needs to practice. He already did some cardio and strength training while I was on my run, but he wants to go through some choreographies while his muscles are still warm.

Jesse tells me I'm welcome to watch, but I am pretty sure watching him dance would wreck me completely. The mere thought is enough to raise my temperature a few degrees higher than the scalding water in the hot tub.

27 Dinner Date

Once Jesse leaves, I walk down to the lake shore and sit on the bench. It should be peaceful. I should be able to sit there and peacefully stare at the lake and enjoy nature.

I am not peaceful.

I'm not in the mood for a walk. I'm not in the mood for anything. I feel like I have energy to burn, but at the same time I've never been more exhausted. I pace back and forth, scuffing the ground with my toe and kicking up little wisps of dirt.

I wish anyone else were here with us. I wish I wasn't waiting here for Jesse to come back, because I really have no idea how to be around him. And I am increasingly convinced that I am going to do irreparable damage to our friendship by saying or doing something asinine. Which would be unacceptable.

After giving up on nature I walk back into the cabin, but there is nothing to do there but stare at the single bed that takes up most of the room. I still can't believe they can't do anything about this at the front desk, but I don't want to hurt Jesse's feelings by making too big a deal out of it. The couch is fine. Not fine, exactly. But acceptable.

I pretend to tidy things up, even though nothing needs tidying. I flop down on the couch and take out my phone, dialing Tea's number.

"Hey Richard. How are things in paradise?"

"I think you mean hell," I mumble.

"Really?"

"Yes. No. Look, I'm calling for an unbiased opinion. Or your opinion anyway. And I don't have a lot of time, so quality, not quantity. I need help figuring out how to survive the weekend."

"Shoot. Tell me why your life is endangered by spending time with your 'friend.'"

"No time for sarcasm. Jesse won't keep his damn hands to himself. And every time he touches me I... Fuck. And I can't tell him to stay away because... he's Jesse. I didn't think it would be any worse than it is every day on campus. That is manageable though. This is hell. His flirty glances, those harmless touches, the way he smiles. And his dark eyes. I can't get away. Plus there's a hot tub. And this—me and Jesse—is all I have to think about here. There are no distractions. I can't not look at him and I don't know what to do because—"

Tea interrupts. "First, you're babbling, which I never thought I'd live to hear. Second, how exactly are things different from the way they were at school?"

I pause. "Nothing is different, I don't think. This is all more of the same. No, there's a difference. It's hard to deal with this— being alone with him—because all of his attention is on me. No one else to interact with. I think that's the problem. And all the little things he does? All the innocent flirtations? The way he looks at me? They don't mean anything special to him. But..."

"They mean something to you."

"We haven't been alone like this since before Ewan. Before I knew how I felt. And now I know. And these harmless little touches are... not harmless to me."

"Mm hmm... Have you ever thought that maybe those innocent touches aren't so innocent? Maybe Jesse has feelings for you. Maybe that's why things feel different now. Have you said anything to him yet?" Tea asks.

"Yes. I don't need to tell him again. He already knows. And this is how he wants things."

"Uh, no offense, but what does Bailey think? Don't take this the wrong way, Richard, but your ability to read people is... not great."

"She thinks Jesse likes me. In a romantic way. She even offered to help me 'get my man.'"

"Uh huh." Tea doesn't say anything after that for a long time. Is she waiting for me to say something? Finally, she lets out a long breath. "Honestly Richard, doesn't he *live* with her? Don't you think she might have the inside scoop?"

"No. It's not like that. Bailey just likes to pair people off. It's like a hobby of hers, only she has a terrible track record. She's been trying to find me a girlfriend forever and now this is her new project. I'm telling you: Jesse doesn't feel that way about me. I would know."

"Okay, *Richie*."

"Richard. Oh. That isn't proof. He's always called me Richie."

"I know. I'll stop teasing you about the name thing. If you really want my advice? I think you should try talking to him again. Now that he didn't just break up with his boyfriend and he's not living in your space. That's when you told him, right? I get why he wouldn't want to risk making things complicated when you were roommates. But things are different now. Why don't you consider the possibility that Bailey is right? Why do you think he agreed to go on this trip with you when everyone else backed out? He could have canceled. Think: has Jesse said or done anything out of the ordinary? Anything that stands out? That might hint at feelings other than friendship?"

I don't mention him calling me his favorite. I'm not sure I heard that correctly anyway. I don't mention the fleeting kisses that I'm sure meant nothing. I say the only other thing that comes to mind: "He told me I sleep like an adorable pill-bug."

Tea snorts. "That boy definitely has feelings for you."

"What makes you say that?"

"You are not adorable."

"Thanks."

Tea laughs at me. Again. "Look, it sounds to me like Jesse is dropping pretty major hints that he is interested in you. In fact, it sounds like he is being Captain Obvious. Also your mutual friend—his *roommate*—thinks he's into you."

"What if you're wrong? What if you're both wrong?"

"What if *you* are? Richard, you need to decide if you want to continue like this—with him driving you crazy whenever you're together—or if you want to take a chance. Isn't it worth the risk?"

"I don't... I don't know."

When Jesse comes back from dance practice he is only wearing a pair of black shorts and a small white towel draped across his shoulders. His skin is glowing with a faint sheen of perspiration and his hair is matted to his forehead.

I don't realize that I'm staring until he throws the towel so it hits me in the face. "Take a picture, it lasts longer." He walks slowly toward the shower with a sashay to his hips. Then he looks back over his shoulder and winks at me.

Maybe Tea and Bailey have a point.

*

Once Jesse is fully clothed I am able to string two words together at least. He has put on a pale pink button down shirt with the cuffs rolled back. "So what's next? If you were Bailey, I'd offer to exchange mani-pedis but I'm pretty sure you wouldn't be up for that."

I look at my nails. "Probably not. Especially if you had nail polish in mind. It burns my eyes."

"You're not supposed to put it in your eyes, sweetie."

"Funny."

"We can't braid each other's hair either," he says, giving my hair a little tug. His fingers graze against my neck and it takes a good deal of effort not to respond in some way. Not to shiver at the sensation.

"We'll dump the sleepover theme, then. Let's jump right to the main course, so to speak. How do you feel about spaghetti with truly amazing primavera sauce?"

"I'll eat anything."

Jesse cracks his knuckles. "Buckle up, cowboy. You're in for a treat. Grab the cutting board and the wider of the two large knives. It has the best edge."

"You tested the knives?"

Jesse looks offended. "Of course. How else can you tell which ones are decent?"

He produces a thick canvas apron that he slips over my head and ties at my waist, coming closer than I really want him to be. He finds a matching apron and asks me to tie it for him. "Thanks sweetie. He turns around while I am still too close, putting us chest to chest. I step back quickly, nearly knocking the bag of onions off the counter.

"Now, follow my lead," Jesse says with a serious expression on his face.

It's not that I can't cook, but pasta primavera is outside my wheelhouse. For a fairly rustic cabin, the kitchen is well stocked with pricey cookware. I arm myself with the requisite cutlery and follow Jesse's directions carefully. Mincing this, dicing that.

I never knew there were different words for the way you cut things other than chopping them large or small. I am absurdly pleased with myself when I manage to julienne the carrots.

Jesse is in charge of assembling all the ingredients and adding them at the right time to the heavy saucepan. Before long the entire cabin is filled with the amazing smell of garlic and onion.

Primavera sauce, at least as made by Jesse, takes much longer to prepare than it does to cook. Before long it's ready for tasting. Jesse blows on a spoonful of sauce, holding it up to my mouth for me to try.

"So…" He ducks his head and looks up at me for approval.

"Damn. I didn't know pasta was a Filipino specialty."

"Everything I do is, by definition, a Filipino specialty," he says in a sultry voice.

The cabin is outfitted with fancy table settings fit for a romantic dinner for two, of course. Jesse finds a tablecloth and lights some candles. All through dinner he sends me seductive looks and does devastating things like run his tongue over his lip after he takes a swallow from his wine glass. Then he swirls his finger around the rim of the glass while saying something that I can't begin to follow because all of my brain cells have fled the vicinity.

So yeah, he has me flustered. And has me thinking it's quite possible that I have been misinterpreting his signals—maybe he is very intentional with his flirting. He looks me directly in the eye as he swallows his last sip of wine, and my mouth goes dry.

Jesse offers to help with the dishes, but I don't let him. "You made dinner. I'll clean up. Those are the rules."

"My hero!" Jesse smiles and rests his head on his hands. He sits there with his elbows on the table, wordlessly staring at me while I wash the dishes and wipe the counters. I feel the hairs on the back of my neck standing on end. When I look in his direction he drags his lower lip between his teeth.

Yeah. Bailey and Tea are definitely onto something. And I am a fucking idiot.

When it's time to turn in for the evening, Jesse grabs a pillow and heads for the couch.

"Wait..." I reach for his arm. "I... You don't need to sleep on the couch."

"Why Richie darlin', are you inviting me into your bed?" He looks down at my hand and raises an eyebrow.

I choke. Literally and figuratively. I let go of his arm. "No. I mean I'll take the couch again. It was surprisingly comfortable. And like I said before—you deserve a break. From sleeping. On couches. Also your shoulder. And I don't want you to get stiff because you know, dancing. I don't want you undoing all my hard work. Massage, you know? And I'll go over there now." I close my mouth, and grab one of the usable pillows.

Either I'm imagining things, or for a fraction of a second Jesse looks disappointed. But despite the fact that I am starting to have very strong suspicions about Jesse's feelings, I don't want to initiate anything out here, where the prospect of rejection based on my own stupid misunderstanding means a long, uncomfortable drive back to campus. Alone. In the car. With him.

Jesse recovers from his disappointment—if that's what it was—very quickly. He stands on tiptoe to give me a quick peck like last time. At least that's what I think he has planned. I steel myself for the feeling of his lips on my cheek. Except he puts his hand under my chin and turns my face to give me a brief, barely-there kiss on the lips. I don't even have time to register what happened before he retreats to the bed.

"Well, if you change your mind, feel free to crawl right in beside me. There's plenty of space under the covers."

I stand there frozen. Again.

"Sweet dreams, darlin'." Jesse has a twinkle in his eye when he pulls the covers up to his chin. He grins at me. "Can you get the lights?"

28 Trouble

I don't mention the kiss and neither does Jesse.

The next morning we pack up and drive back to campus as if nothing happened. Jesse points out charming roadside details and maintains control of the road trip soundtrack as usual. He doesn't suggest any detours. He's perky and happy. And I am... quiet. I don't know what to say. I don't know what to do. I feel like I missed my opportunity to say or do anything. And now I'm stuck again.

"Thank you for the fantastic trip, sweetie," Jesse says when I drop him off at Bailey's dorm. He shoos me away when I offer to carry his luggage up to the room. "I'm fine. But you? You toddle off to bed now. You look like you're ready to drop. That was a longer drive straight through than with our charming little detour."

I nod my head. I am tired. When I get back to my room I lie face down on my bed, prepared to sleep fully clothed. I don't even know if it's physical exhaustion or emotional exhaustion that's worse. I feel like a limp dishrag.

I close my eyes and take a series of slow, deep breaths, only to be interrupted by sudden pounding on my door. "Richard, you utter waste of space, I know you're in there!" Bailey shouts. I don't want to let her in, but I do. Because I know she won't leave. She storms in with her eyes on fire. "Why the *fuck* is your boyfriend still camping out on my couch? Didn't you just come back from your honeymoon?"

"Not a honeymoon. Although I think you know you booked us in the honeymoon suite." I glare at her. She doesn't bother feigning innocence.

"I was going to say you're welcome, but clearly you botched everything." She sits down on my desk and glares up at me.

"Yes."

"I mean you... wait, you're agreeing with me? What the hell happened out there?"

"You said it. I botched everything. Tea told me to look for signs that Jesse had feelings for me. And there were signs. I think."

"Why don't you just kiss him already, or better yet, fuck him and get it over with. Then he'll know for sure that you're not some straight dude stringing him along. He'll know that your earlier confessions still stands, and you're not some confused idiot."

"He kissed me."

Bailey throws her hands in the air. "What! Then—and I cannot say this any more emphatically—why the hell am I the one in your room right now? What should be happening is some very X-rated action between you and your man. What the hell is the matter with you, Richard?"

"He kissed me, but it happened so fast. And it makes me wonder if maybe I'm wrong. It was kind of a nothing kiss. I mean I think it was nothing for him, but not for me. And yes I have had sex before, but not this kind."

"Gay sex?" she asks.

I snort. "No. Although I haven't had sex with a dude. That's not the problem, though. What I mean is I haven't had sex that matters. I haven't done any of this—haven't even kissed someone I'm in love with. Sex has always been more… utilitarian. I want this to be different. It is different. Everything is different."

"Aha. I can pretty much guarantee the same kind of inner monologue is going on with your prince charming over there. He's waiting for you to make the first move. Chickenshit. You too, by the way. The two of you are very trying on my nerves." She pinches the bridge of her nose. "Just tell him, already! Say, 'Jesse, I am in love with you.'"

"I…" Nothing could be more terrifying.

"Okay. I get it. That didn't turn out so well for you last time. Right. Your next best bet is seduction. Turn the tables on him. Go full-out on the flirtation. Get your game on. Scare the crap out of him."

"I don't think so."

Bailey ignores my objection. "Let's go over a few ideas: outrageous pick up lines." She pulls out her phone and scrolls through some idiotic list.

"Try these on for size… If you think I look good in this, you should see how I look good out of this."

"No. I don't know if he likes how I look."

"Oh please," Bailey says, rolling her eyes. "First, you are a tasty snack. And furthermore you must be the only person this side of the Mississippi who can't read the way he looks at you." She goes back to the pick-up lines.

"Hey, I lost my underwear. Can I see yours?"

"I've seen his underwear. They're not that interesting."

"When I'm around you, I can't think straight."

"It will remind him that he thinks I'm straight."

"Those clothes would look great in a crumpled heap on my bedroom floor."

"He doesn't like his clothes on the floor. Even when they're dirty."

"My name is Richie. Remember that; you'll be screaming it later."

"Hell no."

Bailey frowns at me. "Hmm. Too direct? Too overtly sexual? How about cheesy?"

I don't even bother to answer her now. I sit there and let her rattle off a list of ridiculous lines that I would never say: "I'm afraid your license has been suspended for driving me crazy… I'm not a hoarder but I really want to keep you forever… I'm an organ donor: I'd like to give you my heart… I'll give up my morning cereal to spoon you instead… I'm not drunk; I'm just intoxicated by you… Four plus four equals eight. But you plus me equals fate.

"Oh wait…" Bailey stops and grins broadly. "This one's perfect for you: You look familiar. Did we meet in class? I swear we have *chemistry* together."

I hold up my hand. "Enough. Can you honestly imagine me saying any of those things?"

Bailey throws her hands in the air. "Of course not! That's what makes it genius. He'll have to admit that there's something going on if you start *coming out* with lines like these. See what I did there?" She smirks.

"It won't work. He'll laugh his ass off and think I'm kidding."

Bailey screws up her mouth and holds her chin with her hand. "Okay. Let's go nonverbal. Trace your fingers down his spine. A tad too low, maybe. Hold his face in your hands. Run your tongue over your lips. Rest your hand on his thigh. Again, a little too high."

Exactly like Jesse does. All the things that make my blood boil and confuse the hell out of me. "Maybe. But... How exactly would that work? Sitting at breakfast I casually start sucking on his neck?"

Bailey snorts. "Point taken. How about this: a night out. You and Jesse. No one else."

"We do that all the time."

"Yes, but this time you'll be the one in charge. Well, *I'll* be the one in charge. We need to turn up the dial on the romance. What you need is a grand, romantic gesture. Something cliche. Corny as hell. That will appeal to his squishy little gay heart and he will fall right into your arms."

I bite my bottom lip.

"Oh! Definitely use that," she says, scribbling in a notebook she stole from my desk.

Bailey twists a coil of pink hair around a finger. "Now for the setup. Let's come up with a list of things that will make him think of the two of you. Shared experiences. Anything you could use from your trip home?"

"Not really. We went to a gay bar and danced." But all I can remember from that is how it felt to see him grinding against someone else. "That wasn't about us."

"Cabin trip is too recent and too much of a romantic failure to bear repeating... Ooh! What about when he moved in with you? That was darling. What was the movie again?"

"*Singin' in the Rain.* But I don't want to use that. It's from when he thought of me as his roommate. We weren't even really friends yet."

"Some other movie, then. That would be perfect, actually. Movie theaters are a great venue for what I have in mind. Plus, your room is right upstairs. Very convenient for the extra-curricular activities sure to follow. Ah, you can bring back all the old classics: pretend to yawn and put your arm around him. Your fingers can touch 'accidentally' while eating popcorn. I can pull some strings; I've got friends in the film studies department and access to their entire catalog of films. So mostly classics, but that could work since that's right up your alley."

I know exactly what to do. I feel a surge of excitement or nerves at the idea. "Perfect," I say.

Bailey actually squeals.

29 Roman Holiday

I love the dusty smell of old theaters. The air feels heavy somehow. The deep red curtains that surround the screen look almost black in the dim light.

We are the only two people in the old basement theater, the site of our first "date." Bailey pulled some strings and signed it out for a private viewing.

"Ooh we have the place to ourselves! How cozy," Jesse says, giving my arm a squeeze. "I'm thrilled to be able to add another Audrey Hepburn film to my gay bingo card."

I nod calmly even though I am nervous as hell. "Not just any film: *Roman Holiday*."

"Oh, Your favorite!" Jesse's smile is brilliant, his eyes bright. I look away from him so I can remember how to speak.

"Yes. Audrey Hepburn's debut. Plus Gregory Peck. I'm about to change your life," I say as the lights go down. That was one of Bailey's lines. It feels odd when I say it. Jesse raises an eyebrow, so I know it sounds strange too. But he's smiling, which I take as a good sign.

When the projector starts up, it reveals dust motes dancing in the air. Bailey was right. This is romantic as hell. I hope I can pull it off. I hope she's right about all of this.

I don't look at the screen. I can't. Instead, I watch Jesse watching the movie. The light of the projector illuminates his face in a pale glow. His dark eyes sparkle. I keep glancing at his lips, wondering again what they taste like. The kiss at the cabin was too fleeting to offer any hints. He kissed me. That has to mean something. Hell, he'd invited me to share his bed, hadn't he?

I can't keep my eyes off him. I can barely keep my hands off him.

I lower my head toward him and speak softly, even though there is no one else around. "Paramount wanted the movie shot in Hollywood. The director didn't. They agreed to filming on location, but scaled back the budget. That's why it was filmed in black and white."

"I'm glad. It would feel somehow wrong in color," Jesse says.

We are so close I can smell the scent of his shampoo. I close my eyes for a moment and take a few breaths before settling back into my seat. Jesse moves his hand so it rests next to mine on the armrest. His fingers brush against mine almost like it's an accident. But I'm pretty sure it's not.

When Audrey makes her first entrance, I lean toward Jesse again. This time I whisper, coming much closer than necessary. My lips brush against his neck. "At the end of the film, she was given all of the gowns, hats, and accessories to keep. They were meant to be a wedding present."

I stay close, breathing on the sensitive spot behind his ear until he shivers.

"Why aren't you a film-studies major again?" Jesse asks breathlessly.

"I don't want to kill the pleasure of watching movies."

"Fair."

Jesse snuggles up against me. "It's cold," he says, with mock innocence. He knows full well what is going on here.

I put my arm behind him and allow my fingers to graze the back of his neck and he gives a barely audible gasp. I pull him toward me slightly. "Better?"

He rests his head on my shoulder. Shortly after that, he places his hand on my thigh. I can't hide my smile. I had been worried that the scheme Bailey helped concoct would scare Jesse off. Or go the other direction and be too subtle.

Bailey had disagreed. "No, the beauty is in the cliché. The whole thing screams romance—totally you. It's golden. And obvious. If he doesn't respond, you'll have your answer. And I will die of shock."

As the movie continues, Jesse begins to trace figures on my leg with the tips of his fingers. I feel like my blood is on fire.

"I can see why this is your favorite." He speaks softly, his lips devastatingly close. His breath is warm against my neck. Everything about him is intoxicating.

I gasp as his hand moves into dangerous territory. "You are cruel."

He grins while keeping his eyes on the screen. "Tell me more about the movie."

"Fine," I hiss. "In the 'mouth of truth' scene Audrey didn't know that Peck was going to pretend his hand had been bitten off, so her screams of surprise were real."

I can't take it anymore. Not with his damn hands on me. I place my lips on Jesse's neck, and he inhales sharply. As I move on to a slightly different location, he moans softly.

"Sweetie, do you know what you are doing?" he asks, his voice much huskier than usual.

"Yes. I am kissing your neck. But not enough to leave any marks."

Jesse swats me on the leg. "No, sweetie. What you are doing, is driving me crazy. Are you sure? About this? About us? I don't want you to feel any pressure."

"Pressure to do what? This?" I put my hand on the back of his neck and draw him toward me.

And I finally know what his lips taste like—sweet and cool and like nothing I can describe. This time it isn't simply a teasing phantom of a kiss. This time I have the chance to savor the feeling as our lips come together. It seems like I've waited forever for this. Years, at least. Jesse's tongue touches my upper lip and I nearly lose my mind.

I pull away from him reluctantly. I hold him at a slight distance from me, one hand on each of his shoulders, so he can't come any closer.

"I think we should be… not here."

Jesse nods once. Definitively.

The movie is still playing when we stand to leave. I grab him by the wrist. He follows me out of the theater and up the stairs.

We don't say anything in the hallway. I'm afraid it will break the spell between us. That he will come to his senses and change his mind. I'm also afraid that I might be having a heart attack. It feels like there are no spaces between heartbeats.

When we get to my room and the door swings shut behind us, I am suddenly lost. I don't know what to do with my hands. I'm not sure where to look. When my eyes are on him I feel like the room is spinning.

He's so far away—even though only inches separate us—and I want him so much closer.

"Jesse, I need to tell you…" My voice catches. My throat closes off. I don't know what to do. The room feels unfamiliar to me. The furniture seems to be in the wrong places. I lean against his empty desk.

"It's okay love," he says gently rubbing his thumb along the knuckles of my hand.

When Jesse speaks, that's enough to allow me to move again, to bring us closer. I lift him and set him down on the desk, his legs on either side of me. I place my hands on his hips and move in slowly. Agonizingly slowly. Then I take his lips in mine again. And it feels like liquid fire in my veins.

I break contact between us, but I only leave enough space that I can speak without losing myself again. "I love you, Jesse." I like the way this feels on my lips. I like the way it sounds when I hear the words out loud. "I am in love with you." I press my forehead against his. My voice is ragged. "I want you to know."

"I know. Well, I know now. I hoped," he says. He runs his finger along my jaw and I shiver. "I'm sorry. I should have said it first. Told you how I felt. I thought you were confused. Before. I'm sorry."

I'm not sure how much longer my legs will support me; they certainly won't hold me the next time our lips come in contact. Or if he touches any part of me. While my legs are still in working order, I lift Jesse from the desk, his legs wrapped around me. I set him on my bed and then kneel in front of him, taking a shaky breath.

We are nearly eye to eye like this. He puts his hands on my head, his fingers combing through my hair. Finally my heart remembers its job. I can relax enough to take a breath. I think he could do this forever. "Jesse, I…"

"We don't have to do anything," he says, his voice serious. "Nothing you're not comfortable with." He puts one hand on either side of my face and lightly feathers kisses across my forehead.

"Same," I tell him as I tease the hem of his shirt, feeling the warmth radiating from his skin. I lift the shirt over his head. Now

I don't have to hide my admiration for his body. I drink in every inch. He shudders as I drag my fingers lightly across his tight abs and up over his ribs. "God, I've wanted to do this for so long." I climb up into the bed beside him.

"I didn't know," he mumbles before nearly killing me by sucking lightly on a spot on my neck just below my ear.

Holy fuck.

"That's because you're an idiot," I say once I can speak again.

"Is this okay?" he asks, tugging at my shirt. As an answer I pull my shirt off over my head. He smooths his hands over my shoulders, down my arms. He pulls me gently toward him as he falls back on the bed. I roll so he is on top of me because I'm afraid I will hurt him.

And then bare skin meets bare skin and lightning shoots directly into my brain stem. I don't move at all. I can't move. I feel the heat between us. I have never wanted anything so much as this feeling, this contact between us. And it's not because he's a guy. It's because he's Jesse. And this is not casual.

Anything more is too much right now. I have been immobilized. I close my eyes and he rests his head on my chest, both of us breathing hard. I toy with the short, velvety hair at the nape of his neck. I hold him like that for a long time.

And then I'm crying. Not a lot, but enough that Jesse notices.

"Shit. I don't know what's wrong," I say. "Nothing's wrong. I'm so fucking happy."

"It's okay." He moves so we are lying side by side. He kisses the tears off my face. He runs his hands up and down my arm, occasionally grazing my ribs, which is at once very calming and intensely distracting.

I feel like such an ass. I've completely ruined the mood. I grasp his hand, intertwining our fingers. I turn my head to look at him, prepared to meet his eyes now.

"You asked me before. And I couldn't answer then. But I've had some time to think. And I do want to fuck you. Or be fucked by you. I don't know if I have a preference." I can tell this is something that I could have said better by the way Jesse is trying to hide his smile.

"I want you." My voice comes out in a husky growl. "So damn much. But not yet. I don't know when..."

"There's no rush, sweetie. We have all the time. And there are plenty of other things we can do," Jesse says, propping himself up on one elbow, tracing the outline of my lips with his thumb.

I stare into his eyes. I could stare at them forever. "I am very gay for you," I say.

"What a relief," he replies. "Because I love you too."

30 Morning

I wake up wrapped around Jesse, my firm dick pressing into his back. I move slightly and he murmurs in his sleep, pushing his ass back against me.

"Fuck. You really are going to kill me," I whisper into his neck. I swear I can feel him grin. "You're awake, you bastard."

"No. Still sleeping. Can we stay like this all day?" His voice is always hoarse in the morning. But now it is even more gravelly than usual because when we rekindled the mood last night— which didn't take long—we had engaged in "plenty of other things." Jesse had been very vocal.

I kiss the back of his neck and hold him tightly. I could stay like this forever. Well, maybe not forever. I'm surprisingly hungry, and I really need to take a piss.

"I'll be back soon." I detangle myself from both Jesse and the bedsheets. "Don't move."

When I get back, Jesse is propped up on his side doing his best sexy pose. "Welcome back, lover," he says, fluttering his lashes.

"Ugh. We are *not* doing that. Or I'll trot out some of the pick-up lines Bailey told me to use on you."

Jesse laughs. "Please do! Kidding. I couldn't help myself. I had to see your expression."

"You mean this one?" I say, pointing at my scowling face.

"Yes. And it is *adorable!*"

"I changed my mind. We can't stay here all day." I pull the blankets off him, leaving him with only the sheet. "Get up. We're gonna miss breakfast."

"Fair enough. Sustenance is required, but no dining hall for me this morning. You are taking me out. Pancakes, fresh strawberries, lots of whipped cream…"

"Fine. But you'll still need to get out of bed. And… crap. Why do you always end up here in need of fresh clothing?" I ask. I look at the floor of the room—yesterday's clothes everywhere in crumpled heaps. So much for what I told Bailey about Jesse caring about whether his clothes ended up on the floor.

Jesse grins. "Wait for it…"

And then there is a knock.

"Special delivery." I hear Bailey's voice at the door.

By the time I get there, Bailey is gone, but there's a brown paper bag full of clothing on the floor with a post-it note featuring a smirking smiley face.

"Well, aren't you resourceful?" I toss the bag to Jesse.

He flashes his amazing smile. "Who knew that early morning clothing delivery was a service they offered on campus."

"It's hardly early."

Jesse has never been shy. And I don't turn away when he changes this time, enjoying the view very much. I never thought it could be so sexy watching someone put *on* clothing. I am practically salivating by the time he has pulled his shirt down to cover his abs.

"Careful, you'll catch flies with that mouth," Jesse says with a wink. "It's okay. I'm used to having that effect on people. When you are as fabulous as I am, it's the price you have to pay. Now, let me freshen up a bit and then we can depart."

While he's gone I pull the "His" and "His" pillows out of storage and place them next to each other on the bed. Sappy. I don't care.

Jesse comes back and admires my handiwork. "I love what you've done with the place!" he says, indicating the pillows.

He tugs at my arm and pulls me after him toward the door. But before he gets very far, I put my arms around his waist and pull him toward me. I crush his body against mine, not wanting any space between us.

"Wait."

"Okay," he whispers.

I rest my head on his, my chest pressed against his back. My heart is dancing in my chest. And not in a good way. "I need to know that this is real. Because it is for me." My voice comes out much quieter than I intend.

"It feels real enough." Jesse turns in my arms and puts his hands around my neck.

His tone is light and playful, but I am deadly serious. "I need to know. I don't want to leave this room if you aren't coming back.

Wait. That came out more melodramatic and stalkery than I intended."

I break free of his arms and back away, but not very far. He doesn't need another possessive asshole in his life. I'm afraid I'll hold him too tight. Jesse steps toward me, closing the distance. He leans into me, his head resting against my chest. I'm sure he can feel my heart beating a crazy rhythm.

He looks up at me. "I'm so sorry. We should have sorted things out between us a long time ago."

"What are you saying Jesse? I need you to be very clear. Will you move back in? I want you here. I want to wake up with you every morning and go to bed with you every night. If you want your own bed, I guess that's okay. But I don't like this room without you here. I don't feel like me without you here."

Jesse doesn't say anything and it takes me a while to realize that he's not laughing. He's crying, his tears dampening my shirt. I lift his chin so I can look him directly in the eyes. "Oh, hell. I didn't mean to make you feel bad. Remember I always say the wrong things."

He wipes away his tears. "No, sweetie. You always say the right things. You always say the truth. Only sometimes it's hard for people to hear."

My heart sinks. Or leaps into my throat. Whatever it does, it makes me feel like shit. I'm sure all the blood has rushed away from my face. The things I said were hard for him to hear. I shouldn't have said anything.

Jesse notices my expression and takes both my hands in his, kissing my knuckles one at a time. "Oh no, honey. I'm not talking about what you said just now. Everything. Absolutely everything. Of course I'll stay. Wild horses couldn't keep me away."

"You are so gay," I say. Which makes him stop crying and punch me in the chest.

He tries to take my hand to leave again, but I spin him around pressing him against the door with his hands above his head. I move toward him slowly, fitting our bodies together so I can feel every inch of him against me.

Then I kiss him until his knees go weak and I'm the only thing supporting him.

*

While waiting for the food to arrive we spend a fair amount of time doing those ridiculous things that new couples do in public: staring into each other's eyes, holding hands, laughing for no reason. I see why people do this kind of crap now—I can't help myself. And I feel happier than I have felt since... ever.

But after our food arrives and breaks the flow, once I take my eyes off him, once our fingers are no longer entwined, I start wondering if I'm wrong about what he meant. What if I misunderstood? We kissed and fooled around a bit, but what if all that means something more to me than it does to him? What if he thinks of me as a "friend with benefits?" I don't want to be a fuck buddy.

"You look worried," Jesse says, smoothing out the wrinkle lines on my forehead. "There. All better." He grins for a moment. But then he frowns as my wrinkles reappear. "What is it? What imaginary anxieties are you concocting?"

I take a breath. "I like that you are with me now. But I don't know what to expect now that we are... together? Are we? Together? Is that what you want?"

Jesse scoots over so he is nearly sitting in my lap and puts his arms around my neck. "Of course that's what I want. How is it that no one scooped you up long ago, darling? You are hot as hell, an amazing kisser—not to mention your magical hands—ever the gentleman, and apparently the most romantic person on God's green Earth."

I shake my head impatiently. "I know you are moving back. And we will be roommates. And also have sex. But what does that mean to you? I need to know. What am I to you? What are we? I need you to say out loud."

"Oh... you mean the b-word?"

"Bitch?" I say reflexively.

Jesse laughs. "At least this unusual case of nerves hasn't blunted your delicious sarcasm. Let me make things very clear and eliminate any confusion on your part. "You are my boyfriend," he whispers in my ear. "And I am your boyfriend." He places a kiss just behind my earlobe. I think the people at the next table can hear my heart thundering. Then he stops and looks up at me with a grin. "Although I have also been called a bitch—"

"I don't share." I interrupt him.

Jesse tilts his head and raises one eyebrow.

"If we are bitches," I say, causing him to choke. "I don't share. With other people I mean, I want you to have friends. Lots of friends. I want you to be yourself and not be afraid." I don't want to be Ewan. "But I don't want you to be with anyone else. For sex, I mean."

Jesse laughs until his body is quaking and tears are streaming down his face. "I love every damn thing about you," he says when he can catch his breath. "Sweetie, let me be very clear: I am yours, and yours alone."

31 Shameless

It's a nice day, and after breakfast we wander around for a while with no real destination in mind. At least I don't think we have a destination in mind. I only want to be near Jesse. I keep brushing up against him, finding any excuse to stay in contact. And I can't stop grinning.

Jesse ruffles my hair. "Richie, you are so adorable when you're drunk!" he says in a funny voice.

"Drunk. You're hilarious." I kiss the top of his head. Although I do feel tipsy. It's his fault for being so fucking adorable. And because I know he's mine. Finally.

"Let's sit for a while," Jesse says, finding a shady spot under a tree on the quad. The rough bark isn't terribly comfortable against my back. And the grass is a bit damp. But when I sit down, Jesse positions himself in between my legs and leans back against me and I hardly notice the damn tree. Or anything else. I bury my head in his hair and clasp my hands around his waist.

"This is my favorite place," he says.

I look around. "Under this tree?"

Jesse turns and pinches my cheek. "No, sweetie. In your arms." I pull him in toward me even tighter and he sighs as he leans back against my chest.

"Here, I'll make you a daisy chain," Jesse says, moving only slightly so he can pluck flowers from around the base of the tree.

"Those are dandelions."

"Oh hush. Don't ruin the mood." Jesse swats my hand in mock annoyance.

As he braids the flowers together I trail my fingers along the tops of his shoulders, down his spine and back up again. Every now and then I kiss his neck or nibble on one of his earlobes.

"That is very distracting," he purrs, pausing his floral project.

"What, this?" I whisper in his ear before tracing a path down the length of his arm.

"Yes," he gasps, letting go of his flowers. Dandelions scatter on the ground.

I kiss his neck again, sucking lightly. "I'm a little distracted too. And just so you know, I'm not sure how much longer I can keep things strictly PG. Or even PG-13." I slip my hand under the hem of his shirt and tease my fingers along the edge of his waistband.

"Well," Jesse says abruptly, leaping to his feet faster than I thought humanly possible. "I think we're done here." He grabs me by the hand and pulls me behind him.

It takes us almost no time to reach my room.

Without pausing, and before the door even has a chance to close completely, Jesse's hands are all over me. I can't hold back the sound that comes out. Half sigh and half moan.

He walks me backward to the bed. "You're too damn tall." He pushes me so I fall against the mattress. Hard. I forget how strong he is sometimes.

"Agreed."

His kisses are hungry, bruising, urgent. I can't get enough of the taste.

Jesse pulls at my shirt. I shiver as the air hits my bare skin. His eyes rake over my body.

"Your turn," I say, my hands shaky as I undo the buttons on his shirt. Once that is dealt with, I smooth my hands across his chest to remove the shirt entirely. It's like unwrapping a present. "You should always wear button down shirts."

Jesse laughs and presses me into the bed again. I run my hands along his arms, down his back, up his ribs. I love feeling the subtle definition of his muscles. I love the way his skin feels beneath my fingertips, smooth and hot.

His dark eyes meet mine, and I see the same intensity that I feel. "You take the lead. Nothing you aren't comfortable with. Nothing you don't want. What do you want, love?" Jesse whispers. He touches the tip of his tongue to a spot just behind my ear and then follows it with a gentle breath.

Apparently that is the key to my complete undoing. I lose the ability to speak for a moment. And once I can manage to utter a few syllables, I'm not very eloquent.

"I want... that." My voice is breathless. I am breathless.

He turns my head and gives some attention to the matching place behind my other ear. I shiver from head to toe, which causes dangerous friction between us.

"What else?" he asks.

I desperately want to answer his question, but I can't think with him so close. "Fewer clothes," is all I can come up with.

Jesse kisses the spot at the base of my throat, gently sucking on the skin before asking, "Mine or yours?"

"Yes."

*

"I don't know why we have to leave the room. As far as I'm concerned we can order delivery straight to the room and stay in bed. Without clothes. Possibly until the end of the school year."

"What about classes?" Jesse pulls the blankets from the bed. I'm tangled up in them so I end up on the floor, on my ass.

I glare up at him. "The hell with classes. I'll email my teachers that I'm terribly ill again and have to do all my work from home."

"And labs?"

"Problematic. True. And I suspect that your performance classes might also throw a wrench in my plans. But it's the weekend. Why are you in such a hurry to leave?"

He's already pulling on clothes. "Because we have already missed breakfast with Bailey and the dudes. And lunch. And if we skip dinner I'm afraid she will come after us. And I'm low-key terrified of her. She's the real reason I agreed to move back in."

I look at him nervously.

"Kidding. Richie, I'm kidding! Sooner or later I hope you forgive me for being so dense. But for now, get a move on. You require sustenance. So do I, for that matter."

I reluctantly get dressed and head to the dining hall with Jesse. He doesn't loop his arm through mine like he used to. His fingers are laced with mine instead.

"Hello you two." Bailey smiles knowingly as we sit down at our usual table. It's not like we're sitting any closer together. Well, Jesse is pretty much sitting on my lap, but that has often been the case. No wonder everyone thought we were together.

"It looks like date night was a big success," she says.

"Yes."

Jesse pulls back the collar of his shirt and tilts his head to show off one of the many marks I'd left. "Quite a success," he says smugly.

Kit and Danny show up in time for the grand hickey reveal. Kit hoots with laughter and Danny gives me a congratulatory slap on the back.

"Soooo…" Kit says, "When can we help you move your crap out of Bailey's room? Wait. You are moving out, aren't you?"

"Yes." I put my hand on top of Jesse's on the table. "Today. He's moving today."

Bailey holds her hands out defensively. "Okay, okay! Far be it from me to come between you and your man."

"His stuff can move later, I suppose." I'm not afraid that Jesse is going to back out of his plan to move back in, but I don't see any reason why there should be any delay. I want things to be the way they should be. Jesse and I should be together.

"Speak for yourself. I need my stuff. It's very important," Jesse says with a pout and those ridiculous puppy eyes.

"Then we should leave now. Start packing." I start to get up but he moves faster than I do, standing behind me and holding me down by the shoulders.

"I'm teasing. Of course I'm moving in today. And they can burn my stuff for all I care."

"Really?" Bailey says, both eyebrows raised.

Kit claps his hands together with delight. "If you don't want your belongings anymore, I call dibs on your racing jacket."

"Do *not* touch his things. Or I will come for you." I glare at Kit. "And no one can have that jacket."

"Oh?" Jesse says looking down at me.

"Yes. It's your favorite. And you look good in it. Very good."

"Aww, thanks, sweetie." Jesse gives my shoulders a squeeze. When I turn to look up at him he gives me a quick kiss on the lips that should be harmless. It's not.

I have to stifle a growl in my throat and I am immediately resentful that there are other people around.

"Let's go get your shit. Now."

32 Found

When Jesse moved out I never expanded to fill the whole space. Now with his things moved in, it is back to normal. No longer half-empty. The scented candles are back on the window ledge. Jesse's batik wall hangings are back up. His wide array of hair and skin care products are lined up neatly on top of the dresser. The room smells like him.

Things are almost exactly like they were before he moved out—which seems like ages ago—but this time the beds are pushed together, with the "His" and "His" pillows side by side. I no longer sleep clear across the room from Jesse. Everything is better here. It's home.

Kit is helping with the decorations, which is good because they are a lot more elaborate than I could pull off on my own. I want things to be memorable. Not just streamers or balloons or whatever. Kit and a bunch of his friends from the theater department came to hang the walls with fabric and install flats painted white and gray to look like stone buildings. They also brought some sort of stage light that removes color from the rest of the room. Or at least desaturates everything. I had no idea that was possible.

"What about your clothes?" Danny asks.

"You don't like my outfit?" I'm wearing baggy black sweatpants and a white T-shirt.

One of the theater techs gives me a scalding side-eye. "That is *not* an outfit. That is the unfortunate garb of an individual who has turned their back on the world and decided to never interact with another human being. Ever."

"He's kidding. Richard is kidding. Don't worry. Bailey's on it," Kit says.

Shortly afterward, Bailey arrives with a light gray suit and a narrow black tie. "Strip." She shows no indication of leaving me any privacy. Fine. I shed my clothing and exchange it for the items she provided.

"Tuck in," she says once I've got the shirt buttoned up. "Belt." I grab the belt from her and thread it through the belt loops. "Spin," she demands, showing off her handiwork to the rest of the room.

Danny whistles. "Nice ass, Richard."

"Leave the boy alone," Kit says. "Also, seconded."

"How can you even see my ass? I'm wearing a jacket."

Kit shakes his head and Danny laughs.

"Okay, finishing touches." Bailey takes a bunch of thick hair goo and slicks my hair back.

"Really?" I wrinkle my nose. It smells weird and makes my hair feel like I haven't showered in days.

"1940's gentleman. Pomade is not optional."

Danny's friend shows up with the final set piece.

The crew finishes up and leaves just in time. Jesse is never late, and he's been bugging me for details about the party for the last week. So of course, he's right on time. I put my hands over his eyes and walk him to the center of the room. He is wearing a black and white houndstooth jacket, sparkly black pants, and his low-heeled patent leather boots. I am slowly becoming an expert on the names of various fashion items.

He looks around the room, his eyes wide in surprise. It is quite a transformation. Kit's friends really delivered.

"I can see there is a theme here. Black and white? Old movies?"

"Yes. And…" I wait for him to notice the details. I wait for him to see the oversized camera. And the iconic Italian buildings painted on the flats. And the "mouth of truth." And as the crowning touch, the Vespa in the corner.

Jesse gasps. "*Roman Holiday!* Wait, this isn't a subtle hint that you're Italian royalty and plan to leave me here alone with the reporters, walking out of my life forever?"

"No. Of course not. I wouldn't… I wanted… I'm not…" I'm tripping over my damn tongue.

Jesse grabs my hands. "I know, sweetie. I'm only teasing. I love it. Completely and utterly love it." He stands on tiptoe and gives me a gentle and completely unsatisfying kiss. He will have to make up for that later. When we don't have guests.

Danny mixes the drinks—ones that were popular in the forties. I play music from classic movie soundtracks. We dance, even though I am still a terrible dancer. I don't care. I like how it feels to dance with Jesse. I like him here. Where he belongs. I like how we fit together. He makes it so easy to dance with him. With the way he moves, I almost feel graceful in his arms.

He dances with everyone. I like to watch him dance. When he moves to music, it's like he becomes a different species from regular people—even other dancers.

Then Bailey decides it's time for gifts.

"Here." She hands us a neatly wrapped present with a giant black and white bow. It's a set of sheets for our shared bed. We already have some. I remember not to tell her that even without Jesse reminding me to keep my mouth closed. These sheets from Bailey are nicer anyway.

"I wanted to get you sex toys, but Kit said it was in poor taste." Danny smirks. "So we got you a picnic basket. There's stuff inside too." Plastic wine glasses, bamboo plates and silverware. A picnic blanket. It reminds me of our trip.

I tap Jesse on the arm and point to the windowsill. "There's a plant. That's from Tea. She made me buy it. Here's my present." I hold out the box.

"Ooh…" Danny says, "Can we guess?"

I turn toward him. "Not sex toys."

Jesse snorts. He unboxes the present while everyone crowds around him. I don't know why they care so much about my present. They didn't do this for anyone else's. The bottle is hand-labeled by the same woman who helped with my last housewarming present. In her curling script, the sticker on the side reads: "Roman Holiday." I couldn't think of a better name.

"It's massage lotion. I went to that place that has custom scents. And I had them mix this. They combined some things that smelled like your cologne with some things that smelled like the stuff you gave me. I had them try a few times until they got it right. It doesn't smell very strong. I hope it's alright."

Jesse removes the cover and puts a drop on the back of his hand. "Richard…" He's speechless for a moment. I used to get nervous when he called me Richard. Now he can call me whatever he wants. "My hopeless romantic."

"You like it? I've never given a gift to someone I'm in love with before. I've never been in love before. I wasn't sure."

"It's perfect," he says. "You are perfect." His eyes have that hungry look that I have come to relish.

But we are surrounded by our idiot friends.

Kit goes to pour himself another drink, but I hand him the bottle instead. "Take it."

"Why Richard, that's so sweet of you." He smiles and taps Danny on the shoulder. "I think it's time to head home."

"You want us to help clean up?" Danny asks.

Kit rolls his eyes. "No. He wants us to leave."

Bailey throws her arms around Jesse. "No!" she wails, "Just one more dance..." Her hair has taken on a life of its own, escaping from the narrow hair band.

"No more dances." Kit grabs Bailey by the arm and maneuvers her towards the door. "Let's not overstay our welcome, or they'll never let us come back."

Danny follows the two of them out the door. He turns to smile at us. "Night, boys. Great party. Enjoy!"

When the door closes behind them I feel a great sense of relief. I have wanted Jesse to myself all evening. This is partially true. I want him to myself all the time. I only grudgingly share him with other people. And now, I am done sharing.

"About damn time," Jesse says, echoing my thoughts. He puts his arms around me and brushes his fingers against my neck, causing me to shiver.

"It was a lovely party," he says softly.

"I had help."

Jesse laughs, nodding at the Vespa. "I can see that."

I look around at the other pieces from the prop shop. "Don't worry. Someone will pick all this up tomorrow."

"I wasn't worried. Do I look worried?" He sways back and forth, dancing to the music that is still playing. Big band music. Romantic music. I put my arms around his waist.

"What should we do now that we have the place to ourselves?" He asks. The top few buttons of his shirt are undone, revealing a tantalizing amount of skin.

"I have a few ideas." I run my thumb along his jawline and tilt his head up so I can look into his eyes. I like seeing my reflection there. I like the way he looks at me. Especially now. Like he can't look away from me. I'm glad. I can't look away from him either.

"How did I get so lucky?" Jesse whispers. Then he leans in and kisses that place on my neck that short-circuits my brain.

"You... I..." I'm not sure why I'm even trying to speak.

I still have my tie on, but I loosened it a long time ago. Jesse uses it to pull me toward the bed. I stumble after him, tripping over my feet. He pushes me so I fall backwards onto the bed.

In one swift motion he straddles my hips and pins my arms over my head with one hand. I can't move. I don't want to move. Very slowly, he removes my tie and unbuttons my shirt. His hand is warm and smooth against my skin.

I try to reach for him, but I can't escape. I close my eyes. "Jesse." I whisper his name.

"Shhh." He puts a finger over my lips before claiming them with his own. After a series of bruising kisses that take my breath away, he finally lets go of my wrists.

My hands fly to the buttons of his shirt. I am impatient to rid him of the damn thing, but there is also something to be said for a slow and tortuous reveal. "God, I love buttons."

Jesse grins. His hands move to my waistband and I raise my hips so he can slide my pants down and pull them off. Soon we have both stripped down to our boxers.

I pause to admire his very fit body. "I like fewer clothes."

Jesse laughs at me again, but his eyes have gone twice as dark as usual; I have seen that look before. I manage to take him by surprise, rolling him so he is lying face down, pinned beneath me.

I whisper softly in his ear: "Stay right there." It's not like he has much of a choice. I remain pressed against his back while I reach for the massage lotion on the bedside table. The heat between us is almost unbearable, and I am painfully reminded of how very not platonic my feelings are toward Jesse. But that can wait.

I warm the massage lotion in my hands, smoothing it over his skin in long, even strokes. I start by running my hands over his back with gentle pressure, followed by his arms, his legs. But I skip over the area still covered by his thin boxers, eliciting a thin whine from Jesse.

"Patience."

I'm not sure which one of us I'm reminding to be patient. I go completely still for a moment, taking some deep breaths to clear my head. Once I can focus again, I run my hands down either side of his spine and then up again. I can feel his body growing heavy as he relaxes into the mattress. Then I tease my fingertips along the sides of his body, barely grazing his ribs, causing him to gasp.

I continue this way, alternating between the moderate pressure of a relaxing massage and light touches that drive him mad. When I slip my fingers under the waistband of his boxers, he moans loud enough that I'm sure the neighbors can hear.

I don't care.

Driving him crazy comes at a cost, though; I'm slowly going mad as well. Eventually I can't take it anymore. "Turn over." My voice comes out like a growl.

*

Later, much much later, Jesse is lying with his head resting on my chest. I tangle my fingers in his hair and lightly massage his scalp with my fingernails.

Jesse sighs with pleasure. "Never leave me," he says, which makes me laugh.

"Why would I do that? You're my person. You were hard to find."

Interlude

33 Fabulous (Middle School)

"Yo, Squeak!"

Berto—who had long lost his position as my favorite brother—had come up with that one. Short for pipsqueak. Because apparently I was too small to be a full-sized pipsqueak. "Yes, your fatassnesshood?" If I was too little to be a pipsqueak, he was too big to be a fatass.

"Get in the car. I'm taking you to practice."

"I told mom I quit. Done with football."

I hadn't exactly quit. I'd been kicked off the team. My brother knew this. He and my dad had covered for me so my mom wouldn't freak out.

Football wasn't exactly my game, but I hadn't minded playing. Football had been fine.

Kind of.

The catching and throwing parts were okay. I was even a decent place kicker. But I was the smallest kid on the field—a head shorter than anyone else—and any physical contact would send me flying.

Still, football had been fine, or at least nearly fine, until Steven Jens decided to call me Jessica. Before it could catch on, the first time he tried that name on for size, I punched him right in the face.

I didn't come out on the winning end of that fight. To be fair, it was my first fight. No broken bones, but I did get bruised ribs. It still hurt to take a deep breath. We both got kicked off the team due to the zero tolerance policy the middle school had on fighting, which I'm sure bothered him a lot more than it bothered me.

I probably could have appealed my expulsion from the team if I wanted to dredge up the whole "Jessica" thing. But I didn't really want to be remembered for that. Better be known as the kid who got busted for fighting. Football was my brothers' game anyway. I only played because my mom wanted me to. She thought it would be good for me. Help me fit in. Make me stronger.

I glared at Berto. "Practice? Whatever it is this time, I quit. Now take me out for ice cream. My treat."

Berto laughed. "Right. Where are you gonna get the money for that? She's signed you up for some martial arts thing."

"Martial arts? What, because we're Asian? Mom is so racist."

Berto scoffed. "You know why she does this."

"Yeah." I know why. I was born ten weeks early, and she almost died. So I get to be her baby for the rest of my life. It's also why I was so much smaller than my brothers. And there was no amount of physical activity that was going to change that.

We pulled up to the rec center with its big green double doors in front and the long steep hill leading down to the track.

"So, what class am I taking?" I asked Berto through the open window after getting out of the car.

"Tae Kwon Do."

"Is that the kicking one?"

"I think they're all kicking ones, Squeak."

It didn't take me long to find the room. The lessons were in a dance studio with one mirrored wall and a barre for ballet. Some of the older students were setting up thick mats to make a practice floor.

"Is this..." I started to say. And then I spotted Steven Jens dragging one of the mats out of the closet. Before the teacher saw me I backed out of the door. From the safety of the hallway I could see that it wasn't Steven Jens after all. Maybe his older brother. He was wearing a purple belt and looked like he was in high school. I didn't want anything to do with another member of the Jens family. Especially not if kicking or punching was involved. He was built.

A tall skinny man with unruly blond hair came flying down the hall with his arms overflowing with... stuff. "Can you carry this?"

"Um... sure?" I took a crate full of headbands with glittery black styrofoam balls. He was still carrying an assortment of portable speakers, a box of tiny ballet shoes, and a clipboard.

"The preschoolers were scheduled after us for some reason. The poor kids will be exhausted by the end of class. I hate it when they fuck things up at the main desk. Pardon my French."

"I... yeah. That sucks."

I followed him down the hall until we came to another practice room identical to the one where they were holding the Tae Kwon Do class. But this one was full of girls my age and a bit younger. Some had their legs up on the barre, stretching before class.

"You need shoes?" The guy set the speakers on a shelf near the window that overlooked the track and the wooded lot beyond the rec center. "Grab a pair from the corner."

I walked over to where he was pointing and found some black canvas shoes with a short heel. They bent in the middle. I have no idea why, but I took off my sneakers and slipped into a pair of these loaner shoes. Some of the girls had the same type of shoes in black or tan. Some had ballet shoes.

There were no boys. Well, except for me and the instructor.

I was naturally flexible, so the stretches weren't a problem. But everyone else had been to dance classes for more than five minutes, so once they started doing any sort of coordinated movement, I was lost.

"Is this your first class?" This girl with a lisp asked me in a whisper. She had her dark hair in a bun like everyone else, and like everyone else was taller than me. She was probably the best dancer there. She was also the one who most often stopped what she was doing to help me figure out what the hell was going on. "You're a natural, if that's the case."

I laughed. "I'm sure that's not true."

"She's right," the instructor said. His name was Ben.

It helped that this was the first of a new series of classes so they didn't have any kind of routine put together.

"You can continue using the center's shoes, but if you'd like to get some of your own, just mention that you're in the class and you can get a discount at the local dance shop."

"Yeah. Okay."

What now? I wasn't signed up for class. I wasn't really sure I wanted to dance. And I for sure didn't want anyone to see me here. If the kids at school knew I was taking a contemporary dance class, Jessica would definitely stick.

The final piece they played for a cool down was one of my favorite songs. My body seemed to absorb the music. I didn't feel awkward like I had at the beginning of class.

The helpful girl, whose name was Ellis, looked at me out of the corner of her eye and mouthed, "Natural." The song ended and I felt an odd sense of calm wash over me.

I'd find a way to make this work.

*

Weeks later, there I was—lurking backstage with my dance class for my first recital—dressed in white stretch pants and a bedazzled jacket with tails. I had even let one of the backstage parents put me in stage makeup. When I looked at myself in the mirror with my smoky eyes, rosy cheeks and blush colored lipstick, I almost didn't recognize my own face. I looked... more like me. Which was a terrifying thought.

The girls in the group had white spandex suits with sequins down one arm. They all had their hair in buns with hair nets to keep everything in place.

"I think you came out with the better deal in the costume department." Ellis eyed me up and down. "You look fabulous."

I didn't want to look fabulous. I wanted to look manly. I studied myself in the mirror. Not manly. I took a tissue to wipe the makeup from my face, but stopped with my hand in mid-air. I didn't want to ruin someone else's work. And there was part of me that was intrigued by the idea: I looked fabulous.

Ours was the first group to perform, followed by the little girls in their ladybug costumes. Their thin braids kept coming loose despite the liberal application of stiff hairspray. They kept twirling around and bumping into each other, losing their bobbly black styrofoam headbands, and falling out of their tiny ballet slippers.

I peeked from the curtains in the wings to see the audience who had come to see us: parents of the studio classes from age four through high school. And then, to my horror, I saw them: Berto, Caesar, Maya, and my mother. In the audience. Third row back. Seats 1-4. I could only be thankful that my dad and the twins weren't there as well.

I nearly ran off when I saw them there. How did they know? Berto spotted me looking at them and then he winked. The fatass bastard. I guess I hadn't fooled him into believing I was taking part in a Tae Kwon Do exhibition this evening after all. He was the one who found out about the recital. Maybe he'd known about the dance classes all along.

Ellis squeezed my hand. "Don't worry. You'll be great. You've got this." She thought it was stage fright. That I was worried I might not do well.

Honestly, it was the opposite. I was afraid that I would do a fine job on stage. And my family would see me. I didn't want them to see me like this, in full makeup with a sparkling jacket and jazz shoes. This was not what men did. Not Filipino men. Not real men. Real men were like my father who worked for the forestry service and had arms the size of tree trunks. And my brothers who had both made it to the varsity football team as freshmen.

I might have felt at home on stage, but it's not where I *wanted* to feel at home. Why did I have to fight and get kicked off the stupid football team? I could have stayed. I could have handled the bruises and the teasing and sitting out every game. It wouldn't be super manly to be benched for the entire season, but manly enough. Maybe I could have been the designated place kicker.

"Breathe," Ellis said beside me. She looked at where my gaze had settled. "You'll do fine. And even if you don't, I'm sure they'll be proud of you."

"They don't know."

"They don't know what?" Ellis's brows came together.

"They don't know I've been taking dance classes. They think I've been taking Tae Kwon Do."

She poked her head out from behind the wings to get a better look. "They're holding programs. Your name is printed right there for them to see. Pretty sure they know."

I shook my hands at my sides. "Well, they know *now*."

Ellis rubbed my shoulders lightly. "Why is that such a bad thing?"

"You don't understand. I look like a girl."

"Nope."

"What?"

"You do *not* look like a girl."

"But…"

Ellis scowled. "*I* look like a girl. You look like a very poised and polished male dancer. What are you really freaking out about? Your family isn't homophobic are they?"

"What!" I shouted, causing all of the ladybugs to stop spinning around and stare at me. "I'm not. I am *not* gay," I whispered to Ellis. But my voice was harsh and loud anyway.

"Oh. I didn't mean to—"

"And *that* is what I'm afraid of. Everyone will think that about me."

"Is that a bad thing? I mean sure, they'd be wrong..." she looked doubtful. "But does that matter? A lot of people think my younger sister is my twin and it kinda bothers me, but it's not that big a deal."

"Being a twin is not the same."

"I think it is, though." Ellis tilted her head and bit her lip. "People can think whatever they want. But you are either a twin or not when you're born. And you are gay or not when you're born. Right?"

"People don't get disowned for being twins. Or beat up."

"Is that what happened? With football?"

I knew it had been a mistake to mention the fight that got me kicked off the team. "No. The guy was just being a dick."

Then they called us out on stage. I honestly considered bolting, but there didn't seem like much of a point. My family already knew I had been taking dance classes. And lying about it. What did it matter if they found out I was good at it?

When I stepped out on the stage and the lights came up, I felt like a different person. Stronger, taller, more self-assured. As the music played I moved effortlessly through our routine. When we stopped at the end to take a bow, I took Ellis's hand. My family looked happy. They looked proud.

At the applause from the crowd, I felt an amazing sense of belonging wash over me. It was like nothing I'd ever experienced.

This was where I was meant to be. This was what I was meant to do.

I was a dancer.

I had always been a dancer.

It had just taken a while to find my way to the stage.

34 Courage (High School)

High school straight up sucked. Being a gay kid in Idaho was pretty much what you'd expect. It was like being a jellyfish in the Mojave desert. Like being an ostrich at the South pole. Like being Ru Paul at an actual drag race.

My family didn't know I was gay, but I wasn't exactly closeted at school: I hung out with the theater crowd, I was studying contemporary dance, I was playing the starring role in Peter Pan for fuck's sake. It didn't get much gayer than that.

Some random jerk "accidentally" bumped into me in the very uncrowded hallway. "Nice pants."

They *were* nice pants: black stretch-denim that fit me like a glove. "Why thank you." I struck a pose with an exaggerated flip of the wrist. "I am glad you appreciate my flawless fashion sense and my fine self. I could style you, if you like. Those are *not* nice pants." I looked him up and down. With a very critical eye.

"Freak," the dude with terrible fashion sense mumbled, turning away from me and scuttling down the hall. Hockey player, if his grotesque mullet was any indication.

I waited by the front office for my mom to pick me up. Berto was away at school, and there was no money for a car of my own. Which meant if I stayed after for play practice I had to listen to my mom's life lessons all the way home.

"Hey sweet potato pie!" My mom couldn't decide on merely one ridiculous endearment for me. It was always something different.

"Hey Ima." I could barely speak a word of Tagalog. That was about it, actually.

"I wanted to talk to you," she said after I was safely strapped in. "You know Tita Darna?"

"Yeah…" Tita Darna was my mom's cousin. I hoped she wasn't about to tell me that my tita was coming to visit. Tita Darna was your stereotypical Filipino auntie who loved to pinch your cheeks a little too hard and give voluminous hugs. She always had the worst flavors of dusty hard candy in the bottom of her giant purse ready to hand out to unsuspecting young relatives. When I went home I wanted a place to relax without fending off such unbridled energy.

"What about Tita Darna? She's not coming over is she?"

"No. She's still in California. But I wanted to tell you she wasn't always your Tita Darna."

"Umm… okay." Had she been adopted into the family maybe? But she looked so much like her brothers and sisters.

"Yes. When we were little children she was Danilo. But we called her Daniel. She was a boy then. Only you can't say those names to her now because they are dead people names and she will be very upset."

"You mean dead names?" The words were slow to come out of my mouth.

"Yes. It's what I said. Dead people names."

"So… Tita Darna is trans?" I felt like someone had clubbed me in the head with a two-by-four. I didn't even know my mom knew that trans people existed.

She nodded her head. "Yes. It's what I'm trying to tell you. She is a transphobic."

I somehow succeeded in not bursting into nervous laughter. My mom spoke excellent English—it was nearly her first language—but occasionally she picked exactly the wrong word.

She didn't notice my stifled laughter and continued on. "So it's fine if you are too."

I choked. "Ma, I'm not. I'm not trans."

"Okay. I mean of course. I just wanted to tell you that if there was something else you wanted to say, that even your grandmother thinks it's fine. You should be who you are and not feel so worried all the time."

I hoped if I didn't say anything, she might forget that she had spoken and I could ignore the fact that my own mother had sort of outed me in the car on the way home from theater practice.

I put in my earbuds and turned the volume up high enough that she could probably hear the music. I hoped it wouldn't make me go deaf between school and home, but I didn't want to risk her saying anything else I wasn't prepared to deal with.

Once we were home I retreated to my room to watch clips of the bands I followed on YouTube, and catch up on social media. I was looking for a particular clip of a solo done by Minjae—one of my all-time favorite dancers—when I came across a post that read: "GRiD members come clean: 'Domino is Real.'"

Minjae and his band mate Do-Hyun (ship name Domino) had been the center of a scandal because some compromising photographs had surfaced. In Korean culture it's okay for two men to act sexy on stage, but it is not okay for two men to kiss each other off stage, which really pissed me off.

Ordinarily I would ignore posts like this as clickbait, but this one came from a reputable source. There was a very short video clip attached to the post. Min and Do stood hand in hand on stage. They weren't acting sexy for the camera. They looked nervous, or maybe a bit giddy. And in their own words they said they were together. A real couple.

Minjae, my dance idol, from a country as homophobic as South Korea, was willing to stand up on the international stage and admit that he was gay. And I couldn't even tell my own mother—who was clearly supportive and not about to kick me out of the house. And yeah, Idaho wasn't the greatest place to be gay. But it wasn't South Korea. I was such a coward.

I made up my mind to tell my mom at least. Particularly because she already seemed to know. I decided to come out to her as soon as I had listened to GRiD's most recent album in its entirety.

I walked into the kitchen as if I were walking on stage with bright lights shining in my eyes. Ready to deliver my lines. "Ima, I'm gay."

"Oh thank God," my brother Berto said from the next room. "Pay up." He grinned at Caesar and held out his hand.

I hadn't noticed my big brothers and my dad sitting in the living room in front of the television.

My dad smiled at me and nodded.

"Wait. I mean… Pay for what?" I squinted at Berto, pretending that I didn't want to fall through the floor with embarrassment.

"We had bets on whether you would wait until graduation to let us know you were gay. I won. Now," he glared at Caesar, "Pay up."

My mom patted me on the arm and handed me a bowl full of chips. "It's nice you are gay, honey. Now take these to your brothers."

35 Swipe Left (College)

I was a bit nervous to meet my roommate that first day on campus, but I thought I'd done a good job of vetting him based on my previous experience of judging people from their online profiles.

It is one hundred percent true that I did some swiping left and swiping right in high school. There were no other ways of finding the gays in small town Idaho. Believe me. I'd tried.

Anyway, I thought I'd gotten pretty good at separating the wheat from the chaff. I should have remembered that most of the guys I hooked up with had turned out to be pathological liars, egotistical bastards, controlling dickwads, or boring as hell.

Nick seemed like a good fit for a starter roommate, at least from what I'd seen. Easy-going. Not super into academics. Handsome, but not distractingly so. I liked my men a little meatier, to be perfectly honest. The boy was skin and bones. We chatted back and forth a bit over the summer. No red flags.

There was a lot of activity on campus when I arrived. Some people were carting stuff around with the help of their parents, but my family hadn't made the journey west. I flew into Indiana on my own. A bunch of my stuff had been shipped ahead, but I still needed to get it from storage up to my room. As soon as I managed to find storage. Or my room.

"Hey there. Welcome to Hanover Hall. Do you know which wing you are in?" This kid with dark brown hair and a face full of freckles came walking up to me. They were wearing an oversized hand-painted name tag: Grey (they/them).

"West. Third floor."

"Fantastic! I'm Grey. That's my wing! I'll be your RA." They quickly noticed I didn't have much with me. "You need some help finding the storage area? I'll walk you there."

Grey kept up a stream of happy banter all the way to the locked cage full of brown cardboard boxes. Then they helped me load up the flatbed cart that had become available.

When I got to my room, the door was propped open and I saw Nick inside, already unpacking. He had on a white T-shirt with some kind of surfer logo and very unflattering gym shorts about three sizes too big. His light brown hair was just long enough that it was curling up on the ends.

"Hey, I'm Jesse. But you probably know that."

"Yeah." Nick looked up and I watched the expression on his face change from something neutral to something far less welcoming. And I was afraid I knew the cause of his hooded expression. But was it the custom embroidered jeans that tipped him off? Or the T-shirt reading "If you're reading this, I'm gay." My friend Ellis got it for me as a going away present.

I dragged the cart in with some effort and no offer of help from my roomie. "Have you picked a side yet?" Things were not getting off to a great start, but I thought I'd withhold judgment. Maybe he was only crabby because moving was a thoroughly exhausting activity.

"I'm taking that one." He pointed to the bed nearest to the window.

"Sure. This one's mine then. Fabulous."

Nick smirked. "Fabulous."

Okay, so some teensy tiny red flags there.

One of the reasons I'd chosen this dorm was its proximity to the dance studio. But the other reason was that the rooms in this dorm had walk-in closets with plenty of space. I'd tried to minimize the clothing I brought with me, but I was quite attached to my wardrobe.

There is a price to pay for beauty.

I started unpacking, taking things from my garment box first.

Nick coughed. "Are those all yours?" he asked.

I surveyed the row of velvet hangers: plain white linen shirts, pima cotton sateen in every color of the rainbow (arranged in the proper order, mind you), several tasteful floral print rayons, silk shirts in navy, black, and royal blue. And my single favorite item of clothing: a vintage leather racing jacket.

"Why, do you want to borrow them?"

"Hell no! You're not some kind of… You're not gay, are you? Not that there's anything wrong with that. But I don't want you trying anything on me. Or staring at me in my sleep."

I raised an eyebrow. "Trust me. No one will be trying *anything* on you."

How had the question, "Are you a raging homophobe?" not made it onto the roommate profile questionnaire?

I finished hanging up my shirts, my jackets, and the pants that should never be forced to live in a drawer. I did this very deliberately. Not at all like I wanted to run screaming from the room to the nice resident assistant to see about changing rooms immediately.

Maybe everything would be fine. Maybe by getting to know me, Nick would magically realize that gays are people too. And maybe I should keep my head down and keep the gay to myself as much as possible in case I was stuck with him for the rest of the year.

"You coming to the orientation thing?" I asked once I had finished unpacking my higher end clothes at least.

"How many pairs of shoes do you even have?" Nick asked with a sneer, ignoring my question.

I would be the bigger person. I kept my tone even. "Enough. I have enough shoes. Are you coming?"

"No. I think I'll enjoy having the room to myself for as long as I can," he said.

This was not going any better. He was not doing anything to convince me that he was not a homophobic ass who would make my life here at least borderline miserable.

"Well, I'm off then," I said too-cheerfully. I decided not to blow him a kiss, though I was sorely tempted. That was the kind of behavior I could reserve for the day when I found out I no longer had to share a room with this charming fellow.

I walked down stairs to the main lobby where Grey was pointing people toward the tables with name tags and pens. "Remember to include your pronouns."

I accidentally bumped into this tall white guy with stunning dark brown eyes and black spiked hair. Not usually my type, but there was something about him. "Oh. Sorry." I had made him smudge his name. But it was still legible: Richard.

"Whatever. I don't like name tags anyway." His voice came out in a low growl.

"My name's Jesse."

"Ok."

Sophomore Year

36 Otherwise Engaged

"Too hard?"

"No, harder. Right there. Yessssss."

But when Jesse inhales sharply, I freeze.

"Oh sweetie don't stop. You know I can take the pain, if you're the one dishing it out."

"Not funny."

"Please." His voice comes out in a husky whisper with a catch at the end. He knows I can't resist anything he says when he talks like that.

The door swings open, creaking on its hinges, and Bailey enters with a bag of groceries, her bright red hair caught loosely in a black ribbon. She drops the grocery bag on the floor dramatically.

"Sweet Mother Mary, you two are an embarrassment. We talked about y'all being naked in the room. Can't you keep your hands off each other for five minutes?"

I shrug. "No. Also, his shoulder was bothering him. And we're not naked." I think it's funny that Bailey is afraid of walking in on us. We have our own room. And if she really cared she wouldn't have given us the spare key.

"A girl has needs," Jesse says with his most flirty voice. "And my thoughtful little sugar muffin was tending to mine." I wipe the excess oil off his back before he slips back into his shirt, leaving enough buttons undone at the top to be very distracting.

"Hey Sugar Muffin!" Danny calls as he walks in, with Kit close behind.

"No."

"Fine." Danny sighs.

"I keep telling you to leave the boy alone!" Kit pokes Danny in the ribs. Danny has lost a lot of weight since freshman year. Kit looks the same though. Today his fake tattoos are patterned after traditional henna designs with swirling loops of flowers. Some of them have hints of color. Which is new.

"You like?" Kit asks. "I thought I'd try some watercolor elements in my designs."

Jesse admires the work. "When are you going to start doing the real thing?" He grabs Kit's arm and turns it so he can see the designs more clearly in the light.

Kit smiles. "I don't have time to do the apprenticeship thing right now. Maybe after graduation. For now I'm just building my portfolio."

The room still smells of white flower oil. Which I prefer to the usual smell of their room. Bailey likes patchouli and burns incense sometimes. The scent alone makes my eyes water and the smoke makes it impossible to breathe.

I don't know how Kit and Danny put up with it. They moved in with Bailey this year, so only Jesse and I are visitors. Their fourth roommate is secretly living with her boyfriend in another dorm, which leaves plenty of space.

Kit goes to the refrigerator and produces two bottles of the cheapest wine it's possible to buy. Bailey's favorite drink is sangria, and the wine doesn't need to be good, apparently. In fact, she insists that bad wine actually improves the flavor. It's far too sweet for me so I don't care one way or another. I'm simply in charge of chopping the fruit, which Bailey puts on the counter.

"How are you holding up?" Kit asks, putting his arm around Bailey's shoulder.

"Great. Fine. I don't care about him anyway. Boys are losers." She glances around the room. "Present company excepted. Oh. But not Richard. He's a complete loser."

"Thanks."

"Any time, sweetheart." She blows me a kiss.

I wash the fruit juice off my hands and clean the knife and cutting board.

"Back off, girlfriend." Jesse puts his arms around me from behind and rests his chin on my shoulder. "This one's mine, remember?"

At least she's back to dishing out insults. I was hazy on the details, but Bailey's heartbreak had something to do with this guy she'd been friends with. He thought they were dating and they weren't. Bailey doesn't date. I don't know how he didn't know that. Even I know that Bailey doesn't date, and I am notoriously bad at reading people.

Now Bailey and the guy aren't even friends anymore and she is heartbroken. So we were there to cheer her up with sangria and indulge her in planning for the upcoming drag ball.

It's one of the biggest social events on campus, which explains why I had no interest in attending last year. It was pre-Jesse, so I had an excuse. Now as his boyfriend, it is a non-optional event. Which is fine with me. I'm looking forward to it, in a way. I already know how fine Jesse looks in a dress. Hell, he looks fine in anything. Or out of anything.

Jesse is entertaining Kit and Danny with tales of something that happened to some friends of theirs in the fine arts department. He looks at me out of the corner of his eye, then puts a hand to the opening of his shirt.

Jesse figured out my weakness early on: those damn shirts of his that show a little too much skin at the neckline. His wardrobe now consists entirely of button-down shirts. And when he wants to drive me mad, he toys with that damn button at the base of his throat.

I wonder how soon we can leave.

"What do you think?" I startle at the sound of Bailey's voice. She is sketching what each of us should wear. Her latest phase is costume design, so this is the perfect diversion. She holds up the sketchbook.

"Is that me?" I'm the only tall white guy with dark hair in our group, but she could be using artistic license.

Bailey nods.

"A suit?" Not what I was expecting.

"Well, I was going to put you in a strapless number with hoop earrings and big hair. But I think you might topple over on the heels required to pull that off. And I'd prefer it if you survived the evening without harming yourself or others."

Jesse snorts. I didn't know he was listening.

Bailey glares at him. "So, we're going Liza Minelli circa 1973."

"Well, the hair is doable, I guess." I run a hand through my hair.

"Absolutely. You can totally pull off Liza," Jesse says, looking over my shoulder at Bailey's sketch.

"What about you, honey?" Bailey smiles sweetly, batting her eyelashes at Jesse.

Jesse winks. "Nice try, but my sweet lips are sealed. You'll have to wait for the big reveal."

He's close enough that I can feel the heat radiating from his body. For no reason whatsoever he ghosts his fingers along the edge of my collar.

I've had enough. What with the provocative commentary during his massage, the damn button, the flirty glances, and now this. I've reached my limit.

I grab him by the sleeve. "We're leaving now."

I know I'm being obvious. I don't care.

Jesse grins at Bailey and shrugs. "Sorry. I guess we're otherwise engaged."

It takes us almost no time to get to our room, but once we get there I am in no rush. Not really. Sometimes I like to take things slow. When the door closes behind us, I walk Jesse backwards into the bedroom. He sits on the edge of the bed, staring up at me with his eyes wide. I get lost in them for a moment before he touches that top button, drawing all of my attention to the exposed skin there.

I bend down to place a series of kisses at the base of his throat. Then I undo the buttons slowly, trailing my fingertips along his shoulders, his arms, his wrists. I follow the same path with my mouth, smelling the faint scent of white flower oil, tasting the salt on his skin.

"Richie..." he whispers, leaning back and arching into my touch. I keep things feather-light, pulling away when he tries to get closer, placing my lips near his, but never allowing them to touch.

Jesse puts up with this for as long as he can bear it, but eventually he loses patience and pulls me flush with his body before turning to pin me beneath him. There is a predatory gleam in his eye as he straddles my hips and laces his fingers through mine, pressing them to the mattress. "That's enough," he says, hovering above me.

I grin. "What, you can tease me all afternoon, but when the tables are turned…"

"Enough teasing," he says. He rolls his hips against mine and I momentarily forget how to breathe.

We miss dinner at the cafeteria. There is no part of me that is sorry about that.

*

The following day I'm scheduled to watch Jesse's rehearsal after class. The chemistry labs are clear on the other side of the campus from the fine arts building, so I'm in a hurry. I gather my things and start to leave the lecture hall when Dr. Lynne, the head of the chemistry department, catches me.

"Richard, do you have an internship set for spring semester or are you putting that off until junior year?" He couldn't look more like a chemistry professor if he tried. White guy, lab coat, glasses. His thinning hair is graying at the temples.

"Dr. Lorris set me up with one of her research projects. I plan to be a lackey."

"Ah. The biomedical composites study?"

"Yes." I glance at the clock on the wall behind him. It's two minutes slow.

"That will be a good placement for you." He pushes his glasses up. They don't seem to fit well.

"Okay. I have to leave."

It is not my most graceful exit. Dr. Lynne is used to this by now. He's not much for graceful exits either.

I'm not happy to be leaving this late. I told Jesse I would be there. His piece is being workshopped today. He mentioned more than once that it would be nice if I could make it. Talking with the prof added minutes to the time it will take me to get there.

I jog to the fine arts building. I can get there in about ten minutes if there isn't much pedestrian traffic. And it's cold enough to keep most people inside.

The fine arts buildings are all new. Gleaming open spaces, lots of light. Jesse's studio is rehearsing in the smaller auditorium. I can hear the sound of his professor's voice all the way from the front atrium.

"Point your goddamn toes. It's like I've never said those words before. Jesse—show him your feet. Beautiful. Just like that. Again."

Sometimes the rehearsals are closed, but the new prof likes to have people in the audience, especially as the date of the recital approaches. She thinks we'll make the dancers nervous and let them experience what it's like during a real performance.

Jesse is on stage with one of the other male dancers—the one who can presumably not point his toes.

The piece they are workshopping is the one he did the choreography for. I've never seen him dance it. He did a walkthrough in our dorm room and tried to explain things to me, which I thought was adorable. He moved around the room and did some turns and pretended to lift an imaginary partner. He described the leaps they used in technical dance terms. It didn't help. I can't picture what dances look like unless I am seeing them with my own eyes—no matter how well they are described. But I loved watching him talk about the whole process. And I loved how his body moved as he tried to show me a dance that clearly required two people. The way he moves his body through space is always magic.

The piece is programmatic, which I appreciate. It's called "Betrayal." Jesse and his partner enter the stage from opposite sides. The guy is a pretty good match for Jesse, although of course he is taller. They are roughly the same build, but this other guy is white with sandy blond hair. At first they take turns assisting one another with lifts. They fly across the stage higher than they could on their own. They leap apart and crash together before spinning away again, their bodies not lighter than air, but somehow powerful enough to defy the force of gravity.

As the dance continues, the lifts begin to fail. Things become awkward and choppy. Neither of them fly as far or as fast. The turns are not smooth. Sometimes they don't connect for the lifts. When they do, Jesse's partner is stiff in his arms. And then toward the end when Jesse runs towards his partner, the other dancer steps aside and Jesse falls to the floor.

I stand up involuntarily, convinced that the jackass fucked up and missed his catch. But I sit down when I realize it's part of the choreography. Things only get worse from there. Jesse keeps getting up. Keeps trusting the guy. But things keep not working out. Finally the other dude drops Jesse in the middle of a lift and leaves him there, crumpled on the floor. He stalks offstage without looking back. Jesse slowly peels himself off the ground.

I have the irrational urge to do physical violence to Jesse's dance partner. Which I would never do. Still. I should not watch dances like this. Either that, or Jesse shouldn't dance so well. Sitting in the audience, I am utterly convinced that he is crushed and injured on the stage.

"Again. Top." His professor claps her hands. "I want more strength at the beginning. More power from both of you."

Jesse and his partner both nod and take their places.

Again they run and turn and leap and catch and fall. They take the prof at her word. Everything is more. Faster, higher, stronger. Only this time Jesse misses one of his catches, which I know from watching earlier is *not* part of the routine. His partner ends up on his ass, laughing it off. No big deal. These things happen. But Jesse looks shaken.

"Well, that was new," the guy on the floor says as he dusts himself off. "You okay there, Nunez? If you need your boyfriend to take you to the trainers' office I'm sure he'd be more than happy to carry you there."

The rest of the studio snickers. I made somewhat of a reputation for myself after spiriting him off the stage last year when he collapsed. I'm still a fixture at the trainers' office, pestering them for what I can do to help with the pain in his shoulder that never seems to go away.

Jesse shakes himself off. He flashes me a quick grin that is meant to be reassuring. "No. I'm good. Let's go again."

They practice again and again. The same lift. The same turn. The same controlled falls. Until the instructor calls an end to the practice. I'm pissed that the prof didn't ask Jesse to see the trainer. He won't go unless someone else forces the issue.

Maybe it was merely fatigue. But what if it's a complication due to his old injury? Or what if it's a new one?

37 Not a Drag Ball

Bailey hands me a padded hanger with my clothes for the dance. "You know the routine. Strip." My outfit—compliments of the theater department—is a three-piece black velvet suit, and a white shirt with an oversized collar. I've already tried it on a few times so Bailey could do alterations. It's pretty comfortable, actually. I've never worn velvet before.

Jesse kicked me out of our room long ago so he could get ready. I'm not allowed to see him until the dance. Kit had Danny are at the fine arts building so they have access to all the stage makeup. Apparently Danny is going all out.

"I think a lighter touch is called for with you," Bailey says. The "light touch" doesn't seem to apply to foundation, though. "Oh, stop whining. You need basic coverage and contouring at least." After she's satisfied with the face, she spends what feels like an hour on my eye makeup. I didn't know there was makeup for eyebrows. I refuse the fake lashes, which really pisses her off, but I reluctantly allow mascara. She threatens to beat me with her pointiest shoes if I smear it.

After all her work, I do resemble Liza Minelli. Or at least I look like the picture Bailey used as a reference. Although I can see why she wanted to use false eyelashes for a more authentic look. Too bad.

Bailey takes almost no time getting herself ready: tan pants and a mustard shirt. She looks like a random dude from the 1970s— bright red hair securely hidden under a hat—fake sideburns, bell bottoms, gold chains. God, I hate disco.

When it's time for the dance, Bailey and I wait just outside the door for the others to arrive. A steady stream of people pass us on their way in. They call it a drag ball, but it seems to be more of a cross-dressing ball. Or a wear-whatever-the-hell-you-want ball.

Danny and Kit find us before long.

"Damn, girl." Danny whistles. "I hardly recognize you."

"Not true." I looked at myself in the mirror and was perfectly recognizable.

Kit laughs. "Take it as a compliment." Kit didn't dress any differently for this thing than normal. He's wearing one of his usual black and white outfits. I think he hand-painted the jacket he's wearing. It has black angel wings on the back. The only substantial difference from his day-to-day appearance is some very impressive nail art including rhinestones.

Danny is the only one of us who is in conventional drag. Big hair, impressive makeup, exaggerated swing to his hips and everything. His dress is a form-fitting sparkly gold thing that looks very uncomfortable. Still, he can manage to walk in his strappy heels without looking like a total ass. Bailey was right. A dress would have been a bad plan for me if it involved being able to walk in shoes like those.

The shoes I have on are fine. They have thick rubber soles and a low heel. It's the makeup that's proving to be a bigger problem; the mascara is driving me crazy. I can feel my eyelashes every time I blink. They feel twice as heavy as normal.

"Hands off the face," Bailey warns as if she can read my thoughts.

"Fine."

Jesse sneaks up behind me and puts his hands over my eyes. I can smell his cologne. "Hello, lover," he says in a sultry voice.

"Nope. Not doing that."

"Wanna see?"

"Yes."

Jesse removes his hand from my eyes and spins me around. I halfway expect Cyd Charisse again. He looked amazing in the green flapper dress freshman year. But this is a whole different level.

He's dressed in white, always a good color on him. And instead of having several buttons undone, exposing a bit of skin? This is a plunging neckline on a 1950s sheath dress. And of course there is a daring slit up the side showing flashes of leg every time he moves. I can't look away.

And I can see it in his eyes—Jesse knows exactly what his outfit is doing to me.

He sashays toward the ballroom and looks back over his shoulder. "I'm glad it meets with your approval, darlin'."

I catch him by the wrist before he can get very far. "How long do we have to stay here?" I whisper in his ear. His wig smells like plastic.

"The whole night," Bailey says loudly. "You have to stay out with us the whole damn night. You can't let all my work go to waste. And yes, we can all guess what you were saying. And thinking."

Jesse grins.

I wonder if it would be in character for Liza Minelli to pass out from lack of oxygen to the brain. I don't think I can take much of this. It isn't that Jesse looks better when he's dressed like a woman. And if Elizabeth Taylor stepped right off the set of *Cat on a Hot Tin Roof* (that's where I'd seen the dress before) I wouldn't look at her twice.

But there's just something about Jesse being so perfectly himself while also being dressed like someone else... And then there is the tantalizing amount of skin on display. I'm pretty sure everyone who walks past us is staring at him.

"Richie darling, you have got to stop growling at everyone who looks in my general direction."

"I'm not growling."

Jesse laughs. "Sure, sweetie. That was very convincing. Shall we?" He loops his arm through mine and we enter the ballroom.

I can dance. It's something I've been doing more and more. Not well. But it's something I enjoy now if Jesse is involved. Hell, I enjoy almost anything if Jesse is involved.

I'm thankful once again for Bailey's costume choice that allows me to wear sensible shoes. Jesse is in heels, but that's not terribly unusual. These are more feminine than the ones he often wears. And higher. Jesse is still nowhere near my height, but the fact that he is taller than normal keeps throwing me off. His lips brush against my neck when we slow dance and he pretends it's an accident. Every damn time.

Two can play at that game. The dress isn't just cut low in the front. It leaves a fair bit of his back exposed too. I trace my fingers along the deep V, starting near the top and venturing lower. Very slowly.

"You little minx," Jesse says breathlessly.

When he puts his arms around my neck for the next slow dance, I feel him wince. I put my hand flat on his back, warming the muscles there. "You need to talk to someone about this. If even raising your arms like this hurts."

"It's nothing but a sore muscle. You saw that duet—maybe I shouldn't have put in quite so many throws. If I give it a solid rest, it will be fine. I'll ice it later. We've all been working so hard getting ready for this end of semester thing."

"It's more than a sore muscle. And it's stupid not to tell someone."

"You're too sweet."

"I'm not sweet. I'm pissed off. You should take better care of yourself. You should let me take care of you. And hiding your pain doesn't mean it isn't there."

"Can I cut in?" Bailey appears out of nowhere.

"No."

"Darling! Don't be rude." Jesse spins away from me and takes Bailey's hand. Shortly afterward, Kit appears by my side.

I glance at him briefly. "I don't want to dance with you."

"Yeah. I figured." Kit grins with one side of his mouth. "I'm here to protect Bailey in case you decide she's getting too close to Jesse."

"Bailey doesn't even like... people. And I'm not... I don't..."

"I'm sorry." Kit puts a hand out and touches my arm briefly to get my attention. "I should know better than to tease you about that. Don't worry. You're not like him."

Kit is the only one I've told. Sometimes I'm afraid I'm too much like Ewan. Because I want Jesse to myself. I like it when it is only the two of us together with no one else. I know I'm overprotective sometimes. But I don't like the feeling—being jealous and possessive.

"Maybe I am, though. I could be."

Kit stops me with a fierce look. "No. You could not. Can you imagine forbidding Jesse to speak to his friends? Controlling where he goes? Can you see yourself hurting him in any w—"

"No." I flash back to the moment behind stage when Ewan had his hands tightening around Jesse's arm and I legitimately wanted to kick the crap out of him. I have a hard time keeping calm even now when I think about it.

"Richard. You are not him. You could never be him."

We stand there silently for a while.

"You sure you don't want to dance?" Kit holds out his hand.

"Fuck no."

Bailey only dances one dance with Jesse. "Out of a sense of self-preservation I thought I'd bring him back to you," she says when she returns on his arm.

I raise one eyebrow. "You can dance all you want, *darling*. He's still coming home with me."

Jesse laughs and grabs me by the hand to drag me out on the dance floor. His eyes meet mine and I can't look away. I don't surrender him for the rest of the evening.

*

We barely get into our room before I have Jesse pressed against the wall, my hands on his shoulders, my lips on his. I feel like all the air has been sucked from the room and I can't quite get a breath. I love the taste of him. I break the kiss, but only to run my lips down his neck.

Now I can take the time to fully appreciate the benefits of a low-cut dress. I run my fingers along the neckline, then spin him around so I am the one with my back to the wall. I play my fingers across his back. He presses his hips against me, pinning me in place. And nearly causing me to forget my own damn name.

I slip my fingers under the edge of the neckline, pushing it off his shoulders. The white fabric frames his tan skin—the contrast somehow starker in the dim light of the room. How is it possible for him to be so heartbreakingly beautiful? And mine?

"Don't stop there, you big tease." Jesse's voice is ragged.

I find the zipper in the back and very slowly pull it down. Only to discover that he's wearing a fucking bra.

"Oh hell." Sexy removal of bras has never been a strong suit of mine. I can't imagine complicated fancy strapless ones are any easier than the regular variety.

Jesse starts to giggle. "Oh no, has my big, strong, manly man been defeated by feminine undergarments?"

"No. But I'm not sure your feminine undergarments will escape unscathed."

I manage to get the damn thing unhooked without too much of a struggle. But this is no longer a smooth seduction. The dress is pooled at his feet. I throw Jesse over my shoulder and toss him on the bed.

"Now that you have me here, what do you plan to do now?" he says with a grin.

I shed the velvet jacket and remove my tie. "I plan to have my way with you. Any complaints?"

"Not a one." He quickly rids me of the remains of my Liza costume. "Do you have any objections to me having my way with you as well?" He whispers this with his lips against my neck before taking my earlobe between his teeth.

"Ah... no. Objections. I mean, that's good."

"And what about this?" He makes his way leisurely down my neck, ending at the base of my throat.

"Yes. Also. Good."

"I'm afraid, sweetie, that I might be leaving marks on your lovely alabaster skin."

"Good. I like when you leave marks."

Jesse laughs, the sound muffled against my chest as he works his way down. "You are shameless."

"What is there to be ashamed of?"

38 Final

The performance finals—where Jesse will dance the piece I saw workshopped—are a week before academic finals. I am much more nervous for Jesse's recital than I am for my own exams. I wish he wasn't dancing. Not like that. Not when he's injured. Even though Jesse says he's fine. Especially because he says he's fine. In my spare time I've been reading up on injuries common to dancers. It's not comforting.

Jesse is curled up in my lap in the big chair in our room. "Will you sit where you usually do? Eighth row back on the right?"

"Yes. Kit will save the seats after setting up the stage." I run my hand through his hair. It slips like silk through my fingers.

"And you know what time to be there?" He looks up at me.

"Yes."

He tugs at my sleeve. "What time?"

"4:15."

Jesse shrieks. "No! 3:45! Oh. *Now* you have a sense of humor."

"I always have a sense of humor. It just takes someone with vast intellect to pick up on it."

"I see."

I rest my hands lightly on his back.

"Yes please," Jesse says, sliding down to the floor to give me better access to his shoulders.

I smooth my hands over his traps and down his arms. He flinches when I apply pressure near his shoulder—not the site of his old injury. Something different. I'm barely touching him.

I frown. "It's that bad?"

"What? No. Keep going."

But this time I stop. "Something is wrong. Maybe you shouldn't dance. I think you should tell the trainer."

"Tell the trainer what? That I'm a whiny brat? My muscles are sore, sweetie. And I'm tired. Everyone is sore at the end of Hell Week. Look, we'll do the show and then I'll have all of break—all of J-term—to recover to one hundred percent. Now... please?" He tugs at my hand and lays it on his shoulder, but there is no way

I am doing any kind of deep tissue work. I use barely enough pressure to undo some of the tension just beneath the surface.

"Darling, that was the world's most lackluster massage. My baby sister could have done better. Once the show is done I expect you to make up for that."

"Get me a trainer's note first."

"We'll discuss this later, young man. You are not off the hook." Jesse stands up and gathers his gym bag.

It's hours before the performance, but they have pre-recital stuff at the studio that includes stretching and warmups, but also a lot of superstitious crap they do before a show.

Maybe it's part of the superstition that we always sit in the same place too. But I think it's really so Jesse can easily find us even when blinded by stage lights. And he finds me every time. I can tell by the expression on his face when he sees me. His smile changes.

I meet Bailey and Danny out on the quad. Kit is already in the theater after having helped set up for the show. He doesn't need to do any of the technical stuff during the production though, so he can sit with us.

"Don't worry, Richard. We'll be on time," Bailey says, I guess because she thinks I'm walking too fast.

"I'm not worried about the time." I don't mention his shoulder. It's Jesse's business. But if he doesn't agree to see someone after the show, I might tell everyone. I'm still not sure I shouldn't run backstage and rat him out to his professor.

We are some of the first people to arrive. The ushers are still folding programs in half when we enter. Bailey scans the program to see how many times she can find Jesse's name. "Wow, our boy is busy tonight."

"Yes."

Jesse is credited as both a dancer and a choreographer this time. He's the only underclassman with pieces that were accepted for the show. That is very unusual. I heard the other dancers talking about it after one of his practices. So I'm not just biased; he is amazing.

When the show finally starts, I watch most of the performances without paying much attention, but when the first dance that credits Jesse comes up, my eyes are fixed on the stage. It's the piece he did for the cute round-faced girl in his studio— Melanie.

She's dressed in a blue evening gown and starts the piece sitting down at an old-fashioned dresser, doing her makeup in the mirror. I think it's a solo until another girl comes out on stage partway through the piece and starts mirroring her every move. At first it looks like they are wearing different colored dresses, but that's a trick of the light. They are dressed identically.

The two of them dance increasingly complicated steps and come closer and closer but never actually touch until the end, when the mirror girl pulls the cute one to the edge of the stage and pushes her off, where she disappears. The second dancer takes a seat at the mirror and begins taking her makeup off.

Jesse also has choreography credit for one of the pieces danced by the entire studio. It's called "Gravity/Synergy." They move like they are one entity. This makes sense. They all spend so much time together.

The dancers are in unison for the most part, except every now and again one of them will fall and be enveloped by the other dancers before reappearing in the center— lifted impossibly high and supported until they return gently to the ground. His is the final lift. The ending image: Jesse in the blinding spotlight held aloft by a sea of dancers.

Bailey hands me a tissue. "Here, honey. You need this more than I do."

I'm confused. "I'm not crying. Oh. Joking."

Bailey laughs and shakes her head.

Kit points out the set pieces that he worked on. Whoever did the lighting is very good. Not just on the duet with the two girls. All the pieces have things that are lit a certain way to really showcase the dancers.

Naturally, "Betrayal" is the final piece. I steel myself for the heartache to come. My worry is also skyrocketing after what happened in the last rehearsal. Of course it's the finale. Of course it will be the best performance of the entire recital. But I'm glad it's late in the show for more personal reasons.

I'm glad that I won't have to wait long after the performance to see Jesse in real life and be reassured that he's okay. That it is only his stage persona that is crushed by his dance partner. That his shoulder isn't worse. I should have made him consult with the goddamn trainer.

Bailey, Kit, and Danny haven't seen the piece before. The moment the music starts, none of us can take our eyes from the stage. And this time there are no mistakes. The performance is flawless. Right down to the sadistic bastard walking away while Jesse is crumpled in a heap on the floor. Bailey needs more than one tissue.

"Did you like the show?" Jesse asks afterwards.

"I liked your pieces."

"Biased much?" Jesse grins. Then he holds both his hands up and spins slowly in front of me. "See, sweetie? No disasters. Everything turned out just fine."

*

At breakfast the next morning, Jesse drops his spoon on the table. This doesn't seem like a big deal. But then he picks up a glass of milk and his hand starts shaking as if the weight of the glass is too much to bear. He sets the glass down heavily on the table, his arm dropping limply to his side.

My heartrate ticks up a notch and I feel suddenly sick to my stomach. Maybe it's not a big deal. It is a big deal; this is not normal.

"Jesse, what the fuck?" Bailey asks him, but she's glaring at me.

I shake my head. "This is new." I lightly run my hand along his arm from his shoulder to his wrist as if that will tell me a damn thing.

"It's nothing. I think I might have strained my shoulder worse than I thought last week. We've all been pushing ourselves hard getting ready for the end-of-semester performances. And you saw that final piece."

"That's not a strain," Bailey says.

Almost at the same time I say, "That's not nothing."

Bailey is still glaring, but now her gaze has fallen on Jesse.

Jesse tries to laugh this off, but when he sees we aren't smiling, he changes tactics. "Darlings, will it make you happy if I go see the trainer?"

"Yes. Now." I shove my chair back hard enough that I nearly knock it to the floor.

Jesse startles. I'm pretty sure he was kidding about the trainer. I'm not. I take care of his tray and mine. When I return, I stand behind him and pull out his chair. I don't want him moving anything.

"Sweetie, I'm fine. We don't need the trainer. No need to bother them at this hour."

"It's working hours. They're working. Let's go."

Bailey nods.

I hadn't even noticed Danny and Kit arriving earlier. They are seated across from Bailey. I wonder how long they've been there. Did they see what happened? Are they as worried as I am? Danny gives me a thumbs up, which seems odd. Kit waves with a sad expression on his face. That seems more appropriate. I feel like I'm going to be sick.

When we get to the office, the door is already open.

Jesse hesitates on the threshold. "You don't need to come with me."

"Yes. I do."

It's the same trainer who I've talked with before when I wanted to make sure my amateur massages wouldn't hurt Jesse. He's a young guy studying sports medicine and seems to know what he's doing. He calls me "Mother Hen," but I don't care. I think it's funny.

"Press against my hand with the side of your arm. Now this way." He makes Jesse do a number of these tests. He doesn't look happy with the results.

"I'm not qualified to make any kind of diagnosis. You'll need to see an actual doctor."

Jesse laughs. "I'm sure that won't be necessary. I'm not in any pain."

I know he's lying; he is always in pain. Sometimes the pain is less. But this seems different. Nothing has ever affected his arm like this—the sudden weakness. Until now most of his issues have been concentrated around that knot near his shoulder blade on the other side that never goes away. Pain that he can ignore while he dances. Not this.

The trainer looks from me to Jesse. "Listen. Go see a doctor. Today. And if you can't get in right away? Don't use the arm until you find out what's going on."

I feel faint, which is not helpful. "What do you think it is?"

The trainer shakes his head. "Like I said, I can't make a diagnosis. And there are too many possibilities—some worse than others. Maybe it is only a strained muscle, maybe it's not. I know from experience though, you should listen to your body when it's screaming at you like this. Just because you ignore the pain, that doesn't mean the injury will go away. Do yourself a favor and don't turn to Dr. Google on this one."

Too late. I've already done my homework. Repetitive motions wear on the joints. Damage can be permanent. I don't say any of these things.

After we leave the trainers' office Jesse loops his arm around mine. His good arm. "Richie, get that horrified expression of your wickedly handsome face. I've had this sort of thing before. The muscles are like overcooked spaghetti from all the extra practice. After I rest for a few days like I said—maybe a week—things will get back to normal."

I don't say anything. Instead, I march him to urgent care. He puts up a minor fuss, but he can tell I'm in no mood for any more excuses.

*

"I don't want you to worry about all the hot doctors here," Jesse says as we are waiting for the results of his x-ray. "I only have eyes for you." When he's nervous he gets even flirtier than usual. I don't.

The doctor who enters the room is not hot. Then again, I'm not a very good gauge of hotness. Jesse is hot. Other people are... other people.

This guy looks like he must be in his late sixties with a bit of a paunch and a large bald spot. He approaches with a carefully controlled expression on his face, which sets me on edge. Jesse tenses on the seat beside me and grabs my hand.

"Hello, Jesse? Nice to meet you." He doesn't offer to shake hands, but I try not to read too much into that. He looks at me as if I'm a puzzle.

"Richard. The boyfriend," I volunteer.

He doesn't look thrilled, but he doesn't ask me to leave, either. "Yes. Now, let's pull these up so I can show you what we're looking at."

The doctor turns the computer monitor in our direction and pulls up x-rays of Jesse's shoulder.

"Do you see this right here?" He zooms in on the clavicle and takes a pen from his pocket. He points to a very faint line crossing the bone. And there it is: the source of his sour expression when he came into the room.

"That's what we call a hairline fracture. A very common injury for young people. Especially athletes. Do you participate in any sports?"

"Contemporary dance. It's my major."

The doctor nods. "You don't even need to have any specific traumatic injury. These things can develop over time with repetitive motion. Especially if you don't allow yourself time to heal between repeated stress to the area."

"But it doesn't hurt. It can't really be broken."

The doctor picks up on my grimace. Even without my silent editorializing, he knows Jesse is lying.

Jesse shakes his head. "I don't understand. I took a bad fall when I was in high school. That hurt a lot more than this."

The doctor's non-smile becomes a frown. "Tell me about that injury."

"It was a strained muscle. I landed wrong and wrenched my arm. I went through physical therapy and it returned to normal. Only sometimes if I overdo it during practice it gives me a little trouble. And that injury was nowhere near my collarbone. It was near the shoulder blade. On the other side."

"Soft tissue damage can have long-term effects. That sounds like a fairly significant tear. And we all take measures to avoid pain. It's possible that compensating for weakness or discomfort in the area you previously injured contributed to this new injury."

Jesse's face falls.

"So what happens now?" I ask.

The doctor turns to the monitor again. "The bones haven't shifted so there's really nothing that needs to happen other than keeping things still while they heal. Six weeks in a sling before you can start some range of motion activities."

"But then I can get back to training? Back to dance?"

Six weeks would put him partway into spring semester. I can hear the note of panic in Jesse's voice.

The doctor hesitates. "I don't want to make any promises about the timeline. I've seen a lot of injuries like yours. Most often, fractures like this heal cleanly and without complication. But to go back to a strenuous activity that involves so much potential strain on the bone? It may take twice as long. Perhaps twelve to sixteen weeks before you are ready to resume your regular activity as an elite athlete."

That virtually eliminates all of spring semester.

"Anything that would make recovery faster?" Jesse's grip tightens on my hand.

The doctor shakes his head. "We could manage things surgically, which would allow you to start physical therapy sooner, but for a hairline fracture like this? Surgery can cause more problems than the injury itself and really wouldn't save you any time. Let's get you set up with a sling and set up a follow-up in a few weeks."

Jesse nods his head slowly.

"A nurse will be in shortly to fit you for your sling. Wear it day and night until you get the okay to remove it. We want to keep the bones from shifting while they heal."

Jesse stares blankly at the door after it closes.

I squeeze his hand. "It will be okay. This is good."

"How is this good?" I've never heard Jesse's voice sound like this before. Empty. Harsh.

"You're hurt and this will help."

221

"That isn't good. Good would be him telling me that it was nothing. That I was cleared to dance right now. That I was okayed for spring semester. Good is *not* that I broke my goddamn shoulder and have to keep my arm still for a minimum of six weeks. Followed by months of recovery."

I nod. "You're right. That is less good. But Jesse... you are in pain all the time. Maybe they can help with that when you are recuperating."

Jesse shakes his head. "I can live with pain..."

What he doesn't say, but I can hear the words anyway, is that he's not sure he can live without dance.

39 Careful

Finals are done. I manage to pull decent scores somehow despite the fact that all I can think about is Jesse. About Jesse's injury. He's gone from being panicked about the doctor's prognosis to imagining it's no big deal. Magical thinking. He thinks he should just go back to dancing. No problem. I'm convinced he's wrong. Broken bones don't heal overnight.

It's our last night in the dorm together. Jesse has an early flight out in the morning. He's lying down on his back, his head resting on my arm. It's cutting off circulation, but I don't care. I want him close to me.

He's wearing the sling like he's supposed to. He's only had it for a week, but it already feels like a part of him. I hate it. The fabric is coarse and black—like nothing Jesse would choose to wear. It chafes against my skin and I can't imagine it's any more comfortable for him. The sling reminds me of all the things I don't want to think about. It reminds me how fragile he is. Broken.

Jesse turns to look up at me, his eyes bright even in the darkened room. "Have you ever noticed the crack in the paint looks a lot like the Mississippi River? See the delta over there? New Orleans in the southeast corner of the room?" Jesse raises his good arm and points at the ceiling.

"It looks like a crack."

Jesse laughs.

I touch my head to his. I hate being so close to him without being able to put my arms around him, but I'm afraid I will do something that will jostle his arm and nudge the bones out of alignment.

"I'm going to miss you like hell." My voice comes out softer than I expected. Weaker.

"I'll miss you too, sweetie." Jesse turns his head and kisses the weak spot behind my ear. "Want something to remember me by?"

"Don't." I warn him. But I don't move.

"What if we're careful?"

I narrow my eyes at him. "No one can be that careful."

"But we'll be away from each other for nearly a month." He shifts on the bed so he is half-sitting. He uses a single finger to outline my body starting at the waistband of my boxers, up my ribs, around my arm, tracing each finger.

I gasp as he trails that one fingertip up my neck, around my ear, then skips down to my lips. I can't stop from pulling his finger into my mouth briefly. I bite gently on the tip.

He groans, and the sound is more than I can bear. I'm rapidly losing the ability to object to anything he suggests. He knows he can get me to do anything he wants, really. I have no restraint where Jesse is concerned.

"What if I'm careful for the both of us?" Jesse gives me a teasing kiss, nibbling on my lower lip. Then he outlines the shell of my ear before breathing into it as he whispers, "I promise to be gentle."

But I don't want gentle. That's the problem. I want to crush him against me. Want to put my hands over every part of his lithe dancer's body. Want to roll him over so I am hovering over him, taking his breath away, making him lose his mind.

But I stay still. I bite my lip almost hard enough to draw blood. I grasp at the bedsheets to keep my hands off him. "Jesse. Please."

"Don't move. See? We can be careful. Let me do all the work." He looks up at me and the gleam in his eyes is my undoing.

"I can't. I…" I'm not even sure what I'm trying to say. And then he robs me of the ability to think or speak.

*

On the drive to the airport I make Jesse sit in the back seat in the middle because I don't want the seat belt cutting across his shoulder. The doctor warned against this so it's not just my being paranoid. Not that Jesse agrees.

"You're being ridiculous. I could use the lap belt in the front and just stick the shoulder strap behind me."

"No. Airbags. Also, we are not on speaking terms. And I don't trust you to keep your hands off me between here and the airport."

"Is this still about the ravishment? You can't tell me you didn't enjoy yourself." I look in the rear-view mirror and catch his wicked grin.

"Of course I enjoyed myself. My boyfriend is hot as hell."

"Yes he is." Jesse's voice is absurdly smug. "But I do feel a teensy bit bad that I overruled your sweet objections. It's only... Sweetie, you could never hurt me."

I shake my head and glare at him in the mirror. "I could. Even if not on purpose. Also, I've decided it's a good thing you are going to Idaho. That's far enough away that I can keep my hands off you for three weeks. Any closer and I can make no promises."

"Why Richie, you charmer! And I have a confession to make: I'm not actually sorry about last night."

I pull into short-term parking and come around to open the door for him.

"How chivalrous. You don't need to walk me in, darling. I can take it myself from here."

"Not happening." I want to keep my eyes on him as long as possible.

Jesse checked in online, his flight is on time, and I can't go to the gate with him. Once his luggage has been checked, it's time for him to go through security on his own.

"Sweetie, take that look off your face." He puts his palm against my cheek. "You're wounding my poor heart with that expression. Break will be over before you know it. Then I'll be back and things will be back to normal." He pulls me in for a brief kiss.

"I love you, Jesse." I put my forehead against his. "Come back to me."

He kisses me again, much more thoroughly. "Wild horses couldn't keep me away."

After he makes it through the security screening he turns and blows me a kiss.

That night our room feels ridiculously empty without him there. It takes me forever to get to sleep. And I wake up hours earlier than I'd planned. Which is not a problem, really. It just means I can get on the road sooner for the long drive back home.

*

"Richard, you look like hell." Tea says when I let her in.

"Is this our new greeting? Because you've looked better too."

"Ha. Behold. I come bearing snacks." She hands me a large bag of kettle corn as she walks toward the kitchen. "I'm relying on you for the liquid refreshment."

Tea came to keep me company for the day again. Now that the holidays are over it helps fill the long boring hours that I would no doubt otherwise spend pacing back and forth worrying about Jesse.

"How is he doing?" She sits down on the couch while I fire up the entertainment system.

"I think you mean how am *I* doing."

She nods. "That was my carefully veiled question, yes."

"Last time we talked—"

"—Which was no doubt thirty seconds ago."

I rifle through my collection of old DVDs. "Nothing much had changed. Still 'managing things conservatively.' No news is good news."

Tea pulls one of the many throw pillows onto her lap, settling in for the movie marathon. "And to answer my real question?"

"This sucks. I should have gone home with him."

She scoffs. "Don't be such a big baby. Jesse is getting time with his family. You would just have been underfoot. And something tells me he'll have an easier time resting without you there."

I hold up my selections. "What are you up for? *Attack of the Killer Tomatoes* or the original *Plan 9 from Outer Space?*"

We watch both of them. I'm debating on the next selection, when I see that Jesse has called. I shouldn't have silenced notifications. It's a reflex when watching movies; I hate interruptions. But now... five missed calls. No messages. No texts.

"Fuck."

Tea sits up straight. "What's wrong?"

"I don't know. It's Jesse." I wait for him to pick up. The fact that it takes more than two rings for me to hear the sound of his voice makes my heart stutter. Something is wrong. I don't know why any good news would merit so many calls.

He finally picks up on the third ring.

"Jesse. What's wrong?"

I desperately want him to say that nothing is wrong, or that he misses me or that he just wants to hear the sound of my voice.

"Richard, thank God. I'm screwed. Things aren't healing like they expected. I need the surgery. Fuck." Jesse's voice is thick with tears. I feel like I'm going to vomit.

"Wait... What happened?" I start pacing back and forth. I have made my way to the front entryway before I realize what I'm doing. I'm headed for my car. I want to get in and drive to Idaho. Now. While still talking to him. And I would, if I could get there in any reasonable length of time.

"I swear I was wearing the sling. All the time. They said things might have shifted while I was sleeping. Anyway, my shoulder started to hurt yesterday. After we talked. And this morning I went in. They told me to see them if anything was different. If things only felt even a little bit off. I thought they'd give me some prescription strength ibuprofen and a better cold pack or something. But they took more x-rays, and things aren't lined up well enough anymore. The bone won't heal straight. They can't rely on external treatment—especially because I want to dance. They want to do the surgery."

"Damn. I mean... But that's good, though. Right? Won't it heal faster then?" Why am I trying to tell him that things are good when they are clearly devastating?

"I don't know. I should have written down what he said. I should have had someone there with me but I thought it was a routine exam."

"When?"

"It's scheduled for the day after tomorrow."

"I'll be there."

"Richie, I can't ask you to..."

"You're not asking. I'm telling. I'll be there. Also, you're not the boss of me."

At least this makes Jesse laugh a little. "Yeah, we'll see about that."

According to Google, it takes twenty hours by car, twenty-nine hours by train, 115 hours by bicycle, or 452 hours on foot. But that seems sketchy because it involves crossing a mountain range to get there.

It's only four hours by plane.

By the time my mom is home from work I already have a plane ticket. The earliest flight out I could find doesn't leave until 8:00 the following morning. It will get me there by noon.

Jesse's brother Berto can pick me up at the airport. I'm not sure where I'll be staying, but he said not to worry about it. I have other things to worry about. Like the wrath of my mother.

"Where do you think you're going?" she asks. After I've explained my plans.

"I need to be there. Not negotiable."

"I know that you care about Jesse, but he's with his family," My mom says with a disapproving frown. "Your... Jesse will be fine. What can you do for him? It's a minor surgery and then he'll be home. And didn't you say he has a large family? Plenty of people to take care of him. We don't get to see you very often. Gabby is home. Your dad took time off from work. We'll all finally be in the same place."

"No. Because I will be in Idaho."

I should have waited until my dad was home to have this conversation, but she caught me packing my suitcase. My dad doesn't have an issue with me and Jesse. My mom—nice woman—doesn't precisely buy into the fact that I am gay. Pan. Whatever.

"Your friend—"

"—boyfriend."

"Jesse is such a nice boy. He's lucky to have you as a—"

"I'm lucky. And stop calling him my friend. I am in love with him. We have sex. Fantastic sex. And if he needs me there with him, that's where I'm going to be."

That's when my dad walks through the door and sets down his computer bag. He looks at my mom's tight lipped expression and then at me.

"What did I miss?"

"Me telling mom that I enjoy having gay sex with my gay boyfriend. Oh. And can I get a ride to the airport tomorrow?"

40 Neanderthal

It takes forever to walk from the gate to the baggage claim. I spot Jesse's brother right away. He looks like Jesse, but twice as heavy and at least a foot taller.

"Hey man, glad you could make it." Berto slaps me on the back. I hope he doesn't do that often. I want to make a good impression on the family so flinching away from physical contact is probably not a great plan.

I don't have any checked luggage so Berto takes me straight to his car. The air smells clean. We can see mountains from the road. No wonder Jesse misses this when he's in Indiana.

"So, you and my brother, huh," Berto says once we're in the car.

"Yes."

"You're all my baby brother can talk about." His voice is deep and smooth. He sounds like a singer when he speaks.

I raise an eyebrow. "He talks a lot."

Berto laughs. "You're a departure from the guys he usually dates."

"Oh?" I bristle at the comment for some reason.

Berto laughs. "That's a good thing. He's usually drawn to these awful Neanderthals."

"So I've heard. But what makes you think I'm not a Neanderthal?"

"Well, let me count the ways. You're a science major, so clearly you've got some brains. You have been together with him for over six months, so this isn't a casual fling. You flew out here at a moment's notice, so obviously my brother is a priority for you. But wait—You don't by any chance have a secret fiancé do you?"

"What?" I say louder than necessary in the confines of the car.

"Don't listen to me. Never mind. Anyway, I would have brought Jesse to pick you up, but the doc doesn't want him moving that arm too much. So we have him confined to quarters until the surgery tomorrow.

"Good."

"See? I knew I liked you." Berto smiles brightly.

It takes about forty minutes to drive from the airport to Jesse's parents' house on the outskirts of Coeur d'Alene. When I see Jesse standing in the driveway I can't breathe.

"See? Not a Neanderthal," Berto says with a grin. "I see how you look at him. Get out of the car and say hello to your boyfriend." He gives me a little shove.

I get out of the car and walk toward Jesse, but I'm afraid to touch him. I slow my steps as I approach.

Jesse walks toward me, impatient for me to reach him. "I won't break. You can kiss me, you bastard."

I bend down and give him a gentle kiss. He tries to deepen it, but I back away. "I missed you too. But..." I gesture at his arm in the sling.

"After the fucking surgery, you will make up for this." He frowns.

"Gladly."

Berto follows us into the house carrying my luggage.

When we enter the kitchen, Jesse's mom gives me a hug. I can see I'll need to get used to people touching me. It seems to be a family thing.

Her dark hair is in a bun, but there are little curls sticking out on the sides. "Richard, please make yourself at home."

"Yes, ma'am. Oh crap. What am I supposed to call your mom? I mean, what should I call you, Mrs. Nunez?" I'm trying here. I'm not really good with people. Especially new people.

"Rose is fine. Or Tita if you like."

"Nice to finally meet you." Jesse's father walks into the room and shakes my hand, grasping my arm at the same time. Jesse clearly takes after his mom. His dad has ruddier skin and looks more Hispanic. He has very large arms and a wide smile.

"Berto, I need a few things at the store. Can you run a quick errand?" Jesse's mom hands him a list. "And Richard, can you set the table?" She points to a stack of plates. "Jesse is not allowed to move things heavier than napkins. Even with his good hand."

"Putting our guest to work, I see," Jesse's dad says in a teasing voice. I don't know what to call him either. I'll probably just avoid addressing either of them directly to avoid any confusion.

"Oh, he's not a guest. After hearing Jesse talk for so long about him, you should know better. Richard is family."

I freeze for a moment at his mom's words. It seems too soon for me to be family. From her perspective, I mean. Of course Jesse feels like family to me. He has for a long time. I'm not sure I'm ready to have a bigger family than that at the moment. I don't know why I'm so worried. It's not like I don't want to belong here. And I have no plans to leave Jesse. But the idea of being included as a family member already?

"Help. Sure. Thanks." I grab a handful of silverware.

Jesse touches my hand. He speaks softly so only I can hear. "Take a breath, sweetie. She doesn't expect you to propose to me. Everyone who's here is family."

The long table takes up more than half the space in the small dining room. I am already overwhelmed, and I have only met three of Jesse's family members. I wonder if it's too late to back out. Maybe I could pretend to be sick. Then I remember how frightening Jesse is when he goes into nurturing mode. I doubt his mom is any less scary. And I'm supposed to be here taking care of *him*.

Jesse's mom is preparing a giant meal. It rivals Thanksgiving at my house, but his mom seems remarkably calm, considering that the entire family is descending upon the house.

It doesn't take Berto long to run his errand. He arrives just before Jesse's older brother Caesar shows up with his wife Christina, who is either naturally round or quite pregnant. Jesse's mom calls the younger kids to the table: Max and Angel—who I can't tell apart to save my life—and Maya, the baby of the family.

Everyone but Maya talks a lot. I'm glad I'm sitting between her and Jesse. When he senses I'm getting overwhelmed, he squeezes my thigh under the table. Maya notices and gives me a half-grin.

I know I'm supposed to say things, but I'm not sure how to get a word in edgewise, and no one seems particularly offended that I haven't said anything.

I focus on the sound of Jesse's voice. And Maya's when she has anything to say. There seems to be a lot of talk about football, which I've never really gotten into.

Christina is seated directly across from me.

"Where are you from, Richard?" she asks.

"Minnesota. You're not Filipino." She looks surprised. That was probably rude.

"No. I'm a garden variety white girl. A mix of pretty much every Northern European country you can think of."

"Yeah. Sounds familiar. Maybe we're related."

She laughs. "Jesse, this one's a keeper."

"That's what I keep saying." Jesse squeezes my hand and kisses me on the cheek.

With surgery scheduled for the following morning, everyone heads for bed on the early side.

"Your parents are cool with this?" I ask as we enter Jesse's bedroom.

"With what?" Jesse raises an eyebrow.

"With my staying here. With you."

Jesse snorts. "Of course. They know we live together at school. Why wouldn't they be okay with you being with me here?'

"Fair." I unroll the sleeping bag next to his bed. He hadn't even tried to convince me to squeeze in beside him on the twin-sized bed. "Does the arm still hurt? I mean more than it did before?"

Jesse nods. "More at night than during the day, actually. Maybe it's because I don't have anything else to think about as I'm drifting off to sleep."

Despite the pain and the anxiety over the surgery, Jesse falls asleep very quickly. It takes me a lot longer.

*

The hospital in Spokane is larger than I expected. It smells like any hospital: antiseptic. I suppose that's a good thing.

The nurses wear all different colors of scrubs. The nurse who is helping us is a petite black woman named Kandi whose scrubs are dark purple. She writes her name in purple pen on the whiteboard so we'd know who to ask for if we need help. I wonder if all nurses color-coded their markers.

We have to wait a long time for the surgeon. Jesse's family tells stories to make him laugh. I don't have anything funny or useful to say. My only job is to be here, sitting beside Jesse's hospital bed, holding his hand. Caesar asks if Jesse wants anything to drink.

Jesse's mom slaps the back of his head lightly. "Nothing before surgery. You should know this. But Richard, do *you* want something?"

I shake my head.

Jesse hasn't let go of my hand since we arrived at the hospital.

When Kandi finally comes back in to wheel him away for the surgery, Jesse reluctantly lets go.

"I'll see you soon." I kiss him on the forehead.

"Damn you two are cute as bugs," Berto says. Why do people in this family think bugs are cute?

I manage to doze off in one of the chairs in his room before they bring him back. Jesse's mom is the one who nudges me awake as he is being wheeled back in. The surgery didn't take long—I must have been exhausted. I guess sleeping on the floor isn't conducive to a restful night's sleep. Neither is anxiety over the operation.

Jesse pats the spot next to him on the bed.

"Is it okay?" I look at Kandi for an answer.

Jesse gives her a pleading face.

She lowers the rails on one side and I perch on the very edge. Jesse grips my hand again.

"Does it hurt?" Maya asks.

"Not a bit. Although I literally just got out of surgery, so it's probably too soon to tell. I'm pretty sure I'm currently high on the best pain meds western medicine can provide."

"I can't believe they are sending you home today." Jesse's mother wrings her hands.

"What would I do here that I can't do at home? Plus the beds are more comfortable there. And the nurses are hotter."

I frown. What nurses?

Jesse's brother Berto elbows me in the side. "He's talking about you, numbnuts. I may have to take back what I said about you not being a Neanderthal. You're a little slow."

"Yup." Jesse grins. "I was going to have to convalesce at my parents' house in that inconveniently small bed where I spent last night. Inconveniencing my sainted parents and infuriating

Angel—my satanic younger brother who gets the room while I'm away. But since you are here to tend to my every need—"

"You have a bunk at my place!" Berto announces. "Well, not literally a bunk. I have a spare room. And a lot less going on at my house. You and Jesse will be more comfortable there."

"Berto works during the day, but if you can be there I feel fine," Jesse's mom adds.

"Are you sure?" I'm surprised she doesn't want to be the one fussing over Jesse as he recovers.

She nods. "Who better than family to care for our Jesse?"

*

Berto lives in a two-bedroom apartment with a large living room separated from the kitchen by a small island. There are two overstuffed chairs on one side of the room and a small sofa on the other facing a large screen TV.

I help Jesse out of his jacket, which is wrapped loosely around him to accommodate his sling. He looks very thin and small wrapped in the weird hospital shirt they sent him home with. It ties in the front like a traditional Chinese jacket so he can get dressed and undressed more easily.

"You can put your crap in the guest bedroom. Second door from the left." Berto throws his keys on the kitchen counter.

The guest room is sparsely furnished with a king sized bed, a dresser, and a bedside table. I set my suitcase on the floor. Jesse is right behind me. He rests his head against my arm. "Thank you again for coming."

"I didn't come here for you. I came here for me."

"I see." He pokes me in the ribs.

"I'm serious. Not everything is about you. Imagine how worried I would have been back in Minnesota with you in surgery."

Jesse turns me to face him and puts his good arm around me.

I'm afraid even this will hurt him. "Are you sure it's okay?"

"Shut up."

When I feel his arm around me in this sort of half-hug I want to laugh or cry or both. Instead I tilt his chin up and kiss him very

235

carefully, our lips barely touching. He puts his hand around my neck. A tightness in my chest I didn't know was there disappears. I feel lighter. We haven't been apart that long. I stayed with him last night, but this all feels different.

I close my eyes and breathe him in. It's good to be home.

41 Range of Motion

"Hey sweetie, I made you some oatmeal," Jesse calls from the kitchen. "Come on. We can't be late. Gina scares me." Gina is his physical therapist. She's the same person who worked with him after his injury in high school.

Berto walks into the kitchen. "Where's my oatmeal?"

"I thought you were working early today," Jesse says.

Berto shakes his head. "I'm off for the day. Compensation for the all-nighter we pulled." I don't remember what he does for a job. I think he's the one who used to tend bar. But now he does something with computers. "I could drive you to your appointment today if you want," he says.

"As if. Keys please." Jesse holds out his hand.

Berto looks at Jesse, but tosses the keys to me. "I trust you will be a ridiculously careful driver with my brother in the car."

"Yes."

The PT office isn't even thirty minutes from Berto's apartment. It's decorated with art made by local artists. Paintings, sculptures, even a mobile hanging from the ceiling. It twirls slowly in the bright and airy room.

The receptionist, a pudgy woman in her mid-thirties, clearly recognizes Jesse. "I swear you get prettier every time I see you," he says.

She smiles and shakes her head. "You tell the sweetest lies. She's ready for you now." The woman waves Jesse in. She seems surprised when I follow. I guess she hadn't noticed me when we came in.

Gina, Jesse's physical therapist, is easily six feet tall with hands that could palm a basketball. Her black hair is loose and goes down past her waist. "I hate to see you back here, my friend."

"It's a real turn off to see you too, hot stuff." Jesse grins.

"You know very well what I mean. What have you done to yourself now? Broken clavicle? Why on earth would you do that to yourself? Such a pain in the ass. Now I have to go through all the trouble of creating a PT regimen for you. And I have to see your ugly mug twice a week."

The bone is not the problem anymore. No worries about it shifting around. They used some composites to knit the bone together like an internal cast. Supposed to be a better outcome than using metal pins. I did a lot of research after the surgery since I didn't have a lot of time to research things before it happened.

Gina starts with a few simple activities that won't be comfortable but shouldn't hurt like hell. That's how Jesse will gauge if he's doing them right and whether he's ready for the next stage. I ask so many questions that Gina hands me an honest-to-god textbook on kinesiology and assigns me homework. "Here you go, boyfriend. I'm gonna quiz you next time. Chapters five through eight. Also, you are my official spy. Make sure he doesn't take any shortcuts."

"You know I would never." Jesse puts his hand over his heart.

Gina gives him an indulgent smile. "He's telling the truth, actually. Jesse is my star pupil."

"Only because whenever I ignore your advice I get worse."

"Smart kid. Richard? Here are the rules. Right now strictly range of motion. Start small. Sling off periodically. No weight bearing activities. See you Wednesday."

"Wait…" I get her attention before she leaves the room. Jesse is already halfway across the office, flirting with the receptionists. "I have a few questions for you."

"Shoot, boyfriend."

*

Berto is standing in the kitchen finishing off a plate of spaghetti when we get back to his place. "Hey y'all. I don't mean to alarm you, but you may need to hold down the fort on your own tonight. At least for a while. I have plans."

Jesse sits down on one of the bar stools at the kitchen island. "Does 'plans' happen to go by the name of Tanya?"

"Wouldn't you like to know." Berto grins.

I stand behind Jesse and he pulls my arm around his waist. I lean toward him, feeling the heat of his back against me.

Berto raises an eyebrow and looks pointedly from me to Jesse. "So if you wanted some privacy for... whatever reason, I thought I'd let you know not to expect me back for quite some time."

"Interesting. Well, all we have on the agenda for the evening is some more physical therapy." Jesse traces his finger along the inside of my arm.

Berto chuckles. "You should know the walls are thin here. Think of the neighbors. Their poor, innocent ears."

Jesse grins. "From physical therapy?"

"Is that what the kids are calling it these days?" Berto winks.

After he leaves, Jesse does go through his physical therapy. Diligently. I read through the directions and spot him. There are a few activities that require an assistant. Gina included them because she counted on my being there to help.

When we are finished, Jesse looks up at me with a wicked smile. "Do you have any ideas about how you might reward me for doing so well today?"

"Yes."

"How about a little kiss?" He stands on tiptoe.

When our lips meet at first the kiss is gentle, his tongue barely grazing my inner lip.

I step backwards and perch against the arm of the couch, putting us at nearly the same height. Then I put my hand behind his neck and draw him closer. Jesse responds instantly, and suddenly there is nothing gentle about the kiss.

After short-circuiting damn near every brain cell I have, Jesse pulls away for a moment. "Wait, no lectures about having to be careful?"

"Sling off periodically, no weight-bearing activities. I got prior approval from your physical therapist. But remember: we have to be careful not to disturb the neighbors."

I pull him in for another searing kiss before scooping him up from the floor. I carry him into the bedroom bridal style and deposit him carefully on the bed.

I bite my lower lip and allow my gaze to rake over him from head to toe before straddling his hips. "Are you comfortable there?

Jesse stares at me as if I am speaking a language he can't quite comprehend. Well, I did just roll my hips against his, which is making it difficult for me to remember how words are supposed to work as well.

"What?" His voice comes out as a whisper.

"You're going to enjoy what comes next. Very much. And I plan to keep you here for a very, very long time. So I want to make sure that you are comfortable."

Jesse closes his eyes and moans in anticipation.

"Now," I say as I painstakingly undo every single button of his shirt, grazing my fingers along his skin as I go, "Let's see how quiet you can be."

*

The receptionist at the PT clinic is named Janice. She thinks I'm funny. I'm not sure why because I haven't said much. Maybe that's why she thinks I'm funny. I've seen her often enough in the last two weeks. There's only a week of J-term left before we go back to school.

I'm looking forward to getting back to normal. Berto's place is nice, and he's good about making sure we have our own space, but it's not the same as our dorm.

I need to fly back to Minnesota to get my car, so we can't go back to school at the same time, which irritates me. I've been spoiled now spending all of my time with Jesse. I want us to leave together.

"How did things go this week?" Gina asks.

"They were fi… Not so good." Jesse amends his answer when he sees the look on my face.

Jesse was in pain while doing his PT between sessions and couldn't complete all the sets. I'm glad he listened to me when I told him to stop. Especially after seeing the look on Gina's face when the same thing happens here when she has him go through his routine. A lot of frowning. A lot more notes scribbled on the clipboard than usual.

At the end of the session, Gina sits down and puts her hands on her knees. She leans forward. "Well cookie, we need to have a little talk. Are you okay with your personal trainer listening in?"

"Of course." Jesse grabs my arm in a death grip. And to be honest I can't imagine that Gina has anything good to say. Not with that tone of voice and that expression on her face.

"Right. Well, I think there might be something else going on. I would expect things to be improving differently than they have so far."

"It's only been a few weeks." Jesse squeezes my arm with what must be all his strength.

"I know, honey. I'm not saying I'd expect you to be a hundred percent by now, but things aren't progressing the particular way I'd expect. Something's slightly off and I don't know what. One of two things could be going on. You might have bursitis from the break, which we can almost certainly treat with cortisone injections if physical therapy doesn't do the trick—although it will take a lot more work to get you back in fighting form than if we were only looking at coming back from the fracture.

"Or you might have a more serious condition involving the cartilage in the ball and socket joint. That would require another surgery. Either one of these things can be caused by overuse of the joint or direct trauma. Hard to tell if it is a new injury or something that has been getting progressively worse."

I think about the pain he has been living with since before I knew him. The difficulty he had raising his arms above his head. The muscle weakness right before they found the hairline fracture. And now things are not healing the way she'd like to see.

I want to swear, but instead I look Gina in the eye and say, "Torn labrum?"

Gina looks up in surprise. "Someone's been doing his homework. That's a possibility, but I can't say. And until this fracture is healed we can't start investigating further."

Jesse grimaces. "I know this story. Can't diagnose me. Need to see a doctor. May be a career ending injury."

"That's not what I said."

Jesse's face is frozen. "What is the recovery time for something like this? What's the outcome if there is damage to the cartilage?"

"I can't really say. You'd need to—"

"Ask the doctor," Jesse says flatly.

He doesn't speak on the way to the car. He doesn't say anything until we get back to Berto's apartment. Jesse sits down on the couch facing the picture window. "You know I can't go back."

"Back to the doctor? But… if you don't go, things might get worse. Or it could be nothing. Maybe you're not ready for the exercises Gina assigned. Maybe you're pushing yourself again."

"No. I can go to the doctor. I will absolutely go to the doctor. But haven't you done the math, sweetie? I can't go back to school."

My stomach drops.

"Why? Don't they have an orthopedist you can see there? And they have physical therapists. The university has an entire department devoted to training them, so there must be facilities nearby, if not on campus. I can drive you to your appointments. We can work things out."

"That's not it. You don't understand."

"So tell me. Explain it so I understand." Tell me why you can't be with me, is what I want to say. But that would be a shitty thing to say. This isn't about me.

"I can't dance for the rest of the spring. Even if it is the best case scenario. I've always known I had to take a leave for the semester."

But I hadn't known. "When were you going to tell me?"

Jesse looks at the floor. He looks over my shoulder. He looks out the window. Anywhere but at me.

"I didn't know how." He still won't look at me.

"How about this: 'Richard, I need to take a break from school.' And then we talk about what your plan is." And then I can know what this means.

"To be honest, I thought you already knew. Richard, I'm at Indiana on a dance scholarship. If I can't dance, there is no scholarship. I was already worried about coming back from the fracture if things went perfectly. But this? What Gina is describing?" He breaks off and stares at the mountains in the distance.

"Jesse, it's too soon to be making these decisions. Your shoulder might respond well to different types of therapy. And if you do need another operation, there are surgeries with very good outcomes. For dancers in particular. A minor tear to the labrum is a very common injury so..."

"Stop. Just stop. It doesn't matter. I won't be able to dance this spring. I'll lose my scholarship. And there will be no point in returning if I can't dance anyway."

I feel like I should say something. "You could take other classes. Non-performance classes. Until your shoulder is—"

"You can't fix this, Richard. You can't fix me, and you can't fix this. I can't be there. I can't go back. You can't ask that of me."

I want to ask. I want so badly to ask.

42 Spring Semester

I'm the one who has to pack up all his shit and send it back to Idaho. He offered to come, but it didn't seem like there was much point to that. A lot of expense for such a short trip.

"Yours or his?" Bailey asks, holding up some lavender house slippers that would barely fit my big toe.

"Funny."

"Hey, someone has to lighten up the mood here. It feels like a fucking wake. And not the good, Irish kind," she says.

Danny pats me on the shoulder. "We're here for you, man." Jesse's friends are very touchy when they want to be supportive. They haven't kept their hands off me since I got back. I have to remember not to snap at them. They're my friends too. They're trying to be kind.

I keep some of his things. The scented candles on the window ledge. Those slippers. The pencil sharpener on his desk. There's no real reason behind the things I keep. I want to have things around the room that I will come across from time to time. Little reminders that he lived here.

*

"Hey sweetie."

"Hey."

"You could start by saying, 'Hello lover.'" Jesse uses his absurdly seductive tone of voice.

"No."

He laughs. "And how is my *fabulous* boyfriend doing? Tell me every little thing about your day."

"I'm fine. I... nothing new." Why don't I ever have anything to say? Partly because I have done nothing since the last time we talked. I'm never good on the phone. When it's my turn to talk, all I want to say is, "When are you coming back?" He isn't coming back. But this is all that's on my one track mind.

I search for something, anything to say. "The snow's gone already so everything is ugly here. Kit has decided to do ultimate frisbee. How are things going with you?"

"Fine, fine. I'm officially living with Berto now, but you know how that is. Other than that, spending my time between Gina and the rec center. Ellis found me a job answering phones there, so I'm keeping myself busy. And you would not believe how adorable Ellis's little preschoolers are. One of the boys locked himself in the bathroom stall the other day and..."

I let the sound of his voice wash over me until suddenly I can't bear it anymore. I have to get off the phone or I will cry. Which is fine. It's not like I think crying is "unmanly." But I don't want Jesse to worry about me. He has enough to worry about.

I can't tell if this is worse than when he was with Ewan or not—my level of pathetic sadness. Of course this is better. I get to talk to Jesse now. We're still together even if we're not in the same place. When Jesse was with Ewan I was worried about him, about his safety. Now he's with people he loves. He's getting better.

I clear my throat. "Well, I should let you go."

"Alright, darling. I don't want to keep you from your studies. Love you more."

"Not possible."

*

When Jesse and I talk now, the conversations are shorter and shorter. I know it's my fault. I can't carry my side of the conversation. I have nothing noteworthy to say. All I can think about is how dull I am over the phone. How I'm not myself. I worry about how long this can last with me here and him clear across the country. He'll decide that long distance doesn't work for him. That I'm not good for him. That we're not worth it.

Of the many things that have changed since Jesse left? I can't bring myself to leave the room. It will mean returning to find it empty. And I can't bear that.

I'm not this pathetically sad because I miss him. I survived the summer, and it hasn't even been two weeks since I saw him. Of course I miss him. But from everything he's told me, it's quite possible that he won't be back next year, or the year after. I have to face the likelihood that he's not coming back. And my coping skills for dealing with that are apparently non-existent.

I don't have a great track record with getting to class on time—or at all this semester. And I think some of the classes have attendance requirements. I hadn't paid much attention when they handed out the syllabi.

I can't keep track of time. When was the last time I showered? When was the last time I ate? Minutes? Hours? Days? The only real measure of time I have is the time between calls with Jesse.

There is a knock on the door. It's a tentative knock, so it can't be Bailey.

"Richard?" It's Kit. I get up to open the door. "You missed dinner again. I brought you some food."

"Thanks. I'm not..." I start to tell him I'm not hungry, which is true, but it will only make me seem more pathetic. I know I missed breakfast. And I got up so late I had to skip lunch too. At least I'd managed to make it to one of my classes. A rare feat these days.

"How are you really, Richard?"

I see myself through Kit's eyes. I'm wearing the same clothes I've had on for the last three days (three calls from Jesse). I'm sure the room smells like dirty clothes. Like old socks. I don't know. I have trouble sleeping so my eyes are probably red and bleary. The double bed is too large, too empty. But I can't bring myself to pull the beds apart again. Sometimes I sleep on the floor, which for some reason is easier.

Bailey told me I could have the spare room in the quad. Their absentee roommate offered to change rooms with me. Then I could stay there all the time. Move my stuff in. Never have to walk into this room on my own.

But as much as I hate it here without Jesse, as hard as it is to bear going back to our room alone... Giving up our room, the room we shared, seems like a formal acknowledgement that he isn't coming back. And that would be truly unbearable.

"Do you want to talk about it?" Kit asks.

"What's there to talk about?" I fix my eyes on his tattoos—a mountain landscape that looks like Japanese ink painting.

"He's not… You're still together, aren't you?" Kit asks softly.

"Yes."

"Spring break isn't so far away…"

I don't have anything to say. I can't really think positively at the moment. Kit's optimism is unrelatable.

"What can I do?" he asks.

I shake my head. "Nothing anyone can do. I need time." I need Jesse.

"Okay." Kit stares at his hands. Then he looks back up at me. "Um… Bailey sent me."

I finally notice the small bag Kit has with him. Presumably an overnight bag so he can spend his turn sleeping on my floor. Bailey has done that a few times. It doesn't help me sleep any better, but at least she reminds me that I should try to close my eyes. She pays attention to the passage of time. I could put up with that from Bailey. But Kit? No.

"Tell Bailey I'm fine."

Bailey can stay. She isn't half of a partnership. Kit's presence here will only remind me of the fact that Danny is waiting for him back in the quad. In the morning, Kit can get up and leave this room and walk into the arms of the one he loves.

And I can't.

*

I don't remember when I last shaved. Long enough that I have more than just a five-o-clock shadow, but not so long ago that it looks intentional. I shave slowly, carefully. I worry that I might have forgotten how to do it properly and will end up with a face full of razor burn.

I use the aftershave that Jesse gave me. The smell reminds me of him, but everything reminds me of him, so that's no surprise. I put on the dark blue button-up shirt that I know he likes. I debate wearing a belt but decide that's too formal. I feel like I'm an inmate preparing to meet with the parole board. Or like I'm getting ready to attend a funeral. Maybe my own.

The cafeteria feels foreign. Which is ridiculous because I eat there every day. But something feels wrong. The lights are different? Or the sounds? Things seem muffled. Or too loud? I can't tell what the problem is. Which means it's probably me. There is something wrong with me. Which I am well aware of.

I think everyone is shocked to see me. They don't hide it very well. A lot of staring. People stop talking when I approach the table. It's the first time in nearly a month that I've been at breakfast without someone dragging me here. Freshly showered and everything.

"How are you doing?" Danny asks as I sit down at our table.

"About like you'd expect."

The pancakes taste like rubber. The syrup is cold. Everyone eats in silence. I don't know what I'm supposed to say.

"Do you want anyone to go with you?" Bailey asks as I'm finishing up my meal.

I shake my head. "I'm the one who didn't get my ass to class. I'm the one who has to face the consequences. Whatever happens, though? Let me be the one to tell Jesse."

Danny nods.

"Of course," Bailey says.

Kit puts his hand on mine. I'm oddly comforted by this gesture. I can't even look at Bailey, because I know she'll have a sympathetic expression on her face that will only make me feel worse.

I leave them at the table and make the long walk to the science building on my own.

My academic advisor is sitting at her desk, frowning as she stares at her computer. I'm glad I remembered to make myself presentable before showing up at her office. She's always very professional looking. The light from the screen illuminates her face. Her graying hair is cut shorter than mine. I'm long overdue for a trim, though.

"Richard, we are rapidly approaching the deadline for dropping a class without penalty. After this week, if you fail a class, that F goes on your permanent record."

"Yes."

"I've spoken with several of your professors. You're skipping classes, you aren't turning in your assignments on time, you missed a unit final in organic, and you haven't been to the chem lab three sessions in a row."

"Yes."

"What's going on with you?"

"I…" I don't want to explain to her that I'm so damn sad because my boyfriend isn't here that I can't function properly. It's true, but pathetic. I can't think about classes. My brain feels like sludge. I don't know what I can possibly say to my advisor, who is impatiently waiting for my answer.

I keep things vague. "I'm going through some stuff right now. I can't seem to keep my mind on my classes."

"Well, you need to make a decision. Is this 'stuff you are going through' something that is likely to change in the next few weeks? Is it something you can deal with in a timely fashion? Get your head back in the game?"

She's not the most emotionally expressive person I've ever met. I usually like that about her. But right now I wish she had a little more empathy.

"I don't know."

"If you fail any of these core classes it will have a significant impact on your GPA and decrease your chances of graduating on time."

"So will dropping the classes."

"I wasn't suggesting you drop all of them. Only the ones that you are at risk of failing."

She studies the screen again. Clearly she doesn't like what she sees. I already know the bad news. In my core classes I have fallen behind. In my electives, there isn't anything in the grade book.

"That would mean all of them," I say. This is confirmed by the expression on her face.

"You can still switch classes. Take an easier course load. It's not too late to make changes to your schedule. That's what I'm trying to get across. You're a bright student, Richard. Don't let whatever is going on with you derail your future."

Last year I would have agreed with her—that biochemistry was my future. That I came to school to get a degree. Period. Now things have changed. I have changed, but it doesn't seem for the better at this point.

My advisor looks at me like I am supposed to say something. "You think I should change classes?"

She nods her head. Then she pushes the course catalog for the science department across the table. She has highlighted some classes that are much less arduous, but still count towards my major.

I'm not sure why I would do any better in a new class than I would in the classes I'm failing now. It's not that the coursework is too difficult. It's leaving my fucking room that's the problem.

"What if I can't do that? What if changing classes doesn't fix the problem?"

She runs a hand through her hair and sighs. "You could take an academic leave for the semester. You'd need to make that decision soon."

I nod. "I can't do this. Not now." When I say the words it's like a weight has lifted. "If I have to double up on classes later or whatever, I can figure that out. But I can't do this now. What do I need to do for the academic leave?"

I call Jesse shortly after leaving her office.

"Oh sweetie, are things that bad?"

"No." It's a lie. I don't want Jesse to blame himself. "But my advisor thought I could use some time away."

As I'm saying this, I hear how ridiculous it sounds. And I realize there are no lies that Jesse will believe. He knows why I'm leaving. He knows why I can't stay. "I'm sorry. It's not your fault," I say.

"You are a terrible liar." Jesse's voice catches and I know he's holding back tears.

"I know. But it's really not. None of this is your fault. It's just the way things are right now, which is temporarily shitty."

"Yeah."

I hate talking on the phone. I hate that I made him cry. I hate that I can't hold him, and that there are so many miles between us. I hate everything about this.

43 Leave

Shortly after I arrive back home—after the long, solitary drive—my mom makes it perfectly clear that there is no acceptable reason for me to be out of school.

"I just don't understand what could be so hard for you." These are the first words she says to me when I walk in the door. Her next words: "You'd better find something to do while you're at home. I'm not going to have my son sitting around in the basement playing video games when he's supposed to be away at college."

My dad doesn't have much to say about my decision. He just says, "Welcome home."

But I don't feel very welcome.

Being home does one very important thing for me: it gets me out of bed every morning for fear my mom will come after me.

I pick up some hours at my old job stocking shelves at the local Target. More as an excuse to leave the house than to make any real money.

I appreciate the mindlessness of the tasks. Doing inventory, pulling things from the back room. I'm not terribly fond of the random customer service part of the job, but most people tend to avoid me. Even on my best days I don't have a welcoming retail face.

Jesse and I still talk every night.

I still miss him like hell. But it helps to be home instead of in our room, surrounded by memories of our time together.

*

Gabby comes home for a visit to check in on me. She insists that I unpack the boxes I brought back from school, even though I tell her I'm fine leaving things packed up and taking out only what I need.

I particularly don't see why she finds it necessary to unbox my books. I don't have a lot of them that aren't textbooks, and I don't plan on looking through those anytime soon.

"Kinesiology?" My sister picks up the textbook from Gina. It's stamped "Eastern Washington University Bookstore." I never noticed that before. I wonder if that's where Gina went to school. It's probably her old textbook.

"Yeah. I got that from Jesse's physical therapist. It's pretty interesting, actually."

She flips through the pages. "Wow. These are really... ew. How can you look at these diagrams without puking?"

I shrug. "It's a gift. Also, if you think that is bad... biology is truly disgusting."

"Okay." Gabby narrows her eyes at me. "But I'm still not clear on why Jesse's physical therapist gave this to you. It's not something you pick up and read for fun."

I take the book from her and place it on the shelf. "I was enough of a pain in the ass at Jesse's physical therapy sessions that she figured I could stand to learn something."

Then I start running down the list of things I found out about the various problems that can occur with injuries like Jesse's, and the way the joints are supposed to move, and what mechanisms can be disrupted depending on the location and the severity of the injury.

Why dancers are prone to these injuries, and the various therapies that can be used—both surgical and nonsurgical. How range of motion can be improved even in the case of severe injuries if the proper therapies are introduced at the right time.

My sister smacks me in the back of the head. "Why is this not your major, you idiot child?"

"What?"

"Physical therapy. Or 'applied kinesiology' or whatever. Seriously. I've never heard you talk about biochem that way."

"What way?"

"Like you are an endless font of knowledge, you can't stop talking about it, and are determined to tell me everything you know. Other than to complain about your lab partner last year, you've never really said much about your current course of study.

So clearly you have a very different relationship with this stuff." She points at the textbook.

I nod. "Of course. It's interesting."

"Aha! The implication being that whatever crap you are studying now is not interesting. People change majors all the time, Richard."

She's one to talk. She's changed majors at least three times, and that's why it's taking her forever to get through school.

"I never considered any alternatives." I hadn't.

"But you originally started as biochem because you couldn't decide between chem and bio, yeah? Now that you have a full year behind you, what do you actually think? Is biochemistry what you want to be doing?"

"I don't know. I thought so. Maybe not?"

"What's your plan here?" she asks.

"My plan is to put my clothes in drawers because you insisted I unpack."

Gabby rolls her eyes. "Right. Okay, let's say you sit on your ass all of spring semester doing nothing. Fine. But what's your plan for the fall? Do you know?"

"I haven't thought about it."

"Really? You haven't thought through every detail? Haven't planned things to the nth degree? Who are you? And what have you done with my asshole of a brother?"

"It's only been a few weeks since I took the leave. I still have some time to figure things out."

Gabby nods impatiently. "Given. And I know that your brain hasn't been fully functioning for a little while here. But... if you go back in the fall to the same classes you aren't taking now, what will be different?"

"I... He'll be back."

You know you're in sad shape when your big sister says, "Oh honey," and gives you a hug.

After she leaves I find myself wondering: what if she's right? What if it was more than just missing my boyfriend that caused me to fail out of my classes? What if I was studying the wrong course?

At night I read Gina's book, occasionally marking pages with post-it tabs for further review. I have to admit it is a lot more interesting than any of my biochem textbooks. It has actual useful information. Things people can use to solve real problems.

It doesn't take me long to make a decision after this conversation with Gabby. I talk things over with Tea, who thinks my plan is brilliant. By the time I tell my parents what my intentions are, everything has already been set in motion. I'm not asking for permission.

*

Gina has a huge grin on her face when I walk into the clinic. "This may possibly be the most romantic thing I have ever heard of."

"Or the stupidest. Are you sure…"

"Don't even finish that sentence." Gina winds her hair around her hand and ties it in a knot. "I've seen the way that boy looks at you. Hell, I've seen the way you look at each other. He talks nonstop about you every time he's here. And there is no way he won't be ecstatic to see you."

That part is a given. But I suddenly wonder if making the whole thing a surprise was a good plan. Everything happened so fast. I made all these decisions without talking to Jesse about them. Maybe I was afraid he'd try to talk me out of this whole thing. Too late now.

Jesse walks into the reception area to check in. I haven't seen him in over a month. His hair is longer. He smiles and winks at the woman behind the desk. God I have missed that smile. And the way he can make anyone blush. She giggles at whatever he said.

He walks over to Gina's station with a huge grin on his face. "And how is the loveliest physical therapist south of the Canadian border doing on this fine morning?"

Jesse doesn't see me standing on the other side of the examination table. He hasn't looked in my direction. Gina is having a hard time holding herself back. She looks like she might explode.

Jesse's eyebrows come together. "Don't take this the wrong way darling, but is something wrong?"

Gina can't stop herself anymore and she starts laughing and crying at the same time. "I'm sorry. I tried." She looks at me and shrugs.

Jesse turns around slowly. When he sees me his eyes go wide. "Richie!" He leaps into my arms, both feet leaving the ground. As I catch him I nearly lose my footing. Once I manage to regain my balance I set him down gently.

"For the love of Beyoncé, why didn't you tell me you were coming to visit! You nearly gave me a heart attack." He gives me a tight squeeze before taking both of my hands in his.

"How did you get here? Why are you here? Wait... I don't care. How long do I have you before you have to go back home?"

I'm honestly not sure how he will take the next bit of news. "Well, I got a job."

Jesse's face falls. "Oh. So you have to go back soon, then."

"No."

"He's working here with me!" Gina says, and then claps her hands over her mouth.

"What? Working? Here?" Jesse looks from Gina to me.

"Technically it's an internship," I say.

Gina can't contain her excitement. "Apparently doing so well on my pop quizzes back in December put ideas in this boy's head and now he wants to see if a career in physical therapy is for him. I put in a good word, pulled a few strings, and here we are."

"Tell me everything!" Jesse squeals. "How long is this internship? Are they paying you? Are you getting credit for this? How does physical therapy fit with your major? When did you decide on this? Why didn't you talk to me about it first? Oh sweetie, this is all too much. I'm not sure if I should swoon at the romance of it all or bite your head off."

Gina claps her hands, suddenly all business. "PT first. Boyfriend later."

After his session, we drive to Berto's house. "I was wondering why Berto insisted on dropping me off at my appointment today. He was in on this."

I make Jesse sit in the back seat, although he insists that he is cleared for shoulder straps. I am not cleared to have his hands on me while driving. It's distracting enough hearing his voice, seeing him in the rear-view mirror, smelling that herbal scent he wears.

It's a good thing Berto's condo is close to Gina's office.

Once we get out of the car, Jesse loops his arm around mine and leans his head against me. "I still can't believe you're here. I can't believe you're staying. And you arranged this whole thing with Gina and my brother? You are lucky I like surprises, sweetie." He walks into the apartment and calls for his brother. "Berto?"

"He's not here."

Jesse looks at me with narrowed eyes. "How do you know?"

I point at the note on the table.

Squeak: figured you could use some privacy. Moving in with a friend for the duration. Tell Richard he can stay as long as he likes. Let's just say I'm happy to have an excuse to stay with this particular friend. Left an extra key. Don't break anything.

"Why didn't you tell me you were coming? Why didn't anyone tell me you were coming? Especially Berto! No, he's an ass. Especially Gina. Never mind I don't care." He puts his arms around me and draws me into a long, sweet kiss that steals my breath.

I feel a little drunk being this close to him again. Dizzy. "So, you liked the surprise?" I smile against his lips.

"Sweetie, this is the best surprise anyone has ever given me."

"Good."

Jesse raises his eyes to meet mine. I could stare into them forever. He raises his hand to brush my hair out of my face.

"I like your hair long like this." I shudder as his fingertips graze my neck.

"I was going to have it cut."

"Don't you dare." Jesse winds a strand around his finger and gives a tug. "So, sweetie... How much did you miss me, exactly."

"You have no idea."

There's fire in his eyes when he looks up at me. "Show me."

I cup his ass and lift him on to the kitchen island, When our lips meet this time there is nothing sweet or tender about the kiss. Sweet is fine. Sweet is the appetizer. This is better.

He puts his legs around my waist and draws me closer until there is no space between us but the thin barrier of our clothes. When he puts his lips against the side of my neck I make a sound deep in my throat that is entirely involuntary.

He slips his hands under my shirt and lightly runs his fingernails along my ribs. "Bedroom?" There is a note of humor in his voice. He knows he's driving me mad.

"Yes. If you can keep your damn hands to yourself for thirty seconds."

"I make no promises." He slides down from the counter—brushing the whole length of his body against mine.

I walk him backwards toward the bedroom, already unsteady on my feet. And he does not keep his damn hands to himself. By the time we get there he has me halfway undressed, shirt long gone, tripping out of my pants.

I undo the buttons on his shirt so fast that a few go flying off.

When we are both finally rid of our clothing it is such a relief. Nothing is better than the feeling of skin on skin when our bodies meet.

44 Job Prospects

"Mr. Archer. I need you to fill out some forms for your physical therapist." Mr. Archer is over seventy. He is a runner. And he is here to work on hip strength and stability. It's all in his chart. What's not in his chart is that he can be a pain in the ass. I'd been warned by the front desk.

"Where's Ms. Gina?" Mr. Archer looks around impatiently. I'm clearly not his first choice.

"She'll be right here. She's training me in." I run through the list of intake questions. Basic stuff. "How did your exercises go this past week?"

"Fine. My ass hurts after three sets of that first exercise though. I can't stand those resistance bands with the stupid board."

"Yeah I can see how that particular exercise might be taxing on the greater and lesser ass muscles."

Mr. Archer barks out a laugh, which I'm not sure is a good thing. He looks at me out of the corner of his eye.

"Anything else you'd like Ms. Gina to know? Any of the exercises too easy or too hard?" I ask.

"My balance is for crap. But that's not new."

I note that on the form. "Hell, my balance isn't great either. Maybe I should steal some of these plans for myself."

Mr. Archer shakes his head. "You're not a regular physical therapist, are you? Seem kinda young."

"I'm not a physical therapist at all. I'm shadowing Gina to see if it's something I'm interested in." I finish filling out his answers on the paperwork.

"And?"

I shrug. "I'll let you know. You're my first patient."

Mr. Archer laughs again. "Seems like you're starting off just fine."

Gina comes to take over then, going over the forms I filled out. "I'm going to get you some bands with more give. I want to see you progressing to some of the more challenging, dynamic exercises but first I want to see some more strength——"

"——in my ass muscles."

"Yes. In your glutes."

After Gina makes some notes and enters instructions into the computer, I fetch the printout. "Do you have any questions before you go?" she asks Mr. Archer.

"Yeah. Can you make sure this young fellow is here next time? He's a hoot."

"Absolutely. I'll make a note of it in your chart."

When Mr. Archer leaves, Gina turns to me with her eyes wide. "That man was laughing."

"Yes."

Gina raises both eyebrows. "That's not typical behavior from him."

"I guess I have a way with crabby old men. Can't imagine why."

The other clients for the day include a high school athlete with a partially fused sacrum working on flexibility, an elite runner learning to use a new prosthetic leg, and a woman with cubital tunnel syndrome who needs hand therapy.

At the end of the day, Gina fixes me with a hard stare. "On a scale of one to ten, how do you feel about the day? Not how well you did. I can rate you on that. Eight out of ten. You make terrible coffee."

"I didn't make any coffee."

"That's what was terrible." She laughs. "But seriously, what did you think of the job? Do you think it's something that interests you?"

"Who can tell after one day. But it seems interesting. Seems like it'll be something different every day."

Gina nods. "You have a real knack for dealing with the difficult ones."

"There were difficult ones? Besides Mr. Archer? Which ones?"

"You have no idea." She shakes her head. "And I'm not about to enlighten you. Come on Richard. Give me a number. How was the day?"

"Solid eight. You make terrible coffee too." I don't even think they have a coffee maker.

*

Jesse comes in the door and makes a beeline for the kitchen where he greets me with a kiss. "You're so sexy when you're domestic. I love the apron." It's Berto's apron. It says "Kiss the Chef." I'm in the middle of making dinner. Jesse gives me a squeeze. "So, how was your day, sweetie?"

"I didn't think I'd be good working with people, but Gina says I'm a natural."

"I can imagine that. People want someone straightforward like you when they are at the clinic. And you're good one on one, Richie. I know you claim not to like people, and it's true you don't do great with groups of more than four. But PT might be perfect. You get to work on your own without being alone. I don't think alone is great for you either."

I can't argue with that. "You and Gina sound like you are reading from the same prayerbook."

Jesse grins. "The gospel according to Gina. I always knew she was brilliant."

I stir the pot of soup. My last attempt had been too bland. I'm worried this batch will be too spicy. "How about your day?"

"Same old, same old. Answered phones. Signed kids up for classes. Checked out basketballs to the high school kids playing pickup games in the gym. Oh, and helped Ellis find one of her missing kids. Those preschoolers are absolutely precious. And I met this new kid. There aren't any classes for him. The boy is far too advanced. He's getting ready for college auditions. Positively heart-breaking that he can't afford private lessons. Ellis lets him have the room at least. I've seen him dance a few times. Beautiful dancer."

I taste the soup. Passable. It's a lot better than my earlier attempts.

Jesse gets himself a glass of ice water. "And in other news, they have such a big class of intermediate girls they need to split the class as soon as they find an instructor. I don't see how anyone can learn a thing in a class of forty. Those rooms fit twenty-five at most. I imagine they must be poking each other in the eyes when they try to do their stretches at the end of class."

"You could do it." I'd been waiting for him to show some interest. I'd talked to Gina about it. Jesse needed dance. He needed to be more involved with the dancers than just answering phones.

"I'm sorry sweetie, do what?" Jesse tilts his head to the side.

I gesture toward him. "You could teach the class."

"But who would answer the phones?"

"Me."

Jesse laughs. But I'm serious.

*

The rec center reminds me of an old junior high. It's a low brick building with a narrow stairway and dim lighting.

"Brings back a lot of memories being here," Jesse says as we walk towards the doors. "It's where I got my start. Pretending to take martial arts classes."

"What?" I raise an eyebrow.

Jesse laughs. "Yeah. I was such a badass."

Ellis is waiting at the receptionist desk for us.

"Richard, you're a lifesaver. Jesse, don't do anything to mess up the rehab or your terrifying boyfriend will come after me." We'd met before. Ellis pretends to be scared when she looks at me. "Registration for spring classes starts today. Expect the phone to be ringing off the hook. Jesse, you don't mind training Richard on phones, do you?"

"No, but... I'm not sure this is such a great idea." Jesse hesitates. "Richie's a big old softy, but that doesn't come across over the phone for whatever reason."

I start to object.

Jesse puts his hand on my arm. "Unless you are talking to me, darling. Then you are sweetness personified. It's only... I don't want you scaring off potential customers. This place is holding on by a thread as it is."

Ellis shakes her head. "You don't even want to know. We got the estimate for what it will take to bring the building up to code. I foresee an endless series of fundraisers in my future."

"Oh honey, I'm so sorry. Is there anything I can do?"

"Conjure up $150,000? Give or take?"

Jesse sits down heavily at the receptionist desk. "Shit."

"Don't worry. It'll work out. It always does. Sorry to run, but I've got kids coming in. Don't worry. Richard will do fine. The phones are all yours. Jesse? When your students start to show up I've given you Studio C. We split the class alphabetically. If anyone gets lost, you're A through H."

Ellis's first customers are toddling through the door. A few run ahead of their parents and start going all over the place like ants who've lost the scent trail.

"Go that way." I point to the classroom. This little Asian kid squeaks and runs down the hall. Away from me, but more or less in the right direction.

"Ah Richie, you have such a way with the youths." Jesse laughs.

"Thanks."

I sit beside him at the desk and he shows me the phone system. There's only one line. I know how to put people on hold if I need to, and the registration system is easy enough to manage.

I answer the phone a few times to prove that I know what I'm doing.

"You're a quick study, sweetie. I'm no longer afraid of leaving the desk in your capable hands."

Before too long the high school kids start arriving for the advanced classes. Mostly girls with their hair in buns. They move like all the dancers I've seen in Jesse's studio. Even when they're walking it looks like they're performing. Their steps are purposeful. They have much better posture than ordinary human beings. I feel short and uncoordinated when I look at them, even though I'm pretty sure I'm a foot taller than most of them.

"Stop drooling, Richie. I'll get jealous."

I turn toward Jesse. "Not drooling. Do all dancers walk like that?"

"With two legs? Yes."

The phones aren't ringing off the hook, which I take as a bad sign given what Ellis said about the finances. But it does mean that when the intermediate girls show up, I am not worried about being able to handle my job.

Jesse puts on a good show of calm when he leads his students down the hall, but I can tell he's nervous. Once he's gone there is a steady stream of people. Parents hang around outside of the practice rooms waiting for their kids to be done. The younger kids come and go. Some high school kids come to sign out a basketball.

At about the time Jesse's class is finishing up, this older kid walks in. He reminds me a lot of Jesse. He has a bright smile and dark hair. And of course he has that dancer's walk. I'm not sure what there is besides that to remind me of Jesse. This dude has pale skin with freckles and is built like a very skinny basketball player.

Jesse comes walking down the hall followed by his new students. "Hey Jacob," Jesse waves. "When is the application due?"

Ah. So this is the kid with the auditions.

"I've still got a few months until the final deadline, but I'd like to get things in earlier."

"Nervous?"

Jacob laughs. "No. Terrified."

"You'll do fine." Jesse smiles. He is very convincing when he smiles. Jacob visibly relaxes before he walks into his practice room

"Did your first day go well?" I ask once we're in the car.

Jesse nods. "It was okay."

"Well, it can't possibly be better than answering phones."

"Shut up."

45 Betrayal

Jesse's class only runs three days a week. On those days I follow along as a substitute receptionist, covering the phones for the time Jesse is teaching. Tuesdays and Thursdays I stay home testing out new recipes. I got some family favorites from Jesse's mom that I'm determined to master.

On one of his teaching days, that Jacob kid arrives right as Jesse is returning to cover the desk.

"Hey Jesse," he says with a shy smile. If I didn't recognize it as hero worship I might be jealous.

Jesse smiles back. "How's it coming?"

Jacob ducks his head. "You know how it is. The closer the deadline gets the worse my nerves are. I'll get there."

I ask without thinking: "You want an audience?"

Jesse looks at me with an eyebrow raised.

"Not me. I don't mean me. But I know when you have a big show coming up you like to have someone there. And I was thinking you could be the one... and maybe you'd have some pointers." I close my mouth. What if watching Jacob is too much? What if it makes Jesse feel terrible. Then again, I'm not sure why teaching would be okay but watching Jacob would be too difficult.

Jacob looks wide eyed at Jesse for an answer. "Would you?" There is a note of awe in his voice. Jesse is a big deal around here.

"Sure." Jesse looks at me pointedly. "If I can convince Richie to cover the phones a bit longer."

"Of course."

There are no calls to answer. I alternate playing games on my phone and reading my textbook as everyone at the rec center goes about their usual business.

Jesse is gone for a long time. All the dance classes finish up and the parents collect their children. The gym closes and the high schoolers playing basketball return the equipment and clear out. Ellis comes to lock the doors.

"They're still going at it?" She looks at her watch. The center is technically closed. "I have to get home in time to pick up my sister from hockey or I wouldn't run off like this. I mean, Jesse's fine to stay late. He's responsible enough. Make sure the door closes all the way, and turn out the lights before you leave." She locks the doors and heads out to her car.

I give it about another ten minutes before heading to the room where Jesse and Jacob have been hiding for over an hour. Jesse is sitting on a stool in the corner with his eyes on Jacob. He sees me peering through the window and looks up at the clock before opening the door for me. "Sorry sweetie, we lost track of time."

"I noticed."

Jacob is very apologetic.

"I told you I would be fine. I was fine," I tell him. I'm not sure that makes him feel any better. But I don't know what else to say.

All the way back to Berto's I get the Jacob report. "He is so quick to pick up on things. I mean, the material he's already prepared is good, but we have a few weeks to get his audition pieces together and I think they could really be spectacular. I have some ideas—things that will not only show off his skills as a technical dancer, but lyrically as well. And I hope to find him a decent partner. He doesn't need to partner with anyone else for the portfolio, but it would strengthen the package for them to see him as an all-around dancer..."

*

"Quick: what are the characteristics of a Grade II ankle sprain?" Gina asks the following morning as we're getting ready to open the clinic for patients.

"Mild joint instability, swelling, loss of mobility, decreased range of motion."

Gina beams. "Nice."

I scoff. "You're going easy on me. I knew that one in high school."

Gina quizzes me every day. "Even easy questions are worth reviewing. This will give you a strong foundation if you want to switch to a physical therapy program. Grab the green book off the shelf. That's your next assignment. Starting with the chapter on sports-related trauma."

I put the book in my bag.

"How's Jesse doing with the dance stuff?" she asks.

I straighten the brochures for the most common injuries: carpal tunnel, plantar fasciitis. I don't know why I'm bothering. They don't need straightening. "Other than the fact that he's not the one dancing?"

"Yeah." She laughs humorlessly. "Other than that. Do you think it's something he could do long term? You think he could stay here and teach?"

I turn to face her. "At the rec center? I think it would be a mistake. He wants to dance. That's still possible, right? Things seem to be getting better. I haven't noticed any symptoms inconsistent with bursitis."

Gina nods thoughtfully. "Possible. Very possible." But she doesn't sound as sure as I'd like her to.

I don't want him to stay here. Maybe not strictly for selfish reasons. "He needs to be somewhere he can dance. Where it's an option anyway. Here he is stuck answering phones and babysitting for middle school girls. He needs to be back in school."

"*You* need to be back in school. But what if he stays here?" She tilts her head to one side.

"Then I stay."

Gina startles. "Well, that was an awfully quick answer."

"I enroll at the University of Washington, find a place for us other than his brother's condo, and stay here. Cheaper than Indiana, so even if my parents hate the idea, I can make it work. I have a good enough GPA for admission since I withdrew before any of this semester went on my record. And they'll take my credits as transfer. Application isn't due until June."

"Wow. Not expected. You've got a plan."

I shrug. "Not everything I do is spur of the moment. Coming here like I did was wildly uncharacteristic. The only problem is if Jesse doesn't want me here…"

"Boyfriend, do not finish that sentence." Gina wags her finger at me. "There must be dance programs here if he's not ready to go back yet."

"Yes. Not as prestigious. And not in Spokane. No dance major. Best option nearby is in Seattle and the deadline for transfer admissions has already passed."

"Richard, you are frighteningly well informed."

"Yes."

*

Ellis found someone to cover phones for Jesse on a more regular basis. She didn't want the park and rec higher ups to discover she was exploiting my unpaid labor, which means I haven't been around the rec center as much lately.

Jesse has been volunteering his time working with Jacob every day for the last week and a half. They need to record his audition pieces soon; the first deadline is still weeks away, but Jesse wants to have everything recorded well before then.

"He is brilliant, you have no idea. And the changes we've made to his program really showcase his strengths. You have got to see him, Richie. Also, I already told him I'd bring an audience. You don't mind, do you?"

"If I minded, I wouldn't be in the car." It's the third time he's asked me if I can sit in on the rehearsal. I smile. "You're cute when you're nervous."

"And did I tell you we found someone to partner with him?" It's a good thing I'm driving. Jesse is clearly unable to think about anything else.

"Yeah. That girl from the advanced class, right? She was working with you last time I came."

"Mai Linh. She's only a sophomore, but the level of maturity in her dance is… I'm babbling." Jesse says, looking at the smile on my face.

"It's adorable."

When we get to the rec center, Jesse takes off for the first of the two classes he's picked up. I find a quiet spot to study. I never watch Jesse's classes when he is teaching, even though I love to see him work with the dancers. Parents of teenage girls get creeped out by a college-age guy peering through the glass. I get that.

After a few hours of studying, I hear Jesse calling me from down the hall.

"Richie! We need you, sweetheart."

I stow my books and make the long walk down the hallway. I take a seat in the back of the room on the single chair available.

Mai Linh has her black hair in two tight braids crossed in the back. When I walk into the room she and Jacob are taking a break, drinking water, stretched out on the floor.

Jesse greets me with a brilliant smile. "Just in time. We're ready for you. All right my darlings, no time like the present. Your audience awaits." He claps his hands exactly like his professor did in studio classes.

Jesse messes with the sound system and the two of them take their places on opposite sides of the room. When the music comes up I freeze. When they move, I feel my heart race.

He could have warned me.

Jesse has redone the choreography for "Betrayal" as a male/female duet. Mai Linh is too slight to do much catching or throwing. But she's strong. And Jesse has found other ways of communicating the partnership. The way she dances this piece, the way she alternates between supporting Jacob in his leaps and casting him aside? She is scary as hell. The expression on her face is chilling—cruelty without malice. Like she doesn't care enough to hate Jacob when she treats him like crap. Like he is beneath her consideration.

There are substantial differences between this piece and the one Jesse danced in the final recital, but the core is the same. Jacob reminds me so much of Jesse when he dances. It's the way he moves—the quality of the movement is the same—the shapes he makes with his body as he crosses the space.

In the end Jacob is ground down into the floor and left there. Mai Linh stalks off without a backwards glance. And I feel my heart breaking again. Because even if he's not the one lying there, I know it is Jesse on the floor. Broken. Unable to dance.

I might feel like my heart is ripped to shreds, but Jesse is all smiles. "Fantastic. Again. Start from the midpoint where you first cause him to stumble. I want even more intention in your movements there. It isn't an accident. Let the audience see that even if Jacob can't."

Jesse circles the room to see things from different angles. He calls out instructions when he sees something he doesn't like. And shouts or jumps up and down when he sees something that he does.

I take out my phone and pull up the camera. I get footage of them dancing, but also of Jesse as he works with them. Pausing to show Mai Linh what shape he wants from her hands. Helping them with blocking so they use the entire space. There is an expression on his face I've rarely seen before. Maybe once or twice when he was on stage. Right before his time to perform. Excitement. Anticipation. Joy.

They go through the complete routine twice before Jesse tells them to pack up.

"See you both next week. Jacob, you're ready. Don't spend all weekend practicing. I want you to come fresh for the recording. We can do takes Monday and Wednesday to give you some recovery time."

Jesse is silent in the car, clearly still thinking through the rehearsal. When we get back to Berto's he turns to me with bright eyes.

"He's good, yeah?"

I hang up my jacket in the closet. "Yes. Why didn't you warn me."

Jesse flops down on the couch. "About? Oh, crap. I forgot that's not your favorite. Sweetie, I'm so sorry."

I sit beside him and he rests his head in my lap.

I run my hands through his hair. "I never said I didn't like it. But it's hard as hell to watch. I thought it was only when you danced the piece that it would get to me. But watching them dance your choreography? Damn. You are amazing."

"Biased much, sweetie?"

"Yes. But also, I'm right. I saw this at the recital and I saw it tonight. The things you create for yourself or other people… you belong on both sides of the stage. Just like your prof said."

Jesse is silent for a moment. His whole body goes still. I've made a mistake bringing up his old studio right now. I feel like punching myself in the mouth.

I don't mention Jesse dancing after that. I never want to be the person to cause him pain.

46 Visit

When I get home from work on Friday I'm surprised to find Jesse waiting for me at the door. "Guess what?" he asks, standing in my way.

"No." I don't like guessing. And for some reason I expect the surprise to be something horrible. But it's not. He opens the door wide to let me in.

"Oh." I look around the room full of backpacks and sleeping bags. Along with Bailey, Kit, and Danny. "What happened?"

Bailey shakes her head. "What happened? Spring break happened, darlin'. Don't tell me Jesse managed to keep this a secret!"

"Yes."

Jesse beams.

I take my shoes off and put my keys on the counter. "But we don't have spring break."

Bailey twists her unruly hair into a knot and fastens it with a black hair tie. It's a pale shade of cotton-candy pink in contrast to her usual bright colors. "Oh I know. We're not staying long. Gotta visit my relatives in Cali. But you have us for the weekend. Lucky you."

She's perched on my favorite chair, knitting something unidentifiable out of prickly green yarn. Kit and Danny are playing cards at the low coffee table. I sit down on the couch and Jesse sits on the floor in front of me, resting his head on my leg. It feels like we're back in the quad. I almost expect Jesse to suddenly realize that he needs to get to a late rehearsal. But of course he doesn't.

Bailey sets down her knitting and folds her legs underneath herself on the chair. "Jesse was just catching us up on how everything is going here. Sounds like you're settling into your new job, enjoying physical therapy work?"

"Yes."

"Gina says he's a real natural." Jesse pats my knee.

Kit smiles. "Glad you're settling in."

"Things aren't the same on campus. Without you two," Danny says.

"Of course not."

Jesse laughs. "Glad no one else has been able to fill our shoes."

"Well, there are plenty of other flirty theater majors," Bailey says, "but no one quite like Richard."

Jesse glares at her for a moment, but then his expression softens. "I have to agree with you there. No one can hold a candle to my Richie."

Danny makes gagging noises and Kit punches him in the arm.

I knew Jesse had been in contact with them. But I hadn't. Or I would have been aware of their plans. We spend time doing nothing. Making jokes. Eating junk food. Playing games. Jesse tells stories about our life away from campus. I sit there and listen. I don't have anything to add and I'm unreasonably tired. I like the way he tells stories. I like the way he makes people laugh. I drift off while listening to the sound of Jesse's voice.

The next morning I wake up on the couch with Jesse snuggled up against me. Everyone else is sprawled on the floor in their sleeping bags. As people start to wake up there is a lot of stretching and yawning. Nobody is quite awake enough to do anything like speaking.

I whip up breakfast for a crowd while our visitors get dressed and ready for the day.

"I suppose you've made plans already," I say as I hand out plates of scrambled eggs and toast to our visitors.

Jesse is on coffee detail. He hands me a mug. "Of course! We have a uniquely Idaho experience on today's agenda."

"Pond skimming." Danny grins. "I know it sounds like a sex act, but it's not."

Kit cuffs him lightly on the back of the head. "Rude."

"Pond skimming?" I squint at Jesse.

"Here." Kit pulls up something on his phone and tries to hand it to me, but Jesse grabs it away from him.

"Oh no you don't! I want it to be a surprise."

After breakfast we pile into my car and head to the nearby ski slopes. When we get there, a crowd is already gathered around a long, narrow stretch of water at the base of the bunny hill.

About half of the spectators are dressed in costumes. Spiderman. Clowns with rainbow wigs. A young couple dressed as a pair of fuzzy dice. I turn around to see Jesse wearing a yellow and black sequined vest with diaphanous wings, and a headband with black styrofoam balls for antennae. I didn't notice him changing. "Will you bee mine?" he asks.

"I'm already yours."

Jesse kisses me on the cheek. "I know, sweetie."

The weather is warm enough to be comfortable in a lightweight jacket. It makes for terrible snow. We join the crowd and watch as a skier goes down the hill. He's dressed in scrubs, with a stethoscope hanging around his neck. After plowing through the slushy snow, he goes almost the length of the narrow strip of water before tipping sideways and falling in. The water is up to his knees.

Pond skimming.

Next up is a kid in jeans and ski jacket. Their ski tips plow under the water when they reach the pond and they pitch face forward in a spectacular belly flop.

"You're scored on distance, style, and costume," Jesse says. "Who's up?"

"Up?" I look at him with one eyebrow raised.

"Yeah. Who wants to try a run across the pond?"

Bailey shakes her head. "I'm here strictly as a spectator."

"Yeah." Danny agrees.

"Kit?" Jesse asks.

"I can't ski, even without the addition of open water."

"Wait," Jesse says. "Aren't you from Vermont? Don't you have skiing graduation ceremonies there?"

Kit shrugs. "What can I say? I'm the black sheep of the family, in more ways than one. That's why they shipped me off to Indiana in the first place."

Jesse shakes his head in mock sadness. "Well then, I guess I'll have to represent."

I put up my hand. "No."

"Oh please... It's completely harmless. Look." He gestures toward the next skier—a gray haired wonder woman who looks like she's my grandma's age. She makes it almost all the way across the pond, then gracefully sinks into the water, still steady on her feet. She finishes with a flourish of her cape and a brilliant smile. The crowd bursts into loud cheers.

"No. Unacceptable risk. Possibility of a bad fall. Chaotic nature of the landing, impossible to predict the impact. If you reinjure yourself here, Gina will fire me. And I like my job."

Bailey raises her eyebrows. "Look at you, Dr. Hargrove."

Jesse pouts. "Fine. I'll make you a deal: I won't take a run down the hill if you do one for me."

I watch the next skier teeter out of control and slide into the audience in slow motion—the slopes are mushy and the skiing isn't fast.

"Fine." It's just a combination of downhill skiing and waterskiing. I've done both, although I'm not great at either. It could be interesting. The real reason I accept is I know Jesse expects me to refuse. I like surprising him.

"I'll need this." I grab the bobbly antenna headband from Jesse and trudge over to be outfitted with skis.

The run toward the pond feels terrible. The skis barely move across the melted snow. It feels like I'm skiing on crushed glass. When I hit the water I almost lose my balance completely as the resistance changes, but I'm able to stay upright for about a third of the way across the pond. Then I fall on my ass, getting completely drenched. I get out of the frigid pond and rejoin my friends, who are applauding enthusiastically along with the rest of the crowd.

Jesse greets me with a towel. "You never cease to amaze me, sweetie."

"Good."

The ride back to Berto's house isn't long, but it is very uncomfortable. I didn't know to bring a change of clothes but at least Jesse has an extra towel for the seat.

After a long hot shower I feel much better. I put on my sweatpants and a shirt I purchased from the rec center. When I walk into the living room, Bailey and Jesse are having a heated argument over who was most egregiously robbed in the most recent Academy Awards. I am not about to wade into the middle of that. I sit near Danny and Kit instead.

Danny hands me a cup of steaming hot coffee. "It's good to see you like this, Richard. You seem… different."

"I'm not."

Kit tilts his head and looks at me. "No, I think he's onto something, Richard. You're more comfortable somehow."

"Less of a mess is what you mean." The last time they saw me I was barely functional.

Kit shakes his head. "No. I mean yes, but you seem relaxed in a way you never were on campus. Maybe being away from academics was exactly what you needed."

Once Bailey and Jesse are done with their argument, she makes her way over to my side of the room. She waits until Jesse is off in the kitchen, loading dishes into the dishwasher. Then she narrows her eyes at me. "So, are you and Jesse coming back? No. Let me rephrase that. *When* are you coming back?"

"I don't know. We might not. It's up to Jesse." Indiana seems like another lifetime. I haven't said anything more to him about going back to school. About his professor, or coaching, or choreography.

"But you can make it happen," she says. "That boy will do whatever you ask of him."

"And that's why I can't ask."

*

We barely have time to enjoy having the place to ourselves again, when Berto announces that he's moving back in. Things didn't work out with whoever he was staying with.

I'm not very excited about the prospect of Berto's return. Jesse's brother is fine, and this is his place, after all. But it's hard to really relax at the end of the day when he's in the kitchen making dinner or talking on the phone with his friends. And we can only fool around in the bedroom when Berto is home. Quietly. Jesse feels weird if his brother hears us, which I think is a little bit ridiculous. It's not like he doesn't know we have sex.

*

"How are things with Berto back home?" Gina asks at work.

"He's fine."

She laughs. "I can read that expression. What about moving into a place of your own?"

I shrug. "Where would we go? It would have to be close. And cheap."

"What if I said I had a lead on a place that fits the bill?"

"I would say thank you."

She takes out her phone. "Let me get you the number. My cousin knows a guy who's looking for someone to sublet his place. Close, cheap, and available immediately."

"Let me ask Jesse first. I don't think I should make money decisions without him."

"You are wise beyond your years, Richard."

When Jesse gets home from the rec center, I broach the subject. "How would you feel about moving to a place of our own? For the semester, I mean."

Jesse hesitates. "It would have to be a *really* good deal," he says.

"It's only for a few months. And we don't have many other expenses…"

"I would love to have our own place. But I'm not sure how likely it is that we could find something affordable and available at this point in the semester."

"But what if we could?" I ask. Eventually I get him to agree on a price range. He even seems cautiously optimistic about our prospects.

Gina takes me to see the apartment after work. It's much better than anything I could have imagined. And yet somehow within our budget. I can't help but wonder if Gina's cousin did some haggling on our behalf.

I don't let Jesse in on any of the details once the money thing is taken care of. I want it to be another surprise. I like surprising him.

Jesse sits beside me in the passenger seat with his eyes closed the whole way. "Sweetie, I am positively beside myself with anticipation. No clues at all?" he asks when I help him out of the car.

"No. Keep your eyes closed. You'll like this."

"Well yes, but I also like not running into walls or tripping over obstacles. I do enough damage to myself with my eyes open," he says.

His arm is firmly linked through mine. I keep him close as we step into the elevator. "I won't let you get hurt."

Jesse smiles. "I know, sweetie. Now, can I open my eyes?"

"Not yet." I fumble with the keys and manage to get the door open finally. I lead him into the room until he is dead center. "Now. Open them."

Jesse opens his eyes and looks around the apartment. I watch his face as he takes in all the details. His eyes are wide and his mouth is slightly open. Surprise. Afternoon light is coming in through the wall of windows, painting everything in a golden glow.

This place is not like Berto's. There are actual matching pieces of furniture—a loveseat and two chairs. The lamp in the corner is made of driftwood and is one of a kind. Gina told me the name of the local designer when we toured the place, but I forgot. The same person made the matching glass-top driftwood coffee table too.

I like the way the apartment smells. Like fresh cut wood and lemons.

The windows face the mountains. If you look down it's just buildings and sidewalks. But this is on the sixth floor. So if you don't look down, the view is all green trees and mountain tops.

"Do you like it?" I ask, suddenly nervous. "I thought you might like it. The guy who usually lives here is a design student. So he paid attention to things. Details. And I thought you would like the apartment. And the view. Gina says he has good taste. I like it. I hope you do too."

Jesse's eyes are wide when he turns to face me. "Like it? Sweetie, I love it! But how did you find this? Do you really mean this is our place? That's... not possible. But... We can't possibly afford it. We should just stay at Berto's place."

But if we stay at Berto's place, it means staying with Berto.

"I like having space that we don't need to share."

Jesse tilts his head to the side. "Well, so do I. But..."

"You don't need to worry about the money. This fits the budget we talked about. It's on the cheaper side, even."

"How?" Jesse walks around the main room. The apartment itself is roughly the same size as Berto's, even though it's technically a single bedroom.

"Emergency sublet. The guy is in Italy or something. Desperate for tenants since it was a last minute thing."

Jesse wanders through the apartment, trailing his hands along the furniture, stopping to admire the art on the walls. They're real paintings, not prints. I think they were done by the guy who usually lives here, or friends of his.

Jesse peers into the bedroom and smiles when he sees I've already put the "His" and "His" pillows on the bed.

"I love it, sweetie. I can't wait to move in." He puts his hand on my neck to bring me in for a kiss. I savor the taste of his lips briefly before pulling away.

"It's good you can't wait. Because I have another surprise."

The doorbell rings. Jesse raises an eyebrow. "We're entertaining already?"

"No."

I open the door. "So, you ready for the delivery?" Berto asks from the hallway, several boxes stacked at his feet.

"What are you doing here?" Jesse narrows his eyes at his brother.

"I'm just the muscle, here to get you settled. Seems like as soon as I moved back in, your boyfriend couldn't wait to move out. Can't imagine why." Berto smirks. He slides the boxes into the apartment.

Jesse tries to follow Berto and me out the door.

Berto holds up his hand. "You are not lifting with that arm."

"But..." Jesse starts.

"No." I walk out the door with Berto, pulling it shut behind me.

It won't take much time to get moved in. Neither of us had much at Berto's house. Most of my stuff is still back in Minnesota. And Jesse didn't take a lot from his parents' house either. Clothes. Toiletries. A ridiculous number of shoes.

When I'm carrying one of the heavier boxes, someone gets in the elevator with me. She's maybe a little older than I am. She smells like baby powder, but the smell is faint, so it doesn't bother me too much even in the confines of the elevator. She has wavy brown hair with blond streaks, and very pale blue eyes.

"You must be taking Dino's room," she says after I set down my box and punch the number for the sixth floor. "He was in such a rush when he left."

"Yes."

She doesn't push any other buttons. Or ask me to push any of them for her.

"Nice to see Dino found an appropriate substitute." She smiles and flips her hair back from her shoulder.

"Yes." I'm not sure why I'm appropriate.

"I'm Kimberly, by the way. It looks like we're neighbors."

"Okay." I don't want to talk to Kimberly. Her voice is high pitched in what seems like a very intentional way.

"So, what should I call you?" she asks.

I don't really want her to call me anything, but I can't think of a reason not to tell her my name. "Richard." I pick up the box. It hasn't gotten any lighter. When I get off the elevator she walks with me toward my apartment. I look at her out of the corner of my eye.

"Relax. My room is just down the hall. I'm not following you."

"Good."

She laughs. "You are quite the charmer, Richie."

"Richard."

She waves over her shoulder as she walks away. "See you around, then... Richie."

I hope I don't see her often.

47 Internships

Just in case we returned to Indiana, I arranged for a new faculty advisor in the biology department. With his help I'd found a way to get my required field work out of the way with an internship at the University of Spokane.

"So, today's the big day," Gina says. "I feel like I'm sending you off to your first day of kindergarten. Maybe I should pin a note to your jacket with a reminder of what bus to ride home."

"I'm driving."

Gina snorts. "What's the study that you're working on again?"

I hadn't paid much attention to the details other than the fact that I could put in the work now and get credit for summer session, since I was still officially withdrawn for the spring. I shrug. "Something to do with mold."

"How very specific," Gina says.

"Yeah."

"I should never have encouraged you to pursue a career in physical therapy. Now I'm losing my best help." She shakes her head.

"I'm your only help. And I'll still be here in the mornings."

Gina makes a big show of being sad that I won't be with her full time. But I know she scrambled to find money to hire me in the first place, and she knows I can use the credits. Whether I go back to Indiana or not.

I arrive early at the university in case I get lost, but finding the lab is no problem. Everything is clearly marked. The building is white and gleaming on the inside with stainless steel accents. It looks like it was designed by an architect to be a modern art museum, but then the scientists took over.

"Hey neighbor!" I hear a voice call from across the lobby. I turn to see a woman in a lab coat with plastic safety glasses perched on top of her head. Brown hair with blond highlights. Kimberly. I haven't seen her since I moved in. And this is the last place I expected to see her.

"Long time no see, Richie. I thought we'd run into each other more often being on the same floor and everything. But I've managed to miss you."

"Richard."

"Right. Richard. I forgot." She laughs and does that hair flip thing. "I take it you're the new intern. Who knew we'd be in the same lab as well as the same apartment building. Must be fate. Let me show you around."

She takes me to get my lab coat and introduces me to Richelle Hindrawati, the PhD student in charge of the project—which is documenting specific genetic markers for a subspecies of slime mold. Implications for pharmacology.

"Welcome, Richard." Richelle says. She's about my height, with close-cropped black hair, and very long fingers. She has a gold nose ring and speaks with a hint of a British accent.

"I'm afraid it isn't a very glamorous job for the undergraduate intern. Mostly you'll be cleaning and sterilizing equipment, fetching things from storage, shipping off samples… I apologize in advance," she says.

"Not a problem." It's only for a few months and it's just for credit. I don't plan to make a career of this.

The afternoon goes by fast enough, even if it isn't the most interesting work. It's mostly getting trained on custom software and learning where they keep everything in the lab. Basic orientation.

"Hey cutie, how did your first day go?" Kimberly asks as I bring in a cart of recently-sterilized glass equipment.

"You can stop flirting. I have a boyfriend."

She pouts. "I was just trying to be friendly."

"Don't."

I'm surprised when she laughs at this. "I like that about you. Straight to the point."

"Yes." I take off my lab coat and hang it up before leaving for the day.

*

After my first few days on the job at the university I can confirm that Richelle is right. It is dull. But I can't complain; it's a paid position. Apparently the university has a policy against unpaid internships, so I'm raking in the money while getting college credit.

The research itself is tedious, so I'm not sure the job would be much more interesting even if I were more involved in the actual study. A lot of the things they do are very old-school. Growing cultures in petri dishes. Looking at samples under a standard microscope before deciding what merits further investigation at a greater magnification.

While I'm loading up a cart with equipment to be sterilized, Kimberly pulls up a stool to sit right next to me. Close enough that I can smell her perfume or soap or whatever. Close enough that the sweetness makes my nose itch. "How's the hot young intern today?" she asks.

"Not hot."

"Oh Richie, you are so funny!" She laughs and touches me on the arm. I don't bother to react anymore. Or correct her when she calls me Richie. She won't stop anyway, and she thinks it's funny to bother me like this.

"Can I get your help for a minute?" she asks.

I've noticed whenever Kimberly needs help, she always needs *my* help. And she wants to talk all the time, which is irritating. She wants to "get to know me." Thankfully I have managed to avoid her in the apartment building, so at least I get a break from her when I'm not in the lab.

I'm not sure how serious she is about the teasing and the flirting and the constant sexual innuendos. Probably as serious as she is about any of the guys she hooks up with. Kimberly has a different hook-up every few days, it seems. Nothing wrong with that. Casual sex is fine. But it's never been my thing. Besides, I don't have an interest in anyone but Jesse.

I finish boxing up the crap that she needs shipped off. Fill out the packing slip. Log all of that in the computer. She doesn't need my help for any of this. It's not like she's doing anything but standing around watching me complete these mundane tasks.

"A bunch of us are headed out for drinks after work. Are you busy?" She's using her ridiculous sultry voice. I've seen it work on a number of other students here—grad and undergrad—and I can see why. Kimberly is hot as hell and she knows it. I'm not tempted. She knows this too.

"Not busy. But I don't want to go out with you or your group of friends."

"Hmm... I don't understand you, Richie. Why do you play so hard to get?" She twirls a strand of golden hair around her finger.

"I'm not playing. I am hard to get."

She continues speaking, but it sounds like she's thinking out loud. "I don't get it. You're not a prude. You're comfortable talking about sex. You don't see anything wrong with people hooking up. But when I leave you an opening? Not a nibble."

"I am not interested in nibbling anything you have to offer."

Kimberly grimaces. "Ouch. I know that. I'm just curious as to why."

"You want to know? I keep telling you, but you don't seem to understand. It's not that I don't find you attractive. You obviously know that you are. But I am completely, ridiculously, head-over-heels, hearts-and-rainbows and all that shit—in love with Jesse. Nothing else, no one else, offers any kind of temptation. I don't care how mind-blowing the sex might be."

"Awww..." One of the female grad students overhears my tirade and presses her hands to her heart. "Why are all the good ones taken?"

"You sure you won't join us?" Kimberly asks.

"No."

She winks at me. "One of these days you'll say yes."

"One of these days you'll stop asking."

Kimberly laughs and walks away, taking her baby powder smell with her.

*

I'm sitting in the lobby of the rec center waiting for Jesse to be done teaching. Most of the staff have left, including the receptionist. It's just Ellis and Jesse closing down the place as usual.

"Jesse's still hard at work, I see. Want me to keep you company for a while?" Ellis asks.

"No."

She rolls her eyes and sits down next to me anyway. "It's nice to have Jesse back. Don't think I'm saying otherwise. But is there any news on what to expect in the fall?"

I look out the window behind her. The dim light of dusk makes all the cars in the parking lot look like different shades of gray. "No."

"That's very helpful, Richard."

"I know."

"Well I guess I don't need an answer right now. I was just curious what his thoughts were on the subject. He hasn't mentioned anything about it?"

I don't say anything.

Ellis scowls. "Fine."

I look at the clock. They should be done now. I walk down the hallway toward the small practice room that Jesse uses to work with Jacob and Mai Linh. He likes that it faces the green space in the back of the building, and it's big enough for the three of them. I look through the glass and see Jesse with his hands beneath Mai Linh's arms, demonstrating a lift.

I knock on the door. Loud enough that Mai Linh jumps in surprise. Jacob looks up with an alarmed expression on his face. He's not the one in trouble, though. He opens the door to let me in. "Sorry. We went over time again."

"Yes," I say. Then I turn to glare at Jesse. "What are you doing?"

He widens his eyes to protest his innocence. "Me? Coaching Jacob and—"

I hold out my hand and count the infractions on my fingers. "No lifts. Minimal load bearing activities. Predictable weight. What about that makes you think this is okay?" I point at Mai Linh, who looks like she's about to cry.

Jesse gives her a brief hug. "It's okay, sweetheart. Richie darling, don't worry. I know what I'm doing."

I shake my head. "*I* know what you are doing. And I know what you should and should not be doing. I can't believe you would risk a relapse when you've come so far."

Jacob raises his hand. "Um... sir? He wasn't lifting her. Just showing me how to position my hands for the lift."

Mai Linh nods. "He's always really careful."

I look at Jesse. "So. No lifts."

He stands on his tiptoes and kisses me on the forehead. "I promise."

Mai Linh and Jacob pack up their things quickly and duck out.

Jesse puts away the sound system before gathering his personal belongings and stuffing them in his gym bag. "You terrified those poor kids for no reason whatsoever."

"There was a reason. I thought you were behaving recklessly." I turn off the light and close the door behind us.

Jesse shakes his head. "I would never. Didn't Gina tell you I'm her star pupil?"

"Yes."

He loops his arm through mine and leans his head against my shoulder. "Sweetie, you know I want to dance again. I won't do anything that might jeopardize that. But it was very dashing of you to come to my rescue. Even if you were rescuing me from myself."

On the drive home Jesse keeps messing with the music, flipping from one song to another before settling on the latest ballad from GRiD. They're not bad. I never object when he plays their stuff, but it makes me worried. He listens to them whenever he's anxious about something.

Once we get home I put my hands on his shoulders and turn him so he is facing me. "I didn't mean to scare your students. And I know you wouldn't do things that would hurt your shoulder. I wasn't thinking."

Jesse smiles and reaches up to cup my cheek. "You worry about me. It's one of your most endearing qualities. But honestly. I'll be good. I promise." He crosses his heart. "Help me with my stretches?"

"Yes."

Together we go through his assignments for physical therapy. I can tell when he pushes himself too hard because his face gets pinched and his eyes squint. He's being careful now. His sessions always end the same way. Jesse takes his shirt off and lies face down on the yoga mat. I run my hands over his back and shoulders. I use just enough pressure that I can find areas of tension and concentrate on those spots.

It still makes me feel terrible to know that I'm causing him pain. But I also know this is good for him. And that even if it hurts in the short term, when I'm done his shoulders and back feel better.

"I wish I could do this for you, Richie. You should know how amazing this feels," Jesse says as he slowly sits up. "It's so relaxing."

I sit down on the couch. "We tried that. It's not relaxing."

"Well… There are other ways to help you relax." Jesse's voice comes out as a low rumble. He crawls up onto the couch with a gleam in his eye.

"What did you have in mind?"

He pushes me back and hovers over me before lowering himself for a kiss. I sweep the tip of my tongue just inside his lips and he groans softly. It's one of my favorite sounds. I grin against his lips. Then I run my hands through his hair and tug gently, baring his neck so I can press my lips to the spot just behind his ear. I nibble on his earlobe for a bit before whispering, "I like your plan." I run my fingertips lightly down his back.

Jesse shivers. "Good, because I'm just getting started." I feel a wave of heat as his eyes meet mine. I pull him toward me, kissing my way to the base of his neck, sucking gently until he moans my name. The sound causes tingles of electricity to travel down my spine.

I can't get enough of the taste of him. I want to explore every inch of his skin. My lips continue traveling down his chest, but I don't get far before Jesse tugs at my shirt.

"This needs to go," he says. I sit halfway up so he can pull it off over my head. His eyes are dark and bright at the same time as he pushes me back onto the couch, trailing his fingers down my ribs. I inhale sharply through my teeth.

Before things go any further I open the drawer of the side table—one of several places I've stashed the necessary supplies. I love having our own place. Jesse grins wickedly and dips his fingers past the waistband of my pants.

"Jesse," I moan. And then I stop speaking because he presses his body against mine and I lose the ability for coherent thought.

48 When it Rains it Pours

It's still raining. It's been raining all week. But it's not raining hard enough that it warrants an umbrella. Jesse pulls into the driveway of his parents' house and turns off the car.

"I hope you're bracing yourself for the onslaught of love and affection," Jesse says as we pull into the driveway.

"Yes."

Saturday dinners are a family tradition. Not every week, but often enough. Jesse's mom and dad are always there, and at least a few of his siblings. I actually look forward to the dinners, for the most part. The people in his family talk a lot, and make jokes that I sometimes pick up on, and every meal seems like Thanksgiving with all the courses.

I have bonded with his sister Maya. She and I are the quiet ones. She waves to me from the stairs when I enter the house, and smiles before disappearing into her room. I don't see the twins.

"If you're looking for Max and Angel, they have some basketball thing," Jesse says. I'm always afraid I'll call them the wrong names. Now at least I don't have to worry about that for today.

The Nunez house always seems crowded even when not everyone is there. Not necessarily in a bad way. But whatever people are there expand to fill the available space, and it makes me a little uncomfortable. I'm getting used to it.

Jesse's mom rushes over to greet us when we walk into the kitchen. She's wearing a floral apron with lace around the edges. She smells like savory herbs, and has some flour in her hair. She wipes her hands on the apron before reaching up to pinch my cheek. "Richard, you are too skinny!"

"Ma, you know he doesn't like that," Berto says before Jesse even opens his mouth to protect me. I don't actually mind anymore when people in his family hug me or slap me on the back, or when his mom touches my face. Which is surprising.

"I mean it, though. What is your brother feeding him?" she says to Berto. Then she turns to Jesse. "Do you want your boyfriend to starve?"

I used to think she was being serious when she said things like this.

"He's fine. He's just perfect the way he is." Jesse gives me a hug from behind.

I like the feeling of his arms around me. I turn to Jesse's mom. "I'm the one cooking, so you should worry about Jesse."

His mom laughs.

Caesar comes into the kitchen to get more glasses for the table. "So, Richard is the cook? How's that going?"

"Fine. I can now make more things than eggs, French toast, and macaroni and cheese," I say.

Jesse gives me a gentle shove. "Don't be modest. Richie is a fantastic cook. He's even mastered a few of the family favorites, thanks to Mom."

I shake my head. "That's not true. I haven't mastered them. I still need to follow the directions."

Jesse's mom rubs both her hands on her apron. "No problem. At least *someone* can follow directions." She narrows her eyes at Jesse.

"What? I follow directions!" He holds up his hands.

When I walk into the dining room, Christine says, "Hey. Do me a favor?" Then she hands me the baby and walks out of the room, leaving me alone with her kid. Alexander.

He's still young enough that his arms and legs aren't coordinated, and when he gets surprised by something his whole body is involved. So I try not to scare him.

I'm not a natural with babies. Jesse's nephew is the first baby I've ever held. Caesar showed me what to do the first time, so I know to support his head. And I know that Alexander likes it when I bounce him and rock from side to side. I do that when it seems like he's going to cry.

"Aw," Jesse says when he enters the room. "You look so good exuding those parental vibes."

Just then Alexander starts making happy burbling noises, which for some reason fills me with a sense of pride.

Christine comes back into the room. "Thanks, Richard. You are a literal lifesaver. I thought my bladder was going to burst. You want me to take the baby now, or are you okay for a while?"

"I'm okay." There's something soothing about holding a happy baby.

Jesse beams at me. "That's my man."

I sit down in the rocking chair while other people finish setting the table. When it's time to eat, Jesse's mom claims Alexander and I find my usual spot between Jesse and Maya.

Christine offers to take the baby. "We can put him in his car seat so you can eat…"

"Don't be ridiculous." Jesse's mom puts the baby up on her shoulder. "Holding my grandchild is the entire point of having these dinners in the first place. In fact, having grandchildren is the entire point of having children in the first place."

"Gee, thanks mom," Caesar says.

"Yes, yes, I love you too. Just not as much as I love your child. You'll understand once you're a grandparent."

"Whoa!" Caesar laughs. "Let me enjoy fatherhood first!"

The food is delicious as always. I help myself to seconds of almost everything.

Jesse's dad clears his throat. "So Richard, how is that physical therapy job going? And how is our Jesse doing with his exercises?"

"Fine. I like the job. And Jesse is very good about doing his physical therapy."

"See, Ma? I follow directions." Jesse leans forward to make eye contact with her.

She shakes her head. "For this maybe. But cooking? No."

"And the rec center? Mom says you're picking up more hours there," Caesar says.

Jesse sits back in his chair. "I have to keep busy somehow with Richard toiling away in Gina's office and the university all day."

"And there's rent money to consider now," Jesse's dad says.

"I told you to continue staying with Berto. Save some money." Jesse's mom shifts Alexander onto her other shoulder.

"Nah, I kicked them out." Berto grins. "In fact, I was about to start charging them rent anyway. Double what they're paying now. They were really cramping my style."

I start to disagree, but Jesse squeezes my leg, which means I don't need to say anything. It's a joke. Jesse's family makes a lot of jokes.

"I like my job," Jesse says. "We're opening up more classes for preschoolers during the day so I might get to do more teaching and less work on the phones."

Jesse's dad helps himself to another dinner roll. "More students means more money for that place. I'm glad to hear that."

Christine takes the baby from Jesse's mom. "Are they still worried about finances?"

"Always." Jesse runs a hand through his hair. "Ellis says major renovations are necessary. We might have to find a temporary location for classes if they can't bring the building up to code before bringing in additional funding."

I help myself to more of the spicy beans. Maya quietly asks me to pass the potatoes.

"It's gonna take more than a few extra classes to fix that place up," Berto says.

Jesse's dad quickly agrees. "That building is a relic."

After dinner it's Jesse's turn to hold Alexander. He sits on the couch. He's careful not to strain his shoulder. I get a pillow to support his arm. Then I help Maya clear the table and wash dishes.

"Thank you for taking such good care of our Jesse." His mom walks over and gives me a big hug.

"Of course. I will always take care of him."

She pats my arm. "Such a good boy."

*

The following morning I wake to an unrelentingly gray view from the window of our apartment. Still raining.

"You think this is bad, go west. There's an actual rainforest closer to the coast," Jesse says when he sees me staring out the window.

"No thanks." I didn't realize how much I would miss the sun until it didn't make an appearance for days at a time.

Jesse and I are having a late breakfast of homemade waffles and fresh orange juice. He's dressed in his favorite fluffy bathrobe.

I'm in boxers and a T-shirt. I feel like we're an old married couple. Well, maybe not. We still have great sex. So maybe this is still our honeymoon.

That idea worries me, suddenly. What if this is all just temporary? What will things be like when we return to the real world?

"What worrying thought just popped into your head?" Jesse sets down his cup of coffee and frowns.

"How long do you think we'll stay together?" I ask.

Jesse walks around the kitchen island to wrap his arms around me. "Where is this coming from, sweetie?"

"I want us to stay together..." I want to say forever, but that sounds too sappy. "Indefinitely."

Jesse spins me around, stands on tiptoe, and kisses me firmly on the lips. "Let's plan for that. Were you entertaining other options?"

"No. But I thought maybe all this was the honeymoon phase. When it's just the two of us. And later you will realize—"

"Do *not* finish that sentence. Unless you were going to say that later I would realize that you are the world's most amazing boyfriend and I love you beyond words, and that we should stay together indefinitely."

I feel less anxious when he says that. Less worried. Also it helps that he is tracing his fingers in calming circles on my back. I close my eyes. "I want to stay like this. With the two of us."

Jesse pulls me close. "I'm sorry we spend so much time apart. I don't think it's good for you to spend so much time alone. If this is the honeymoon, someone did a terrible job planning it."

"True."

"If this were the honeymoon we'd have a lot more time for this." He slips his hands under my shirt and runs them up my spine. When his phone rings I am tempted to throw it out the window—except our windows don't open.

"Don't answer that."

Jesse doesn't say anything. He is too busy kissing my neck, making my knees go weak. There is the ping of a text message and then another call. He ignores all of these.

But then *my* phone starts to ring. Which can't be a good thing. I pull back from Jesse reluctantly. I pick up my phone. It's a call from the rec center. "Aren't they closed on Sundays?"

Jesse nods his head. He holds up his phone. "She called me too."

"Hello?" I answer the phone.

It's Ellis, of course. "Thank God. Give Jesse the phone. And get dressed. I need both of you. It's all hands on deck."

I hand the phone to Jesse. He listens briefly before swearing softly and hanging up. "The center is flooding. Pack up all our towels. And grab the fan from the closet."

I throw on some clothes and gather supplies.

Jesse doesn't say anything on the way to the rec center. The rain is still coming down hard. We stop on the way to pick up a wet/dry vac from Berto's. By the time we arrive, Ellis is in full crisis mode, marshaling her small army of emergency workers. I recognize a lot of the dance instructors. I think the other people are parents of the dancers. Jacob is there too.

I set down the box of towels and the fan as Jesse wheels in the vacuum cleaner.

Ellis comes to meet us and catches us up on the situation. "The roof is leaking in studios A and B, and there's flooding on the lower level. Right now it's just in the hall there. Maybe coming up through the foundation? It's hard to tell. Wanna keep the gym dry. Called maintenance, but no one's working today."

"What are *you* doing here," Jesse asks.

"Had a bad feeling. One of the parents thought there was a wet spot in the ceiling Friday."

Whoever decided to put a flat roof on a building in this area was crazy. Between the snow in the winter and the rain the rest of the year, it's just asking for trouble.

Because I'm one of the taller volunteers, Ellis sends me to practice room A. One of the parents who comes along has some experience in construction and takes charge of the situation. The water is dripping from two different spots. The ceiling tiles there are bowed down, heavy with water.

"We're better off relieving the water pressure on the tiles now and dealing with what comes next than waiting for the inevitable," he says.

We take everything out of the room that can be moved. I get up on a ladder and put a hole in the lowest part of the tile with a screwdriver, spilling water on the studio floor. That sets the rest of the crew to work with towels, mopping things up as fast as they can.

"How are you with heights?" the guy asks.

I get down from the ladder. "Not bad. Why?"

He wipes his wet hands on his jeans. "We need someone to put a tarp over the area that's leaking to see if we can block some of the rain from coming in. There must be a low spot."

"I've been sent for a tarp," I tell Ellis. "Two, actually. For the roof."

She nods. "I'll get you some weights too."

I put my windbreaker on and go out in the rain. The wind has picked up and the raindrops are nearly horizontal. In this case I am glad of a flat roof and the permanent ladder that I can climb to get there. Even so, it's a struggle to make the climb with the things I'm carrying. And I might be fine with heights, but I would not be fine clinging to a sloping surface slick with rain.

I find the problematic spots without a problem. There are two giant puddles on the west side of the building. I try to sweep away the water, but of course it comes right back. So I cover them and secure the tarps in place with the weights.

When I get back inside, Ellis is taking pictures of all of the areas damaged by the water. "For insurance purposes. Their answering service said they can have someone out by tomorrow morning."

Until then, the rooms have trash cans underneath the leaking areas and there are fans and dehumidifiers in the basement. Jesse was on the contingent that helped mop up the lower level and wedge towels under the doors to the gym in the hopes of preventing water from entering there.

When he finds out that I climbed onto the roof he isn't happy. "I'm glad you helped, but how could they ask you to do that in this weather?"

"I volunteered. Also, it wasn't that dangerous."

We are some of the last people to leave. "You can't stay here," Jesse tells Ellis. "There's nothing you can do that we haven't done already."

Ellis nods, exhausted, and locks the door behind us. "This better be covered by insurance, or we are well and truly fucked."

49 Surprise

At work the next day I walk from the printer back to the examination room with instructions for Mr. Arthur's new series of exercises, but it's the wrong room. It's one of the rooms where Ben, the other PT, sees patients. He wears shoes with velcro closures that squeak when he walks.

"Sorry. Wrong turn."

Ben looks up at me and laughs. It's not really possible to get lost here. There are only four rooms—two for each physical therapist.

Gina looks at me with one eyebrow raised when she sees me coming out of Ben's room.

Mr. Arthur looks over the sheets with a frown on his face. "You're trying to kill me, aren't you?"

"Yes. No. Gina is trying to kill you. I'm just the messenger."

He folds the papers in half and stuffs them in the pocket of his jacket. "You don't seem as sharp as usual. Skip your morning coffee?"

"No."

After he leaves, Gina whirls on me. "Spill, boyfriend. You look like the walking dead."

I take a seat across from her in the exam room. "The rec center flooded. We didn't get a lot of sleep."

Gina's face collapses. "Oh. Poor Jesse. He loved that place."

"He *loves* that place." I correct her. "We were there trying to deal with the worst of the damage until... I don't know when."

"Is that why you can barely put one foot in front of the other and are trying to leave me for another physical therapist? You know I don't stand for cheaters. I demand 100% loyalty from my assistants."

"I'm loyal. Just tired." I rub my face with my hands. It feels like there's sand in my eyes.

"Lie down." Gina points to the exam table, a fierce look on her face.

I tilt my head to one side. "I don't need an examination. I'm fine."

Gina snorts. "You're no good to me if you fall asleep standing up. You'll probably knock over some expensive equipment that we can't afford to replace, or accidentally impale one of our patients. And while that could ultimately bring us more revenue in the way of copays, I don't think it's a great business model. Take a nap. I can handle things for a while."

I consider defying her instructions for a moment, but I suddenly realize how tired I really am. "Fine. But I'm using the chair. I might roll off the table. They're not designed for naps."

"Deal. I'll come get you in twenty minutes."

Gina doesn't keep her word. She lets me sleep through the rest of my shift and wakes me ten minutes before I need to go to the lab.

"That was not twenty minutes."

She pats me on the shoulder. "Sorry, honey. I looked in on you and thought about waking you up, but I just couldn't. You looked too precious. Now make yourself presentable so you can run out on me and go to the university."

Jesse catches me at Gina's office just before I leave. He never calls during my workday. It can't be good news.

"Hey, sweetie."

"How bad is it?" I ask. But it's obvious from his tone of voice.

Apparently flood insurance was not included in the rec center's package.

"They're closed for classes this week to try and sort out what they can. They're searching for a temporary location," Jesse says.

"So how soon can they make repairs? Where will the money come from?"

"You know what I know. Ellis isn't an expert on insurance either. All I know is we're gonna have a real fight on our hands to keep the place open. The board would need to chip in quite a bit to make these repairs, and they could very well decide it's just not worth it. The building is one of the older ones. They were already on the fence about the place." He sounds so tired.

"Maybe..." I'm about to say maybe it's better if they close it. But I know how important the place is to Jesse. It's where he learned how to dance. It's where he learned how to be himself. I don't want him to lose that. "Maybe they'll think of something."

"Maybe." He's quiet for long enough that I wonder if the phone went dead. His voice when he does speak is so quiet. "I miss you."

It does things to my heart. I want to be there with him, to hold him, to make him worry less. "It's okay. You'll see me before too long. It's only a few hours."

"But they'll be the longest hours of the entire day. Plus I'm staying late today to keep Ellis from working herself to death. Don't wait on dinner for me... I hate our schedules sometimes."

"Me too. See you tonight."

Jesse sighs. "Already counting the hours."

I manage to make it through my shift at the lab without falling asleep. When I get home, the apartment is cold and empty. It's not the first time Jesse will be home late. I've gotten used to it. But I still don't like it.

I eat cold leftovers from the fridge. I pull up a movie and sit down in front of my computer. I'm not at all interested in watching whatever it is. I plan to fall asleep on the couch waiting for Jesse to come home. I know it's ridiculous, but it's hard for me to get to sleep without him.

I wake to the sound of keys being set on the kitchen counter.

The room is dark except for the faint moonlight coming in through the windows. The rain has finally let up.

"I didn't mean to wake you," Jesse says.

"Always wake me." I sit up straight and tilt my head from side to side. It's stiff from sleeping crooked even for a short time.

"But you looked so peaceful. I was just going to grab a blanket and tuck you in."

"No. I'd miss you."

He smiles. "In your sleep?"

"Yes." I stumble into the bedroom and get undressed.

"We found a new space," Jesse says after he's done getting ready for bed. "A temporary one, I mean."

"That's good."

"Yeah." Jesse snuggles against me and I pull the covers around us. "It's actually at my old high school. We'll have to get there early to clear the desks so we have practice rooms. And stay later to put the rooms back together. But they aren't charging us rent, so that's a bonus."

"Good."

"We've had to put a hold on the preschool classes we were offering during the day though. Since actual high school classes apparently take priority for use of the space. I'm sorry. You're asleep," Jesse says in a quiet voice.

"No. I'm awake and listening to you. It's nice. Keep talking."

"I'll still field calls from the rec during the day while Ellis works on overseeing the repairs. The major drawback, other than having to set up the rooms every afternoon, is that it's a lot farther away. It'll be almost an hour each way. I'm afraid…"

"More dinners on my own, then."

Jesse gives me a squeeze, "Don't sound so sad. You're breaking my heart."

I turn so I can put both arms around him. "Dinners are fine. I'm not sad as long as you come home at the end of the day."

Jesse touches his forehead to mine. "Always."

*

The university has surprisingly good food. I'm lazy enough that I rely on the cafeteria for lunch most days instead of bringing anything from home. Today it's chicken tenders and French fries.

The cafeteria is busy, but I manage to find an empty table. Shortly after I settle in, Kimberly plops down in the seat right next to me. She always manages to find me. I should have chosen somewhere more crowded to avoid this problem.

"There are other tables," I point out.

"But this is the best seat in the house." Kimberly grabs one of the fries off my tray and dips it in ketchup.

I narrow my eyes at her. "Get your own fries."

"Nah, I've already eaten. And besides, you can spare a few for your favorite colleague." She rests a hand on my arm.

Kimberly likes to see if she can make me flustered with her outrageous flirting. She can't. But she keeps trying. I am about to warn her away from my fries again when I see Jesse standing behind her holding two bento boxes.

He's dressed in a navy blue track suit with red and white stripes down the side. He looks from me to Kimberly and back again. "Surprise," he says in a small voice.

She takes her hand off my arm. "Oh! You must be Jesse?"

"Of course he is. Who else would he be?"

"I can see my reputation precedes me," Jesse says with a wink as he sits down on the other side of me.

Kimberly's eyes rake over Jesse. "He's cute."

"Yes." I don't like the way she's looking at him. Even though I know it doesn't mean anything.

She laughs. "I'm Kimberly, by the way—"

I interrupt before she can start any kind of conversation. "She was just leaving."

Jesse swats my arm. "Don't be rude, sweetie. Feel free to stay. You can give me all the gossip." Jesse puts his elbows on the table and leans on his hands.

Kimberly laughs again. "Yeah, I can't imagine Richie spilling juicy lab secrets."

Jesse looks at her with an odd expression on his face. "No. Richie is no help whatsoever in that department. In fact, he's never even mentioned anyone he works with."

I open the bento box that Jesse brought. Rolled egg, tempura green beans, onigiri with spicy seaweed, and pickled ginger— takeout from one of my favorite sushi shops.

Kimberly stands up. "Well, much as I'd love to stay, I don't want to be a third wheel. Plus my lunch hour is over. Enjoy yours. It was nice to meet you, Jesse."

"A pleasure," Jesse says.

When she leaves, I notice two people at the next table staring at Jesse. I don't know either of them. But apparently they know me.

"I had no idea Richard was gay," one of them says in a voice that is not as quiet as she thinks.

The woman seated next to her shrugs. "Maybe they're just friends."

I turn to face them directly. "We are *not* just friends."

Jesse smiles and waves theatrically. "Sorry folks, this one's taken."

They smile nervously and look away.

"Oh, stop glaring sweetie. They're harmless. By the way, Kimberly is absolutely stunning. You didn't tell me about her."

I shrug. "What's to say? She's stunning, she's on the same study as I am, and she's irritating as hell."

Jesse helps polish off the rest of my fries. "Best eat these while they're still hot. I have to say I'm a little bit disappointed... I thought I'd get to see you in your lab coat. Scientists are sexy," he says in a stage whisper.

"We leave them in the lab." Food and lab coats don't mix. For a variety of reasons.

"Well then, I'll have to come see you in the lab sometime." He turns his attention to his own lunch for a while, but then looks up. "Oh, I forgot the second half of why I came by today—other than wanting to lay eyes on my fabulous boyfriend. We've got kind of a big favor to ask. I told Ellis you were in band back in high school. And I might have let slip that you are good at repairs."

"Why?"

Jesse claps his hands together. "Brilliant idea: an instrument donation fundraiser. Just think about how many people have old instruments sitting around at home in near-playable condition. They donate, you fix, we sell!"

"I don't think that will make enough money." I don't know how much used instruments go for, but it won't bring in the kind of funds they'll need for the repairs and renovation.

Jesse laughs. "Of course not, sweetie. The silent auction will most likely give the biggest bang for our buck. A lot of local businesses and individuals have stepped up already. Between that and outright donations... I know the instrument sale won't bring in a ton of money, but it will bring more publicity to the rec, and that can't hurt."

"Okay."

Jesse claps his hands. "I knew you'd say yes!"

"Of course."

"Fabulous! Ellis already talked to the band director about this. We can use any tools they have. And if you let them know what other supplies you might need, the band parents can probably scrounge up whatever is necessary." Jesse glances at the large clock on the wall. "Crap. I promised Ellis I'd meet with her before the trailer shows up to move things over to the high school."

"Do you want me there? I could take the rest of the afternoon." I stand up to clear the table.

Jesse shakes his head. "You're sweet, but we've got this covered."

"I'll walk you to the car." I don't want him to go yet, even though I need to get back to work as well.

I hold his hand as we walk through the cafeteria. It seems like a lot of people are looking at us. They're probably looking at Jesse. I know I can't keep my eyes off him.

"Ooh, you are going to be the talk of the lab for some time, sweetie," Jesse says under his breath.

"Why?"

He laces his fingers through mine. "Because your boyfriend is such a catch. And because apparently it's shocking that you're gay."

"You *are* a catch. And why do they care whether I'm gay or not?"

He squeezes my hand. "They care because you are hot as hell, sweetie. Everyone loves a tall, dark-haired, brooding man. I'm going to have to keep an eye on you or one of these sexy scientists will scoop you up."

We are nearly at the car. I tug on his hand to stop him. "Jesse. I don't want you thinking like that. I would never..."

"Oh I know. I was just joking," Jesse says with a fleeting smile.

I tilt his head up and give him a kiss. Not a peck. The kind of kiss that makes people stop and swivel their heads to stare. Whatever. I don't stop kissing him until he goes weak in the knees and melts into my arms.

"Don't joke," I say. "Not about that."

50 Repairs

We are allowed into the high school on the weekend to get things fully ready for classes. And to help prepare for the upcoming fundraisers. Jesse is helping Ellis with setting up the storage spaces in the classrooms. The makeshift practice spaces are clustered together in the fine arts wing. They can't hold dance classes in the band room, though. It has risers built into the floor. That's where I am.

"This is such a fantastic idea. I'm so glad I can help." The band director's name is Cynthia. She has bleached blond hair caught up in a plastic clip. She's wearing jeans and a black linen shirt. Without heels she wouldn't be much taller than Jesse. She hasn't been here for long. She looks like she's maybe in her mid-twenties.

"We don't have a lot of donations yet, but I thought you could start with some of the old instruments that belong to the school. Give you a chance to train in your crew." She nods her head toward Jacob and Mai Linh, who were the only two who volunteered to work with me. I guess I don't scare them anymore.

Cynthia shows us some old drums with broken heads and stretched out snares. "Do you have new parts for these?" I can't do anything but use them for parts if we don't have new materials.

"Not on hand. You'll know more than I do about what's worth fixing. In the percussion department anyway. I was a clarinet major. I can triage the reeds and brass fairly easily. But you're the expert here."

I nod. "I can make a list of which things are worth saving and do a parts inventory of what we'd need to make them playable."

She hands me a clipboard and retreats to her office. I walk through the scattering of battle-scarred percussion instruments and put yellow post-its on most of them: Do Not Resuscitate. Then I beckon Jacob and Mai Linh over. "Grab one of the marked instruments. They're only good for parts."

I set them up at the table with the requisite tools: screw drivers, exacto blades, needle-nosed pliers, and wooden mallets. The school also provided us with leather straps, mouthpiece-pullers and WD-40 to help with brass instruments, but we're doing one section at a time, beginning with the drums.

"Most parts of a drum are designed to come apart," I say. "If you make a mistake, don't worry. These are no good to anyone except for the parts. Cheap instruments not worth repairing. Just don't get hurt." I glare at both of them.

Jacob grins and Mai Linh nods her head.

I leave them to demolition while I assess the more playable instruments. We work in silence for a while until Mai Linh asks if it's okay to put on some music. "Sure. As long as you make good choices."

She looks nervous until Jacob says, "He's kidding. Jesse says he listens to almost everything."

Mai Linh looks relieved and routes her playlist through a portable speaker. Not bad. More pop music than I would have included, but a fair amount of the classics as well. I recognize one of Jesse's favorite songs. When I hear the opening chords it makes me smile.

"You know them?" Mai Linh asks, surprised.

"Only because of Jesse."

"Only because of me what?" Jesse asks as he enters the room. "Oh! I love this song." He starts dancing, using the risers as part of the dance. He moves effortlessly from one level to the next. The piece is a slow, lyrical number. His movements are controlled. He moves from one flawless pose to the next. Fluid snapshots.

When the piece ends, he freezes on the top step. Jacob and Mai Linh both applaud.

"Stop staring, sweetie. It's like you've never seen me dance before."

Of course I have, but it's been a long time since I've seen him dance like that. He dances for fun around the apartment. He dances with me. He dances to show his students how to do a particular move. Careful of his shoulder. Mindful of his limitations. But it's been forever since I've seen him move like this—a full piece from beginning to end, designed to be performed for an audience. I love watching him move.

"What's the progress here?" he asks.

I take him on a tour of the instrument graveyard. I think I'll do some maintenance on their regular equipment as well. No one has been taking care of the percussion instruments since long before Cynthia started working here. I tap the head of the snare drum next to me with my fingernail. It sounds like crap. I tighten the snares. Better. Still not quite right.

Jesse giggles. "Let me guess. It's a little off."

"A lot off. I want to come talk to their percussion section."

"Uh oh…" Jesse pretends to look scared.

I shake my head. "Not like that. I could come out and show them how to take care of things better. The band director is a clarinet player."

"Heaven protect us!" Jesse clutches his hands to his chest.

I shrug. "She's not a percussionist. Do you know her at all?"

"No. There was some really old guy here when I was in school. Ms. Pitman is new. From what I hear the kids really like her. But anyone would be a step up from Mr. Meineke. He was famous for spitting on students when he talked to them and he always told people what a relief it would be when he could finally retire. He made a habit of kicking out one or two kids every semester to ensure good behavior. Where is she, by the way? I want to thank her personally for helping us out."

I look through the window to the band office, but she's not there. "She'll be back at some point. Are you all set up with the practice rooms?"

"Yeah. We're ready to pack it in for the afternoon. Maintenance wants to lock up the building by 3:00. I can help you put this disaster away," he says, looking at the table full of what looks like a lot of shrapnel.

It doesn't take the four of us long to get things packed up in large plastic tubs that can be stored in the back of the band room. I need to find Cynthia so I can give her my list. And Jesse still wants to thank her. Luckily we run into her on our way to the main doors.

"Thank you so much, Richard. And you must be Jesse!" She takes the clipboard from me. "I'm so happy to meet you in person. I hear you're a fabulous dancer."

Jesse waves off her compliments. "I don't know who you've been talking to…"

Cynthia smiles. "My husband told me about you. And it's no small feat to be accepted to Indiana."

"Your husband?" Jesse raises one eyebrow.

"Yes. Oh, Sorry. I didn't change my name so people don't always make the connection. My husband Rob. Robert Hanson."

Jesse goes absolutely still. He isn't breathing. I take his hand and he squeezes mine so tightly it hurts. He takes a shallow breath.

"Oh."

It's all he says before dragging me out of the building.

Jesse is quiet. All the way home. For almost an hour. I put on a playlist full of music I know he likes, but he doesn't seem to register what's playing anyway. Doesn't fiddle with the music like he usually does. No singing along. I don't know if I should say anything.

The afternoon sun is irritating, and not just because it is glinting off the road into my eyes. It's too bright. Too cheerful. It should be cloudy at the very least. Why is it sunny now? It's been overcast for weeks. I should have left a pair of sunglasses in the car.

I keep glancing over at Jesse. Checking on him. Looking for signs that I should say something. I don't know what those signs might be. For part of the ride he pretends to be asleep. Tea does this when she's too stressed to talk about things. I figure this might be the same.

When we get home, I park the car in the garage, relieved to finally be out of the sun. It takes my eyes a while to adjust to the dim light indoors.

As we walk into the building, Jesse holds my hand with the same intensity he did back at the school. Like he's afraid I might run away. I squeeze his hand gently, but he doesn't seem to notice. His eyes are focused straight ahead, fixed on our destination. Almost as if—aside from the connection of our hands—he is unaware of my presence.

"Jesse, I…"

We're barely in the door when Jesse spins me around and grabs the collar of my jacket, pulling me toward him and slamming his lips against mine. His teeth graze against my lower lip and I taste blood. I try to put my arms around him, but he has no patience for that. He pushes me backwards toward the bedroom. Jesse pulls at my clothing, frustrated when my jacket refuses to come off quickly enough. He tears at the fabric without any success. I fend him off long enough to remove the jacket myself. He has my shirt off in no time.

His lips are all over me, not gentle, not sweet. My heart is hammering in my chest, but more from concern for Jesse than anything else. There is nothing intimate in our connection. It's like he's not fully there. His mind is somewhere else. Not on me. Not on us.

Jesse rakes his fingernails down my back, leaving marks. I inhale sharply. My body reacts to him of its own accord, but nothing about this feels right. His eyes are shut tightly, his lips in a thin line. His actions seem desperate somehow.

"Jesse," I whisper, bringing my hand up to cup his cheek. And that gesture breaks him. He opens his eyes, looks directly at me and dissolves into tears. His whole body is shaking. I fold him in my arms and hold him tightly.

He takes a few gulping breaths. He looks me in the eyes finally. "I'm sorry. I…"

"Nothing to be sorry about."

I lower him to the bed and crawl in after him. His small body curls against mine. I wrap the both of us in blankets. I keep my arms around him while he cries until there are no tears and all that is left is wracking, painful sobs that shake his whole body.

Eventually Jesse falls asleep, his breathing deep and even. I lie there next to him, watching the rise and fall of his chest. I smooth his hair back from his forehead. I wish I knew what was wrong. Wish I knew how I could make things better. Jesse doesn't even stir when I disentangle myself to get out of bed. I tuck the blankets around him more securely and kiss him lightly on the forehead.

What happened in Jesse's past with this Rob person? I should have made Cynthia tell me before we left. I should have had Jesse go to the car while I stayed behind to find out. Part of me doesn't want to know. Because whoever this Rob person is, whatever he did to Jesse… I'm pretty sure I won't take it well.

I text Ellis. She'll know.

Me: Who the fuck is Rob?

I don't hear anything back right away. I pace back and forth in the living room. I scroll through crap on my phone, failing to find anything of interest. I tidy things up even though they don't need tidying.

Eventually I go to the kitchen and pull out the ingredients for waffles, Jesse's favorite comfort food. This much I can do for him—even if it only makes things slightly better—I can have a stack of waffles from scratch ready by the time he wakes for dinner. If he wakes for dinner.

I'm in the middle of beating the egg whites when my phone pings.

Ellis: POS

For a moment I think she's calling me a piece of shit. But then realize it's a response to my question.

Me: More
Ellis: Ask Jesse
Me: Rob married the band director
Ellis: Fuck
Me: Who is Rob
Ellis: Can't. Promised Jesse
Me: He cried himself to sleep
Ellis: Fuck. Don't leave him alone
Me: I'm not an idiot
Ellis: Jury's out. Give him time

It's the smell of bacon that lures Jesse from the room. I wanted to be at his side when he woke. His eyes are puffy, his face is swollen and pink. He's wearing one of my hoodies. The sleeves cover his hands.

I smile, in case that's what he needs. "You look good with my sweatshirt. But yours fits better."

Jesse pulls the sweatshirt around himself. "This one smells like my boyfriend, though. It's a tradeoff. Ooh… waffles."

"Yes."

I want to ask him about Rob. But this doesn't seem like the time. I don't want to ask him what's wrong just to have him melt down again. Jesse is calm now, at least on the surface. This seems less like a time for interrogation and more like a time for comfort food.

So I dish him up a plate of waffles with fresh raspberries. When he sits down I put my arms around his waist and kiss the top of his head.

"Mmmm. You have really mastered the one true breakfast-for-dinner, sweetie," he says around a mouthful of waffle. "These are perfect. Just what the doctor ordered." When he's finished, he turns to give me a quick kiss. "Do you know what else the doctor ordered?"

"No."

"*Roman Holiday.* Or something else Audrey-related. Your choice."

I pull up *How to Steal a Million* because I figure a good heist movie will take Jesse out of whatever weird headspace he's in. Jesse settles between my legs on the floor and I rest my hands on his shoulders, automatically kneading them. Doing my best to decrease the tension.

He asks for commentary on the film and I oblige.

"When they were filming this scene, Audrey wasn't dressed for the weather. She was given some brandy to help her warm up, but she wasn't used to alcohol. So by the time she was wanted, she was tipsy. She knocked over the lights when she had to drive the car."

Jesse moves from his spot on the floor to curl up on the couch with his head on my lap. It seems like the movie is over in no time. Once the credits are done, he sits up and stretches.

I feel like I have to ask. "Do you—"

But Jesse interrupts before the words are out of my mouth. "No. I do not want to talk about it."

51 Visitor

It was a long day at the university. I stayed late since I was in no real hurry to get home. By the time I reach the apartment, it's already getting dark, but it will still be hours before Jesse gets home. Trying to teach classes while simultaneously helping raise funds for the rec center means a lot of late nights for Jesse. And solitary dinners for me.

I'm just heating water for my instant noodles when the power goes out. When I look out the window I can see lights out all around. Not just our apartment. I register the outage with the power company, but they already know about the issue. Their automated system lets me know that the problem should be resolved in two to five hours. Which means no noodles.

I fetch the candles from the bedroom—the nice-smelling ones I got for Jesse. When I light them, they fill the room with an herbal smell. A hint of pine. Slightly spicy. The candlelight makes the room seem even more empty. I wish Jesse were here. But wishing won't make that happen.

I'm about to make myself a sandwich when there's a knock on the door. I'm tempted to ignore it—it can't possibly be anyone I'm interested in seeing. But whoever it is knocks again. Louder this time.

I look through the peephole. I can't make out who it is in the darkness.

"Richie. It's me. Kimberly." She shines the flashlight from her phone toward her face.

"What do you want?" I ask her through the closed door.

"Can you at least open the door and talk to me face to face?" Her voice sounds odd. Not flirty.

"Fine." I open the door, but I don't move to allow her in.

She shifts from one foot to another. "I hate to impose on you like this, but can I come in?" She sounds nervous.

"Why?"

She opens her hands and gestures to the dark hallway. "I know this is going to sound stupid or like I'm making things up but... I have trouble with the dark. Can I please come in?"

She honestly looks scared. I open the door and move aside. "Okay."

"Thanks." She breathes a sigh of relief. "I know it seems ridiculous. But there was a guy on campus in undergrad. He used to cut the power to student housing and find his way in. There were five... attacks on female students. They did finally catch him. And I know it's not rational..."

"Stay until the lights come on." I might not like Kimberly, but it seems like a dick move to ask her to leave. If Jesse were here he would let her stay. It's the right thing to do. Even if I don't like her very much.

"Great. Thanks. I promise to be on my best behavior." She doesn't even smirk when she says this. "Have you eaten?"

"No."

"How about we order a pizza?"

I can't think of a reason to object. "Fine."

Kimberly pulls up the menu on her phone. "You want pepperoni or should I get a veggie option?"

"Meat is fine."

She tilts her head to the side. "Hmm... I'll get half and half. They make a gourmet veggie that's to die for." After she's done ordering, she takes one of the candles and sets it on the coffee table, sitting down on the couch.

I don't join her in the living room. I'm already second-guessing my decision to let her in. Now I'm stuck with her for several hours, when all I want to do is have dinner in peace and maybe play games or watch something until Jesse gets home.

I refuse to play host.

While we're waiting for the pizza to arrive, she looks at crap on her phone and presumably communicates with the outside world. Posting pictures of herself or arranging to meet up with one of her many admirers. Whatever.

I listen to music with my good headphones. I empty the dishwasher. I sweep the floor. I wipe the already-clean counters. Time wasters. Before long, the pizza arrives.

"Do you have anything to drink?" Kimberly asks.

"There's Coke, I think. Maybe some cider in the back."

She sighs. "Don't go anywhere. I'll be right back. On second thought, come with me. I have some wine in my fridge."

"Who drinks wine with pizza?"

She rolls her eyes. "I do."

"Fine."

I walk with her to the door of her apartment. I even go inside with her. The only light is coming from Kimberly's cell phone. She grabs a bottle of wine in one hand and two wine glasses in the other. It doesn't take long before we're back at the kitchen table with the pizza. She pours me a glass of wine even though I say I don't want one.

"This is so romantic," she says. "Eating pizza by candlelight."

"No."

She laughs. "You know I'm just kidding."

"Stop." It would be romantic, I suppose. If she weren't the one here. There is nothing romantic about this. I help myself to a slice of the pepperoni.

"Oh Richie, you have to try this." She holds a slice of the gourmet veggie pizza as if she's going to feed it to me, but in the process she knocks over my untouched glass of red wine, spilling it on me.

"I'm so sorry," she tries to help mop up the spill, pressing napkins against my shirt and working her way lower.

I reach out and grab her wrist. "I've got this. You wipe up the spill."

I set a roll of paper towels on the counter before heading to the bedroom to change. When I'm standing there in nothing but my boxers, Kimberly comes running into the bedroom.

"There's someone trying to get in!" she says, real fear in her voice.

I hear the sound of the door closing. Keys on the kitchen counter. Footsteps to the bedroom. And then Jesse is standing in the doorway.

"Hi honey. I'm home." His voice is flat. "I thought I'd come home early to surprise you. But apparently you had a different surprise for me." He looks from me to Kimberly.

The power comes back on just then, along with the lights in the kitchen and living room. We're still shrouded in darkness, though.

"It's not what you think," Kimberly says, waving her hands. "Nothing is going on here. I was just…"

I only realize how bad things look once she starts apologizing. I'm nearly naked. Two wine glasses. Candlelight.

Jesse turns away from me to look squarely at Kimberly. "You should go home," he says. "Now."

He hasn't taken off his coat yet. I take a step toward him. "Jesse…"

He holds up his hand. "Don't touch me. You smell like wine."

"Yes. Kimberly spilled on my shirt." I point at the hamper, hoping that will be enough of an explanation. It should be.

"I don't want to hear excuses. And I certainly don't want to hear about Kimberly, your adorably perfect 'coworker.' Put some clothes on." He yanks open the dresser and throws a pair of pants at me. I pull them on and grab a T-shirt.

I follow Jesse out to the kitchen. There are bags of takeout from our favorite restaurant on the floor. Kimberly had taken the pizza with her. And the wine glasses. Good.

"Jesse," I reach out my hand, but he backs away. "You know I would never do anything to hurt you. It doesn't make sense."

He shakes his head. "No. It makes perfect sense. What doesn't make sense is you coming here in the first place, now that I think about it."

"What?"

"Classes got too difficult for you? You got bored? Needed a break? I might understand all that. But why did you come out here in the first place? That's what I can't figure out. Why didn't you just stay in Minnesota?"

I am speechless for a moment. "I came because of you."

"Did you really think I needed you here?" He sneers.

"What the hell!" My voice sounds so loud in the small space. "Maybe you didn't need me. And yeah I could have stayed back home. But I wanted to be here with you."

"Sweet talker." He spits the words out like they're curses.

"Why else would I move here?" I step closer with my arms wide. Maybe if he'll let me hold him things will be different. He'll understand. But Jesse stiffens when I approach him, and I stop in my tracks.

"What I don't understand is why here? Why not at her house at least. But... in our bedroom." He almost sounds like he's talking to himself now.

I have trouble getting the words out because I'm so shocked by his accusation. I take a breath before I speak. I struggle to keep my voice level. "She wasn't... in our bedroom." Except she was. Moments before Jesse walked in. Which was the whole problem. "She came by once the lights went out. We ordered pizza. She brought wine. I don't even like spending time with her."

Jesse throws his hands in the air. "Then why have her over? And what does the lights going out have to do with you inviting her here for dinner and more?"

"I didn't invite her. Not for dinner. Not for anything else. Whatever you're thinking? Never happened."

Jesse's face is twisted in a scowl. "No really, why did she have to come here from the lab instead of going home?"

I realize then how little I've talked about Kimberly; I've never mentioned where we met. "She lives here."

Jesse's eyes widen. "What do you mean here?"

"In our apartment. On our floor." I'm surprised they've never run into each other. Then again, we have very different schedules.

Jesse rubs his forehead. "Right. Which you conveniently never mentioned. Even after I interrupted the two of you at lunch. How long?"

"How long has she lived here?" Why does he want to know that?

Jesse scoffs. "No. How long has this been going on? The two of you."

I can feel my pulse beating in my temple. I look him in the eyes. "*Nothing* is going on. There is a zero percent chance I would do that to you. And I have no interest in anyone else. Ever. You know that."

"Do I?" he asks.

"Yes. You fucking well better. Have I ever done anything, said anything, that would make you doubt me?"

Jesse doesn't answer.

"Then believe me now." My voice is tight. We've never fought. I don't know how to fight. Not with someone I care about. It scares me.

He remains quiet.

"What the hell!" I shout. Jesse flinches. I take another long breath so I won't shout more. But then I realize there's nothing left for me to say.

I stop to unpack the food from the takeout bags: grilled sandwiches from Sidney's, already growing cold. I get a plate from the cupboard, unwrap my food, and have a seat at the counter.

Jesse stares at me. "You're just going to sit there eating dinner at a time like this?"

"A time like what? When you are leaping to ridiculous conclusions and making crap accusations?" I take a bite of food. I figure if my mouth is full I won't say anything I will regret. Because right now I am furious. Yes, things hadn't looked great. But for him to go right to the idea that I was fooling around with Kimberly makes my blood boil.

"Unbelievable." He turns his back on me and walks into the bedroom, slamming the door shut behind him. I hear the lock click into place.

I set down my food and stomp across the apartment after him. "You're being fucking ridiculous!" I pound on the door. "Come out here and talk to me." I need him to look in my eyes and know I'm telling the truth.

"I thought you were busy having dinner," he says.

"You need to listen to me."

There is a long silence before he says, "I can't do this right now, Richard."

I hate that he's calling me Richard. He sounds distant. Formal. He sounds unlike himself. I think I hear the sound of sobs.

I feel sick. Torn in two. Part of me wants to fold him in my arms and tell him everything is fine. The other part wants to pound on the door and continue shouting.

He should feel bad. He is in the wrong.

But I feel terrible. I'm hurting him.

I can hear quiet sniffles from inside the bedroom. As angry as I am, the sound still breaks my heart.

"Jesse. I…" My voice breaks off. I don't know what I can say that he will listen to at this point. I'm too angry to comfort him and too sad to shout. I back away from the door, away from the sounds of Jesse weeping.

My sandwich is still on the counter. The scented candles are still there with their blackened wicks. If I could go back in time… No. He should believe me. That Kimberly is no one to me. And I did the right thing letting her in. The rest had been bad luck.

I'm uncomfortable in my own skin. I know if I keep pounding on the door it won't help Jesse believe me. And it probably won't make me feel any better. But I want to shout. Loud.

I pace back and forth, but it doesn't do anything to help my racing brain or my thundering heart. I haven't been this angry in a long time. I've never been this angry with Jesse.

I have to get away.

Everything I need… Everything I want is locked away in the bedroom. It doesn't matter.

Without another word, I pick up my keys and walk out the door.

52 Away

Of course it's still raining. I drive for a long time with no destination in mind. I drive in meandering circles further and further from our apartment. First it's densely packed apartment buildings and offices. Then residential neighborhoods. Then scatterings of houses with long stretches of road in between. And finally it's just empty. Desolate.

I'm living some horrible movie cliché: the empty road, the rain against the windshield, darkness closing in. Alone.

Why didn't he listen to me?

I'm used to people misunderstanding me. I'm used to people being offended at things I say. Confused about my real meaning. But Jesse? With the exception of my clumsy confession, he has always understood the truth behind my words.

And he knows how I feel about him. He *knows*.

So why was it so easy for him to believe the worst of me? I go back over all of my interactions with Kimberly. Meeting her in the elevator with her perfect hair and her too-friendly smile. The sweet smell of baby powder lingering in the hall behind her. Should I have mentioned her to Jesse then?

What about her constant innuendos at work? Pressing me to see if I might be interested in a little side action. Should I have mentioned that? I didn't like dealing with her crap in the lab. The last thing I wanted to do was think about it when I was at home. But maybe I should have.

Jesse had seemed upset when he met her that day at lunch, which didn't make sense at the time. Was he always afraid I would do something to betray him? Was that the real beginning of tonight's argument?

And finally my decision to invite her into the apartment. I had never wanted her there. Which is what made everything worse. All of this was because I took her in on a whim. She would have been fine in the dark. I would only have felt a little bit guilty. Nothing would have happened to her.

What's funny is I let her in partly because I was thinking about what Jesse would do. He would help people. Because it was the right thing to do. He was always considerate. Always kind.

About forty-five minutes into my drive I realize two things: I'm running low on gas, and I never did eat dinner. I fill my car's tank first and then pull into the parking lot of some random diner in the middle of nowhere. We had places like this back home on roads just like this. Roads that were empty for miles and then had a small town stuck near a train stop or something. Here it is forests and mountains instead of prairies and farms.

The restaurant is mostly empty. It has brown and orange vinyl booths. Cheerful curtains with orange and white checks. Fake flowers on every table. The music playing is instrumental covers of 90s rock: "Smells Like Teen Spirit." Jesse would think it was hilarious.

The menu is printed on tan-colored card stock. The specials are listed on a chalkboard above the cash register. There's a display of pies featuring pumpkin, apple, and sour-cream raisin.

The server's name is Jeanine. Her outfit matches the decor. A brown polyester dress with an orange and white name tag. She smells like hot metal and has stubby fingers with multiple rings that make them look even shorter.

"Can I bring you some coffee?" she asks. "Regular, or decaf?"

"Regular is fine." I order a ham and cheese omelet and hash browns without looking at the menu. While sipping my scaldingly hot coffee and waiting for my food, I call Tea.

"How do you know if you're broken up?" I ask.

Tea chokes. "Richard, you can't just start a conversation like that. I thought you were talking about you and Jesse."

"Yes."

"Wait, what?" Her voice goes up several pitches. "What the hell happened, Richard?"

"We had a fight. You know Kimberly? From work? She was at our apartment. It looked bad." I fill her in on the details.

"Well, it doesn't sound great. But Jesse knows you. He knows you wouldn't cheat on him. He'll come around once he has a chance to think things through."

I unfold and refold my napkin so the crease is in the right place. "I don't know. You didn't see him. Maybe he won't."

"Richard. People fight. It doesn't mean it's the end of the relationship."

I move the salt and pepper shakers so they're in the center of the table on either side of the ketchup. "I don't fight. Not with Jesse. We don't fight."

"People fight," Tea insists. Even people who love each other."

"I'm afraid if I see him now I'll say something I can't take back. How could he not believe me?"

There is a long silence. "I don't know what to say, Richard."

"Maybe there is nothing to say."

Jeanine arrives with my food. "Here you go, darlin'."

The omelet is greasy and the hash browns are cold, but they fill me up anyway. I sit at the booth for a long time, taking advantage of their bottomless cup of coffee. It tastes like scorched cardboard. If we're not broken up, this is not a place I will be taking Jesse for dinner.

Jeanine brings me the check. "You pay whenever you're ready, hon." She smiles at me sadly. I must seem as pathetic as I feel. First darlin' and now hon. She reminds me of Bailey.

The rain is still coming down. I run to the car to try and avoid getting too wet by pulling my jacket over my head. I check GPS to see where in the hell I am. About midway between Spokane and Coeur d'Alene. I'm sick of driving. I'm sick of everything. I thought talking to Tea would make me feel better. It usually does, but not this time.

It's Jesse's voice I want to hear.

Why didn't he listen to me?

I pound on the steering wheel. I can feel the anger in me bubbling up. The kind of anger that makes my blood sing in my veins. The kind of anger that makes my skin itch. I can feel my heart beating in my chest. It feels like I've just run five miles uphill. I turn up the music in the hopes that the rhythm of the drums will somehow counteract this feeling. That the pounding of the bass will distract me from all this. That the wailing of the guitar will crowd out my racing thoughts.

It works, to some extent. I focus on driving. On the menial tasks of keeping the car on the road. I keep driving without a destination in mind, but autopilot brings me to a familiar place.

I don't know what possesses me to ring the doorbell. But I do.

Moments later, Berto opens the door a crack. His eyes are narrowed at me as he speaks from just inside the door. "I was wondering if you'd show up here. Jesse called. Please tell me you're not the flaming dickwad my brother thinks you are."

"I'm not."

Berto opens the door wide. "Come in. Let's hear your side."

I take a seat in the living room and he hands me a glass of ice water.

I tell him the whole story, from meeting Kimberly in the hallway, working with her at the lab, her constant flirtations, culminating with what happened tonight when the power went out.

Berto sighs. "Richard, you might not be an ass, but you are unlucky as hell." He rests his elbows on his knees. "What do you know about my brother's dating history?"

"Only what you and everyone else have mentioned: that he has terrible taste in men. Oh. And I met Ewan, his most recent disaster." I hold up the hand I broke when punching the wall after the infamous backstage encounter.

"Yeah. He told me about that. Part of what made me think you were a good guy—helping him get away from that situation."

"I didn't. It was our friends."

Berto looks at me with eyes eerily similar to Jesse's. "It was you. Jesse told me. Maybe they helped him move, but you are the one who convinced him to leave. You two are good together. If it helps at all, I'm willing to bet this misunderstanding has very little to do with you. And a whole lot to do with a previous relationship."

"Rob?"

Berto freezes at the name. "He told you?"

I swirl my glass of water, ice clinking against the sides. "No. Rob's wife works at the high school. We met her last week. It was weird, and then Jesse wouldn't tell me anything."

"Fuck," Berto slams his fist down on the table. "Sorry. No wonder my little bro is shutting you out."

I set down my glass of water. "I need to know. Tell me what happened."

"Okay. I'm only telling you because I know how you feel about my brother. And I think you need to know." Berto cracks his knuckles one at a time. "You came to the right place for this information. Jesse only told me and Ellis before swearing us to secrecy. And knowing Ellis, she'd kill you for hurting Jesse before telling you anything. Doesn't matter you weren't at fault. She's more of a shoot first, ask questions later kind of gal."

"Yes. She is."

Berto takes a moment before continuing. "Rob was Jesse's first serious boyfriend. He was older. He and Jesse dated in secret—Rob's idea. Because of the age difference. So my brother didn't tell anyone until afterwards. When it all went to hell."

Berto presses his lips together. "Turns out Rob was engaged. He'd been cheating on his future wife with Jesse the entire time. Yeah. The jackass was going through an 'experimental phase' before marriage and he used my brother—a kid in high school— to figure out his own sexuality. Predatorial bastard."

Berto runs a hand through his hair. "Jesse was a mess after that. Stopped talking to his friends. Lost a lot of weight. Pushed himself during rehearsals so hard he collapsed. Eventually Ellis dragged the secret out of him. Got him some help."

My heart is racing. I'm having a hard time breathing, but I force myself to breathe normally so I can speak. "Jesse isn't an experiment. And I would never hurt him like that."

Berto pats me on the back. "I know, man."

Both of us are quiet for a very long time. I look around the apartment where Jesse and I used to stay.

"You need a place to sleep tonight?" Berto asks.

I look up, surprised.

"He'll come around, Richard. Don't worry. But he might need some time."

"Yeah. Okay."

I know there are reasons for Jesse's actions that have nothing to do with me. But I'm still not okay with the fact that he doesn't trust me. I'm still mad. And I don't really want to go back to shouting.

53 Sorry

At the lab the next day, Kimberly finds me the moment I arrive. "Richard, I am so sorry. Is everything okay between you and Jesse?" Something in my expression gives things away. "Oh no! Do you want me to talk to him? I'm sure I can clear things up." She isn't using her high-pitched voice for once. Just her regular one. It sounds much better.

"No." Anything she has to say will only make things worse.

Kimberly avoids me for the rest of the day. I'm glad. I don't have the patience to deal with her, even if she is no longer pretending to pursue me.

I drive past our apartment on the way to Berto's. Jesse's car is gone. He's at work, so I won't have to face him yet. I want to pick up a few things. Spare clothes at least. When I walk in, the place seems empty. As if Jesse is the one who left.

I almost expect to see the closet empty when I go into the bedroom. I even check. But no, all of his things are still there. Hanging neatly. Organized by color. The "His" and "His" pillows are still on the bed, but they're turned over so you can't see the words. I wonder if that means anything or if it was just an accident.

I pack only a few items of clothing. I'm not moving out. I just can't move back in yet. When I turn to leave the room I pause. Before I leave, I turn the pillows right side up. "His" and "His."

I remember the words Jesse threw at me just before I left: "Why did you come here? Why didn't you just stay in Minnesota?" At the time I came because I was sick with worry. There was nothing to hold me in Minnesota. And I needed him.

I was no longer sick with worry, partly because I had studied up on his condition and had been part of his rehab. Jesse was progressing well with his physical therapy, although it was slow progress that I knew was frustrating for him.

Now I had different reasons to stay, too.

Back at school it seemed everything revolved around Jesse—further proof that I was not studying the right major. Here I have more of a life outside of our relationship. And as much as I don't like that our schedules leave us so little time together, maybe a bit of time apart is good, in a way.

But not like this.

I leave a note for him on the counter. "I miss you. Please talk to me." It's not enough. I call Jesse's number. Of course the phone goes right to voicemail. He's teaching.

I don't know what to say the first time, so I hang up. The next time I call, I'm ready. "Remember. I love you." I don't want to say anything else over the phone. I don't want to make excuses or apologize or tell him that once we talk everything will be miraculously better.

I want him to hear the sound of my voice.

I want him to know I'm thinking about him.

I want him to call.

*

Gina knows something is wrong because Jesse rescheduled his physical therapy appointments for afternoons—when I won't be in the office. She hasn't asked me about it, though. Not except to ask if I'm okay. Which I appreciate. We pretend everything is fine. That helps me make it through the day. I barely even see Kimberly anymore.

It's been three days since I started crashing at Berto's house. He tells me not to worry, still. But I'm not sure he's been in communication with Jesse. I don't think Berto has any more information than I do.

I call him once a day. Straight to voicemail. The same message each time: *Remember. I love you.* I don't ask him to call. He already knows I want him to talk to me. I'm not sure what else to do.

I miss him. I miss the sound of his voice and his bright smile and the way he sneaks up on me to give me a hug from behind when I'm not quite awake. I feel the loss of contact with him like a missing limb.

I pick up my phone. I'm about to call him when Tea calls to check in on me. Which is at once comforting and irritating.

"How are things going with you and Jesse?" she asks.

"They're not." I pace back and forth in Berto's living room.

"Hmm... have you tried talking to him?"

I stop to part the curtains and look out the window of Berto's apartment. Still raining. Just a light drizzle. "I wrote him a note. I've left him voicemails. He hasn't called back."

"What about in person?"

"I haven't been home. I'm still staying with Berto."

"Really? That's... unexpected. His own brother is on Team Richard? Well, maybe it's the right decision to give Jesse a little space. Some time to think things through."

"It's what Berto says. But how much time?" I ask.

Tea sighs. "I don't know. Maintaining relationships is an art, not a science. And you'll note I couldn't salvage my own love life."

"Maybe it's already too late. Maybe we're already broken up. I need to know how much time to give him."

I hear a sound behind me and turn to see what it is. I assume it's Berto home early for some reason.

It's not.

I drop the phone from nerveless fingers. It clatters off the coffee table before landing softly on the carpet. My entire body is frozen in place. Jesse is standing in the middle of Berto's living room, hands held out in front of himself.

"Hey there. I didn't mean to scare you. But if you want to know how much time you need to give me to realize what an ass I've been? This is enough time. It's been enough time. More than enough."

I'm frozen in place. "I thought you were at work." It's not at all what I want to say.

Jesse gives me a very small smile. "Time off for good behavior?"

"I'm not sure your behavior has been that good."

"Touché." He comes closer. "I got your messages."

"Good."

"And, I'm sorry." He takes another step. "I should never—"

"I just need to know that you believe me," I interrupt.

Jesse winces. "I made a mistake. I opened my big damn mouth when I was too tired and too stupid to see things clearly."

"You were stupid. But there were reasons."

Jesse raises an eyebrow. "Berto?"

"Yeah. And it's good you know you made a mistake. But I need to know that when you look at me you can see me. What I'm saying. I don't lie. I would never lie to you."

He's almost within arm's reach now. "I know that. I remember. And sweetie... We aren't broken up. Unless... that's what you want?" His voice ends in a whisper.

I still can't move. "No. I..."

Jesse puts his arms around me and buries his head in my chest. "Next time I'm an ass, can you stay? Yell at me. Call me a fucking idiot. But don't walk out."

I put my arm around his waist. "I don't know how to argue. I don't want to say things that hurt you. But I did want to say them at the time."

Jesse holds me tighter. "They're just words, sweetie. Leaving hurts more than anything you could say."

"I'm not sure. I was angry."

"Yeah, so was I. Promise you'll stay. We can figure things out together. It's part of being a couple." He looks up at me. His eyes are so dark.

I reach up to touch his face. "I promise. I don't like being apart."

"Then let's go home."

"Yes. I didn't bring enough clothes to last the week. And Berto uses the wrong kind of detergent."

Jesse laughs and kisses me on the lips. I notice the kiss is salty, which is when I notice he is crying.

"Don't." I wipe the tears from his face with my thumbs. "Our fight is over now."

"Yes," he says, pulling me in for a tight hug.

"Then let's go home."

We drive in my car, leaving Jesse's in the parking lot of Berto's building. We can get it later. He doesn't stop touching me all the way home. Not in a distracting way, though. His hand on my leg is an anchor. A reminder of his presence.

When we walk into our apartment I notice a bottle of wine on the kitchen counter.

"It's from Kimberly. She sent it along with a heartfelt apology. I guess it's the traditional 'I'm sorry you made a complete ass of yourself and jumped to ridiculous conclusions about your amazing boyfriend' gift," Jesse says.

"Yes."

He hasn't let go of my hand since we left the car, his fingers laced through mine. It feels strange to be back even though I was only gone for a few nights.

He looks into my eyes and cups my face in his hand. "Can I kiss you?"

"You never have to ask that."

"Yes I do," Jesse says. "You're too tall." He tugs on my hand and leads me to the bedroom. I sit down on the edge of the bed and pull him toward me.

"Better?" I wrap my arms around him and bury my face in his neck.

"Much better." He rests his cheek against mine and whispers in my ear. "I missed you so much."

"Yes. I missed you too." I feel almost dizzy from being in his presence again.

He cups my face in his hands. When our lips meet, the kiss is long and sweet. He tangles his fingers in my hair. He climbs into my lap and curls up with his head against my chest.

My heart is beating faster and I am exquisitely aware of his every move. But I don't want us to have sex. Not yet. I don't want it to seem like that's what I missed about him.

I lean back against the pillows and cradle him in my arms. "Can we just stay like this? For a while?"

"As long as you like," Jesse says.

I pull him closer, hold him tighter, and pull the blankets up to cover both of us. "I like you here."

"I like being here," he says, nuzzling his cheek against mine.

"Good."

The next morning I wake up still curled around Jesse, surrounded by the faint scent of his cologne.

"I am never getting out of bed," Jesse says, rolling over so he is lying half on top of me, resting his chin on his hands.

"Yes. Never get out of bed. As long as I don't have to leave."

Jesse kisses the tip of my nose. "Darling, that would completely defeat the purpose. Easily 90% of the appeal of staying in bed is your presence."

"What's the other ten percent?"

Jesse props himself up on his elbow, ticking off points on one hand. "Five percent pima-cotton, two percent cold floors, and two percent sheer laziness."

"You're missing one percent."

"I guess you are ninety-one percent of the charm."

"Good. Be lazy. Stay here."

He groans. "We can't. Not all day, anyway. We both have work commitments."

"But not right now. We don't need to leave now." I pull him down on top of me, bringing his chest flush against mine.

"No. We don't." His voice is a whisper.

"We could call in sick…" I place my lips gently at the base of his throat. I love the hollow between his collarbones.

"Okay." He speaks the words against my skin and I feel vibrations all the way to my toes.

"That was easy." I grin.

"What can I say? You are very persuasive."

I wrap my arms around him and pull him tight. My lips find his. He sucks on my upper lip and I savor the taste of him. The kisses grow more heated and my hand slips beneath his shirt.

Jesse shivers when I trace circles over his ribs. And then he loses patience with me. Rolling me onto my back, he makes short work of removing my clothing and his. His lips and hands are everywhere.

"Jesse." I can't find what I was going to say. I can't form any words but his name.

54 Silent

Jesse made me buy a suit. It's a second-hand gray pinstripe. Jesse calls it vintage. But I don't think it's old enough to be vintage. I borrowed shoes from Caesar. They're more comfortable than they look.

Jesse looks stunning as always in his own formalwear: black with white satin trim and patent leather shoes with a two inch heel. He spins to let me take in the full effect.

"You look good," I say.

Jesse smiles. "Yeah I do. I have to dress the part since I'm going as eye candy. I need to look good on your arm."

"You always look good."

Jesse swats my arm. "Flatterer."

The silent auction is being held in the spacious lobby of the high school theater. The tables are laid with white tablecloths. Small spotlights are positioned to draw attention to the various auction items.

The school provided an ensemble to play music in the background. It's a surprisingly good string quartet. Of course string players usually start when they're three so I shouldn't be surprised that they are competent after fifteen years performing in public.

Jesse tugs on my sleeve. "I'll be right back, sweetie. I need to check in with Ellis on some last-minute details."

I decide to check on some details myself. I walk over to the table where we have some of the more expensive donated instruments on auction. There are a few wooden clarinets, and an older violin in fantastic condition. Niche items, but if someone knows what they're looking at—could be a steal. I eye the pages with bids. Volunteers were allowed to bid before the auction officially opened. A few people had put down low numbers, but nothing that would meet the minimum bid.

Cynthia stops by the table as well. She's wearing a hot pink dress with matching pumps. "I can't thank you enough for the work you and the kids put in on the instruments. I hope the sale brings in a lot of money for the center."

"Yes."

"Anything exciting yet?" she asks.

"No." I don't want to talk to her.

Cynthia looks around the room as if she's trying to find someone, which gives me a bad feeling. "Your husband isn't here, is he?"

She looks surprised. "Rob?"

"Do you have another husband?"

She laughs, but she sounds nervous. "No. He couldn't make it."

"Good."

Cynthia looks at the floor. She knows. But how much does she know? I wonder if she was the original fiancé that Rob was cheating on or if she's a newer model. I don't care.

"Um…" She searches for something to say.

I don't want to hear whatever it is, so I turn and walk away.

There's a commotion at the door as the camera crew for the local news arrives. Jesse told me they were coming to get more publicity for the center. He appears at my side and grabs my elbow. "Ah! They're early! Stall them. I need to put my face on."

"Your face is fine."

Jesse slips his arm through mine and looks up at me with a huge smile on his face. "You always know just the right thing to say."

"I'm only telling the truth."

Ellis points out our location to the crew and they make their way over.

"Jesse." The reporter approaches and shakes his hand. "Good to meet you in person finally." Anna, the reporter, is Gina's second cousin or something like that. They look like they could be twins. Except Anna has dark gray eyes and lighter skin. Jesse says something I can't hear that makes her blush and laugh.

She goes over things with Jesse before they start shooting. "I'll ask Ellis a few questions about the history of the rec center and the building itself. Then we'll go to you for information on the silent auction and your personal statements. Speak from the heart, but don't feel like you need to share anything you're uncomfortable with. Do you have any questions for me?" He doesn't. Jesse already knows all the things they'll ask him. They sent him the questions ahead of time. I helped him practice.

They record Ellis's spot first. I find out that the rec center building was part of the WPA, constructed during the New Deal. And that it used to be the city hall until a new one was built closer to the center of town in the 1970s. She talks about the various programs that use the space and the demographics of the people served by them. I'm only half listening. Ellis gets flustered several times and they have to stop and redo those parts.

They're still doing Ellis's portion of the interview when I catch something out of the corner of my eye. It's Cynthia, standing next to a tall white man with light brown hair and a neatly trimmed beard. He's looking right at us. Right at Jesse. I wait until Ellis is done and Jesse is getting situated under the lights before slipping away.

Cynthia doesn't see me until I'm right in front of her. I spare her a glance before turning to her husband. "You need to leave."

"Who are you?" he asks, puzzled.

I don't bother to answer his question. "Stop looking over there. He doesn't need to see you. He needs not to see you. I'm asking you to leave."

Rob looks from me to Jesse. I see realization dawn on his face. "You know, I never meant to—"

"I don't give a fuck. Just get out."

Rob opens his mouth like he's going to say something. But then he decides against it and walks away, with Cynthia close behind him. He pretends to look at auction items on his way out. Pretends it was his decision to leave. When he's finally out of sight I walk back to the filming location.

I congratulate myself on not making a scene and not breaking anything. Not even raising my voice. Still, my heart is racing from the confrontation in which nothing much happened. I make it back in time to catch part of Jesse's interview.

He's telling the story about trying to fool his parents into thinking he was taking martial arts classes instead of dance. He makes the interviewer laugh.

"This place was important to you when you were growing up for other reasons as well," the interviewer says in a soft voice.

Jesse takes a breath and smiles one of his sadder smiles. "This wasn't an easy place to be a gay kid. But the center was always a safe place for me. Before and after I came out. And every kid deserves to have a place where they feel like that—like they belong. That they can be their authentic selves."

The interview concludes and Jesse comes to stand beside me again. "Thank God and all her angels that's over," he says.

"You did a good job."

"Thanks, sweetie. So did you."

I look at him, raising an eyebrow.

"I saw what you did."

Rob. He'd seen me with Rob. "I—"

Jesse squeezes my hand. "It's okay. I'm fine. It actually really gave me a sense of closure to watch my hot as hell, sweet as sin boyfriend literally chasing my ugly past away."

*

"Sweet Mary, mother of Jesus!" Jesse shouts at his phone the next morning.

"Is she the one texting you this early on a Sunday?"

Jesse rolls his eyes at me, but he has a wide smile on his face. "No. It's Ellis. She says the rec made its goal. The auction brought in about half of what we were looking for, and after the interview, someone called in to the station with an anonymous donation covering the rest."

"It wasn't me."

Jesse laughs. "I figured that much."

I'm writing up a mid-semester report on my internship for my prof. I have to find things to say besides, "It's boring as hell and has only succeeded in convincing me that a career in physical therapy is the right choice." Because that probably will not get me a passing grade. More detail will be necessary.

Jesse is sitting beside me, drinking a cup of coffee and basking in the fantastic success of the rec center's fund raising project.

When he finishes with his coffee, he sets the mug in the sink. "Don't move. I have something to show you."

His tone makes me nervous. Suddenly serious. Jesse goes to get something from the bedroom before returning to the kitchen. He's carrying a large envelope. He sits down beside me and sets it down on the counter.

"At my last therapy appointment, Gina said things were looking good. She tentatively said that I could start more dynamic work. Building strength, not just increasing my range of motion. My trainer at the gym agrees." He touches his bad shoulder. "Working toward lifts, even."

"What's this?" I tap the envelope with one finger. I can see it's hand addressed to him from the School of Performing Arts at Indiana.

Jesse takes a deep breath. "Open it."

I carefully open the envelope and spill its contents out on the table. I sift through the documents carefully. There is a form letter welcoming him to the newly established dual choreography/performance program at the university. There's a handwritten note from the head of the dance department liberally peppered with exclamation points. And a slim fine-arts course catalog with post-it flags highlighting classes for fall semester.

"Shit, Jesse... This is amazing. It's amazing, right?" I study Jesse's face for some kind of reaction, but he is unreadable. I'm not sure he's taken a breath since I started looking through the contents of the envelope.

"Yeah..." Jesse sounds hesitant. "I've had that hiding in the bottom of the dresser for weeks. I didn't open it until my last appointment with Gina. At her office."

I feel a ridiculous pang of jealousy that he chose her instead of me. That she was the first to hear this news. But that only lasts a moment. "Do you want to go back?" I pick up the course catalog and page through it. I want him to go back. I want him to say yes. Please say yes.

Jesse wrings his hands together. He takes a shaky breath. "I want to dance."

"I know. But... What about this?" I point to the program description and the enthusiastic letter from his professor.

"Choreography. Coaching. Do you want that too?" I remember the look on his face when he was working with Jacob and Mai Linh.

Jesse doesn't answer right away. When he speaks his voice sounds far away. "What if Gina's wrong? Or what if she's half right—I can dance without doing further damage, but I can't dance for shit anymore? What if the surgery changed something?"

"Stop." I gently press on Jesse's back and he slides down to sit on the floor in front of me. I smooth my hands over his shoulders and he relaxes against me.

Using only slight pressure I can feel the tension in his muscles release. There are still signs of his old injury—but it is much less pronounced. "The surgery did change something. Or rather, the extensive rehab afterwards did. You can now move without causing progressive damage. And before? You danced well despite the pain, not because of it."

Jesse hesitates. "I could stay here, though. I could stay and teach classes at the rec center. There will be more Jacobs who can use my help."

"Yes, but…"

He twists around to face me. "But I'm a dancer. If there is even a slight chance that I can be on stage again—"

"You have to try." My voice is quiet. I don't want to seem like I'm pushing him to make a decision.

Jesse pushes away from the couch. He suddenly stands up and begins pacing back and forth in the living room. "What if it's the case that I really can't dance?"

"Then you try again later after more rehab. Or you go strictly choreography. Or you try something else entirely. And whatever you choose, I'll be there. Assuming you want that."

"I can't ask that of you, Richard." Jesse stops in his tracks. "You've already lost a semester at school because of me."

"Is that what you think?" I get up from the couch and put my arms around him from behind. "How can you think that?" I rest my chin on the top of his head. "You didn't take anything from me. I took this time to figure out what I wanted to do. I didn't waste an entire semester taking classes I would never use."

I can feel Jesse trembling in my arms. I hold him tighter.

"Jesse. Do you remember what you asked me the first day we met? When I dropped my books and we had breakfast? You asked me where I found myself when I closed my eyes and clicked my heels together."

Jesse turns in my arms and looks up at me. "Do you remember every conversation we've had?"

I stroke my thumb along his cheek. "Only the important ones. At the time my answer was Minnesota. That was home. My answer changed. It's with you. When I click my heels together? There's no place like home? That's where I am. I'm with you. You want to stay here and keep teaching? I've filled out my application for Washington. Not due yet. Gina wrote me a letter of recommendation. They have a good PT program."

Jesse looks stunned. "And what if I want to go back? What if I want to try?"

"Easy. I'm only on leave so I don't even need to apply. I re-enroll for fall. Drop chem, load up with applied courses and go straight-up biology. I've already spoken to my new advisor. Still works as preparation for a degree in physical therapy."

"As simple as that?" He still looks surprised. I don't know why.

"I already told you. Home is where you are. Whatever you want. Your decision."

Jesse twines his arms around my neck. "Have I mentioned how much I love you?"

"Yes. It's very convenient. I love you too."

Epilogue — Junior Year

55 Home

The lights come up, and the stage is bathed in a cool silver-blue. There is a spindly tree on the left side of the stage. I don't recognize the female dancer. Maybe she's from a different studio. She's dressed in a flowing pale blue dress. Or maybe it's a trick of the light. Jacob's outfit is olive drab; it looks natural on him.

It takes me a little while to see that the piece is a mirror image of "Betrayal." There is an equality between the two dancers even though the way they support each other is very different. Jacob has the strength to support her while she twines around him slowly, slipping to the floor. But he never lets her touch the ground. And she is flexible enough that she is there to meet him as the choreography becomes ever more complex. She is always there in time to make sure the dance is smooth, that he is never alone.

When the piece gets a standing ovation, they call Jesse up to the stage. As they should. The head of the department thinks he should start entering his pieces in competitions. Everyone says he's brilliant. He goes back to watching from backstage.

I know Jesse has a few more pieces in the recital. He played all the songs for me, but didn't let me watch any of the rehearsals because he wants all the dances to be a surprise.

A bunch of other people dance. They're good. Well, a bunch of them are actually not that good. It's the first recital of the semester, after all.

Bailey pinches me. Hard.

"What the hell?" My voice comes out louder than I mean it to and a few of the audience members snicker. She points at the stage.

The lights don't fade. They are extinguished without warning. Then a single spotlight. Just like the first time I saw him on stage.

His costume is simple. Bare feet. Black pants. A white shirt—sleeves intended for cufflinks left open. His smooth black hair is pulled back from his face. His eyes look impossibly dark under the lights, the stage makeup accentuating their intensity.

The auditorium is utterly silent as he takes his initial pose—one hand at the base of his throat and the other reaching toward the sky. I hold my breath.

Only his hands move at first, as if he is coming to life gradually. His movements are smooth, with occasional choppy breaks that mirror the music.

His whole body comes to life then, graceful leaps showcasing his ability to become weightless. A fantastic mix of isolated movements and long flowing lines. He doesn't need anyone to catch him. He barely touches the floor before taking off once more.

I am struck again how he dances like no one else—like air is the water he swims in. As the music slows toward the end, he spins on one leg until he comes to an absolute standstill and it's as if time itself has stopped.

I don't remember to clap when the dance is over.

Kit waves a hand in front of my face. "Your man is trying to get your attention." I look up at the stage to see Jesse smiling brightly, looking straight at me. I give him a thumbs up. Still in shock.

"You really didn't know?" Kit asks. "He told us not to tell you, but I was sure you would have guessed. Why else do you think you were banned from rehearsals?"

"He said I was a distraction while he was coaching. And that everyone but Jacob was afraid of me."

Bailey laughs. "As if. You are such a softy."

"Jesse, that was goddamn brilliant!" Danny picks Jesse up in a big bear hug and spins him around. Then he looks at me with a guilty expression on his face.

I nod my head. "It's fine. Trainer approved post-recital congratulations."

Bailey elbows me in the ribs. "Your time away made you so much funnier, Richard. What did they do to you in Idaho?"

"Washington."

"Well, that explains it." She rolls her eyes. "Cocktails chez nous?"

The last thing I want to do is spend time with a group of people, even if they are my friends. I want Jesse to myself. But I don't say anything. I don't have to.

Jesse wraps his arm around mine, giving it a squeeze. "Sorry my darlings, we have other plans." He waves as the three of them move on.

Jesse lets go of my arm and skips around to walk backward facing me. "Were you really surprised, sweetie?"

I hadn't seen him dance for nearly a year. Not like this. On stage, under the lights, in front of an audience. The way he moves when he dances... "You're lucky the shock didn't kill me."

"I was sure Kit had spilled the tea when he talked about the set for my solo."

"I thought he meant something you choreographed for someone else."

When we reach our house, Jesse unlocks the door and I follow him in. We don't live far from campus, and it's only a few blocks from the house that Bailey, Kit, and Danny share. But I appreciate the privacy. With no shared walls.

Jesse removes his jacket and I see that the clothes he changed into are remarkably similar to those he wore on stage: crisp white shirt and black pants. Jesse's hand drifts to his collar, then drifts away almost subconsciously. Too late. My mind flashes to the opening image with his fingers at the base of his throat. I trap his hand before it can wander back up into dangerous territory.

"I thought you'd appreciate the choreography. And the costuming." Jesse raises one eyebrow.

"Yes." I move toward him, trailing my finger along the opening of his shirt.

His eyes gleam. "I know how much you love me in white."

I bend to kiss the hollow at the base of his throat, tasting the salt of his skin. "I love you in everything."

Jesse groans and I feel the vibration against my lips.

"And I love you in nothing at all." I spin him around so his back is facing me, putting my arms around him tightly so there is no space between us. Then I whisper in his ear: "You are exquisite."

Jesse gasps as I suck on my favorite spot behind his left ear. He has a small birthmark there as if to mark the spot for me. I begin unbuttoning his shirt from the bottom. With each button, I move my lips to another spot on his neck. "You don't mind if I leave a few marks, do you?"

Jesse tries to say no, but it comes out as more of a moan.

Once I have undone every button of his shirt he spins to face me, neatly escaping the sleeves. He moves so quickly I have no time to react. He pins me to the wall, holding my arms in place. I am struck again by how strong he is.

"My turn." He grins.

*

I wake up late the next morning with Jesse wrapped around me like a blanket. We did finally make it to the bed. One of the best benefits of not sharing our space is that there is never any hurry to get to the bedroom. And no need to be quiet.

"I'm glad we stayed in last night," I say once Jesse opens his eyes.

Jesse uncurls enough so that he can prop himself up to look at me. "Yeah. Me too." He gives me a leisurely morning kiss.

"Spending time with you is ten times more enjoyable than spending time with anyone else. Even if sex is not involved."

Jesse chuckles. "Glad to know I'm more than just a piece of ass. Oh don't look so horrified, sweetie. I know what you're trying to say."

"Good. Because what I'm trying to say is I love everything about you. And I love every minute spent with you."

Jesse gives me a long, slow kiss. An unhurried kiss. The kind that saps all my energy and makes me want to stay in bed forever.

He stops to rest his head against my shoulder, lazily tracing each of my ribs with a finger.

"How did I get so lucky to find you, Richie? What if someone else had swooped in first."

I shake my head. "I have never felt about anyone the way I feel about you. No swooping possible."

"There he is. My hopelessly romantic boyfriend." Jesse snuggles against my side, pulling the covers around us so we are in a cocoon. "Can we stay here forever? I never want to leave."

"We only have this place until May."

Jesse gets a wicked gleam in his eye. "Better make the most of it then.

Made in the USA
Middletown, DE
19 September 2022